THE WINTER GUEST

Also by Pam Jenoff

The Kommandant's Girl
The Diplomat's Wife
The Ambassador's Daughter
The Last Summer at Chelsea Beach
The Orphan's Tale
The Lost Girls of Paris
The Woman with the Blue Star

PAM JENOFF

THE WINTER GUEST

PARK
ROW
BOOKS

PARK
ROW
BOOKS™

Recycling programs
for this product may
not exist in your area.

ISBN-13: 978-0-7783-1157-7
ISBN-13: 9780778312109 (Library Exclusive Edition)

The Winter Guest

First published in 2014. This edition published in 2021.
Copyright © 2014 by Pam Jenoff

This edition published by arrangement with Harlequin Books S.A.

Park Row Books
22 Adelaide St. West, 41st Floor
Toronto, Ontario M5H 4E3, Canada
ParkRowBooks.com
BookClubbish.com

Printed in U.S.A.

For Mom, who still makes our lives better every single day.

THE WINTER GUEST

Prologue

New York
· 2013 ·

"They're coming around again," Cookie says in a hushed voice. "Knocking on doors and asking questions." I do not answer, but nod as a tightness forms in my throat.

I settle into the worn floral chair and tilt my head back, studying the stucco ceiling, the plaster whipped into waves and points like a frothy meringue. Whoever said, "There's no place like home" has obviously never been to the Westchester Senior Center. One hundred and forty cookie-cutter units over ten floors, each a six hundred and twenty square foot L-shape, interlocking like an enormous dill-scented honeycomb.

Despite my issue with the sameness, it isn't an awful place to live. The food is fresh, if a little bland, with plenty of the fruit and vegetables I still do not take for granted, even after so many years. Outside there's a courtyard with a fountain and walking paths along plush green lawns. And the staff, perhaps better paid than others who perform this type of dirty and patience-trying work, are not unkind.

Like the white-haired black woman who has just finished

mopping the kitchen floor and is now rinsing her bucket in the bathtub. "Thank you, Cookie," I say from my seat by the window as she turns off the water and wipes the tub dry. She should be in a place like this with someone caring for her, instead of cleaning for me.

Coming closer, Cookie points to my sturdy brown shoes by the bed. "Walking today?"

"Yes, I am."

Cookie's eyes flicker out the window to the gray November sky, darkening with the almost-promise of a storm. I walk almost every day down to the very edge of the path until one of the aides comes to coax me back. As I stroll beneath the timeless canopy of clouds, the noises of the highway and the planes overhead fade. I am no longer shuffling and bent, but a young woman striding upward through the woods, surrounded by those who once walked with me.

And I keep a set of shoes by the bed all of the time, even when snow or rain forces me to stay indoors. Some habits die hard. "How's Luis?" I ask, shifting topics.

At the mention of her twelve-year-old grandson, Cookie's eyes widen. Most of the residents do not bother to learn the names of the ever-changing staff, much less their families'. She smiles with pride. As she raises a hand to her breast, the bracelet around her wrist jangles like ancient bones. "He made honor roll again. I'm about to go get him, actually, if you don't need anything else..."

When she has gone, I look around the apartment at the bland white walls, the venetian blinds a shade yellower with age. Not bad, but not home. Home was a brownstone in Park Slope, bought before the neighborhood had grown trendy. It had interesting cracks in the ceiling, and walls so close I could touch both sides of our bedroom if I stretched my arms straight out. But there had been stairs, narrow and steep, and when my old-lady hips could no longer manage the climb, I knew it was time to go. Kari and Scott invited me to move into their Chappaqua house; they certainly have the room. But I refused—even a place like this is better than being a burden.

I look across the parkway at a strip mall now past its prime and half-vacant, wondering how to spend the day. The rest of my life rushed by in an instant, but time stretches here, demanding to be filled. There are activities, if one is inclined, knitting and Yiddish and aqua fitness and day trips to see shows. But I prefer to keep my own company. Even back then, I never minded the silence.

One drop, then another, comes from the kitchen faucet that Cookie did not manage to shut. I stand with effort, grimacing at the dull pain that shoots through my thigh, the wound that has never quite healed properly over more than a half century. It hurts more intensely now that the days have grown shorter and chilled.

Outside a siren wails and grows closer, coming for someone here. I cringe. Now, it is not death I fear; each of us will get there soon enough. But the sound takes me back to earlier times, when sirens meant only danger and saving ourselves mattered.

As I start across the room, I catch a glimpse of my reflection in the mirror. My hair has migrated to that short curly style all women my age seem to wear, a fuzzy white football helmet. Ruth would have resisted, I'm sure, keeping hers long and flowing. I smile at the thought. Beauty was always her thing. It was never mine, and certainly not now, though I'm comfortable in my skin in a way that I lacked in my younger years, as if released from an expectation I could never meet. I did feel beautiful once. My eyes travel to the lone photograph on the windowsill of a young man in a crisp army uniform, his dark hair short and expression earnest. It is the only picture I have from that time. But the faces of the others are as fresh in my mind, as though I had seen them yesterday.

A knock at the door jars me from my thoughts. The staff

has keys but they do not just walk in, an attempt to maintain the deteriorating charade of autonomy. I'm not expecting anyone, though, and it is too early for lunch. Perhaps Cookie forgot something.

I make my way to the door and look through the peephole, another habit that has never left me. Outside stand a young woman and a uniformed policeman. My stomach tightens. Once the police only meant trouble. But they cannot hurt me here. Do they mean to bring me bad news?

I open the door a few inches. "Yes?"

"Mrs. Nowak?" the policeman asks.

The name slaps me across the cheek like a cold cloth. "No," I blurt.

"Your maiden name was Nowak, wasn't it?" the woman presses gently. I try to place how old she might be. Her low, dishwater ponytail is girlish, but there are faint lines at the corners of her eyes, suggesting years behind her. There is a kind of guardedness that I recognize from myself, a haunted look that says she has known grief.

"Yes," I say finally. There is no reason to hide who I am anymore, nothing that anyone can take from me.

"And you're from a village in southern Poland called… Biekowice?"

"Biekowice," I repeat, reflexively correcting her pronunciation so one can hear the short *e* at the end. The word is as familiar as my own name, though I have not uttered it in decades.

I study the woman's nondescript navy pantsuit, trying to discern what she might do for a living, why she is asking me about a village half a world away that few people ever heard of in the first place. But no one dresses like what they are anymore, the doctors eschewing white coats, other professionals shedding their suits for something called "business casual." Is she a writer perhaps, or one of the filmmakers Cookie referenced? Documentary crews and journalists are not an uncommon site in the lobby and hallways. They come for the stories, picking through our memories like rats through the rubble, trying to find a few morsels in the refuse before the rain washes it all away.

No one has ever come to see me, though, and I have never minded or volunteered. They simply do not know who I am. Mine is not the story of the ghettos and the camps, but of a small village in the hills, a chapel in the darkness of the night. I should write it down, I suppose. The younger ones do not remember, and when I am gone there will be no one else. The history and those who lived it will disappear with the wind. But I cannot. It is not that the memories are too painful—I live them over and over each night, a perennial film in my mind. But I cannot find the words to do justice to the people that lived, and the things that had transpired among us.

No, the filmmakers do not come for me—and they do not bring police escorts.

The woman clears her throat. "So Biekowice—you know of it?"

Every step and path, I want to say. "Yes. Why?" I summon up the courage to ask, half suspecting as I do so that I might not want to know the answer. My accent, buried years ago, seems to have suddenly returned.

"Bones," the policeman interjects.

"I'm sorry…" Though I am uncertain what he means, I grasp the door frame, suddenly light-headed.

The woman shoots the policeman a look, as though she wishes he had not spoken. Then, acknowledging it is too late to turn back, she nods. "Some human bones have been found at a development site near Biekowice," she says. "And we think you might know something about them."

1

Poland
1940

The low rumbling did not rouse Helena from her sleep. She had been dreaming of *makowiec*, the poppy seed rolls Mama used to make, thick and warm with a dusting of sugar. So when the noise grew louder, intruding on her dream and causing her hands to tremble, she clung tighter to the bread, drawing it hurriedly to her mouth. But before she could take a bite, a crash rattled the house and a dish in the kitchen fell and shattered.

She sat bolt upright, trying to see through the darkness. "Ruth!" Helena shook her sister. Ruth, who was curled up in a warm ball with her arms wrapped around the three slumbering children between them, had always slept more soundly. "Bombs!" Immediately awake, Ruth leaped up and grabbed one of their younger sisters under each arm. Helena followed, tugging a groggy Michal by the hand, and they raced toward the cellar as they had rehearsed dozens of times, not bothering to stop for the shoes lined up at the foot of the bed.

Helena scrambled down the ladder first, followed by Michal. Then Ruth passed five-year-old Dorie below before climbing down herself, the baby wrapped around her neck. Helena dropped to the ground and pulled Dorie onto her lap, smelling the sour milk on the child's breath. She cringed as the inevitable wetness of the muddy earth seeped through her nightclothes, then braced herself for the next explosion. She recalled the horrors she'd heard of the Warsaw bombings and hoped that the cottage could withstand it.

"Is it a storm?" Dorie asked, her voice hushed with apprehension.

"*Nie, kochana.*" The child's body relaxed palpably in Helena's arms. Dorie could not imagine something worse than a storm. If only it were that simple.

Beside her, Ruth trembled. *"Jeste's pewna?" Are you certain there were bombs?*

Helena nodded, then realized Ruth could not see her. *"Tak."* Ruth would not second-guess her. The sisters trusted each other implicitly and Ruth deferred to her where their safety was concerned. Michal leaned his tangle of curls against her shoulder and she hugged him tightly, feeling his ribs protrude beneath his skin. Twelve years old, he seemed to grow taller every day and their meager rations simply couldn't keep up.

Ten minutes passed, then twenty, without further noise. "I guess it's over," Helena said, feeling foolish.

"Not bombs, then."

Helena could sense her sister's lips curling in the darkness. "No." She waited for Ruth's rebuke for having dragged them needlessly from bed. When it did not come, Helena stood and helped Dorie up the ladder. Together they all climbed back into the bed that had once belonged to their parents.

Helena thought of the noises early the next morning as she made her way up the tree-covered hill that rose before their house. The early-December air was crisp, the sky heavy with foreboding of the harsher weather that would soon come. It had not been her imagination—she was sure of that. She had heard the drone of the airplane flying too low and the sound that followed had been an explosion. But she could see for miles from this vantage point, and when she peered back over her shoulder, the tiny town and rolling countryside were untouched, the faded rooftops and brown late-autumn brush she had known all her life showing no signs of damage.

She was halfway up the hill when a rooster crowed. Helena smiled smugly, as though she had outplayed the animal at its own game. Pausing, she turned and scanned the horizon again, gazing out at the rolling Małopolska hills. Beyond them to the south sat the High Tatras, their snowcapped peaks obscured by mist. She gazed up at the half crescent moon that lingered against the pale early-morning sky. The wind blew then and the moon seemed to duck behind some silvery gray clouds, casting light around the edges.

Helena bent to untangle the frayed hem of her skirt from the tops of her boots with annoyance. Her eyes dropped once more. Biekowice was just one of a dozen or so villages surrounding the larger town of My´slenice, spokes on a wheel fanning across the countryside. The entire region had been part of the Austrian empire not thirty years earlier and the latticed, red roof houses still gave it a slightly Germanic feel. There was one road into town, feeding into a cluster of streets, which wound claustrophobically around the market square like a noose. Another road led out just as quickly. A patchwork of farms dotted the outskirts, gray smoke wafting from their chimneys to form a halo above.

Shifting the small satchel she carried, Helena continued along the western path, a pebble-strewn route that climbed upward toward the main road. In the stream that ran alongside the path, water gurgled. Her footsteps fell into an easy rhythm. Despite her mother's admonitions, Helena had escaped to the woods frequently as a child. In the confines of their small cottage, she bounced about restlessly like a rubber ball, with nowhere for her energy to go. But this was the one place she could be by herself and truly feel free.

Pine needles crackled beneath her feet, breaking the stillness, their scent mixing with more than a hint of smoke. What brush or refuse could the farmers be burning now? Everything, even items once discarded, might have some use. Leaves and twigs could, if not fuel a fire, at least make it burn longer, stretch the logs or make them hotter when the wood in the pile was damp. She scoured the ground now as she walked, looking for dropped berries or nuts or even acorns that might be used for tea. But the earth here was picked bare by the animals, as ravenous and desperate as she.

The war had broken out more than fifteen months earlier, and for a while, despite the warnings that crackled nonstop across the radio, first in Polish and later in German, it seemed as though it might not have happened at all. Though their small village was less than twenty kilometers from Kraków, little had changed other than the occasional passing of military trucks on the high road outside town. It was the blessing, Helena reflected, of living in a place so sleepy as to be of no strategic value. But the hardships had come, if not the Germans themselves: herds of cattle and other livestock disappeared in the night, reportedly over the western border. Coal stores were requisitioned and sent to the front to help the war effort. And an unusually cruel summer drought had contributed to the misery, leaving little to be canned for winter storage.

She reached the paved road that led toward the city. It was deserted now, but exhaust hung freshly in the air, suggesting a car or wagon had passed recently. Helena's skin prickled. She could not afford to encounter anyone now. She looked longingly back toward the trees, but taking the steep, winding forest path would only slow her down.

As she started forward, Helena's thoughts turned to the previous evening. "Don't go," Ruth had begged as they readied the children for bed. They'd worked seamlessly in tandem as they'd completed the familiar grooming chores, like two appendages of the same body. "It's dangerous." She accidentally pulled Dorie's braid too hard, causing her to squeal.

Ruth's objection was familiar. She had fought Helena since she'd first proposed going to the city, continuing Tata's weekly pilgrimage after his death. It was not so much that the half-day trek was physically demanding; Helena had navigated the steep, rocky countryside with her father all her life. But the Nazis had forbidden Poles from traveling beyond the borders of their own provinces without work passes. If they noticed Helena and asked questions, she could be arrested.

"What other choice do we have?" Helena had asked practically, pulling the nightdress over Karolina's hair, savoring her freshly washed smell. They did baths twice a week, Karolina first, then the older children and Ruth and finally Helena, scrubbing as well as she could in the cool, filmy water after the rest had gone to bed. "We have to make sure Mama eats." And is not mistreated, she added silently. The care at the sanatorium was minimal, the resources scarce. She hadn't told Ruth of the times she'd turned up to find their mother missing her socks or lying in her own excrement, risking infection of the bedsores she persistently developed from not being turned.

Ruth had not answered, but continued unbraiding Dorie's hair, lips pursed in conflict. Helena knew that Ruth found the notion of Mama shut away in some city hospital alone unbearable, and that Helena checking on her each week gave her some comfort. Ruth feared the outside world, though. She had responded to everything that had happened by closing off and drawing within.

Helena, on the other hand, wanted to see the world. Her mind reeled back to an earlier trip to the city. It was a fine fall day, some leaves still orange on the trees, others giving a satisfying crunch beneath her feet. She had passed the turnoff for the city and it was a good two kilometers down the road before she realized she was on the path that would lead away from Biekowice for good. Ruth's face had flashed in her mind then and Helena had stopped, guilt-stricken. She had been distracted, she told herself, and accidentally missed the turn. But she knew it was something more—for a moment she was actually leaving, without looking back. She had not taken that path again, but each trip she stopped and looked longingly down the road, wondering how far she could actually go.

Helena was jolted from her thoughts by a loud noise, a giant's foot crunching down on a house. Ahead, a German jeep, machine gun mounted on the front, blocked the roadway. Helena leaped back into the roadside brush, catching her hand on something jagged. She stifled a cry as a thorn cut through her worn glove and into her skin.

As blood seeped through the wool, Helena berated herself silently for her carelessness in not clinging to the cover of the trees that lined the road. She crouched low to the ground, not daring to breathe. But it was too late: the gun mounted atop the jeep turned toward her with a creak. A soldier stood behind it, his gaze seeming to focus just above her. He shielded his eyes, searching the forest. This was the closest Helena had come to the war and, despite her terror, she found herself studying the man. He was ruddy faced and ordinary; save for the uniform and gun, he might have been one of the loggers down at the mill.

The soldier's eyes narrowed, a mountain wolf hunting its prey. A hand seemed to grip Helena's throat, squeezing. Would he arrest her or shoot her here? She was suddenly desperate to be in the house that an hour ago she had so eagerly escaped. Her heart pounded as she imagined her death. Ruth would be sad, or maybe cross. "I told you so," her twin might say if she were here now, a smug smile playing about her full lips. Ruth liked to be right more than just about anything and Helena seemed to always give her reason by spilling or breaking something.

Helena pictured Michal, wise beyond his years, comforting his sisters. But the little ones were closer to Ruth, depended on her for their care. And they had been so battered by the loss of their parents that they might weather this additional blow without much grief.

Helena felt against her side the cool metal of the knife she'd taken from Tata's hunting kit and tucked in the waist of her skirt. She carried it in case she encountered a wolf, but now an image seized her of drawing it and slashing the German's throat.

A minute passed, then another. Finally, the man sat down and started the ignition. As the jeep started in the other direction, Helena slumped against a tree, trying to catch her breath.

When the sound of the engine had faded, Helena stepped out from the bushes and scanned the now-deserted road. She didn't dare continue this way now. Perhaps Ruth had been right about the danger of the trip and she should return home. But she imagined Mama alone in the hospital and knew that she had no choice. She doubled back to the path where it emerged from the woods. Steeling herself, Helena stepped into the forest and the welcome shelter of the trees that loomed overhead as she started toward the steep pass over the hills.

2

At the sound of the door clicking shut, Ruth snapped her eyes open and tightened her arms around the children. She strained without success to see in the darkness, instantly struck by the sense of emptiness beside her. The bed was a bit cooler and the mattress did not sink as heavily as usual. Helena was gone. She had left for the city, this time without nudging Ruth as she usually did. And she had gone earlier, though perhaps that was not so strange, given the shortening days and the need to get back more quickly before nightfall.

Ruth shifted with effort, weighing the void she always felt in Helena's absence. Michal's head was on her shoulder, Dorie holding to her ankle and Karolina flung across her chest. The children seemed to gravitate toward her instinctively, even while sleeping. They were curled around her like puppies now, sweaty fingers clinging to her arm, cold toes pressing against her side. They had slept like this since their parents had gone, not only for warmth and to comfort the little ones, but also to keep everyone near in case of bombs like the ones Helena thought she had heard the previous night, or God only knew what else. Usually she found comfort in their closeness. But now they seemed cloying and heavy, making each breath an effort.

Disentangling herself carefully, Ruth donned her housecoat and slippers. She made her way to the kitchen, savoring the easy movements of her now-free limbs. She pulled back the shutters to watch as her sister climbed the hill. Her stomach fluttered anxiously. She had never quite gotten used to Helena's absences. They had always been together, and in some hazy memory she could remember looking up from her mother's breast to see the roundness of her sister's head, eyes locking as they fed. Being without her was an appendage missing.

"Don't go," she wanted to shout as Helena grew smaller. They had sworn to Mama that they would keep the family together, and each time Helena ventured out to Kraków, risking arrest or worse, they were putting that promise in jeopardy. Her mind cascaded, as it always did, to the worst-case scenario: without Helena, Ruth would not be able to sustain the family and the children would have to be placed in an orphanage, where they would surely remain because no one was taking on extra mouths to feed these days.

As Helena disappeared, seemingly swallowed by the thick pine trees, Ruth was struck by an unexpected touch of envy. What was it like to just walk away, escape the house and the children and their needs for a few hours? Generally Ruth liked the comfort of their home with all of its memories and had no interest in venturing beyond the front gate. But now she imagined striding through the brisk morning air, arms free and footsteps light. Did Helena ever want to keep going and not come back?

Pushing away her uneasiness, Ruth walked to the kitchen and began preparing the ersatz coffee, knowing even as she did that the bitter mixture of ground acorns and grain would do little to stave off her exhaustion. She slept so poorly these days, waking at every creak. Helena had always been the one with the vivid dreams, while her own sleep was deep and uninterrupted. Now her nights were shattered with dark images of holding on to a tree, trying not to get blown away by a storm with winds so fierce they lifted her from her feet, seeming to pull her by the ankles and threatening to tear her in two.

She dreamed of the odd things, too—not food dreams like the ones Helena and the children often discussed, describing in mouthwatering detail the cakes and breads as if doing so might cause them to actually appear. Instead, Ruth dreamed of stockings, the smooth silk kind, well-woven without any holes or pulls. *Nylons*, she'd heard them called on the radio. They talked of German soldiers giving them to the girls. She sniffed. Piotr had not given her any gifts, even when she'd knitted him the scarf. He had talked about making her something for her birthday or Christmas, but their courtship hadn't lasted that long.

Setting the coffeepot with the rusted handle on the stove, she looked around the house, their one saving grace. Built by their grandfather over the course of a decade, it was made of stone, and sturdy enough to keep out the harshest of weather. There was a large living room with a wide-beam oak floor and fireplace, and the lone bedroom off the back. Beside a faded picture of the Virgin Mary, a ladder climbed to the loft where the children had slept when their family had still been whole. Ruth saw an image like a long-forgotten dream of Tata playing with Helena on the floor, roaring with laughter as she and Mama looked on. They had been too happy to know how poor they were. Ruth had joined in, too, sometimes when the play was not as rough. Other times, she had watched from the side, wishing she could be a part of the game but too timid to play.

Seeing the house clearly now, Ruth began mentally inventorying the cleaning and decorating that needed to be done for Christmas. Once she had looked forward to the holiday so eagerly. Now it felt an effort, the idea of celebrating without their parents inconceivable. But they had to keep to their traditions as much as possible for the little ones' sake.

There were other things that had to be done before deep winter set in, too: Helena would have to reseal the windows and repair the chimney crack their father had neglected to fix. Tata had promised grander things, too, like plumbing pipes for an indoor toilet. He had always tried so very hard to please Mama, but the basic chores to keep the house running and the odd jobs he took when he could get them seemed to fill every waking hour. Mama did not complain when such extra things did not materialize.

Once Ruth had imagined a home of her own—nothing terribly grand, just a bit bigger than this, with a flower garden. But that vision had walked off over the hill with Piotr, and remembering it now, she felt frivolous. Daydreams were not a luxury she could afford anymore, and wanting too much, well, maybe that was what had caused all the trouble in the first place.

Ruth uncovered the plate of peas that she'd left by the sink the previous evening and began shelling them for the soup she would make for lunch. A year earlier, the broth would have been thick with sour cream and pieces of lard. Now it would be mostly water. There was a bit of beetroot, too; she could shred and mix it with some vinegar and call it salad.

She pulled out the radio that sat hidden beneath the sink, adjusting the volume so as not to wake the children. Radios had been forbidden by the Germans, and keeping it was her one act of defiance, a link with the outside world. Only heavy static came through. Whether the radio was dying or the Germans had jammed the signal, she did not know. She made a note to ask if Helena could fix it. An unintelligible voice crackled then, growing clearer in time for her to hear the announcer warn in a low gravelly voice that Jews were no longer to ride the trolley cars.

Reaching for the coffeepot, Ruth stifled a laugh. There was no trolley in Biekowice, and no Jews, either. She had seen Jews only once in her life on a trip with her parents to the market in My´slenice. *"Dorfjuden,"* she'd heard them called on the radio recently. *Village Jews.* Their cluster of dismal, tar-roofed shacks made her family's own cottage seem luxurious by comparison.

"I'm surprised we haven't seen more of them, really, with all of the trouble," Helena had remarked a few weeks earlier over breakfast, in that vague manner of speech they tended to use around the children.

"Better that they stay where they are," Ruth had replied, her own voice sounding harsh. She did not mean it unkindly, nor did she harbor any special animosity toward the Jews. But while the Germans seldom seemed to trifle with Poles, they had enacted an endless series of laws aimed at the Jews, forbidding them from doing ordinary things and making their already-miserable lives harder. Ruth just didn't want, as Mama would have said, to borrow trouble by having them around.

But Helena had a point, Ruth reflected now. Why didn't the Jews scatter and flee the Germans? Though they probably thought there was strength in numbers, staying in their small compact centers just made them an easier target.

There was no mention of the bombing on the radio that Helena had thought she had heard the previous evening. Ruth smiled with satisfaction, glad that her sister, who always accused her of having an overactive imagination, had this time been wrong.

She finished shelling the peas and transferred them to a smaller bowl. From the bedroom came the sound of Michal's snoring, the girls breathing gently beside him. She sighed. No one saw the work she did, the little things that kept them going. Helena deemed the chores she did outside and in the barn so much harder, scoffing at what she called "woman's work." Perhaps that was because Mama had made it look so easy, doing things twice as well and without complaint. To Ruth, though, it sometimes felt like too much.

Ruth washed the plate and dried it carefully, setting it back in its place in the cupboard. She tried to keep everything exactly as Mama had, as though she might walk through the door at any moment and inspect everything with a sweeping eye and issue Ruth a grade. Not like Helena, who blew through a room like a storm, sending things scattering. *Borrowed* was how the house seemed to Ruth, though she had grown up here herself. Like a sweater she kept carefully because she would one day be expected to return it. To acknowledge anything more would mean that Mama might not come back, and the thought was more than she could bear.

Ruth was suddenly restless. It was not like her. Usually Helena was the one hopping around like a chimpanzee. "Bored?" Ruth had replied incredulously once when her sister remarked upon it. The notion seemed absurd, especially when there was so much work to be done. But now the house felt small and confining. She wanted to go—not into the woods, rough and deep, like Helena, but somewhere else.

Ruth tiptoed back into the bedroom to the washbasin, studying her reflection in the pale early light that just illuminated the cracked mirror. She took in her thick auburn hair and round blue eyes with a twinge of self-admiration, avoiding the scar that marred her neck. She combed her hair and patted a bit of Mama's old lotion onto her cheeks, fighting the tears that welled up at the familiar, flowery smell. The jar of lotion Mama had given her was one of Ruth's most prized possessions and she loved the way it soothed her cheeks and eased the redness brought on by the wind and cold. She did not know where the cream had come from or how she would replace it when the last precious drops were gone.

It was important, Mama had said, to always look one's best, even for the most mundane of occasions. Ruth did not wear the lotion every day, though; she used to save it for Sundays when Piotr came. Her mind reeled back to one of his visits a few months earlier. The weather had been unseasonably warm and he had cajoled her into the shadows of the trees, persuaded her to let his hands wander lower and longer than they had before. But she had pushed him away a minute later and he had not tried again. Her cheeks stung now, remembering.

Turning from the mirror, she looked down at the sleeping children and a wave of affection passed over her. She had been sixteen when Karolina was born, old enough to have a family of her own if things had worked out differently. At the sight of the squiggling bundle in their mother's arms, she'd felt a longing she could not remember with Dorie or Michal—and more than a twinge of envy as Tata hovered above, glazed eyes proud and happy. Not that Ruth was jealous of his attention—she had long since resigned herself to being the daughter he did not see, his main interest in Helena because she would walk the woods and do rugged things with him. But Ruth wanted to be the center of her own family, an adoring husband standing anxiously above her. Now she had the family, the responsibility of caring for the children, only with none of the love or affection of a husband.

"Watch the others," she whispered into Michal's ear, judging by the way the covers shifted that he had heard her. The girls did not move. *Let me go with you*, Dorie would have pled through the long, uneven fringe of hair that fell into her eyes. Having lost both parents, she was afraid to let Ruth out of her sight, for fear she, too, might not return.

Nearing the front door, Ruth frowned at a brown footprint she had somehow missed when sweeping in the dim light the previous evening. Keeping the house was an endless battle against dirt tracked in under feet, crumbs and milk spilled on the table. But she persisted doggedly in her attempts to keep the house as neat as Mama had. What would happen, she wondered now, if she simply stopped trying?

Ruth donned her coat. It was more of a cape, really, great swaths of billowing fabric where the sleeves should have been.

She had found it in the back of her mother's armoire two years earlier, and had been instantly captivated by the soft, flowing garment, which was more fitting of what she imagined a night at the opera to be than anything in their roughshod farm life. "Where did you get it, Mama?"

Her mother had stared at the cape, as though it was part of another lifetime. "I don't remember." It was not just her vague tone that told Ruth she was lying—surely one could not forget acquiring such an extraordinary thing.

"Can I keep it?" Mama shrugged, seemingly divorced from whatever part of her life she had worn it. After that, Ruth wore the cape from October to April.

"So impractical," Helena chided each winter. "Not very warm. And you're going to trip." Ruth's first impulse was always to take it off to escape Helena's disdain. But she persisted in wearing it, navigating the extra folds of cloth like a second skin. She pulled the hood high and close around her face now, her own personal coat of armor. Mama's lavender scent enveloped her like the arms she had not felt in more than a year. It was growing fainter, though, muted by her own smell and the passage of time. She had to burrow deeper, stick her nose in the collar, to really find it anymore.

Ruth stepped outside and breathed in the crisp, coal-tinged air like a drink of water she had not known she needed. She had not realized how much she craved this bit of solitude, a few minutes just for herself. Their wounded goat, Bolek, one of the last two animals still living in the barn, limped hopefully to the fence and she patted his nose in silent apology for the lack of the treat he was seeking. She paused at the gate to arrange some twigs on the ground, pointing in the direction of the barn. It was a game she and Dorie played, Ruth leaving clues that led around the house and yard. Once they might have ended with the discovery of a piece of fruit or hard candy, but with none to be had she would have to come up with another sort of treasure.

Closing the gate, Ruth gazed up at the hill where her sister had traveled a few hours earlier, trying to picture the hospital. They would make Mama well, though how they would go about it, she could not fathom. Helena was always so vague in her descriptions of the nurses and Mama's treatment, and Ruth did not like to ask too much and admit that she did not know. But there was a plan, she had always believed, and that plan could surely not be to leave the children with neither parent. No, Mama would not be going to the Other Place with Tata. Not now.

"The other place," Helena repeated, with that one eyebrow arched, after overhearing Ruth using the expression to explain to Michal where their father had gone.

"Heaven, or whatever you would call it, where they go after they die…" Ruth kept speaking, using too many words, spilling them on top of one another like a drink carried too quickly across the room.

"I thought that was something you'd made up just for the children," Helena replied. Ruth looked over her shoulder to make sure the little ones were out of earshot. "Surely you don't believe it."

Ruth faltered. "Don't you?" Helena had gone to church and sat beside her as the priest talked about heaven each week.

"I believe we put Tata in the ground. And that is where he is." Stifling a gasp, Ruth crossed herself. She had pushed away the image of the coffin being lowered into the earth, holding Dorie back so she didn't throw herself in the hole after it. To Helena, dead was dead. They had not spoken of it again.

Ruth continued walking along the narrow band of water that wound along the edge of town like a ribbon. Farther down, it passed between high banks of peat moss under a crude wooden bridge where children played in summer as their mothers washed clothes. It quickly disappeared around the bend where it widened into the gorge. When they were younger, she and Helena would climb the bluff holding hands and watch the logs travel downstream to the mill.

An image flashed through Ruth's mind of her and Helena standing in this very spot when they were seven. A snowstorm had come suddenly on their way home from school and Helena had been transfixed by the way the forest was suddenly coated in white. "Come," Ruth had urged, tugging her toward home, but Helena stood still. Ruth's gaze followed her sister's upward to where the treetops and sky became one. They remained motionless, for how long Ruth did not know, hand in hand, the two of them alone in that snow globe of a world.

"*Dziewczyny!*" *Girls*, a voice called like a sharp wind, blowing her into place. Only then had Ruth noticed the coating of ice on Helena's face, and the way her own feet had gone numb. A neighboring farmer had found them and carried them home. They might have died, Mama scolded. But together they had not been afraid. How she wished for just another moment like that, the two of them alone in a white, silent world.

At the adjacent Slomir farm, an old man pulled a wagon with both hands, taking the place where his horse had once been. Though his land was ten times the size of theirs, Pan Slomir had always looked enviously across the fence at their plush, fertile patch, which seemed to draw energy from the stream like a child from its mother's breast. Now he glared at her, not bothering to mask his disdain. Ruth hunched her shoulders slightly to avoid making eye contact. Once she had loved the walk into town, soaking up the approving looks like sunshine warm on her face. She could almost hear him thinking: *What would become of the Nowaks?* It was a question that Ruth herself did not like to ask.

Closer to town, she focused on the familiar things—the way the houses, set close to the road, slatted at exactly the same angle, the birds seeming to dart from rafter to rafter in identical patterns, as though performing a dance. Twigs and roots poked out persistently between the paving stones. Biekowice was not a place that one ever left. Children grew up and married and raised their families in the same house, or maybe their husband's house if it had more room. Sons worked at the same jobs their fathers had before them. Marriage just above one's original station was the best to be hoped for a daughter. Every ten years or so, some headstrong young person would head off to the city never to be heard of again. Rumors of doom and destruction always followed. There had been a story once of a girl who had left and found her fortune, but Ruth didn't know her personally.

She passed the school, now closed by German decree. A group of girls, twelve or thirteen years old, played around the wide base of a tree. Ruth envied the easy way they laughed and joked. She and Helena had gone to school for a few years when they were younger, before Mama decided to teach them at home. But the village schoolgirls regarded the identical twin sisters, who sat in the back of the classroom together holding hands, as an oddity. Helena had never seemed to mind much, deeming the other girls "silly." Ruth would have liked to have been included in their secrets and games, though. She had never quite fit in here, felt an outlier from the others. But that couldn't be right, for she had never been anywhere else. Was it possible simply to belong nowhere?

She approached the main square. Market was a modest affair, a dozen or so canvas-covered tables smelling of carp in stale water and odd bits of too-old meat. Beside the stalls, Gorale women who had come from the sharp mountain peaks to the south sat on the ground, selling crude wool sweaters and salty sheep cheese from burlap sacks, their weather-hardened faces turned upward.

At the dairyman's stall, Ruth gave her most appreciative smile, hoping that he might move the wire over a bit to make the cut of cheese more generous. But he simply looked down at his work. She turned away, feeling foolish. Once her smiles seemed to buy everything. Now it was as if her prettiness had faded, making her a tarnished coin. It wasn't just that, of course—the war had taken the men to the front. There were so many more women that even a tired old merchant failed to notice.

She passed the dairyman the ration cards and moved on. Behind the vegetable stall, Pani Kowalska sorted potatoes and did not look up. She had been a contemporary of Mama's and could not be more than forty-five, but the hair tucked beneath her kerchief was white and she had many chins, making her look much older. What was it about the women in the village who seemed to age overnight? One day they were young and beautiful, with the promise of a future before them, and the next they were crones. Mama had never made the transition—she had not had the chance before taking ill. But Ruth knew that one day she would wake up looking exactly as Pani Kowalska, and then any remaining hope for a future would be gone for good.

She appraised the selection of fruits and vegetables. Even before the war it had not been good, the cool climate and short growing season inhospitable for vegetables like tomatoes and peppers. Now all that remained were a few mottled onions and potatoes already sprouting roots.

"Three apples," Ruth requested. An unfamiliar police car sat at the edge of the market, engine idling despite the lack of a driver. Ruth shivered uneasily. The fact that the provincial police had come to town had nothing to do with her, but it was different, and change seldom meant anything good.

"Did you hear about the Garzels?" Pani Kowalska asked as she weighed the fruit on the scale. The mole on her nose, which seemed to have doubled in size since Ruth had last visited the stall, bobbed as she spoke.

Ruth shook her head as though the woman was watching. Life in a small village reminded Ruth of what a zoo might be like, though she had only read about such places. Homes transparent, lives exposed to one another. Everyone knew everyone else's business, almost before it had happened. *"Nie."* Ruth suspected that she did not want to hear the answer. She inspected the apples the woman handed her, which were mottled and bruised. She did not protest, knowing the rest in the barrel would be no better.

Pani Kowalska wiped her hands on her skirt. "Gone."

"Perhaps they went to find Leopold," Ruth suggested. The elderly couple's son, just a few years older than Michal, had disappeared ahead of a transport of conscripted men to the front. The call-ups had taken place with alarming frequency of late, young men ordered to report for either military service or other forced labor for the Reich.

"Not if he went to forest they didn't." Ruth did not want to admit that she was unfamiliar with the term. "To the woods to fight," Pani Kowalska clarified unbidden. Ruth had heard the rumors of soldiers from the decimated Polish army who had gone underground to wage war against the Germans.

Ruth searched for another plausible explanation. "Without him to work the farm, they must have decided to go to relatives."

Pani Kowalska shook her head, chins jiggling. "They left with the door open, all of their belongings still inside. Who on earth does that?"

Who indeed? One would board up the house if truly going for a while and planning it—unless one did not want anyone to know or to attract too much attention.

"And then there are the goings-on in Nowy S¸acz," Pani Kowalska added, gaining steam even as she returned to sorting potatoes. "They arrested all of the Jews." How had the woman heard such things? The news on the radio would not have spoken of them. But gossip, even about those they did not know, seemed to travel with the wind like pollen. "Good riddance, I say," the old woman spat with more bile than Ruth might have thought she could muster. Ruth did not respond, but sadness tugged at her. Why did Pani Kowalska sound so angry about a handful of Jews in another town? Ruth did not have any particular affinity for the Jews, but it was the ugliness of it all that bothered her.

"Christ killing heathens. Always driving down my prices," Pani Kowalska added, as if answering the unspoken question. So that was the real reason. Her hatred of the Jews stemmed less from purported drinking of baby's blood than the price of turnips.

The Jews weren't all hard-charging vegetable merchants, Ruth wanted to point out. "Surely just the men have been taken," she offered instead.

Pani Kowalska shook her head. "All of them." What would the Germans want with the women and children? And what could they possibly do with so many people? Ruth's arms suddenly ached for her brother and sisters. But before she could ask, the old woman looked past Ruth's shoulder at another customer. *"Tak?"*

Ruth stepped aside and surveyed the rest of the market. Taking in the flies that swarmed above the meat stand as though it were August, she decided to save the rest of their ration coupons for her next visit.

At the corner, she spied a familiar figure approaching, a sallow, fiftyish women who stared vacantly ahead and carried her empty basket as though it bore rocks. Ruth started quickly in the opposite direction. Her foot caught on the curb and she stumbled, catching herself before she fell to the ground. Piotr's mother turned toward her, then looked away quickly, no more wanting the encounter than Ruth did. But it was unavoidable. Ruth brushed her hands on her skirt and took a step toward the woman.

A moment of silence passed between them. *It was your fault,* Ruth wanted to yell, seized with the urge to slap her sagging cheek. Piotr's mother had welcomed Ruth warmly in her home, professing that Ruth was the daughter that she'd never had. But at the first opportunity, she had turned on Ruth, casting her out.

"Dzie'n dobry," Ruth greeted instead over the dryness in her throat, cursing her own lack of nerve. She eyed the stitching of the woman's scarf, tighter and of a better quality wool than her own. Had she knitted it herself or was it a gift from Piotr's new fiancée? Her pale blue eyes were a mirror of her son's, but Ruth had not noticed until just now how cold and unfeeling they could be. "How is Piotr?" she asked, in spite of herself. His name stuck in her throat.

A slight wince crossed the woman's face. "He's been sent to the front."

A knife shot through her and she knew in that instant he would not be coming back. Her eyes stung. "I'm sorry," Ruth said awkwardly, as though she had been personally responsible for his conscription. She stumbled past Piotr's mother and continued on, struggling to keep her back straight and head high. He was not hers to worry about anymore.

3

Helena reached the top of the forested hills that rose high above the city of Kraków. A fine perspiration coated her skin from the climb, causing the wool collar of her coat to itch unpleasantly. From here, shrouded by the tall clusters of perennially flush pine trees that pointed defiantly toward the sky, she could see whether the winding streets below were clear and it was safe to go down.

The panorama of the city unfurled before her. Wawel Castle sat upon a hill, presiding over the sea of slate roofs and spires below. Months ago, the city had looked untouched from here, the cobblestone passageways timeless, save for a handful of cars. But the war now seemed everywhere. The streets were choked with trucks and soldiers, like the big black ants that appeared in the kitchen at the first sign of spring.

After charting her course to avoid any checkpoints, Helena began the descent into the city. She emerged from the woods onto the path that quickly became a dirt road, trying to walk normally as the trees thinned and the houses grew more clustered. Closer in, the paved streets were speckled with harried pedestrians, darting between the shops, eager to scurry back to the safety of their homes. The air was thick with exhaust from a delivery truck idling at the curbside. Workers in overalls carried their dinner pails, eyes low.

She crossed the bridge and started down *ulica Dietla*. Once Roma children had played instruments at the corner of the wide thoroughfare, open violin cases turned upward in hope of a few coins. But now only a hapless gray-haired *babcia* sat propped against the base of a building, seemingly oblivious to the cold. Her eyes were closed and toothless mouth agape, as though she might already be dead.

Helena slipped into the crowd, her skin prickling as she viewed the city with more trepidation than ever. She caught a glimpse of herself in a shop window. Beneath her faded, nondescript coat, her dress hung like a baggy sack and her reddish-brown hair was hastily pulled back in a knot. Anxiety formed in her stomach. She looked like a girl from the countryside, *"na wsi"* as she had heard the city dwellers call it derisively—not at all like she fit in. Certainly a passerby would recognize any moment now that she did not belong here and summon the police.

Steeling herself, she pressed onward. Twenty minutes later, she reached Kazimierz, which was the Jewish quarter, or at least what was left of it. There were no Jews in the village back home, and when she had first journeyed to the city, Helena had enjoyed walking through the streets here, smelling the chicken fat and dill from the butcher mix with the aroma of cinnamon and raisins from a nearby bakery. The loud voices, speaking a language she did not understand, had made Kazimierz seem like a foreign country. But the streets were nearly deserted now, as if the population of Kazimierz was dwindling, or simply too afraid to be out on the streets. Many of the shops were boarded up, windows that had not been shattered slashed in yellow paint with the word *Żyd. Jew.*

The building that housed the hospital had once been grand,

its marble steps and tall columns suggesting a bank or perhaps a government office. Now its stone facade was black with soot and the steps covered with droppings from the pigeons that occupied the eaves. Helena walked through the vacant lobby, past the front desk nobody bothered to man anymore, down the lone gray corridor redolent with old plaster, urine and bile.

When Tata had told them that he'd placed their mother in a Jewish hospital, the only facility with a bed they could afford, Helena had imagined somewhere dark and exotic, with shrouded men performing strange rituals. She had been surprised on her first visit by just how unremarkable it was—the white walls were bare and the nurses wore simple dresses and caps. The gowned patients were undistinguishable by faith, time and illness stripping away all social division. Save for the tarnished ornaments affixed to each doorway (mezuzahs, she'd heard them called on a past visit) and the occasional rabbi or other visitor in religious garb, one would not know it was a Jewish place at all.

Helena crossed the ward. Though it was a dismal affair, there were little touches, light-filled windows and slightly wider-than-average beds that said the people who ran it had once cared. Nearing her mother, Helena's heart sank. Mama had been a beauty, tall and slender with alabaster skin. Now her green eyes were clouded and her chestnut hair dulled to a lifeless gray. The skin below her cheekbones had caved in, giving her a ghoulish look. "Mama," Helena said, touching her hand. Her mother did not move or respond, but stared vacantly at the ceiling.

The elderly woman in the next bed listed to one side, her gown hanging open to expose a withered breast. Helena walked over to her and straightened the woman's head, keeping her own eyes averted as she fixed the woman's gown. "Excuse me," Helena said gently, hoping she did not mind the intrusion. The woman blinked, conveying with the simple movement an ocean of gratitude and relief.

A nurse moved swiftly at the other end of the ward, folding

blankets, shifting patients from side to side with deft hands as she freshened the beds. Her name was Wanda, Helena recalled. She was more capable than most of the other staff, and kinder when time allowed it.

"*Dzie'n dobry,*" Helena greeted as Wanda neared. The heavy-boned nurse did not respond, but stared downward at the fresh red wound on Helena's hand.

As if on cue, the cut from the thorny bush, which Helena had rinsed hurriedly in the icy stream, began to throb. Wanda disappeared into a closet across the room and emerged a moment later with a piece of damp gauze, which she gave to Helena. She closed the closet door swiftly, as though something might escape.

"Thank you." As Helena cleaned the wound, alcohol stinging the raw skin, she waited for Wanda to ask how she had hurt herself.

"She sat up this morning," Wanda informed her instead, too busy to take further interest in maladies not her own. "Took a bit of broth and even said hello to me." The words, offered to make Helena feel better, slammed her in the chest. Her mother had been cognizant for a fleeting moment and Helena had missed it. Had Mama felt all alone, confused about where she was and why no one was there with her?

"Perhaps in the spring when the weather is nicer, I can wheel her outside in one of the chairs," Helena offered.

A strange look crossed Wanda's face. Did she not think that Mama would still be here then, or was her concern larger than that? "With so many Jews gone…" Wanda faltered in her explanation.

"Where have they gone?" Helena was glad to have the opportunity to ask.

Wanda lowered her voice. "Some have left the city, or even gone abroad, if they were able. Others have been ordered to the ghetto."

Helena shook her head. "Ghetto?"

"The walled neighborhood in Podgórze." Helena had passed by the industrial neighborhood across the river and seen the streets that the Germans had begun to cordon off. She had surmised that some Jews from the villages were to live there. But it seemed odd to relocate the Kazimierz Jews, who already had a neighborhood of their own. And if the Jews were going, what future could the hospital have here? "Will they all go?"

"I doubt it. There are still a good number of Jews living in Kazimierz."

Mama coughed once, then again. "Is Dr. Ackerman here today?" Helena asked. "I need to speak with him about my mother's medicine."

Wanda frowned. "He's been called away." Helena sensed that it was better not to ask when he would return. At first the war had seemed a boon to the hospital—the Jewish doctors, forbidden from treating Gentile Poles, had flocked eagerly to work here. But their numbers had diminished ominously in the preceding weeks. "And I'm sorry about the medicine. We haven't been able to get any new shipments of the laudanum and so we've had to dilute what we have left in order to make it last."

They had decreased Mama's dosage, Helena reflected, and yet she was no more lucid—further proof that wherever her mind had gone with the illness, it wasn't coming back. "Then perhaps another medicine," she suggested. "Something that doesn't make her so drowsy."

"I'll ask." But Wanda's tone made clear that there were no other drugs to be had.

"The medicine supply," Helena persisted, "is there truly nothing to be done?"

Wanda's forehead crinkled. "I've tried the other hospitals, even gone to the Mariacki Cathedral to see if any could be bought."

She was talking about the black market, Helena realized, caught off guard by the casual way in which the nurse mentioned procuring illegal goods, in a church no less. Helena considered the nurse: Wanda did not wear the yellow star of a Jew. Yet she had chosen to remain working here. Helena was touched by the nurse's effort, risking her personal safety to help her patients. "Here." Helena fished in her pocket for a coin. She could ill-afford to give away money now, but in addition to expressing her gratitude, it might buy Mama an extra moment's care. She watched the conflict that washed over Wanda's face, wanting to refuse the offering because taking care of Helena's mother was her job.

But no one could afford to be that proud in times like this. Wanda took the coin and shoved it into her pocket. *"Dzieki."* She shuffled past, continuing on her rounds.

Helena settled into the chair beside the bed. Mama had suffered silently for months with what she presumed were just the normal aches and tugs of a body that had borne five children trying to pull itself back into place. But the pain grew worse and her appetite waned and by the time the village's lone doctor came he could feel the lump in her belly, larger than an apple. She might have stayed at home until the end of her days, had fought for it. But then her mind started to slip, as though the cancer had spread there, or perhaps the fate she was going to face was simply too much to contemplate. One night they'd found her over the baby's crib holding a pot of hot water and they knew the time had come for her to go.

Helena pulled out the bread wrapped in paper. She tore it into small pieces and held it out. "Look, Mama," she offered, bringing the dry, flat bread close to her mother's nose. "Ruth baked this for you yesterday." Even Ruth's best efforts could not come close to the bread Mama had once made, but it was hardly a fair comparison, given the lack of good flour these days.

When Mama did not respond, Helena leaned forward and dipped the bread into the glass of tepid water that sat on the table beside the bed. Then she lifted her mother's head and put a small piece in her mouth, willing her to eat it. But the bread lay between her slack lips. Finally, Helena removed it again, fearful that she would choke. A sour smell came from between her lips, the teeth Mama had maintained with such care beginning to rot. Helena stared at the remaining fistful of bread uncertainly. No one would take the time to feed it to her once Helena was gone; it would just be taken by one of the nurses or other patients. She tucked it back in her bag.

Helena gazed out the window, grateful yet again that the ward in which her mother was located looked into the interior courtyard. From here, Mama could not see the military vehicles that rumbled by or the German soldiers in the streets. A different room would have made the pretense of normalcy impossible.

"You aren't going to tell her about the war, are you?" Ruth had asked their father the first time he prepared to set out for the city after the invasion. Overhearing, Helena had been surprised. It was a war, for goodness' sake, and their mother was at the heart of it. But Tata hadn't said anything. Looking around the sanatorium now, Helena was struck by how little had changed—the machines still hummed and the patients still moaned, trapped in their own private battles. So the fiction had persisted.

Beside Helena, her mother stirred. "Mama?" Helena leaned forward, hope rising in her as she kissed her mother on her papery cheek.

But her mother only looked at her blankly. Did she wonder why her beloved husband no longer came to visit, or had she not noticed? *"Ruti?"* she asked, using her pet name for Helena's sister.

Helena blanched. No, it wasn't Ruth who was sturdy enough to make the journey, or brave enough to try. But if thinking it was so brought their mother comfort, Helena would play along. "Yes, Mama, it's me." It should have been Ruth here, Helena reflected. She had always been closer to Mama, sitting at their mother's side, learning with rapt attention how to cook and sew while thick-fingered Helena followed Tata into the woods, gathering kindling and roots. Sometimes it seemed as though she and Ruth had been cast into those roles at birth. "The pretty one," she'd heard people remark more than once about Ruth—but how was that possible when they were twins and meant to look just the same? She herself had been deemed sturdy and capable for so long she could not fathom where the idea had first arisen. Had their parents noted these differences in them from the start and nurtured them, or had they grown to play the parts they had been given?

"Jealous, even as a baby," their mother had remarked of Helena more than once over the years. "You would give me such a look when I held your sister instead of you." *I wasn't jealous*, Helena had wanted to respond later, when she was old enough to understand. *I just wanted to be held, too, to be a part of things before you had to set us down and move on to the next task or chore.* But it was always that way with twins, never enough time or arms to go around, and the extra always seemed to go to sweet, helpful Ruth.

The sisters had always been a great source of curiosity in the town, the first set of twins seen there in more than a generation. "And after, when the midwife put you both in the cradle, the first thing you did was hold hands," Mama was fond of recalling. "She'd said she'd never heard of such a thing."

Whenever they went out, people made sport of trying to guess which one was which. "No, no, don't tell me!" In fact, the sisters had subtle differences: Ruth had a rounder face and large blue eyes while Helena's own features were plainer, her skin more ruddy than luminescent. And there was the birthmark, too, heart-shaped just below Ruth's right ear, which Ruth desperately tried to conceal, that made them impossible to confuse if one looked closely. But to the casual observer, they were indistinguishable.

Helena sat in silence for several minutes. There were things she wanted to ask her mother now, about how to make a good poultice for the goat's wounded leg, and the way to get the cabinet above the stove to stop sticking. She wanted to tell her mother that Dorie had lost another tooth, how Karolina was starting to speak a bit. But she was never sure if hearing about the children would make Mama happy or more forlorn, or even if she remembered them at all.

She searched her mother's face, looking for some words that would change it all. But she had stopped believing in magic years ago, and prayers were Ruth's province. "Come back to us," she said plaintively, knowing there would be no response.

Helena opened the drawer on the night table and busied herself taking inventory of the scant contents, taking note of the spare sock that was missing. She picked up her mother's extra housecoat, which someone had shoved in the drawer without bothering to fold. There was blood at the collar. Helena bent hurriedly to check for a wound, and Mama winced, as though accustomed to a rough touch.

"Shh," Helena soothed, willing herself to move more slowly. But there was no mark on her mother's neck. Had the blood come from an old wound or had someone else worn the gown? She put it in her knapsack, replacing it with the fresh one she had brought with her.

"I should go," she said finally. Guilt rose in her then as it always did at the notion that after she left Mama would again be all alone in this sad place. But she had to get home to help Ruth, and if she didn't leave now she would not make it before dark. She searched her mother's face for some reaction, but found none. No, the sadness about parting was all hers. Mama was already alone.

Helena left the hospital, retracing her steps through Kazimierz as she made her way from the city. The gray clouds had grown thick and ominous now, the air biting. The earlier dampness under her clothes had dried to an uncomfortable chill. As she wound her way around the base of Wawel Castle, Helena peered over her shoulder, inexplicably fearful that someone might be following her. Spotting nothing unusual, she pressed forward, heart beating just a bit too quickly. Despite her anxiety, she could not help but feel a touch of excitement. For so long it had seemed that everything moved around her while she stood in place like the moon behind the clouds. Now with the explosion she was sure she had heard the previous night and the sighting of the German jeep, the world had shifted slightly and suddenly life felt different.

As she crossed the wide bridge that spanned the river, her thoughts turned to her father. The priest had called Tata a hero for stepping in front of the runaway wagon and blocking it from hitting a child. Helena knew he was the furthest thing from that, though. Tadeusz Nowak was a drunk and he had most likely gotten hit because he was too inebriated to move out of the wagon's path, even at ten o'clock in the morning. But she said nothing, accepting the neighbors' gifts of sympathy, the soups and baked goods that flowed much more generously than if he had been found lying in a pile of vodka and vomit.

Helena was the one who had answered the knock the day they came about Tata and followed the constable to the site. There were details she would spare Ruth and the others about the way he had soiled himself, how his neck hung at a funny angle like a broken doll. She had focused instead at the hands and arms that were as familiar as her own.

Tata had been her counterpart, the one most like her, and with his death a part of her had died, too. But after he was gone she discovered a newfound clarity and purpose, slipping into his role, taking charge of the wood and the hunting and their safety. She found she was capable of doing things that she had never been taught, as though a part of Tata had left his body in the moment he was struck down and leaped into hers.

An hour later, Helena reached the edge of the forest. She rubbed at the back of her hand where a bit of pine tar had stuck above the wound, contemplating her route. The road would have been faster, but she would take the high pass over the mountain so as not to risk encountering more Germans. She started forward. The terrain ahead was much more difficult, the rolling hills deceptive. It gave no indication of the steep slope, or the sharp stones that jutted out from the ground, marring the path. Helena navigated through the rocks, finding the familiar footholds. She had come this way every week as a child on walks with Tata. She had loved the springtime best when they would gather mushrooms, father and daughter making their way through the woods in the predawn darkness, the silence only broken by the sloshing of his flask.

The goodwill of the neighbors had evaporated quickly after their father's death, as people pulled back to whisper about how the Nowak children—now virtually orphans—would survive. Helena did not mind—she preferred their distance to the over-kindness she had never quite believed. There was speculation, too, about the lack of a possible suitor for either twin. Ruth had had someone for a time, a big strapping boy called Piotr. He had called on her faithfully each week, bringing the odd bit of candy for the children. But then the business with their father had happened and Piotr had come one last time to speak with Ruth. Helena had not been able to hear their conversation, but when she had peered around the side of the barn she spied them down by the stream, Piotr handing back the brown scarf her sister had knitted for him, Ruth pushing it away so that it dropped to the ground. Helena had rushed out afterward to collect it so the scarce wool could be reused.

When Ruth had come back inside the house, Helena had faltered. She put her arm around Ruth's shoulder, cringing at her own stiffness. "I'm sorry."

Ruth shrugged off her arm and stepped away. "You never liked him." Ruth's tone was accusing. Helena wanted to deny it, but Ruth was right: she had not liked Piotr, and had resented that Ruth had something beyond their family. She had not wanted him to stay. But now he had hurt Ruth, though, and for that she wanted to kill him.

Though Ruth had not said, Helena knew that it was the children who had caused Piotr to run. No man wanted to take on the responsibility of caring for someone else's family, especially not one with young mouths needing to be fed for so many years yet. There would be no marriage for her or Ruth now; of that she was sure. So they would go on working and keeping the children alive until they were big enough to fend for themselves. Michal perhaps would support them in a few years or the younger girls might someday marry; they were pretty enough. What else? Helena could plant a good-size garden in the spring and sell the extra bounty in town. She'd heard that the war had opened up jobs for the women left behind by the men forced to go and fight. But even if she could secure a work pass, traveling to the city once a week was hard enough; she could not commute daily and she could not leave Ruth alone with the children for longer than that.

As Helena paused to catch her breath, an unfamiliar scent tickled her nose. It was sweet yet acrid, like when the farmers burned brush in early autumn and something unintended got tossed into the fire, a dead squirrel perhaps. No one was burning this late in the season, though. Looking west, she noticed then a thick finger of dark smoke curling toward the sky. Where was it coming from? There were no factories in that direction and it was too far beyond the trees to be a forest fire.

A sudden rustling noise from the bushes made her jump. Recalling the German she'd encountered earlier, her heart pounded. But the noise had not come from the road. She scanned the side of the path. There had been stories of hungry wolves in these parts, but it was more likely a dog or raccoon. Something she might kill for food, if it was not too wounded or rabid. She heard the noise come again, this time more of a wheeze.

She reached for her knife. A voice not entirely her own told her to run. But instead, she drew closer to the bushes, curious. Beneath a scraggly pine tree there was a lump, too long to be an animal, huddled in a pile of leaves. As she neared, the air grew thick with the metallic smell of blood. She pushed aside the branches, then stopped with surprise. A man lay on his side, almost hidden by the leaves. He didn't move, but his torso rose and fell with labored breaths.

Helena stared at him. Before today, she had not encountered anyone on her treks through the forest. "Who are you?" she demanded, hoping to sound braver than she felt. He did not respond. Fear rose up in her. No good could come of a meeting with a stranger and she was far from any help. "Who are you?" she repeated. A low, guttural moan escaped his throat. Helena studied the man, whose dark hair was pasted tight to his head by a mixture of blood and sweat. She relaxed slightly; he was in no shape to do her harm.

"Show me where you are hurt," she said, more gently now. His arm, which had been covering his midsection, flopped in the direction of his right leg, but there was no visible injury. The stranger wore a uniform of some sort, dirt-caked and torn. She recalled the explosion from the previous night that she had taken to be a bomb. The Nazi jeep she'd encountered earlier had not been looking for her. The full danger of the situation crashed down upon her and she turned to flee.

"Please," he croaked just above a whisper, and somewhere in her mind she registered the word as English. Her mind whirled: what was an American or British soldier doing here?

Freezing, was her first thought as she turned back to him in spite of herself. He lay on the ground and his skin was a shade of blue-gray that she had never seen before. He needed shelter if he was to live. Without thinking, she reached for his arm and pulled as though to lift him, her fingers not quite wrapping around its thick girth. The man was heavier than she expected and did not move, but shrieked with pain, his cry echoing against the bareness of the trees.

"*Spokój!*" she hissed, and he looked up, his brown eyes meeting hers, long lashes fluttering with fear. But she could tell from his expression that he did not speak Polish or was too disoriented to understand, so she raised her finger to her lips and shook her head to silence him.

The church, she remembered then. There was an old wooden chapel, about fifty meters farther along the path into the woods. But if she could not move him, how could she possibly get him there? "Come." She knelt and put her arm around his shoulder, close to the stranger in a way that made her shiver. Then she tried to stand, more gently this time. But she stumbled under his weight. He fell forward, and as she went to lift him again he waved her off, dragging himself along the ground in a half crawl.

As he inched forward, she glanced over her shoulder nervously, willing him to move faster. Her skin prickled. A sharp barking cut through the stillness. "Hide," she whispered frantically, pushing him into the thick bushes. There came a dull thud from the other side, followed by a cry. She crawled through the brush toward him. He had rolled down a steep ravine and into the stream that ran alongside the path. There was another bark, followed by footsteps. She peered out from the bushes, jumping back as a man with a shotgun appeared, an underfed German shepherd on a leash by his side. He did not wear a uniform like the German soldier she had encountered earlier on the road, but the clothes of an ordinary farmer (albeit one she did not recognize from the village). Perhaps he was just hunting or trapping.

A second man appeared from the opposite direction. "Anything?" His Polish was thick and peasantlike.

"A small chapel. But I found nothing there," the other man replied. Helena's anger rose. These men were searching for the soldier, doing the Germans' bidding. Panic quickly overshadowed her fury as the dog sniffed along the edge of the path, drawing closer. Surely the animal would smell the soldier's wounds.

Her heart raced as the dog stopped, its ugly snout just inches from her own face. *"Chocz!"* ordered the man holding the leash, tugging at it and forcing the dog to follow. They continued deeper into the forest.

A rasping noise came from behind her. Helena turned back toward the soldier, who lay on his back in the stream, seemingly oblivious to the icy water that trickled around him. Hurriedly she moved to him, pressing her hand to his mouth to muffle the sound. She looked over her shoulder, hoping the men had not heard. She wanted to admonish the man to be quiet once more, but he was too far gone for that. His face was ghostly white and he seemed to be struggling for each breath.

Quickly she reached down with both arms and, using her legs to brace, pulled him from the water onto the incline of the bank. "You have to help me get you to shelter," she said. But his eyes were half-closed and she had no idea if he understood.

She checked the now-empty path once more. The men knew about the chapel. Did she still dare to take the soldier there? Though the men had already checked it, they could still come back. But she could not take him to her house—even if he could make the journey, the road out of the forest to their cottage was open and exposed. And leaving him out here meant certain death. There was no other choice—the chapel was his only hope.

She wrapped the soldier's arm around her shoulder, cold water dripping from his hair and seeping into her collar. Bracing herself anew, she maneuvered him back onto the path. The force of his weight brought her to her knees once more. "Help me," she pleaded, her voice a whisper. She held her breath as he dragged himself slowly the last few meters down the path, certain the men would return to discover them.

At last they reached chapel. It was no bigger than Helena's cottage, but taller with an elongated knave. A wood-shingled roof overhung the building like a cap drawn close around the brow. The top of the steeple was completely gone, the mounted cross threatening to topple at any second. She had discovered the abandoned chapel as a child and played around it many times despite her mother's admonishment lest the roof cave in and crush them. She had often wondered who would have cared enough to build a chapel, not big enough for more than a handful of worshippers, here in the woods, instead of just going to the church in town. And why had they stopped coming?

Helena opened the door and peered inside. The air was thick with the scent of moldy wood and damp earth. She had not been here in years and the structure had deteriorated further with time. The floor had rotted to a few remaining planks over dirt and much of the roof had peeled away, revealing the gray sky above.

Helena turned back to help the man through the doorway, propping him against the nearest wall. Her hand brushed against something hard at his waist and she pulled back his shirt to reveal a pistol that had somehow survived his ordeal. She did not know why she was surprised—he was a soldier, after all. For a moment, she considered taking it, then decided to leave him his one defense, if it even still worked. She ran her hands over his torso, feeling for other injuries, not sure what she would do if she found any. Then she pulled her hands back, wondering if he minded the intimacy of her stranger's touch. But he lay with his eyes closed, still laboring to breathe.

She shivered, not entirely sure it was from the cold. There was something exciting and dangerous about him that made her take a step backward, that made her want to run and yet unable to look away at the same time. She peered in her satchel, pulling out the small loaf of bread she had tried to feed to her mother and placing it on the ground beside him. He needed a fire, but there was no wood and nothing else to burn.

"I'll get help," she offered. But even before he shook his head she knew that it was impossible. There was no one to be trusted and telling anyone would only put them both in danger. She looked around desperately. There was nothing more she could do for him here, and if she waited longer it would be dark and she would be unable to make the rest of the trip home.

She started to stand and he clung to the hem of her skirt in a way that might have been improper if he'd had the strength to mean it. *Don't go*, the helpless look in his eyes seemed to say. She took his hand from her dress and placed it back on his chest, struck by the warmth of his fingers, and the strong muscle beneath the torn uniform. "I'll be back," she promised. And then she turned on her heel and ran.

4

<hr />

"I'm going to see Mama again today," Helena announced two days later as she fed breakfast to Karolina. She held a spoonful of coarse oat cereal suspended midair a few inches short of the baby's open mouth, watching for Ruth's reaction.

Ruth stopped dressing Dorie, the skirt stuck awkwardly over the child's head. "Why? Is she worse?"

"She's fine." Helena immediately recognized the lack of truth in her response. "Fine" would have meant Mama recognizing her own daughter or chewing a mouthful of bread. Helena didn't like to lie.

But Ruth tended to view the world as she wanted to see it. "When Mama comes back…" she would often say. At first Helena had wanted to correct her—how could she possibly believe that would ever happen? Denial was Ruth's means of survival, though, and there was no harm in pretending as long as she didn't rely on it. So Helena sometimes spared her from the worst.

"Me!" Karolina squawked, grabbing the spoon. As the child tried to feed herself, Helena considered telling Ruth about the soldier she had found. Ruth was better with salves and bandages and such, and she might have some other ways they could help the man. But something stopped her.

"Her doctor wasn't there last time and I wanted to ask him about her medicine," Helena added instead, stretching the story. She had never gone to see Mama more than once a week before. Surely Ruth would see through the lie. But Ruth just yanked the skirt over Dorie's head, then sat the child in the chair to braid her hair, which had more than a hint of red to it, without reaction.

Helena took the spoon back from Karolina and scraped a last spoonful of cereal for her. "Drink your milk," she said, more sternly than she intended. Waste could not be tolerated, even by the children.

"Mook," Karolina offered. She had been a quiet baby for so long they had fretted something might be wrong, a deficit caused perhaps by the trauma of her parents' disappearance. But she had begun speaking a few months earlier, gathering new words each day and trying them on for size. She took a sip from her cup, then smiled brightly, searching her sister's face for praise. She was, like Ruth, too dependent on the approval of others—approval that seldom came anymore for any of them.

Helena looked across the crude wooden table at Michal, who had finished eating and now rested his chin on his hands, staring into the space. None of the children played during meals as she and Ruth had in happier times, giggling and whispering until their parents would scold them. Rather, they sat and ate gravely, as though they realized the scarcity of food and were unwilling to take it for granted.

The wind blew more strongly today than it had in months, howling around the house like a wolf looking for an entry point. Helena's thoughts shifted to the soldier, alone in the cold, damp chapel. She had helped him without thinking, the same instinct that had prompted her to bring home a wounded squirrel she'd found as a child. Though his ripped uniform had not born any markings, she suspected that he was American, or perhaps British. Her heart skipped as she remembered the bit of pale flesh that she had glimpsed through the fabric. Enough, she admonished herself. This was not a schoolgirl's crush, like Ruth always seemed to have on various boys when they were younger—this was about the soldier's survival. Was he in pain? Was he even still alive? Helena had wanted to get away sooner to check on him. But Karolina had come down with a brief, soaring fever the night she'd returned, and Ruth couldn't handle the three children alone when one was sick.

What if she didn't go back to the chapel? She had brought the soldier to safety, and surely that was as much as anyone could expect from her. Anything else would put their family in danger. But he was already dependent on her, and without her help he would die of cold or starvation or something worse.

Across the table, Michal's hazel eyes met hers. He had been born with wisdom beyond his years and had never gone through a childish phase. Though she did not believe in such things, it sometimes seemed as though he was an old soul who had seen all of this a thousand times before, and his understanding of the world made him somber. The day she'd almost taken the leaving path, Michal had peered at her deeply when she returned, as if aware of her near-transgression. He was staring at Helena now in a way that made her wonder if he had read her mind and knew about the soldier at the church. But of course, that was impossible.

She reached across the table and put her hand on his. He looked up, surprised at her rare display of affection. Perhaps more so than the girls, it was Michal to whom she was closest and had tried to shield. It had not always been that way—at first, she'd hated him. "A boy," Tata had announced the day Michal was born, his face beaming with pride. Then six, Helena looked at the tiny infant with a mix of resentment and love. He would grow into the son who would take her place as their father's favorite. Over the years, she had fought to stay stronger and more useful, always a step ahead, even as Michal grew taller.

One morning when she was twelve, she'd awakened to a squawk of dismay as Tata pulled her six-year-old brother from his bed for his first hunting trip. Jealousy nagged at her—before Michal, it had been she who had accompanied Tata on his dark forays into the cold woods to set traps and shoot deer. Now he had his son. But Michal sat on the floor, skin white and eyes wide as their father tugged at his collar, trying to force him to his feet. Michal looked up at her imploringly. He had always loved animals, had all but stopped eating meat as a child once he'd realized where it came from. Tata loomed over him, unwilling to be dissuaded. "Come," she said, helping Michal to dress. Tata did not object when she tagged along, holding her brother's hand as they trudged wordlessly through the dark, still woods.

There was nothing to be caught that day. When they had returned home, Tata stomped into the barn and emerged holding a flailing chicken by the neck. "Kill it," he instructed Michal, unwilling to be placated until the lesson was complete. The boy stood back, trembling. Several seconds passed. "Do it." Tears streamed down Michal's cheeks.

Helena stepped forward and grabbed the chicken from her father, snapping its neck beneath the warm feathers with one swift movement. Her eyes met Tata's defiantly and for a moment she feared he was going to return to the barn to get another chicken, their last, for Michal to kill. But he had simply walked away. "Come," she'd said again to her brother. Together they went to clean the bird, Helena gently but persistently showing him how to remove the feathers and separate the bones.

It was perhaps hardest on him now, Helena reflected as the memory cleared. Michal was old enough to remember faint glimpses of the happiness that had once been theirs, not like Dorie and Karolina, who didn't know what they had missed.

But he had been too young to understand why it had all gone away, leaving him alone in a house full of girls.

"Here." Helena pushed the rest of her bread toward him, trying to ignore her stomach, which grumbled in protest. As she did, she noticed a stain on her sleeve left by spilled milk and cereal.

Michal hesitated, then devoured the bread in two bites, hardly bothering to chew. "May I be excused?"

"No," said Ruth.

"Yes," said Helena in near-unison, their voices clashing against each other. They looked at each other uneasily. It was a tacit understanding that, despite their differences, they would not disagree in front of the children. For all of the hard times, she could not recall her parents quarreling, at least not when they thought the children could hear, and she and Ruth had tried to maintain that unified front. But the sisters seemed to differ more of late, their opposition laid bare for the children to see.

"Yes," Ruth relented quickly. "Check on the animals, will you?"

"Come on, Dorie," Michal said, holding out his hand.

Dorie followed him, her gait stilted. Her right leg had grown more slowly and was now an inch shorter than her left, causing her to limp. "It will even out," Mama had predicted optimistically when Dorie had started walking and the problem first became apparent. But the difference had become more pronounced with time.

Last spring, Helena had cut down a block of wood and affixed it to Dorie's right shoe to compensate. It worked, and the limp had been all but gone when she had worn it. But a day later, Dorie had pulled the wood from her shoe. "It just doesn't feel right." Around the house, her limp had become so much a part of things they scarcely noticed it. As Helena watched Dorie hobble now along Michal's long, foal-like gait, she seemed so vulnerable.

Michal and Dorie bounded through the door, spurred by the brisk morning air, their two heads bobbing auburn. Helena opened the shutters to let in the light. Ruth kept the children immaculate, Helena conceded inwardly. Their clothes were not torn or stained, the darned bits hidden so well they could scarcely be seen. She brushed their teeth with baking soda each night, insisted that their baths be thorough. Helena sometimes wondered why she bothered when they so seldom saw anyone but one another.

Outside the children ran in circles, Michal pretending to exert himself but really going much slower than he might have, allowing Dorie to catch him and feel that she was doing well. They chased a chipmunk around the yard, nearly colliding into the dwindling woodpile as the animal ducked beneath. Watching them play together, Helena was flooded with pride—despite their thinness and simple clothing, there was a light about them, a kind of strength other children did not possess. And they had a way of instinctively protecting each other, always had, even before they could walk or speak.

Was it different for them somehow because they weren't twins? Helena wondered. With her and Ruth, it had always been a competition, who had spoken first (Ruth) and walked first (Helena), and later who was prettier, smarter, could sew or cook better. But it wasn't any easier having older or younger siblings, she supposed, someone always ahead of you in the queue or behind in the scramble for food or attention. It was the plight of being one of many. Big families were the norm in these parts, even families like their own that could ill-afford them.

As the children disappeared into the barn, she smiled at Michal's awkwardness, the way he had not quite grown into the long legs and broad shoulders he'd inherited from their father. "I heard something at market the other day," Ruth said in a hushed tone, even though only little Karolina was there to hear them. Helena's breath caught. Had Ruth learned—or somehow guessed—about the soldier? Guilt nagged at her suddenly. Until now, she always told Ruth everything. Yet this time something had held her back. It was as if, by discovering the man in the woods, she had taken a step apart from her siblings.

Helena licked her lips. "What is it?"

"The Garzels disappeared—Pani Kowalska said maybe they were arrested."

Helena's brow arched. "She said that?"

Ruth bristled. "Well, she didn't exactly say it, but she suggested that was the case."

Helena waved her hand dismissively. "Just silly gossip from an old woman with too much time on her hands."

Ruth tried again. "She said that they arrested the Jews in Nowy Sącz, too. People couldn't make up such awful things from whole cloth, could they? There must be some truth to it." She sounded as if she really needed Helena to believe her.

"Perhaps," Helena said, trying to take the idea seriously. She started to lift Karolina down from the chair before she began to fuss, demanding to climb down herself.

"Here," Helena said, relenting and letting her do it, but keeping a protective hand close behind. Karolina looked at her in disbelief—it was Ruth, not Helena, who usually gave in. But the child's smile, so rare these days, was reward enough. Karolina scampered down. She had always shown physical prowess beyond the others, rolling over at three months and walking at nine months, almost as if she knew that the world was testing her, and despite her small size she would need to get around on her own two feet. Helena checked her forehead and noted with relief that her skin was now cool to the touch, then released her to play on the floor.

"People wouldn't stand for it," she replied to Ruth, resuming their conversation in that fractured way that happened frequently while they were caring for the children. A lack of confidence eroded her voice. In fact, the war had stripped away so many civilities, given people a license to act on their deeper, baser selves. Many, she suspected with an uneasy feeling, would be only too happy to let the Germans get rid of not just Jews but neighbors they had never really wanted in the first place.

Helena's eyes traveled to the corner by the fireplace, where the scarf Ruth had knitted for Piotr still lay crumpled in a ball, untouched though months had passed. She kicked it out of the way, hoping Ruth had not seen. Anger rose within her as she thought of the boy who had broken her sister's heart. "He's not worth it," she had wanted to say many times since Piotr last had come. But she held back, knowing such sentiments would only bring Ruth more pain.

Helena gestured to Karolina's thick hair, which Ruth had cowed earlier into two luminous pigtails. Karolina was the outlier in their auburn-haired cluster—thick locks the color of cornstalks made her shine like the sun. "Do mine next?" she asked.

"Really?" Ruth's brow lifted. Helena held her breath, wondering if she'd gone too far. She'd never had the patience to sit, instead pulling her hair into a scraggly knot at the back of her neck. She worried that this, coupled with her announcement of an extra visit to their mother, might arouse Ruth's suspicion. But Ruth just shrugged. "Sit down." Helena dropped into the chair. Ruth's touch was gentle, her movements soothing as she coaxed the stubborn wisps into place with deft fingers. Helena fought the urge to fidget—it was all she could do not to leap from the chair and run out the door into the forest.

"Mischa needs shoes," she announced grimly when Ruth had finished braiding. Ruth's brow wrinkled. For the girls, there was always an old pair to be handed down, but Michal would not be big enough to wear Tata's boots for at least another year or two, and there was no money for new ones. "What about your knitting? You could sell some pieces."

Ruth cocked her head, as if she had not considered that her handiwork would have value to anyone outside of the house.

"Perhaps with Christmas coming I can barter something knitted for a pair at market."

Christmas. The word sounded foreign, as if from another lifetime. "Remember how Mama would decorate the house with mistletoe?"

"Holly," her sister corrected, her voice crackling with authority. With Ruth, there was always a rejoinder. "And we would sing carols until she would give us a coin to stop." Helena smiled fondly at the memory, one of many that only she and Ruth shared. "Then we would open our gifts and Tata would pretend to fall asleep early..."

"He didn't..." Helena began. Tata hadn't pretended to sleep; he had passed out from the half bottle of homemade potato vodka he consumed during *Wigilia*, their Christmas Eve feast. Even as a young child, Helena had known the truth. How could two people live the same moment but remember it so differently?

"Of course he did," she relented, allowing Ruth to win. Ruth sniffed with quiet satisfaction.

Helena brushed aside the memories, forcing herself to focus on more practical matters. "Or we could sell it," she said, gesturing with her head toward the corner. The sewing machine, which Tata had bought for their mother as a wedding present, had been her most prized possession. It would fetch a fair price, even from someone who wanted to use the parts for scrap.

"No!"

"Ruti, we must be practical. We need food and coal."

But Ruth shook her head. "We need it. That's why Mama left it to me. She knew you wouldn't keep it safe."

A lump of anger formed in Helena's throat. Had Mama actually bequeathed the sewing machine to Ruth while she was still coherent enough? More likely, Ruth had simply presumed. Helena swallowed, struggling not to retort. Ruth clung to the machine because letting it go meant acknowledging that things had changed permanently, and that Mama was not coming back.

Helena walked back to the fireplace where Karolina played by the hearth. "Let's get you dressed." She held out her arms, but the child hung back, looking up uncertainly at Ruth. It was Ruth from whom the children sought care and affection, preferring her softer voice and gentle, uncalloused hands.

Ruth crossed the room gracefully, appearing to swirl rather than walk, her skirt a gentle halo around her—not like Helena, who seemed to crash headlong at full force. She scooped Karolina up with effort. "She's getting too old to be carried all of the time," Helena scolded. "You'll spoil her." Ruth did not reply, but smiled sweetly, smoothing her hair and kissing the top of her head. Dorie and Karolina had had so much less of their parents than the others. Ruth tried to make up for it, fashioning little treats when she could and singing to them and rocking them at night. Karolina eyed Helena reproachfully now as Ruth carried her past. Helena opened her mouth, searching for the right words. She loved the children, too, though perhaps she never told them as much. But they needed to be strong in these times.

Helena walked past her sisters to the bedroom. Fingering the stain on her sleeve, Helena's eyes roamed longingly toward the armoire. She opened the door. Mama's clothing still hung neatly, as clean and pressed as the day she had gone to the hospital. Her church dress was practically new, the gleaming buttons kept immaculately. Even her two everyday dresses were nicer than Helena's, having been spared the hardships of the woods these many months.

Helena reached inside and pulled one of the dresses out. She remembered Christmas two years earlier, when Ruth had opened a box to reveal a new skirt, pink and crisp. "There was only money for one," Mama explained. "And Ruth's bigger. You'll have her old one." It had been a pretext. Though Ruth was a bit fuller figured, the truth was that she was the prettier one with the better chance of marriage, and it was always presumed that she should have the nicer, more feminine things.

There had never been any talk of a suitor for Helena, even in happier times.

"What are you doing?" Helena jumped and spun around. Ruth had appeared behind her, stealthily as a cat.

Helena held up the dress. "I was thinking of borrowing this."

"Nonsense," Ruth snapped. "Yours is good enough for traipsing through the woods and doing chores. You'd only soil it and we need to leave it for when Mama comes home." She eyed Helena warily, daring her to argue. Then Ruth took the dress from her and returned it to the armoire, closing the door firmly behind her.

5

The sun was dropping low to the trees later that afternoon as Helena neared the chapel and pushed open the door. *"Dzie'n dobry...?"* she called into the dank semidarkness. Silence greeted her. Surely the soldier could not have fled in his condition. For a second, she wondered if she'd imagined him. He could be dead, she thought with more dismay than she should have felt for someone she'd only met once. His wounds had seemed serious enough.

She pulled back the shutter that covered one of the broken windows to allow the pale light to filter in. The soldier was curled up in a tight ball on the ground, much as he had been when she found him, but farther from the door. She hesitated as excitement and alarm rose in her. What was she thinking by coming here? She didn't know this man, or whether he was here to help or do harm.

Helena walked over and knelt to feel his cheek, caught off guard by the softness of his skin. She was relieved to find he was still warm. Then she remembered Karolina's illness, barely passed. Had she made a mistake by coming and possibly bringing sickness to this man in his already-weakened state?

The soldier moved suddenly beneath her hand and she jumped. His eyes snapped open. He stiffened, almost as Mama had when she feared pain in the hospital.

"It's okay," Helena said, holding her hands low and open. "I'm the one who brought you here."

He forced himself to a sitting position, trying without success to stifle a whimper. "Who are you?" His Polish was stiff and a bit accented.

"I'm called Helena. I live close to the village. You should rest," she added.

But he sat even straighter, clenching and unclenching his hands. His chocolate eyes, set just a shade too close together, darted back and forth. "Does anyone else know that I'm here?"

"Not that I'm aware," she replied quickly. "I haven't told anyone." She wanted to say that someone else might have heard the crash, but it seemed unwise to upset him more.

He stared at her, disbelieving. "Are you sure?"

"I haven't told anyone," she repeated, suddenly annoyed. "Why would I have gone to all of the trouble to save you just to turn you in?"

He shrugged, somewhat calmer now. "A reward, maybe. Who knows why people do anything these days?"

"No one knows that you're here," she replied, her voice soothing.

"Where is 'here' exactly?" he asked.

"Southern Poland, Małopolska. You're about twenty kilometers from the city."

"Kraków?" Helena nodded, sensing from his expression that her answer was not what he expected. "That puts us about an hour from the southern border, doesn't it?"

"Roughly, yes. Perhaps a bit more."

His face relaxed slightly. "You're real." She cocked her head.

"I thought I might have been delirious and dreamed you. And then I wasn't sure you were coming back."

"I'm sorry," she replied quickly. "It's hard to get away." He had rugged features, an uneven nose and a chin that jutted forth defiantly. But his eyelashes were longer than she knew a man could have, and there was a softness to his gaze that kept him from being too intimidating.

"I didn't mean it that way," the man added. "Just that I'm glad to see you again." A warm flush seemed to wash over her then, and she could feel her cheeks color. "I don't think I introduced myself properly. Sam Rosen." He held out his hand. "I'm American." His deep voice had a lyrical quality to it, the words nearly a song.

"But you're speaking Polish."

"Yes, my grandparents were from one of those eastern parts by the border that was Poland when it wasn't Russia. They used to speak Polish with my mother when they didn't want the children to understand what they were saying. So I had a reason to try to figure it out." The corners of his mouth rose with amusement.

She shook his outstretched hand awkwardly. He had wiped the blood from his face, she noticed, leaving a narrow gash across his forehead. "You're looking better," she remarked, meaning it. There was a ruddiness to his complexion that had not been there before. His hair was darker than she remembered it, almost black. A healed scar ran pale and deep from the right corner of his mouth to his chin.

"Thanks to you," he replied, his eyes warm. "Bringing me here saved my life. And the food you left did me a world of good." He made it sound as though she had left him an entire feast and not just a handful of bread.

"A bit more," she said, passing him another piece of bread, slightly larger. His fingers brushed against her own, coarse and unfamiliar. "I'm sorry that's all I could manage." She could not take any of the scarce sheep's cheese or lard they needed for the children.

"You're very kind." His voice was full with gratitude. He tore into the bread with an urgency that suggested true hunger. Of course, the morsel she'd left him last time would not have lasted a day, once he was able to eat. She noticed then a pile of leaves—he must have dragged himself outside to forage. "They taught us in training which things we could eat, roots and such. And I've managed to drink some rainwater." He gestured across the chapel to a puddle that had formed where it had rained through the opening in the roof. "I'm sorry not to get up," he added. "My leg is still a mess. But I don't think it needs to be set."

She looked around the chapel—the wooden pews had rotted to the floor and there was no sign of any pulpit, but fine engravings were still visible on the walls, faded images of angels and the Virgin Mary at the front. "It's a good thing I found you," she said, sounding more pleased with herself than she intended. "The path is just off the main road. Someone else might have turned you in to the police for favors or food."

"What about animals?" he asked. "Are there wolves?"

She hesitated. "Yes." His eyes widened. She did not want to alarm him, but other than sparing Ruth the occasional bit of reality, it was not in Helena's nature to lie. Once the wild animals had clung to the high hills, content to feed on small prey. But with food sources growing scarce, they'd become bolder, venturing down to the outskirts of the village to steal livestock.

"Here." Helena opened her bag. She had looked around the hospital ward while visiting her mother earlier, searching for whatever supplies she could take to help him. There had only been a few rags and a small bottle of alcohol lying on one of the nurse's carts and she didn't dare to risk looking in the supply closet or any of the cupboards. She handed the bottle to him. "I brought you these, too." She pulled out the wool coat and thick gray sweater that had been her father's. Sam took the

sweater and put it on, swimming in its massive girth. She hoped
he could not detect the smell of liquor that lingered, even after
it had been washed.

"Thank you. My jacket must have been stripped off with the
parachute. It's probably hanging from a tree somewhere."

So he had fallen from the sky, after all. "So you jumped?"

He nodded. "Before the plane crashed. The weather forced
us to fly farther north than we should have, I think, and the
pilot had to go off course. At first we received orders to turn
back, but we had all agreed that we were too far gone for that—
we wanted to see the mission through. Then something went
wrong with the plane. We knew we were going to have to wild
jump, that means just land anywhere, as well as we could." She
imagined it, leaping from the plane in darkness and mist, not
knowing what lay below. "I wasn't sure my chute was going
to have time to open. It did, but I got caught in a tree. When
I was trying to free my chute, I fell from the tree and, well…"
He gestured to his leg. "The rest you know."

Sam opened the bottle and doused the cloth, then pressed it
against the gash on his forehead, grimacing. He shivered and
there was a sudden air of vulnerability about him, as though all
of the foreign bits had been stripped away.

"I'll be right back," she announced. Before he could respond, Helena rushed outside to the grassy patch above the
chapel, collecting an armful of sticks to make a fire. She stopped
abruptly. What was she doing coming to the woods to tend to
this stranger, risking discovery at any moment? Caretaking had
never been in her nature. It was Ruth who nurtured the others, Michal that cared for small, hurt animals. And she had her
family's well-being to think about. She had done enough, too
much, her sister would surely say.

Helena eyed the path back toward the village. She could just
turn and go, now. But then she remembered the gratitude in
the soldier's eyes as he had taken the food from her. She was his

only hope. If the Germans came, though, she would be arrested, leaving her family helpless. She had to think of them first. One had to be practical in order to survive in these times. She would build the soldier a fire before going and that was all.

She returned with her armful of kindling, which she carried to the small stove in the corner. He frowned. "It isn't right, you hauling wood for me."

Helena fought the urge to laugh. She carried enough wood to keep her family warm—the small pile of kindling was nothing. Still, she was touched by his concern. "It's fine." The wood was too damp, she fretted as she broke it into pieces. But when she struck the match she'd brought from home and touched it to the pile, it began to burn merrily.

"Thank you," Sam said, sliding closer along the floor as she closed the grate. The tiny flames seemed to make his dark eyes dance. He winced.

"Is it very painful?" she asked.

"It isn't so bad when I'm still, but when I move, it's awful."

"Let me." She walked to him and slowly helped him inch closer to the fire, letting him lean on her for support, feeling his muscles strain with the effort of each movement.

"There is one other thing…" He hesitated. "I'm so sorry to ask, but I'd like to wash if that's somehow possible." She'd noticed it earlier, his own masculine earthy scent, stronger than it had been last time she was here. "Perhaps some water?"

"Let me see what I can find." Helena went back outside to where she had seen a rusty bucket lying by the drain. She picked up the bucket and walked uphill several meters to the stream. She moved slowly on her return, taking care not to spill. "It's cold," she cautioned as Sam took it from her, his hand brushing hers.

He cupped his hand and drank from the bucket hurriedly. Then he splashed the water on his face, not seeming to mind as the icy droplets trickled down his neck. "That feels great."

He pulled off the sweater and unbuttoned his shirt. She

blushed and half turned away; out of the corner of her eye she caught a glimpse of his back where it met his shoulder, muscle and bone working against the bare, pale skin as he bathed. She sucked in her breath quickly, then held it, hoping he hadn't heard.

Her heart hammered against her ribs. "Pan Rosen..." she began, lowering herself to the ground as he dried himself with his torn shirt.

"Sam," he corrected. Sam. In that moment, he was not a soldier, but a man, with an open face and broad smooth cheeks she wanted to touch. He pulled on the sweater she had given him once more. "And may I call you Hel..." He faltered.

"Helena," she prompted.

"Helena," he repeated, as if trying it on for size. "That's quite a mouthful. May I call you Lena?"

"Y-yes," she replied, caught off guard. All of the other children had pet names, Ruti, Mischa—but she had always been Helena.

"Lena," he said again, a slight smile playing at the corners of his lips. His shoulders were broad, forearms strong. Sitting beside him, she felt oddly small and delicate.

She struggled to remember what she wanted to say. "What are you doing here, Sam? Are the Americans coming to help us?"

"No." Her heart sank. The talk of the Americans entering the war had been growing in recent months, whispered everywhere from the hospital corridors to the market in the town square. And if the Americans weren't coming yet, then what was he doing here? "That is, I mean..." He broke off. "I really can't say too much," he added apologetically. Then he frowned again. "You must be taking a terrible risk coming here."

Not really, she wanted to say, but that would be untrue. "Everything is dangerous now," she replied instead. In truth, finding him was the most exciting thing that had happened to her in years, maybe ever, and she had been eager to return. "Especially going to see my mother." She told him then about sneaking in and out of Kraków, her near-encounter with the jeep. "Of course, if not for the German I would never have come this way and found you." She could feel herself blush again.

He did not seem to notice, though, but continued staring at her, his brow crinkled. "I wish you wouldn't go to the city again."

Helena was touched by his concern, more than she might have expected from a man she just met. "That's what my…" She stopped herself from telling him about Ruth, the fact that she had a twin. She did not want to acknowledge her prettier sister. "There are five children in the family, including me. I'm the one who has to go check on Mama. My father is gone and there's no one else to make sure she's cared for."

Helena's thoughts turned to her mother. She'd actually seemed better today. For once she'd been awake and hadn't mistaken Helena for her sister. And she had reached for the bread that Helena offered. For a second, Helena had hesitated; she had hoped to keep the extra food for the soldier. She was overcome with shame and had quickly broken the bread and moistened it. "Pani Kasia says that they're going to kill us," Mama had announced abruptly as she chewed, gesturing to the woman in the bed next to hers. She had an unworried, slightly gossipy tone as though discussing the latest rumor about one of the neighbors back home.

Inwardly, Helena had blanched. She had worked so hard to shield Mama from the outside world. But the hospital was a porous place and news seeped through the cracks. "She's a crazy old woman," Helena replied carefully in a low voice. For months she had done her best to keep the truth from her mother without actually lying to her, and she didn't want to cross that line now.

"And sour to boot," Mama added, smiling faintly. There was a flicker of clarity to her eyes and for a second Helena glimpsed the mother of old, the one who had baked sweet cakes and rubbed their feet on frigid winter nights. There were so many things she wanted to ask her mother about her childhood and the past and what her hopes and dreams had been.

"Mama..." She turned back, then stopped. Her mother was staring out the window, once more the cloud pulled down over her face like a veil, and Helena knew that she was gone and could not be reached.

"It's so brave of you to make that journey every week," Sam said, drawing her from her thoughts. His voice was full with admiration.

"Brave?" She was unaccustomed to thinking of herself that way. "You're the brave one, leaving your family to come all the way over here."

"That's different," he replied, and a shadow seemed to pass across his face.

"How old are you, anyway?" she asked, hearing her sister's phantom admonition that the question was too blunt.

"Eighteen."

"Same as me," she marveled.

"Almost nineteen. I enlisted the day after my birthday."

"Did you always want to be a soldier?"

"No." His face clouded over. "But I had to come."

"Why?"

He bit his lip, not answering. Then he lifted his shoulders, straightening. "When I joined the army, they sent me to school in Georgia, that's in the southern part of the United States, for nearly a year. I had to learn to be a soldier, you see, and then how to be a paratrooper."

Helena processed the information. She had never thought about someone *becoming* a soldier; it seemed like they were already that way. But now she pictured it, Sam donning his uniform and getting his hair cut short. "Is that why it's taking so long for the Americans to come?" It came out sounding wrong, as though she was holding him personally responsible for his country.

But he seemed to understand what she meant. "In part, yes." His brow wrinkled. "Some people don't want us to enter the war at all." How could the Americans not help? Helena wanted to ask. Sam continued, "Everyone has to be trained, they have to plan the missions…" He paused. "I probably shouldn't say too much. It's nothing personal," he hastened to add. "I'm not supposed to talk about it with anyone."

"I understand." But the moment hung heavy between them. She was a Pole and not to be trusted.

"They don't know," he explained earnestly. "I mean, the American people know about Hitler, of course, and the Jews there are concerned for their relatives, trying to get them out. Until I came to Europe, I had no idea…" He stopped abruptly.

"No idea about what?"

Sam bit his lip. "Nothing." Helena could tell from his voice that there were things that she, even in the middle of it all, had not seen. Things he would not share with her. "Anyway, our rabbi back home said that—"

"You're Jewish?" she interrupted. He nodded. She was surprised—he didn't look anything like the Jews she'd seen in the city, shawl covered and stooped. But there was something unmistakably different about him, a slight arch to his nose, chin just a shade sharper than the people around here. His dark hair was curly and so thick it seemed that water could not penetrate it. "You don't look it," she blurted. Her face flushed. "That is, the Jews around here…"

He smiled, not offended. "There are different kinds of Jews. Some, like the Orthodox, are more observant than others, and they dress differently."

That was not quite what Helena had meant, but she was grateful to let it be. Thinking of the empty streets and shuttered shops of Kazimierz, and what the nurse had told her about the ghetto and her sister about the Jews of Nowy Sącz, she was suddenly nervous for him. Not just a foreigner, but a Jew. The full danger of his situation crashed down upon her. "Did they make you come?"

"No, I volunteered." He cleared his throat. "That is, the kind of work I do…" She wanted to ask what that was exactly, but she knew he wouldn't say. "It's a really big honor and I raised my hand to be considered. At first they said no—they were worried that being Jewish I might let emotions get in the way." His face was open and honest in a way that she liked, as if he could not hide a single feeling. So unlike here, where everyone kept their eyes low to avoid trouble. "Are you Catholic?"

Helena nodded, picturing the worn old rosary Mama kept in her bed stand drawer, even at the hospital. She had insisted on dressing the children in their best clothes and going to Mass each Sunday. Helena always dreaded the stares of the other villagers, wondering where their father was, speculating that he was sleeping off another night of drinking. After Mama got sick and had gone to the sanatorium, Ruth had stubbornly persisted in herding the children to church. But then their better clothes became too small and threadbare to wear and after Tata died they stopped going altogether. "Everyone is here, more or less."

He did not speak further, but stared off into the distance. "What are you going to do now?" she asked finally.

He paused. "I don't know. Stay here for now, I guess. I don't have much choice with this leg." He finished the bread and looked at her with a serious expression. "When you found me, was there any sign of anyone else?"

She shook her head. "No one. You were by yourself in the woods. No other people, no plane. And the night before, when I heard the crash, I never saw anything." She did not have the heart to tell him about the force with which the crash had shaken their house, making the likelihood that anyone else had survived virtually nil.

"No, you wouldn't have. We flew in low with lights down. It was an engine problem, I think, maybe birds, that got us—not the Germans." The distinction seemed to matter to him a great deal. "The plane was too low for our chutes to open properly. I doubt the others were as lucky." Pain washed over his face. His own injuries had been awful, but surely his fellow soldiers had suffered worse. She was seized with the urge to put her arms around him and comfort him, as Ruth might Dorie when she scraped a knee. But offering comfort did not come naturally to Helena and she stopped, caught off guard by the unfamiliar impulse.

He cleared his throat and took her hand in his. "You cut yourself." The spot where she had caught her hand on the thorny bush while fleeing had reopened from the cold, dry air.

She pulled back sharply. "I'm sorry," he said quickly. "I didn't mean to offend you."

"It isn't that." She was ashamed of the rough calluses, the places where her knuckles had split from chopping wood. Ruth always scolded her to take care of her hands. She kept her own soft by wearing an old pair of Tata's work gloves as she washed and cleaned, rubbing lanolin into her palms and pushing back her cuticles. Ruth took time to do the little things, as though it still mattered and there were young men looking for wives and not that Piotr, her last best hope, had disappeared into the abyss. For once Helena wished that she had listened.

"May I?" He reached out once more. Helena nodded, then extended her hand, allowing him to cradle it in the warmth of his own. He examined it carefully. She felt silly having him worrying about such a little cut, when he was so much more seriously wounded. He dropped her hand and she wondered if he was repulsed by its coarseness. But he reached in his pocket and pulled out a small tube, uncapped it. "It's a salve," he explained as he squeezed some into his palm. "Hard to believe that I lost almost everything but managed to keep this."

"Plus your flashlight and your gun," she replied pointedly.

He blinked with surprise. "Yeah, that, too." A moment of awkward distrust passed between them, then evaporated. He took her hand in his own once more, sending shivers of unfamiliar warmth through her as he rubbed the lotion into her skin.

She pulled away again. "I can do it."

"Of course." Sam held out the tube. He had strong wrists, flat on top with a few dark hairs curling toward the backs of his hands. She was suddenly mindful of her thick stockings, the darning where they had torn at the knee impossible to conceal.

She finished rubbing in the lotion, studying him more closely now. "Your scar—is it from the war?"

"No, I fell when I was younger," he answered, a beat too quickly.

She recapped the tube and tried to hand it back. "You keep it," he said.

"Oh, I couldn't…"

"Okay, then I'll give you some more next time." *Next time.* The two words hung in the air, waiting for her to refute them.

She looked up, noticing then how the sun had dipped low. "I have to go." She stood reluctantly. Talking with Sam had been such a reprieve from the dreariness of the rest of her life. "Do you need anything else?"

"Some longer branches, if you wouldn't mind. I can use them to make a crutch."

"I saw some out by the knoll." She returned a few minutes later with several pieces of wood.

"Thank you," Sam said. "I didn't expect… That is, I didn't think people here would be nice."

"Oh." She brought her hand to her mouth, feeling her cheeks flush.

"That was thoughtless of me to say," he recovered hastily. "You have to understand, the Jews who came to America from Poland, well, they left for a reason and maybe they didn't have the best experience here, or leave with the best impression of the people." He was talking quickly now, stumbling over his words. But it was more than just awkwardness, or embarrassment over what he had said. He was nervous. "Thank you," he repeated, somehow making the words sound like something more. She nodded and started toward the door.

"Please wait." She turned back. "It's important, you understand, that no one else know I am here." His voice was grave and she knew he was talking about something larger than his personal safety.

"I promise."

He opened his mouth to argue and then closed it again and stood reluctantly. "Lena, wait…" She turned back as he struggled to stand, holding on to the wall of the chapel. "The trains," he said. "Can you see them from where you live?"

Helena hesitated, puzzled. She nodded. From the window of the barn loft where she had always hidden as a child when things got bad one could see the tracks. She went there still when she needed a moment of quiet. The trains had changed lately, increasing their frequency, seeming to move with grim determination. "You can tell a lot from the rail lines—how often they go, in which direction, what kind of cars they are carrying, if they are empty or full."

"I'll watch," she promised.

She noticed the dark stubble on his cheeks and chin, which seemed to have grown thicker during her visit. "I can bring a razor next time," she said, remembering her father's, which sat in a tin cup in the cupboard, waiting for the soft peach fuzz on Michal's upper lip to evolve.

"You mean you'll… That is…" He paused, conflict washing over his face. "No, you mustn't come again. It isn't safe," he added, and she saw then that he was worried for her safety. He was setting her free, giving her permission to go and not come back. Could she take it? Her shoulders slumped and she

was suddenly overwhelmed and saddened, by all that had happened and that she had taken on in coming here—and by the
fact that she was now leaving him.

"I'll see you soon," she replied firmly, not realizing that she
was making the promise until the words had flown from her
mouth. Then, before he could argue further, she turned and
started down the hill.

6

After Helena disappeared into the forest, Ruth set Karolina down to play with wooden blocks by the fire and busied herself cleaning up the breakfast dishes. When she finished, she dried her hands and opened the cupboard. In the back, exactly as Mama had kept it, was the glass jar of honey. Ruth had discovered the jar when she was eight, and Mama (whose sweet tooth was her one weakness) had shared a bit with her in exchange for keeping it a secret. Ruth dipped a finger in it now and then put it in her mouth, the familiar sweetness a reminder of happier times. How wonderful it had been to have something that was just hers, instead of split between her and Helena. Guilt surged through her. She should share it with the children, a rare treat for all of them. But then it would be gone. It was all right to keep this one thing as hers alone, wasn't it? Better for them not to get used to such things, anyway, when they likely would not have any more.

Checking on Karolina, who was still playing contentedly, Ruth poured a cup of coffee and carried it to the seat by the

window. The wind whistled, seeping through the cracks. Outside Michal and Dorie continued to run, undeterred by the cold.
As Ruth looked around the cottage, a sense of foreboding overcame her. "Things are changing," Helena had observed cryp-
tically the previous evening. Why did she say this as though it
were a good thing? Ruth had liked the old world with its seasons and predictable expectations. Now everything was topsy-
turvy, uncertain.

She shifted uncomfortably, thinking of Piotr. The memory
of his face had grown fuzzy in her mind since the last time he'd
come to see her. She had taken the time that morning to roll
her hair into a fine braided knot. "Ruth, you look like a princess!" Dorie had exclaimed. Touched, Ruth had glowed with
a bit of nearly forgotten pride. "Princess" was Dorie's highest
honor, and one she had only bestowed on Mama—until now.

Piotr had appeared across the field from town at one o'clock,
as he had each Sunday, head bowed low against an autumn
wind. He was not bad looking, Ruth had reflected. Taller than
her by a head and broad-shouldered, he had thick features and
colorless blond hair. Balled in one hand was the scarf she had
knitted for him and she wondered why he wasn't wearing it.
She might have kept it for Christmas and given it to him as a
gift, but she'd wanted him to have it exactly for days like this.

"*Cze's'c.*" He greeted her with an awkward kiss that did not
quite reach her cheek. She waited for him to notice her hair,
but he did not remark upon it.

"Shall we walk?" she asked, speaking a bit more quickly
than usual. Their courtship had been unremarkable, consisting
mostly of strolls by the stream when the weather permitted it.
"Or would you prefer to come in and warm up by the fire?" He
did not answer but peered uneasily over her shoulder. It was the
others, she decided. Piotr was an only child and more comfortable around a calf or foal than human little ones.

Ruth put on her cape and followed him outside in the direction of the stream. The water was low, pulled back to reveal dry muddy banks littered with pebbles and branches. A mossy smell rose from the muck. The stream would swell again when the snows came and melted, then rise perilously with the spring rain showers. She pointed to a bend in the stream, just beyond the edge of their property. "Helena says that is a fine place for catching trout. Perhaps in the spring…"

Piotr stopped and turned to her abruptly. "I can't. That is, my father doesn't want me to come anymore." He faltered, face reddening like a beet.

"I don't understand." Her stomach burned ominously.

"Things are going so poorly with the farm. And now there are the quotas." He was referring to the percentage that the Germans now exacted from each farmer's yield. The sisters' own garden was too small to offer much, but from a farm like Piotr's, the demand would be severe. "There isn't enough to support a family."

It was a lie, of course—she and Helena managed to feed the children with so much less. But he was offering it as a reason— an excuse, really—as to why they could not go forward. Ruth watched him, contemplating what to do, which smile or touch might cajole him to change his mind. She'd learned from observing Mama how to charm a man into doing what she wanted. A few minutes ago he was just an ordinary boy; now he was all she had, and she was suddenly desperate to keep him.

"The war has just made things so difficult," Piotr began again. He broke off and thrust the scarf in her direction so quickly that it fell to the ground, then he stomped off in the opposite direction with a gait too clumsy to be a run.

She took a step forward, stumbling over a tree root. "Piotr!" Her voice echoed against the stillness of the trees. It was not until he had disappeared across the field that she realized he would not be coming again.

Staring at the emptiness before her, so new and yet so per-

manent, Ruth recalled how just a week earlier he had kissed
her behind the barn. She had pushed his fumbling hands away,
partly because it was the right thing to do, and also because once
she gave him that, he would no longer want her. But he had left
her, anyway. Had Piotr broken off things because she had let
him go too far, or because she had stopped him?

Neither, she decided now, gazing out the window at the very
spot where their courtship had ended. It had not been about sex,
but money. Piotr's family just didn't want to be saddled with
supporting so many children who were not their own. Piotr's
mother had undoubtedly told him to get rid of dead wood while
he still had the chance, that Ruth and her family would never
be anything but a burden. But if Piotr had been a stronger man,
he would have stayed in spite of his mother's opinion—and for
that weakness Ruth hated him most of all.

Piotr had begun courting the liveryman's daughter, beautiful
and unencumbered by anyone, just three weeks later, confirming Ruth's suspicions. Her cheeks burned now as she relived the
rejection. It wasn't so much Piotr she missed, Ruth reflected.
She hadn't really wanted to go live in his big cold house on the
other side of town, and there was a roughness to his touch that
had made her dread what lay ahead. No, it was the idea of him,
the now-gone promise of having a place secured, which filled
her with a sense of loss.

Worst of all that day, she'd had to return to the house to face
Helena. Though she had not said a word, her sister's expression
indicated that she'd known it would end poorly all along. She
did not want to accept Helena's sympathy—or acknowledge
the fact that they were the same again, alone without anyone.

There was a knock at the door. Ruth started, setting down
her coffee cup so quickly that a bit splashed high over the edge
onto the table. No one came calling unannounced, or at all
these days. For a fleeting second she thought that it might be
Piotr, conjured from her thoughts. Perhaps he had come to beg

her forgiveness and tell her that he had made a mistake. She would take him back, if his apology was sincere, although not right away. She had given things too easily before, a mistake she did not intend to repeat. But of course, Piotr was off fighting somewhere. Helena, she decided. She must have come back for something and forgotten her key—again.

Ruth opened the door, then stepped back at the sight of an unfamiliar woman whose dark hair was streaked with silver. Though she did not wear the yellow star, something about her shawl suggested that she was a Jew, from a neighboring village, perhaps. *"Tak?"*

The woman did not speak, but looked over Ruth's shoulder, assessing the house, which despite its modest size and furnishings must have seemed luxurious. Ruth cringed, wondering if for a moment the woman would ask for food or money, or worse yet, shelter. They had nothing extra to spare and letting the woman in would surely invite trouble. She noticed that the woman wore no gloves or hat, but seemed oblivious to the cold. "Can I help you?" Ruth asked more softly. Karolina toddled up behind her, tugging at the hem of her dress. Ruth lifted her protectively.

"My child," the woman croaked, her voice younger than her careworn face might have suggested. Was the woman deluded and thinking that Karolina was hers? Ruth hugged the child tighter to her breast. "I have a little girl." The woman held her hand up to just below her waist. "Wearing a red plaid scarf with an eagle on it. Have you seen her?"

For a moment, Ruth thought she must have misunderstood, for who misplaced a child? But the woman's eyes, ringed with circles from her not having slept or rested in her search, were sincere. "I'm sorry, I haven't." She eyed the woman. She had only seen Jews from afar, dark, mysterious creatures that seemed to confirm Father Dominik's admonitions in his sermons that they were shrewd and cunning and drank the blood of Christian infants. But the woman before her just looked like any mother, tired and bedraggled and desperate.

"They said a camp…" the woman began feebly, and before Ruth could ask, the woman turned and started off across the hill.

"I'm sorry," Ruth said again into the empty space before her, with more feeling than she had expected. Though the woman might look different, a child was a child, and Ruth could not help but pity her. Still, Ruth had her own family to think about and could not afford to become involved.

She closed the door and sat down with Karolina on her lap, shaken by the lingering image of the woman's face. They knew families that had lost children in the traditional sense, born too small or taken by influenza or some other illness—not the odd way this woman had just described. She had seen the grieving mothers at market with their hollow eyes, disbelieving, despite the odds, that it had happened to them. The merchants seemed to speak softly and cut more generously for those women, but other villagers stepped back, as if the loss might somehow be contagious. Ruth's throat tightened. She would take the squabbling and competition and hardships of a large family if it meant that they were safe—and together.

Suddenly anxious, Ruth rapped on the window, gesturing for Michal and Dorie to come inside. "Take your boots off," she instructed, closing the door quickly behind them. "I'll warm some milk." As she set Karolina in her high chair, she hoped they would not ask about the woman.

The children darted beneath the table and around the chairs, as though the colder weather had made them unusually restless. "Where's Helena?" Dorie asked, seeming to notice her sister's absence for the first time.

"She's gone to the city," Ruth replied absently.

"Nooo!" the child wailed, her face seeming to crumple. She swung her braids from side to side, tears streaming down her cheeks.

Ruth stopped in surprise, milk pitcher suspended midair. The children seldom noticed, much less minded, Helena's absences. She set the pitcher down and knelt. "There, there," she soothed, stroking Dorie's hair. The child's breath was improbably sweet like cinnamon. "She'll be back by tonight. You'll see. She's only gone to visit Mama." She usually refrained from mentioning their mother, not wanting to remind the children and cause them distress or answer their many questions. But now she added the information, hoping it would bring further plausibility to her explanation of Helena's absence.

"You know Christmas is coming," Ruth offered, trying to change the subject.

"Are we having a tree?" Michal asked.

"I don't think so, darling," Ruth said, a knife going through her as she watched his face fall. It seemed frivolous, cutting down a pine tree when there was so much else to worry about. "But we'll have a lovely meal and all of the songs and stories."

"And Mama?" Dorie looked up hopefully, eyes brightening. "Will she be back for Christmas, too? Did Helena go to get her?" Ruth understood then that for some reason today, Dorie had equated Helena's going to the city with Mama's disappearance, a trip was taken in one direction only. She imagined that Helena, too, wasn't coming back.

"Mama," Karolina repeated absently, asking for the mother she surely could not remember.

Inwardly, Ruth crumbled. This was the conversation she had been avoiding. "No," she said gently, knowing that there was no way to avoid breaking Dorie's heart again. She pushed a cup of milk toward her sister. "Mama needs to stay in the hospital where there are doctors and medicine that can make her feel better."

"Just like we were playing outside, Dor," Michal offered. Ruth braced herself for further questions about their mother's recovery, tried to anticipate and come up with answers that were not quite lies but spared the child from the truth. But Dorie turned away and began playing with her rag doll on the floor.

"What were you playing outside?" Ruth asked, grateful to Michal for redirecting the conversation. When she and Helena were little, theirs were simple pretend games, like house and school. Ruth was always the mother or the teacher, taking charge in a way that now seemed prophetic.

"Hospital," Michal replied. "Dorie's the nurse. I was the patient and Dorie cured me." She wondered what the unseen hospital life must look like in his mind.

"Doctor," his little sister corrected quickly. "I'm going to become a doctor for real."

Ruth started to tell Dorie that to be a doctor you need to go to school and then college, which would take money they did not have. That even under better circumstances, it would be nearly impossible for a woman. But Dorie's eyes shone at the idea, a childlike dream not yet deterred by the war or realities of their situation, and Ruth would not take that from her. "That sounds wonderful."

Dorie's expression dampened. "Ruti, what are Nazis?" she asked, shifting topics without warning.

"Why do you ask?"

"I heard you talking to Helena about them." Inwardly, Ruth sighed. She already knew better than to speak in front of Michal about matters from which she wanted to shield the children. But Dorie was getting older now, and speaking guardedly or spelling out words did not work anymore.

"They're Germans, darling—German soldiers." The last word—too good for them, really—stuck in her throat.

"Why have they come?" Dorie had a need to know why things were a certain way, how they worked, to scratch beneath the surface. It was a fierce intellect that in another time and place might have been nurtured to greatness. But Ruth did not know how to channel it, and after taking care of their basic survival needs, she seldom had the energy.

Ruth stopped, stymied by the impossibility of explaining war to children. Why indeed? "They want to be in charge. It's all about politics and government. But they haven't come to Biekowice so they won't bother us."

"But what about the Garzels?" Dorie had been outside playing when she and Helena had spoken of their neighbors' disappearance. Had Helena told her about it? "Did the Germans make them leave the village?" Dorie persisted.

"Never you mind about the Garzels. Tend your own garden, as Mama used to say." Karolina giggled from her high chair, as though Ruth had said something funny. Ruth wiped the milk that had dribbled onto her chin, then picked her up and set her on the floor by the fire.

Dorie's forehead lifted in that way Ruth's used to, before Mama had cautioned it would leave wrinkles. "But it's winter," she said. "The garden has gone all withery."

Ruth smiled at the child's literal interpretation. "Not an actual garden, silly. It means that we should take care of our own family and our own business instead of worrying about what others are doing."

"Okay." Dorie downed her milk with a gulp, then hopped down and joined Karolina playing blocks.

"And what about Mama?" Michal asked, swiping aside the lock of hair that had fallen across his forehead. "Are the Germans in Kraków, too?"

On this point she could not lie. "Yes, they are. But the hospital is safe."

"Good." Michal's voice was trusting, devoid of suspicion. He drank his milk, seemingly satisfied.

Ruth noticed then that the button at his collar had fallen off. She reached out to examine it. "If you change into your other shirt and bring me this one I can fix it for you." As Michal disappeared into the bedroom, she went to the kitchen to fetch her sewing kit.

There was another knock at the door. Ruth turned. The Jewish woman must have come back, like one of the persistent Roma beggars that passed through the village each spring, so used to being told "no" that they had almost become immune. Had she not believed that Ruth did not know where her child had gone, or was she seeking something else now, money perhaps or food?

Ruth walked to the door and started to open it to tell the woman that she could not help her. Then she stopped, halted by an unseen hand. She peered through the crack in the door. It was not the Jewish woman, but a strange man in uniform. She inhaled sharply. Had the Nazis finally come to Biekowice? No, not a German, she realized, taking in the insignia on his chest. He was a policeman from My´slenice. But she was hardly relieved. Biekowice had no police force of its own, and the uniformed officers from the regional headquarters seldom ventured into the village. For a minute, she considered not answering. But he could see through the window that the fire blazed merrily, belying the fact that someone was home.

She swiveled back. The girls were on the floor, quiet and obscured from sight at the window. "To the loft," Ruth whispered low and urgent over her shoulder to Michal, who, hearing the knock, had stuck his head out from the bedroom. She waved her hand frantically behind her. She could not imagine what the policeman wanted, but she sensed it best they not be seen. She picked up Karolina and threw her at Michal, whose eyes widened. "Take Dorie, too, and don't make a sound." Too surprised to question her order, he obeyed.

She kicked Karolina's blocks under a chair with her foot, then turned back to the door and opened it, heart pounding. *"D-dzie´n dobry,"* she managed. The man was fortyish and scarcely taller than her, with a barrel chest and paunched midsection.

"I'm Sergeant Wojski, from the Voivoda police department," he puffed. He did not bother with formalities, but spoke to her in familiar language, asserting his power. *Sergeant*. Under other circumstances, the man would be a desk clerk. But the war had given power to those who were most willing to cooperate, not those who were most fit.

He did not produce credentials, but took a step forward. Ruth held up her hand, stopping him. "There's illness in the house," she lied, not yielding. He retreated to the doorstep. "Can I help you?"

"Let me speak to your husband," he instructed in a voice too firm to be called a request.

She hesitated, then shook her head. "It's just me and my sister." The children had been out of sight, but she prayed he had not heard them before knocking. There were records of the whole family, including the children, if one looked in the provincial office. It seemed wise, though, not to draw attention to the youngsters, living here without parents—especially Michal, who was as tall as a sixteen-year-old. In a flash, she imagined him conscripted to help with the war effort, given one of the awful jobs that Helena had said were relegated to the youngest, like scampering to the front lines to collect the unexploded shells.

"Your parents?" Clearly the notion of a woman living alone here was unfathomable.

"Died," she blurted out. She felt instantly guilty. Mama was alive, but it seemed like the safest thing to say, and correcting it now would just raise more questions.

"Papers?" the man asked, questions staccato and unrelenting. As he extended his hand, a glint of something silver flashed about his wrist. A watch. Even from a distance she could tell it was expensive, too grand for someone of his station, and she wondered where he had gotten it.

She turned toward the fireplace, feeling the man's eyes on her as she moved, and pulled from her bag her *kennkarte*, the identification card she had been issued with the rest of the family shortly after the start of the war. She handed it to the man, fingers trembling. He shook his head. "I want your parents' papers." The Germans, and the police on their behalf, seemed more concerned with those who could not be accounted for, worried that they might have disappeared into hiding.

Ruth went to the box in the kitchen where Mama had kept the important papers. She pulled out the coroner's certificate denoting Tata's death, willing her hands not to shake as she turned it over. "My mother's papers have not come yet from the hospital." She prayed he would not ask which one.

The policeman handed the paper back to her. "We are looking for some people traveling through the region. Outsiders. Have you seen anyone unfamiliar?"

Ruth hesitated. Was he talking about the Jewish woman? Surely if she pointed him in the direction that the woman had gone, he would leave to follow after her.

"Strangers," Sergeant Wojski pressed when she did not answer. "Men who aren't from these parts, in uniform perhaps. Have you seen anyone like that?"

"No, of course not." The surprise in her voice was genuine. A lone Jewish woman passing through was odd enough. But foreign soldiers… She had heard the rumors like everyone else of a military plane crashing. No one had ever found the plane, though, and something like that couldn't just disappear into thin air.

"If you see anything…" He dropped a card on the table so hastily it fluttered to the ground. *"Do widzenia." Until we meet again.* Though he used the customary parting, it felt more like a threat.

Ruth remained motionless as he turned and walked to the gate. She picked up the card and, when the man had disappeared from sight, closed the door behind her. "It's all right," she called. There was no response, but a moment later she heard the scuffling of the children, playing in the rafters above. It really was fine, she told herself as Karolina's giggle rang out. She picked up the now-cold coffee with shaking hands. Two disconcerting visits in a day were merely a coincidence. That they were ordinary Poles with nothing of interest to anyone was their one saving grace. None of this, not the Jewish woman or the soldiers the policeman was looking for, had anything to do with them. Still, she wished Helena was here to help her make sense of it all.

As she raised the fresh cup of coffee she had just poured, a thudding sound came from the loft followed by a cry. With a sigh, she set down the cup once more, then went to check on the children.

7

"Dzie'n dobry." Helena was surprised to find Sam standing outside the chapel, leaning against a tree. Though he had grown increasingly mobile over the past two weeks, this was the first time she had seen him venture beyond the chapel walls. Warmth rose in her as she took in the full length of his thinning frame, set against the lush pine forest.

Several emotions seemed to wash over his face at once as he saw her—concern that she had risked her safety to come yet again, but relief and happiness, too. At last he smiled widely. "Lena! I'm glad you're here." He reached out and placed his hand on her shoulder, then paused. She held her breath, wondering as she did each time she arrived if he might kiss her cheek in greeting. But his expression clouded over once more.

"Let's eat," she said, hoping to forestall any argument about her coming.

She followed Sam into the chapel. There was a fire lit in the woodstove. He kept it burning as low as possible, generating just enough warmth to survive without sending too much smoke up the chimney and attracting attention. Helena spread the cloth on the ground before her, producing the usual bread plus the extra cheese and potato she'd been able to save, and setting them out as though preparing a great feast. She did not take food from the children, of course, but rather slipped a bit of her own dinner into her pocket each night and nabbed every uneaten morsel she could find around the house without being noticed. It wasn't enough; she could see that Sam's clothes hung more loosely on him than they had when she first found him. But it was the best she could do.

"Here." She pulled out the two cracked teacups. Dorie had been using them to play with her doll and Helena hoped the child would not miss them. Sam had used a tin bowl she'd brought previously as a pot to heat some water and now he steeped a few of the tea leaves she had given him in it.

She poured the tea into the cups and handed one to him. Their fingers brushed and she shivered involuntarily, then hoped he had not noticed. He wrapped his hands around the cup. "Thank you. This is almost civilized."

Helena picked up a morsel of bread and pretended to eat it for Sam's benefit as he devoured the rest of the food. They sat without speaking for several minutes, the silence comfortable between them. She studied his profile as he chewed, the strong, angular jaw and full lips now as familiar as her own face. Though only two weeks had passed since she'd found Sam, it felt to her as though she had known him all her life. She'd stopped faithfully at the chapel on her way back from visiting her mother last week, and slipped away a few other times to see him, pretending that she had gone to check the traps in the woods. It was all she could do to resist the urge to come every day. In these moments she and Sam shared, sitting on the damp floor of the dilapidated church, she could forget about the dreariness and worry of the outside world.

Even when she could not get to the church, she thought of

Sam constantly. At home, she imagined him alone, wondering how he passed the hours, whether he was safe. The previous evening, as a heavy rain had fallen steadily on the roof of their house, she had lain awake shivering, as if she was cold and wet beside him. Was it really possible to feel so much so fast for a man she had met just days ago? She hated that this part of her life had to remain separate and hidden. She pictured Sam coming down from the chapel to their house. Michal, constantly surrounded by women, would be overjoyed. Mama would have approved of his manners, Tata his strength. But the picture was all jumbled, the pretense of normalcy impossible, for if her father hadn't died and she hadn't been going to visit her ailing mother in his stead, she never would have discovered Sam in the first place.

He tilted his head back, looking at the chapel roof, gray sky visible through the crumbling rafters. "I wonder who built this place."

She considered the question. "I don't know." There were small cabins scattered throughout the hills, designed to offer shelter to hikers and hunters caught in bad weather or between towns for an evening. But this chapel was too big and ornate to have been built for that purpose. "A hundred years ago, this land was owned by a wealthy baron before it was partitioned. He might have put it here for himself, or those who worked for him."

"Churches made me so uncomfortable as a child," Sam remarked. She cocked her head, not understanding. "I thought if I went inside lightning would strike. And if I passed by on the way home from school, kids would throw rocks at me and call me Jew." She marveled that the same prejudices could exist halfway around the world, where things were meant to be better. "But here I am, staying in one."

"Why do you think people dislike Jews so much?" Helena cringed at the bluntness of her own question.

He shrugged. "Some people hate Jews because they see us as

successful," he offered. She stifled a laugh. The Jews in the villages with their drab tattered clothes were even poorer than her
own family. "But my folks are just plain working class."

"What about you? What kind of work did you do?"

"Odd jobs mostly." An uneasy look crossed his face. "I don't
know what I'm going to do after the war. I suppose I could stay
in the army."

"Do you like it?" She found herself emboldened, asking more
personal questions than on her previous visits. "The army, I
mean."

"I do, actually," he said, warming to the conversation. "Some
parts of it, anyway. The army throws together some really different kinds of people." He rubbed the back of his neck and she
noticed for the first time how his once-close-cropped hair had
grown a bit, the way it curled at the collar. His eyes were deep,
his voice thoughtful. Something inside Helena stirred and she
was seized with the need to stroke the smoothness of his cheek.
She had never been interested in boys before; the ones she saw
like Piotr seemed crude and silly, less good at all of the things
she could do for herself. But with Sam she craved his company.
It was like pulling back the paper from a present to find out
what was inside.

A feeling rose from deep inside her that for a moment she
could not articulate. *Happiness.* She understood then why people yearned, why her sister wanted things. Helena simply had
not understood that life was supposed to have these extra good
bits, too. Or maybe because she was too afraid that this feeling
might swallow her whole. Guilt surged through her. She had
no right to be thinking of such things, not now, when survival
was all that mattered.

He continued. "These weren't fellas I would have been close
with back home. But in the army you gotta be able to count
on the guy next to you. Sometimes you like your brother and
sometimes he drives you crazy but he's still your brother and

you love him." She nodded, recognizing the truth in what he'd said from her own family. "Now, I'd say we're friends."

Friends. She considered the word. She had never had a friend outside the family. She and her siblings were insular, removed from the other children in town, especially once she and Ruth had stopped going to school. But even before then they had been separate, understanding somehow that they did not belong. Were she and Ruth friends? They worked together as a team to take care of the children and she loved her sister, but they were hardly companions or confidantes.

Sam cleared his throat. "So I like the guys, and I've gotten to see a bit of the world I surely never would have otherwise. And I've met you." He looked away shyly. Helena's heart skipped a beat. Over the past two weeks, her own feelings for Sam had become impossible to ignore, the way she waited for each visiting day so eagerly. He seemed to like her coming, as well, but she had told herself he was just grateful for the food and other assistance she provided. But now a tiny flame of hope tickled at her insides. Was it possible that he liked her, as well?

"But I've seen terrible things," he said. "The fighting, that's not for me." There was a helplessness to his voice that made Helena want to draw him close, comfort him as Ruth did the little ones. "So I'll get out and as for what I'll do after, maybe I'll go to school to learn a trade and open my own shop for woodworking or furniture. I'm good with my hands. What do you think?" he asked.

Helena hesitated, caught off guard by the question. No one ever asked her opinion, not her parents when she was little and certainly not Ruth now, since their talk seldom ventured beyond practical matters. She straightened, enjoying the unfamiliar sensation that her views mattered.

"It sounds like a fine idea," she said, not sure if it was the answer he was looking for. "Christmas is coming in a few days," she added, changing the subject.

"Jews don't celebrate Christmas," he replied.

"Of course, how stupid of me." She brought her hand to her mouth, embarrassed by the mistake.

But his face showed no sign of offense. "We celebrate Hanukkah. It's not a major holiday but it celebrates the retaking of the temple in ancient times, and the miracle of a bit of oil that burned for eight nights."

"I had no idea." There was so much about his religion she did not know and she bit her lips, trying to formulate a question. But before she could speak, there was a sudden thudding noise outside, once, then again and again, growing louder. *Footsteps.* Her eyes darted desperately from corner to corner, searching for a hiding place in the bare, exposed chapel and finding none. Sam grabbed her and pulled her to the ground beside him, as though trying to make them disappear into the earth. He half lay on top of her, not breathing. It was not necessarily the Germans, she told herself. But a passerby discovering them here would be nearly as bad.

Sam's heart pounded through his shirt, racing alongside her own. The sound came again, closer to the outer wall. They lay motionless for several seconds, his cheek warm against hers. A minute later, the sound faded and was gone.

"Just an animal," she said. "Raccoon, probably."

"Sorry." As if noticing for the first time how intimately he was holding her, he straightened and moved away.

"That's all right," she replied quickly, the air growing cold around her. Despite her relief that the danger had passed, she wished he might have stayed close for just a moment longer. The situation was too serious for such silliness, she admonished herself silently. Sam's expression was grave and his skin nearly as pale as the day she had found him. She saw anew the fear he lived with every minute and the danger that worsened the longer he was here. It was easy when she was with Sam to forget everything and talk as though they were safe. But this was not a game—if someone found them, they would be arrested, or even killed.

"I watched the trains again yesterday," she said to relieve the awkward tension. The previous day, Helena had been able to slip away to the barn. She had climbed into the loft, the hay scratchy and familiar beneath her skirt.

His eyebrows lifted. "And?"

Helena wasn't sure what Sam was looking for, or what she was supposed to tell him about it. "They seem to be going east and they have a lot of freight cars, though what are in them I can't say. But when they come back they're always empty."

"They must be moving munitions to the front, preparing for a possible break with the Soviets. This is helpful—or would be, if I could get word to my unit." His face locked with frustration. As his strength returned, Sam seemed to grow more restless with each of her visits.

"There was something else..." She hesitated. "I think I saw where your plane crashed." She had deliberated whether to tell him at all. The first few times she had come to the chapel, the plane was the first thing he had asked as to whether it had been found. But she had heard nothing. The state-controlled radio broadcasts would not have mentioned it, though surely if Ruth had heard it discussed in the gossip at market, she would have said. Then in the loft yesterday morning, she had noticed something out of the corner of her eye. "There are some trees sheared off at the tops about two kilometers east of here."

"That would be it." His jaw set grimly. "I need to get to the crash site."

She touched his arm. "Surely you can't think that anyone else might have survived." He did not answer.

They sat in silence beside one another. Helena's thoughts turned to her visit with her mother earlier that day. The bed beside hers where the elderly woman had long lay was empty. She wondered sadly if the older woman had finally passed but when she'd asked Wanda about it, she shook her head. "Relocated," she mouthed before moving on.

Helena had been puzzled by the response; the woman would not have chosen to be moved. She noticed then around the ward a handful of now-empty beds. There were all kinds of restrictions for the Jews, she knew from the signs around town, prohibiting them from going to restaurants and riding on trolleys. But this was a hospital, and a Jewish one at that. Surely the Germans would not bother with a few old people.

"What is it?" Sam asked, noticing her quiet.

"Nothing." She saw then the dead leaves piled thick on the ground by the stove where he slept, a futile attempt to keep dry in the previous night's storm.

"What is it? You can tell me."

Helena hesitated, feeling foolish. She did not want to burden him with her concerns when he was stranded up here behind enemy lines, just trying to survive each day. "My mother is in the city and I'm worried."

"The Germans won't bother the hospital," he assured her. "They have other concerns. Anyway, there's always the chance that the Soviets may break from the Germans and invade," he added, a note of hopefulness to his voice.

Helena shivered. "You say that as if it would be a good thing."

"Wouldn't it?"

She shook her head emphatically. The Russians were rumored to be so barbaric as to make the Germans look kind. "I can understand why the Jews might find this helpful, with so many being communist."

He flushed. "We aren't communist." Suddenly, the conversation had taken an awkward turn. "That's a rumor the Germans propagated to raise hatred of the Jews. But the Russians, they can't be any worse than the Germans, can they? The atrocities the Nazis are committing…" He slammed his fist against the wall. "I've got to get out of here," he said, his voice more intense than she'd ever heard.

A noise at the door to the church made Helena jump. Her eyes darted across the room and she braced herself to hide once more. This time, though, Sam did not seem alarmed. It was not footsteps, but an animal scratching. "Look!" He whistled and a second later a medium-size, scraggly dog pushed through the door and bounded over to where Sam sat on the ground. Sam laughed as it nuzzled him, throaty and deep, and the sound seemed to lift her above all of the worry and despair. His face was animated like Michal's had been on Christmas morning in better times.

Helena opened her mouth to warn him—the dog was a stray, one she had seen roaming the outskirts of town in a pack that she had admonished the children to avoid. Lately there were rumors that the dogs, unable to find the usual scraps of food in the garbage, had gone feral and attacked a child, that they might have rabies. Then, watching Sam stroke the dog's fur, she sighed inwardly. There were so many things to worry about these days; strays hardly seemed to be one of them.

"You like dogs?" he asked.

"I don't know. I guess so." She'd never had a dog. The children would have loved one. Pets were a luxury, though, another mouth to feed when there already wasn't enough to go around.

"Here." Sam gestured toward the dog. Helena hesitated fearfully. But the animal lay tamely in Sam's lap. "He won't bite." Sam had brushed the dog, she noticed, perhaps even washed it somehow. She lowered her hand to pet the animal, and as she did, her fingers met Sam's beneath the fur.

"I have a Labrador at home," he said, smiling as a faraway look crept into his eyes. His hand rested lightly on hers and lingered, too firmly to be accidental. Her heartbeat quickened. "A yellow pup, just over three years old. He would love this place, with the trees and hills and so much room to run." Helena had not really considered his life beyond the walls of the chapel before today. But now a picture emerged of pets and day trips to the countryside. Was there a girl who might go along with him?

Sam continued. "The first thing I'm going to do when I get home is take Scoop—that's his name—out of the city for a swim down at Johnson's farm and…" He stopped as her expression fell. "Lena, what is it? What's wrong?"

"Nothing." Helena pulled her hand away, stiffening. Sam sounded so excited about leaving. She could hardly blame him for not wanting to stay, cold and in danger, thousands of miles from home. But the idea still nagged at her stomach. She had gotten used to Sam being here and he was going to leave, just like Piotr had left Ruth, and Tata had left them all.

Suddenly she could not hold back. "It's just that when you go, I'll be sad." He did not answer and she felt foolish for having said anything. "You must go, of course, and it's all very selfish of me, but I've gotten rather used to our visits."

"Have you?" He smiled brightly. "I would have thought you'd be glad not to traipse halfway up a mountainside with food."

She opened her mouth to protest, then saw that he was teasing. "Not funny." She reached out to swat at his arm playfully, but he caught her hand and intertwined his fingers with her own, sending tiny shocks of electricity through her. "When do you think you'll go?"

"Soon." The word cut through Helena like a knife. "I'll wait long enough to let my leg heal a bit more and then make a break for the border," he replied, so quickly she could tell he had been thinking about it for some time. That couldn't be terribly long, she calculated, judging by the ease with which he'd moved outside the chapel today. "I've got to get out before the heavier snows fall." She nodded. He could never survive the winter in the chapel, even with the provisions she brought. And at some point the trail would become impassable, either for him to get out or her to visit. Helena had wondered about that even before finding Sam, how she would get to her mother when the weather got bad. She would have to leave extra food, bribe Wanda or one of the other nurses to make sure Mama got some of it. "Probably in another week, maybe two," he added.

"So soon!" she cried out before she could stop herself, the immediacy of his planned departure a blow. She had not realized until that very minute how much these visits—and Sam himself—had come to mean to her, the space they had taken in her life. She looked away, not wanting him to see the tears that welled up uncontrollably. Anger rose unexpectedly within her. She had been just fine before he had come here and made her want things that without him she never would have missed— things that simply could not be.

"Lena," Sam said, the use of the pet name familiar now. He grasped her hand once more.

Astonishment replaced her anger. She swallowed, sensing a moment coming that she had lived a hundred times in her dreams. "Y-yes," she managed, looking up at him.

He lowered his head, bringing his lips to hers, warm and rough. She froze, caught off guard by the tingling sensation that seemed to envelop her all at once. His lips tasted improbably like apples just a day too ripe. She leaned in, eager for more.

Then just as quickly, he pulled away. "I'm sorry," he said, flustered. "I never should have done that."

"I don't mind," she replied breathlessly, reaching for him, still light-headed. Her skin tingled.

But he straightened, moving farther from her. "No, we can't."

"Why not?" She stiffened at the sudden rejection, then stood up, eyes burning.

Sam leaned forward and caught her hand, sending the dog scurrying from his lap. "Helena, wait." He pulled up to one knee, grimacing, and drew her back down. "I'll be leaving," he said, and his words slammed into her. He cupped her chin in one hand, his lips so close she could smell the sweetness she had tasted a moment ago.

"But you're here now," she protested.

"At some point soon, though, I'll have to go and..." He clutched her fingers tighter in his own. "And I don't want to make this harder on either of us."

Helena stared hard at the wall, too proud to push the matter further. "I wonder what it would have been like if we'd met somewhere else." Then hearing the unintended weight behind her words, she blushed. "Not that we would have, of course."

"I think about it all the time," Sam replied quickly, sensing her discomfort and hastening to ease it. "If we'd met back home, I would have asked you out. Courting, my mother says." He laughed. "No one our age calls it that anymore. I would've taken you to Nickel's soda shop for an ice cream soda, or maybe an egg cream. They have a television and everything." Helena had seen a film once, on a projector in the town hall, but television had not come to the village. He continued. "And then maybe I might have worked up the guts—I mean, the nerve—to ask you to one of the dances they have at the lodge on Saturday. Nothing fancy—just an old guy on a piano, and the ladies' auxiliary sells punch and cookies." He stopped speaking and she wondered if he was lost in memories. But then he stood with difficulty, leaning on his makeshift crutch and extending his hand down to her.

"Shall we?" She hesitated. Did he really mean for them to dance, right here? Then she stood, her body about a foot from his, looking at him uncertainly. She had whirled Dorie around the room in play and she had seen her parents dance once many years ago when they thought no one was watching. But she had not, in fact, ever done it properly herself.

"Here." Sam reached out and took her hands gently, placing one on each of his shoulders. Then he put his own hands on her waist, just above the hip. "Is that okay?" She nodded, suddenly unable to find her voice. "Good." He inched nearer to her. "I might even come closer, if the chaperones allowed it," he joked. She did not respond but instead rested her head on his shoulder, surprised at her own boldness, and at the same time feeling she had been doing this her entire life. The damp stone of the chapel walls and Sam's unwashed smell and the liquor that clung to Tata's coat melded together into a kind of cologne.

He began to hum a few bars of a song she'd heard on the radio, before they'd stopped playing music. "I'll be seeing you in all the old familiar places..."

A minute later, Sam stopped humming. They stood motionless, not quite dancing but swaying, bodies pressed close. His face was just inches from hers now, his breath warm on the rise of her cheek, and she wondered whether he might kiss her again, what he would do if she kissed him.

"Well, I guess that's it," Sam said a moment later, a note of reluctance to his voice. He straightened and she pulled away. Helena was suddenly chilled, as though the fire in the stove had gone out. They sat down again. "Of course, if we were back home I'd have competition." She cocked her head, not understanding. "Other boys, wanting to ask you out and dance with you. I'm sure it's no different in your village." She stifled a laugh. If only he knew.

"I dated, of course," he confessed, though she had not asked. "The usual sorts of things." Helena had no idea what that meant—and she wasn't sure she wanted to know. Had he taken girls to dances or movies or had it been something more? Such things, which Ruth spoke of longingly, once seemed silly to Helena. Now she was fiercely jealous of the faceless girls who had been there with Sam—and who would be there again after he went home.

He continued. "But it wasn't like this. I like you, Lena, and I think—" he swallowed "—that you like me, too."

"I do." The words came out too bluntly, something Ruth said

was a particular flaw of hers. Helena had to be honest, though, especially now staring into Sam's rich chocolate eyes. "But once you go, this will all be gone, too." She waved her hand around the chapel, then between the two of them to clarify.

He put a hand on her shoulder. "You could come with me."

She inhaled sharply. "Me?" He had mentioned imagining them somewhere else, but she had not thought him serious.

"It wouldn't be easy, but there are ways. We have to get to the border."

We. Her breath caught as she comprehended the audacity of his idea. He was talking not just about leaving, but about leaving *with* her. A portrait unfurled in her mind of the two of them living together in a modest house, although where she could not fathom. The very idea of it filled her with happiness. She saw it in that instant, she and Sam walking from the chapel, not looking back. But how could that possibly be? Mama and her siblings and all of the reasons they could not be together came crashing down upon her then, water dousing a flame.

"I can't leave my family."

"You could go first and send for them."

"My mother would never be well enough."

Sam pressed his lips together, his silence confirming the grim truth. There was nothing he could say that would give her hope, and he would not lie to her. "Then I won't go, either," he said stubbornly. "I won't leave you." He wanted to protect her, she knew. The notion that, trapped in this chapel, he could prevent any danger seemed ludicrous. But just his being here made her feel safer somehow. "Not after all that you've risked for me."

"You can't stay," she countered. Every day he remained here made his discovery more imminent.

He opened his mouth to protest, then closed it again, unable to argue. The air fell flat and silent between them. A pigeon fluttered in the rafters above.

"The timing," he said. "It's awful, isn't it?"

"I suppose." Timing had never been on her side—Mama taking sick, then losing Tata, leaving them alone as the war worsened.

"Goddamned war," he added ruefully, forgetting not to swear.

"But if it wasn't for the war, we never would have met," she pointed out.

"Well, I'm not going just now," he said, forcing a smile. She nodded—whatever time they had together would have to be enough.

"Do you have a photo?" he asked. "Of yourself, I mean. I should like to have one."

"I'll look for one." Did he mean for now to keep company in the chapel, or to take with him when he was gone?

"I don't want to know," she announced suddenly. He cocked his head, confused. "When you're planning to go, I mean. Just leave. To say goodbye... I couldn't bear it." She brushed at the stinging of tears in her eyes, ashamed. He did not answer, but drew her into his embrace. Nestled in the warmth of his arms, she felt a safety and comfort she had not known since childhood, or maybe even then.

"It's late," she said, noticing through the window how the sun had dropped behind the trees.

"Too late for walking. You should stay."

In an instant, she could see it, a night lying beside Sam under the coat, huddled close for warmth. But she shook her head. "I must get back." She had never been gone overnight before. Ruth would be beside herself with worry.

"Here," he said, holding up his flashlight. He fiddled with the object and it gave off a faint yellow beam as he pressed it cool and hard against her palm.

"I can't take that." Without his flashlight, he would be alone in the darkness of the chapel.

"I insist." Her hand brushed his as it closed around the metal. "You need some light to make it home."

"Fine," she said, relenting somewhat. On this point, she could see that he was right.

At the door to the chapel she wondered for a second if he would try to kiss her again. Instead, he drew her close to his chest, his arms forming a fortress around her that she never wanted to leave. A moment later, he released her. Helena stood motionless for several seconds, wanting to hold on to everything between them in case it did not come again. "You need to go now, before it gets any darker," he said.

Reluctantly she turned and started through the woods, the air away from Sam colder than ever. Even with the light, it was almost impossible to see and she moved more slowly, taking care not to catch her feet on the tree roots. Her skin still tingled from his last embrace. Thoughts leaped through her mind, colliding with one another midflight: *Sam cares for me, too… I could go with him… I cannot.*

For the first time in her life, Helena wanted something that was real and something for herself. She could not have it, though, without betraying those closest to her. She pushed down her thoughts, trying to focus on the path before her. But she could not contain her sadness. It was only a matter of time before she came back to the chapel and found him gone.

8

Helena arose late the next morning. Gray light was already filtering in through the yellowed curtains and a clattering in the kitchen told her she was the last one to rise—something which almost never happened. The room was colder than normal, as if the fire had gone low. Helena drew the blanket up to her neck. She closed her eyes again and lay still for a moment, pretending that she was at the chapel, Sam beside her. Her breath grew deeper as she imagined his hands on her waist.

A loud bang drew her from her thoughts. Reluctantly she stood and dressed. She walked from the bedroom. Ruth was struggling to get the large washtub up the ladder from the cellar. Cold air whooshed in through the open door. Helena groaned inwardly. She had forgotten that it was washing day. Laundry was one of Helena's least favorite tasks, made more onerous in winter by the fact that they could not do it outdoors. But Ruth persisted in gathering the bits of soap that remained to clean their clothes and sheets.

"Help me," Ruth said, holding out her hand before Helena

could escape again. Helena turned to look for Michal, but he was engrossed in play with Karolina. And Dorie was too small to be useful. Helena scampered down the basement stairs and pushed the tub up to Ruth, who pulled it into the room. Helena climbed back up, brushing the dirt from her sleeves, and added more wood to the fire to take away the chill.

There came a sudden yelp from the bedroom. Alarmed, Helena rushed toward it. Dorie, who had been trying to help with the wash by removing the bedding, sat on the floor, a fresh red scrape on her right arm. Helena brought out the kit that held the salves and bandages. As she cleaned the wound, she was taken by her sister's arm, which had a shape reminiscent of Mama's and seemed to have lengthened overnight. The children grew quickly, like weeds sprouting in the garden after a soaking rain. They had changed so much in the past several months, Mama and Tata would hardly have recognized them.

This thought, more than any other, saddened Helena. Sometimes, recalling Tata's face was so immediate it was as if he was just here and had gone out hunting. But then she remembered everything that had happened since he was last here, all of the growth and changes in the world, and it was as if he were very far away, or perhaps had never existed at all.

"There." She pressed a bandage firmly against Dorie's elbow, grateful that at least for this one thing she could help.

"Here, let me." Ruth rushed into the bedroom with a damp towel, then stopped as she looked down at the wound, which Helena had already tended. A hurt look erased her surprise, as though Helena had taken something that was hers.

But Dorie raised her arms to Ruth, seeming to forget Helena and the aid she had just given. Ruth scooped her up with effort and murmured into her hair. "There, there, little one." It was the comfort more than anything else that the child had needed. Helena closed the kit and took the sheets from the bed, then followed Ruth from the room.

"Ruti…" As Ruth filled the tub with water and began to submerge the clothing, Helena considered once again if she should tell her sister about Sam. It had been easier to say nothing when it had just been one or two visits. But each time she saw him, the secret grew, burning inside her. It was more than just guilt—Helena wanted to tell someone about Sam, talk about him aloud and make him real. Despite their imperfect relationship, Ruth was the closest thing she had ever had to a confidante. Ruth would be angry she had kept the truth from her for this long, though. She would demand Helena stop seeing Sam. No, Helena could not risk ruining everything now. She swallowed the secret back down, an insufferable lump in her throat.

Ruth wrung out a shirt, then turned toward her expectantly. "What is it?"

"N-nothing," Helena managed. Then another thought occurred to her. "With everything that is happening, maybe we should pack some bags." Dorie had gone back to the bedroom to get the pillowcases, but Helena spoke low so that Michal would not hear.

"Bags?"

Watching her sister's eyes widen, Helena realized just how outrageous the suggestion must have sounded. They had never spent a single night away from the cottage. "Just in case."

"In case what?"

Helena faltered, not at all sure. In case the Germans came, she wanted to say. In case they had to leave. But the ideas seemed far-fetched, like the wild speculation and dramatics for which she had so often chastised Ruth. "I don't know."

"And where would we go?" Ruth said impatiently, and turned back to the wash. Again Helena had no answers.

Helena looked at the pile of laundry, which seemed to regenerate itself each time Ruth washed a garment, instead of growing smaller. "I need to tend to the animals," Helena said, more eager than ever to escape the chore. Not waiting for an answer, she grabbed her coat. Outside she gazed wistfully into the forest. It felt so much longer than a day since her last visit to the chapel, perhaps because they had talked about him leaving. She did not have a pretext to go again so soon, though, without making Ruth suspicious. Her insides grew warm as she pictured Sam. What was he doing right now? Was he thinking of her?

If she couldn't go see Sam today, at least she could check the trains again. Looking over her shoulder to make sure no one was watching from the house, Helena walked into the barn. She hitched her skirt and climbed up the ladder into the hayloft. She and Ruth had played here often as girls, creating mountains and oceans out of the stiff, browned grass, games that only the two of them understood. One day Ruth had minded how it got in her hair and declared it too scratchy. She had not played there with Helena again. It was not she, but Ruth, who had changed, trying to act ladylike and look nice for boys. She had left Helena behind. But now Piotr was gone and Helena had something with Sam, though what she was not sure.

Leaning back, Helena stared up at the gray morning sky that traveled boundlessly over the mountains to the south. A whistle sounded in the distance, pulling her from her thoughts. A train, the ordinary sort with a dozen or so boxcars that she had seen her entire life, puffed slowly around the corner, steam rising. Unlike the empty train she had told Sam about, the boxcars on this one were closed. Through a slat in one of the closed doors, she thought she glimpsed the very oddest sight: an arm sticking out. But she blinked and then it was gone.

The train moved around a curve and disappeared from sight. She would tell Sam what she had seen on her next visit and see if he could make any sense of it. Turning in the direction of the chapel, Helena scanned the tree line. Something moved, breaking the stillness of the forest. A dog, or wolf perhaps… No, it was bigger than an animal, she realized, squinting. *A man?* Helena leaned forward, her concern growing. Was he looking for Sam?

The figure was headed away from the chapel, though, walking toward the village. As it drew closer and came into focus, Helena gasped at the familiar limp. *Sam!* He had left the chapel and somehow made his way through the woods. Did he mean to come here to the cottage? No, he was walking parallel to the tree line, headed doggedly for something. But he was out in full view of anyone who might look in that direction. She climbed down the ladder from the loft and raced across the barnyard. She had to stop him.

At the ground level, Helena paused, unable to see him through the trees. She started toward the forest in the direction he seemed to have gone. Moments later she spied him, some fifty meters ahead. He was trying to move quietly, but his awkward limp, magnified out here in the rough terrain, caused branches to snap, threatening to betray him at any second. She started after him, sliding in her haste. Then she righted herself and stepped forward more carefully, using the trees on either side for support, making up ground between them. She wanted to call after him but didn't dare.

"*Sam,*" she whispered finally as she neared him. He turned, surprise and then stubborn defiance setting his face. Perspiration coated the delicate curve of his upper lip. "Are you mad? Where are you going?"

He opened his mouth to speak and then, seeming to think better of it, turned and started walking again, heading east. Now she understood—she had told him where the crash site was. She followed him, watching his shoulders square with determination and his muscles strain. Warmth surged through her. Though she was frustrated that he had risked everything by leaving the chapel, she could not help but be glad to see him again. But her annoyance persisted. "Your leg isn't healed. You're going to make it worse. And it's broad daylight. Anyone could see you, or the Germans could come back."

"I can't just sit around waiting. I have to find the plane."

"Why? You can't think someone might still be alive?" After all the time that had passed, he could not possibly have hope.

His eyes darted back and forth desperately and she knew then it was more than that. "There's information in the plane, things that the Germans must not discover." It was the most he had said about why he had come to Poland. Her curiosity grew.

"What information?" He bit his lip. Her frustration rose. "I'm risking my life helping you, Sam. I would think you might trust me by now."

"The longer I wait here, the greater jeopardy for the mission."

She wanted to tell him that his mission, whatever it was, had ended the minute his plane had crashed, that it was madness to do this. But she knew he would not be dissuaded and standing here arguing made the risk of discovery even greater. "Fine, I'll help you."

Helena held out her hand and he took it, leaning on her slightly for support. She led the way, trying to clear a navigable path for him while clinging to the bit of forest where the pine trees were most dense so as not to be seen. They made their way through the forest, their footsteps breaking the silence.

They reached the swath of forest she had seen from the loft. Trees had fallen or were sheared off midway, as if taken down by loggers and improbably left. The destruction was much more massive than Helena had imagined, even having heard the crash. There was a tangle of metal larger than her house, so twisted it scarcely resembled the planes she'd seen flying overhead. It sat deep in the crater it had made upon impact, covered lightly with the snow that had fallen since. The roof had been peeled off like an open can and one of the wings was missing. A faint burning smell hung in the air, suggesting someone had been here more recently than the night of the crash. Of course, the Germans had found the site—the fact that Sam had jumped and landed miles away was the only reason he was still alive.

Sam stood silently for a moment, staring at the wreckage. Pain rolled over his face as he imagined the crash and what his fellow soldiers must have suffered. He dropped her hand and raced forward. "Careful," she said as he moved awkwardly through the jagged, unsteady pieces.

He disappeared into the front of the plane, leaving Helena alone. Her skin prickled knowing the Germans could come back anytime.

Sam emerged, his face ashen.

"What is it?" He did not speak as he made his way back toward her. "Come," she said, taking his hand. Together they returned to the shelter of the unbroken trees. "Did you find what you were looking for?"

"One of the men, John…he was still in there." He shook his head, distraught over seeing his friend. "We're soldiers, I know. We're supposed to expect these things and be able to handle them." His face crumpled, sadder than she had ever seen it. She put her arm around him, searching for words to ease his pain but finding none. "John was the most eager of all of us to get home. His wife was having a baby." He straightened. "The others could be alive. I should go look for them." He started forward, pulling at her hand.

She stopped. "Sam, wait. That's impossible. Where would you look?" She did not wait for him to answer. "If they jumped like you did, they could be across a hundred miles of countryside. And if they were arrested, to go after them would be suicide." He was silent, acknowledging that she was right. But his eyes darted wildly.

"Did you find what you were looking for inside the plane?" she repeated in a low voice, changing the subject.

"Gone."

A chill ran through Helena. "What was it?" she could not help but ask, unsure if he would answer.

He bit his lip. "It was information," he whispered, "that would have helped the partisans—and shown them that they could trust us."

Partisans. Helena had heard stories of pockets of resistance, groups of young men who had taken to the woods in hopes of fighting back. The Home Army, they were called. There was even a rumor that some rebels had thrown a bomb into a German military truck, killing several soldiers. But such hopeful anecdotes were few and unsubstantiated. And even if they were true, what difference could a few schoolboys make throwing rocks at tanks? It was David versus Goliath. Surely the American army had not come all this way for that.

He continued. "Information for the partisans about positions, ways we could help them fight. The documents were encrypted, of course, with a key that we had to memorize. So the documents would be useless to the Germans, unless..." *Unless one of the men talked.* "If the Germans got their hands on the documents and the code, it would be devastating," he added.

Her stomach twisted. "Do you think they did?"

"I don't know. We were trained to destroy the information if captured, so one of the men might have done that if he had time. You see now why I had to come here."

She processed the information. Sam was not just the ordinary soldier he had made out to be. If he had lied to her about this, what else? He had been cautious and rightfully so. But he trusted her now.

"You could have asked me. I would have gone to the plane for you."

"After all that you've done, I couldn't put you in further danger."

They were traveling parallel to the village now and for a moment Helena considered taking Sam to their house. Just for the night. She could hide him in the barn and Ruth wouldn't even have to know. But that would make the danger even worse, bring it perilously close to the children. Instead, she started toward the forest.

A figure appeared suddenly on the path in front of them. Helena jumped. A man in a constable's uniform stood blocking their way. *"Dobry wieczór, pani."* He directed his greeting to Helena, bidding her good evening as casually as though they had met crossing the market square. But his eyes watched Sam closely, a predator tracking its prey. Who was he? He did not look familiar but his tone suggested they had met before. She wondered where he had come from, and whether he had seen them at the crash site. Her heart raced.

"What are you doing here?" the constable demanded. Helena searched for a plausible explanation.

"Dobry wieczór, Pan Constable." Helena turned in surprise as Sam spoke. His Polish was smoother and more flawless than it had been in any of their previous conversations, the accent undistinguishable from her own. "I'm Mirosław Sendecki, a cousin of the Nowaks and I've come from Rzeszów to pay respects for the loss of their mother, my aunt." His intelligence training must have prepared him for scenarios just like this, she realized. "We're going to the cemetery to pay a visit to my uncle, as well, and we're hoping to make it before dark. If you'll excuse us…"

"Papers?" the constable asked. Helena reached into her coat pocket and pulled hers out, but the man waved her away and gestured to Sam.

"My cousin's papers are at my house," she blurted out, then instantly regretted making her own family a target.

The policeman stared at her and Sam for several seconds, weighing her story. Failure to present one's papers was a crime in itself. They might both be arrested. "I'll call by the house to check them later," the policeman finally said sharply. He stepped aside, but continued to stare after her as they walked past and continued along the path.

When they had rounded the bend and the policeman had disappeared from site, Helena stopped, trying to figure out what to do. "What will you do when he comes looking for my papers?" Sam asked in a low voice.

"I'll think of something."

"You never should have come with me," he said regretfully.

"You never should have left the chapel!" She looked around— she could not take Sam back up to the chapel while the policeman was still on patrol. Sam had told the policeman they were heading to the cemetery, but that was in the middle of the village and they could not actually go there, either, without attracting attention. Her earlier idea, of taking him to the cottage, popped into her mind once more. "Come."

Sam was limping more now as he followed her, worn out from the trek to the plane. Helena hoped he would have the strength to make it back up to the chapel when it was time. As they reached the gate to her house, she looked longingly toward the cottage, wishing she could simply bring him inside. But who knew what impetuous Ruth might do when confronted with Helena's secret? Instead, she hurried him into the barn and pulled up a door cut into the floorboards that led to a shallow cellar. She gestured for him to climb down into the empty space and he did so, crouching beneath the low ceiling. "Wait here."

She raced into the house, where the fire blazed merrily now, giving the room a too-warm feel. Ruth had nearly finished the laundry and she and Dorie were wringing out the last of it. Helena waited for Ruth to rebuke her for being gone for nearly two hours and not helping with the wash. Ruth did not look up, but raised her finger to her lips and then pointed toward the bedroom, indicating that Karolina was napping.

"I'm going back out to finish some work," Helena said in a low voice.

"Again?" Ruth asked mildly, not looking up.

"Can I come?" Michal asked.

"No!" she said too harshly, instantly regretting it as his face fell. "I think I saw a squirrel in one of the old traps and I'm going after it," she lied, knowing Michal would not volunteer to help.

"Well, at least take a potato to warm yourself if you aren't going to be here for lunch," Ruth said. Helena went to the stove and gingerly selected a potato, which was almost too-hot to touch, wishing she might have two. She grabbed some extra bread from the cupboard, hoping Ruth would not notice, and slipped from the house once more.

In the cellar, Sam was rubbing his wounded leg. "Serves you right," she said, handing him the food without keeping any for herself. "What were you thinking, going like that?"

"I told you, I had to try to find the documents. I'm sorry I didn't tell you sooner."

"I understand. But no more secrets, okay?" He nodded, taking her in with a long look. She had rushed after him into the forest without the care she usually took before visiting the chapel, and was suddenly mindful of her disheveled hair and soiled work dress. He did not seem to notice, but touched her shoulder, warming her. "The fact that the documents are gone, does that make things worse for you?"

Conflicting expressions crossed his face, unable to protect her from the truth without lying. "Perhaps. If they access the code, they'll be able to figure out who we are, and what we were planning to do. And sooner or later they're going to realize that there were more of us than they've accounted for."

She shivered. "You have to get out of here."

He nodded in agreement. "My leg is just about strong enough."

"So I've given it some thought," she began, then she paused, licking her lips. Helping him go was the only choice she had, but doing so could not be harder. "The mountains to the south are heavily fortified but if we could get you on a train north, a freighter perhaps to Gda'nsk, it might be possible to escape by sea."

His brow furrowed. "I don't understand."

"You said you wanted to leave."

"I do, but not to escape. I need to get to the partisans."

She stared at him, mouth agape, stunned by the audacity of his plan. To make it out of Poland, an enemy soldier getting across the border, was one thing. But to stay and keep fighting... "That's madness!" she blurted out. His face seemed to crumple a bit, as if her confidence in him was something he sorely needed.

"If the Germans crack those documents, it is going to reveal key information about the partisans—who won't know they've been exposed. I have to get to them. I never should have said anything," he added grimly, before she could protest. "The less you know, the better."

She persisted, ignoring his last remark. "I mean, first of all you're wounded."

"I'm nearly healed," he insisted stubbornly.

"But how? Where will you go?"

"Southeast." He hesitated, then lowered his voice as if someone else might hear. "We were supposed to drop into a clearing on the Czechoslovakian side of the border." It was the most he had said about his mission. "The objective was to make contact with the partisans in the woods there."

He continued. "We want to help them organize. The resistance is very fragmented. There are different factions, each with their own interests. There's dissent among their leaders—whether to attack now before things get worse or wait until they've amassed more weapons..." He stopped suddenly, and she wondered if he was worried about trusting her again. "I don't want to bore you."

"Not at all." She was fascinated by this world, which until now she had not realized existed. People doing something real, something that mattered. Suddenly, she felt hope.

"Plus, if I can find them, perhaps they know what happened to the rest of my team. I know it's unlikely any of them survived," he conceded, seeing the conflicted look on her face. "But there were other units operating with us. If any of them made it to the partisans…"

"And if they didn't?"

"Then it is so much more important that I do. I can help provide lines of communication, and the intelligence that they sorely need. Reinforcing the partisans is critical to holding the Eastern front." Suddenly, the whole world seemed to hang in the balance of what he was trying to do and she could see the bigger picture, thousands of little pieces like themselves contributing to the whole.

Helena pictured the rugged border region to the south. The High Tatras, which separated the two countries, were not like the rolling hills north of Biekowice. Rather, they were tall, snowcapped mountains, almost impossible to traverse on foot. "There couldn't be a more dangerous route," she protested. "Even if you could make it across the mountains, the border is guarded heavily."

"Do you think you're telling me something I don't know? I don't have a choice." He set his jaw.

"But if they capture you…the things you know."

"I'll never tell," he said resolutely, his eyes far away. He would sooner die than betray his men, or the people he was trying to help. She had to get him out to make sure that did not happen.

"They'll kill you," she ended, her voice nearly a wail. Usually the calm one, Helena could feel herself reaching a level of panic that reminded her of Ruth.

He grasped her by both shoulders. "Which is why I have to get out. And you, too," he added. "I want to get you and your family to safety. But first I have to make contact with the partisans. Setting off blindly without some idea of their whereabouts would be, as you say, madness." She nodded, for once in agreement. "The problem is that the partisans are so scattered across the countryside. We don't know who's in charge or how to make contact."

She forced herself to breathe more calmly now. "Then how are we to find them?" *We.* His mission had become her own. She waited for him to rebuke her that it was not her fight, that or it was too dangerous for her to become involved.

"I'm told that the resistance in the city operates through the churches. If I could make it to Kraków and try to contact the underground, they might have some idea as to the whereabouts of the partisans."

Sam could not, Helena reflected, go to the city. Though his Polish had been good enough to pass muster with a country policeman, his dark complexion would make him suspect as a Jew immediately. More to the point, he did not have papers to pass as a Pole if he was stopped. Her fear rose up again. She could not lose him. She wanted to ask him not to do this. Wasn't just surviving enough under the circumstances? But seeing the stubborn way his jaw set, the dogged expression in his eyes, she knew that it was futile. No matter how much they felt for each other, or how much she wanted to keep him safe, this was about something bigger than the two of them, and he would not give up.

"Helena?" Ruth's voice came across the barnyard, getting closer.

"Stay down," Helena hissed. She climbed from the cellar in time to see Ruth's head appear in the barn.

"Did you get it?" Ruth was talking about the squirrel, she realized.

"The trap was empty. I must have been wrong." Her guilt rose at having gotten Ruth's hopes up for more food.

"What on earth are you doing down there? It's filthy."

Helena noticed then that her dress was black with soot. "I found some old tools of Tata's," she lied. "I'm seeing if there is anything useful."

A second passed, then another. From below came a scuffling

sound and Helena coughed loudly to muffle it. "Well, come inside when you're done," Ruth said before turning back toward the house.

"My sister," she explained when Ruth had disappeared back in the house. She was grateful that Sam had not seen her.

"She sounds like you."

Helena ignored the comment. "I could go for you," she offered tentatively, returning to the original subject. "To the city, I mean."

His eyes widened with horror. "No." His tone was firmer than she had ever heard him use. "I mean, that is very kind of you to offer, but it is much too dangerous."

"But I can get into the city easily. I know how and no one will question me."

He put his hand on her shoulder. "Helena, no. It's out of the question."

She looked at him levelly. "So you're saying no women are helping?"

He looked down, avoiding her gaze. "No," he said, unable to lie to her. "There are women in these resistance movements, couriers and such. But they have experience."

"No one trains for this sort of thing," she countered. "I'm strong…"

"And you're smart and resourceful," he added.

She felt herself blush. "And I know how to get around the city without being detected. I can do this."

"You would be really good at it," he agreed, and she found herself sitting a bit straighter. "But I've already endangered you enough. This isn't your problem."

"Not my problem," she repeated slowly, her voice thick with disbelief. She jumped to her feet, anger flaring. "How can you say that to me? After all that I have done, everything I have risked for you, you still don't consider me an ally. You came here because you wanted to help. Don't I have to do that, too?"

He did not answer and she could see him wrestling with the dilemma—the undeniable truth of what she had said versus his desire to keep her safe. "I can't lose you. Please don't do this."

"I have to." She could no longer hold back the emotion in her voice. "Don't you see? If I don't follow this through it will have all been for nothing." It was not just about him anymore, she reflected. The fight had become hers, too. "You don't have a choice," she added. "I'm your only hope or else you stay here until the Germans find you or the weather gets too bad for me to reach you and you are cut off and starve."

"Or the war ends," he countered. But his face clouded; the idea of remaining here and leaving the fight to others was unbearable to him.

"I'm your only chance," she insisted. He sat back, relenting silently. "So what is it you need me to do?"

"You've got to go to the city and make contact with the resistance. But I'm not certain where. You must watch out, too, for impostors. There are German spies who infiltrate the resistance and then turn them in to be killed. There are criminals who pretend to be partisans to take advantage of people." She nodded, understanding then the magnitude of what she was about to undertake.

"What do you want me to do if I make contact?"

"Tell them that I am trying to reach the Slovak partisans." He paused, looking around the cellar, then crawled over to a bag of animal feed that stood in the corner. He ripped off a piece of the paper bag, then picked up a scrap of coal from the ground and used it to scribble something on the paper. He handed it to her. Reading the note, her eyes widened. "But that's everything— your name, your exact location. If it fell into the wrong hands…"

He nodded. "Which is precisely why I am counting on you to make sure that it doesn't."

Despite Sam's concerns, he was depending upon her. Helena's

chest tightened. "I can do it," she said, forcing more bravado into her voice than she felt.

"I know you can," he replied sincerely. "But goddammit, I wish you didn't have to." He took her hands in his. "I need you to understand something—intelligence work requires a cool head." *Intelligence work.* Suddenly there was a name for what she was doing. Her shoulders squared with new purpose.

"I do have one lead," he said slowly. "There's a man, Alek Landesberg." He spoke in a low voice now. "Landesberg is the head of the Jewish resistance. His group is small and tight-knit, and most importantly, he's solid. He can be trusted."

"So if I can find Alek, I give him the note, right?"

"It isn't that simple. Landesberg is a shadow. It took us months just to learn his name."

"But you said his group operates in Kraków."

"It's a big city. What are you going to do, just ask for him on the street?"

He had a point. "I'll think of something. In the meantime, we have to get you back to the chapel." She desperately wanted to keep him here, close to her. But he couldn't stay in the cellar, when Michal and Ruth might find him. And it would be im-possible here to build him a fire—there was no way she could keep him warm. They crept from the cellar and across the field and started up the hill silently. "Promise me that you won't do anything stupid again." He opened his mouth to argue, then closed it again, seeming to think better of it.

They moved swiftly across the field that separated the barn from the forest, clinging close to the cover of the trees. Her skin prickled as they neared the spot where they had encoun-tered the policeman an hour earlier. "I can make it the rest of the way myself," he said. His words stung. He did not need her as much as he once had to get around—but he needed her help more than ever. "You should go home." They stood awkwardly in place, not wanting to part, but unable to go farther together.

She wanted to kiss him, or at least touch him once more, but she did not dare.

"Promise me," she said, "that if I do this for you, you will stay in the chapel. It's too dangerous for you to go out again." She watched the conflict roll over his face, torn between his inability to sit still and do nothing and the fact that he knew she was right. "Trust me," she said.

"Fine. When?" he asked, the conflict apparent in his voice. He was urgent to make contact but did not want to press for more than she could give.

"Soon," she promised. "You should go."

He looked puzzled at her changed demeanor. "Are you still angry?"

She shook her head. She did not want him to linger and risk his safety, or to ask more questions about her plans—questions to which she herself was not quite sure how to answer.

9

Ruth's step was lighter than it had been in some time. Her basket was a bit fuller after recent trips to market with an unexpected boon of carrots, apples and nuts that would help make for a festive holiday dinner. Snow had begun to fall, pale white against the trees. She stuck out her tongue to catch flakes as she had done when she was a child. It tasted bitter now, like cold ash.

As Ruth reached the base of the hill where it rose behind their house, her twin's face appeared in her mind. That morning when Helena left to go see Mama, her cheeks were flushed, eyes glowing in a way that made her plainness almost pretty. Envy tugged at the edges of Ruth's stomach. Pretty had always been her thing. Helena had promised to return early to help with baths. But it was nearly midday now and Ruth wondered what "early" meant. Helena's trips seemed to get longer each time. She had always enjoyed getting away, but she was different now, nearly giddy when she left. Was life at home really that bad?

Her mood more somber now, Ruth neared the house. A loud banging noise came from inside. Alarmed, she froze, her hand hovering above the doorknob. Then, hearing Michal's shout, she flung the door open and stepped inside. "What's wrong?" The table was piled high with dirty bowls and spoons that had not been there an hour ago, and it was covered with a fine coat of powder, as if it had begun to snow indoors, as well. The children had tried to make breakfast, she realized. A metal bowl had crashed to the floor, sending flour everywhere.

Annoyance quickly replaced her relief. "Let me," she said, setting down her basket and taking the pitcher of milk Michal was holding. The pale blue porcelain had been one of Mama's favorites and she had saved it for special occasions, not everyday cooking.

"Can I help?" Dorie had attempted to do her own hair and now her thick braids stuck out diagonally in either direction, like two hands pointing. The delicate slope of her nose was dusted with flour.

"*Nie,*" Ruth replied crossly. But Dorie reached for the pitcher, anyway, pulling it from Ruth's hands. It fell to the floor, shattering and sending an arc of milk mixed with blue shards sailing across the floor. Ruth leaped back, yelping with dismay.

Suddenly the weight of it all crashed down upon her. "Get out!" The children looked up at her, eyes wide, mouths agape. It was Helena who lost patience and snapped on occasion, never Ruth. "Go!"

Michal started for the door. Dorie stumbled as she followed, her shorter leg buckling. She flailed forward, banging her chin on the table as she fell. "Oh!" Ruth cried, instantly remorseful. She rushed forward as a crumpled Dorie began to wail. "I'm sorry." How could she have been so cruel?

"I broke Mama's pitcher," Dorie lamented, more despondent about her blunder than the fall.

"I'll fix it," Ruth lied, knowing that was impossible. She pictured Mama, tried to summon from her image a fraction of her patience and strength. "It's just a pitcher. But are you hurt?" She

examined Dorie's face, which showed no sign of injury. Ruth
wrapped her arms around the child, desperate to take away her
pain and shame.

"Come on, Dor," Michal said casually, extending his hand.
Dorie dried her eyes. "Let's go out back and play tag in the field.
It's your turn to be it." He sensed that, with her pride wounded,
she needed distraction, not sympathy.

Ignoring him, Dorie stood and reached for the broom. Ruth
started to protest, then thought better of it. The child needed to
feel as though she was helping in order to redeem herself from
what she had done. "Well done," Ruth said a few minutes later,
though Dorie's clumsy strokes had only spread the mess further.
"I'll finish up here. You go play."

As the door closed behind them, Ruth picked up the broom.
Porcelain crunched beneath her feet as she began to sweep the
soppy mixture that had formed on the floor. There would be
no milk for at least another day, Ruth fretted, glancing toward
the cradle where Karolina slept undisturbed. The baby let out
a contented half sigh, lost for a moment in a world that didn't
know hunger or worry.

Ruth paused, looking at the dishes strewn across the table.
The children had been trying to help but they had wasted flour
they could ill-afford to spare. Food seemed to disappear more
quickly these days, loaves of bread and pieces of cheese dimin-
ishing as if being eaten by mice. Perhaps it was only her own
hunger that made it seem as though their food supply was shrink-
ing on its own.

Finished sweeping, Ruth grabbed a rag and knelt wearily to
clean up the rest of the mess. She straightened, a sense of power-
lessness overcoming her as she replayed Dorie's fall in her mind.
There was simply no way for her to protect them from all of the
hurt and danger in life, even at home. But behind the house,
the children played as though nothing had happened, their faces
bathed in light. She smiled, relaxing slightly.

A scream jarred her from her thoughts. In the cradle by the fireplace where she slept during the day, Karolina had awoken from an early nap. Pulled from the breast too young due to Mama's illness and forced to drink powdered milk that was hardly a substitute, she had been a colicky baby. But this was different. She thrashed about, face red. Was she sick again? Ruth lifted her, shuffling from side to side, but the child would not be comforted, so Ruth carried her into the bedroom and pulled back her diaper. Beneath the cloth, Karolina's skin was red and chapped. Once Ruth would have made a cornstarch paste to soothe her bottom, but they could not spare the tiny bit they had left now.

Ruth's eyes traveled to the dresser where Mama's jar of lotion sat. It had run low; only a few drops remained and when it was gone there would be no more. But it would ease Karolina's distress. Sadly, Ruth opened the jar and applied the last bit of cream to Karolina's skin, then reclosed the diaper and picked the child up. Karolina rested her head on her shoulder and sighed, now content.

Inhaling the child's powdery scent, a strange mix of affection and resentment washed over Ruth. *Without you, I could have everything. Without you, I would have nothing.* Had her own mother felt that way? Mama had seemed content to live this life. But now for the first time Ruth saw her as a woman, complete with her own private dreams and desires.

Ruth lay Karolina across the bed once more. She wiped off a bit of the breakfast porridge that Helena had missed on the child's chin, then sighed. Ruth did not mean to be critical of her sister. But Helena brought chaos where calm was needed, playing with the children on the floor in loud ways that dirtied their clothes and made them restless. No one could do as well by the children as Mama had, though, and even Ruth's own efforts were a poor second choice. Watching Karolina sleep, Ruth's resolve to do better strengthened. They were being tested, she believed. God helped those who helped themselves, Mama always said. So they would persevere. Because surely if they did, God would not—could not—let anything bad happen to them.

There was a knock at the door. Ruth moved to answer it before the sound disturbed Karolina, peering through the crack in the way that had become her habit in recent weeks. Her breathing stopped. The policeman, Wojski, stood on the doorstep once more. She had pushed the memory of his strange visit from her mind. When the children had asked, she'd said only that the policeman was looking for someone, hoping they would not speak of it again. She had not mentioned it to Helena, not wanting to hear her views on how she would have handled it differently. It was in the past, she'd told herself.

Yet here he was. Reluctantly she opened the door, willing herself to breathe normally. *"Dzie'n dobry, pani,"* he said. "Everyone is well now, I presume?" Not waiting for her to respond, the policeman stepped forward. She moved aside, knowing that she did not dare refuse him access. He removed his hat, revealing a wide swath of bald scalp through the gray strands he'd attempted to comb over it. The stale odor of cheap cologne hung unpleasantly around him.

"Herbata?" She offered tea, hoping to conceal her nervousness. He peered around the cottage, as though searching for something, not bothering to conceal his interest.

Over the man's shoulder, Ruth could see Michal and Dorie through the window, oblivious to what was going on inside. Had the policeman come from another direction he might have seen them playing out back, but thankfully it seemed he had not. She looked desperately toward the woods, willing Helena to magically appear. But her sister would be gone for some time yet.

She moved into the kitchen, trying to steer the policeman's gaze from the back window so he would not notice the children. "I haven't seen anyone like the men you described," she offered, eager to give him what he wanted so he would leave quickly. On the stove behind the policeman, the kettle was nearly boiling.

She fought the urge to reach over and turn it off, not wanting to draw his attention toward the window.

But he shook his head. "It's another matter, I'm afraid." Her breath caught. What could he possibly want now? "We've also had reports of hoarding." Ruth's eyes traveled to her basket containing the items she had purchased at market. She had heard stories of what happened to those who squirreled away food beyond what the ration cards permitted. But they had taken nothing extra. "I've been sent to investigate suspects."

His words reverberated in her mind. *Investigate suspects.* What did he mean to do? "I have no idea what you're talking about."

The kettle was still on, the water boiling to a fever pitch. Steam shot forth, forming a cloud over the policeman's shoulder. In a moment it would begin to whistle. With a deft movement, Ruth reached behind him. Her arm touched his waist and his eyebrows rose, misreading her intentions. She flicked the stove off and turned back to face him.

The policeman licked his lips and took a step forward. "Of course, I was pleased to question such an attractive suspect." The man's voice was gravelly. He took her in with a sweeping head-to-toe gaze, and for the first time in her whole life her looks seemed a liability. "Are you alone?"

She swallowed, searching for the right answer. "Yes."

"Your cousin has gone, then?" Ruth cocked her head, puzzled, and started to say that she did not understand. Perhaps he had her confused with someone else. She decided instead to play along.

He took a step toward her. "It must be quite lonely here all by yourself."

"I have a sister. She's not here right now," Ruth added quickly.

"But without a man…" His hand grazed her hair, his breath wafting sour upon her. Then he stroked her cheek. It was a gesture so bold that she thought she might have imagined it. She froze, not pulling away for fear of angering him. Mistaking her silence for acquiescence, he lowered his hand, tracing a line from her cheek to her neck to her collarbone and nudging back the fabric of her dress to expose her skin.

She flushed at the memory of Piotr's furtive touch behind the barn, his clumsy gropes going farther than they properly should have before she pushed him away. It seemed now that she was being punished for the earlier transgression.

Ruth bit her lip, willing herself not to scream and attract the attention of the children. The policeman's tobacco-stained fingers dangled above the edge of her breast, hovering, waiting to strike. She braced for the shame of what would surely come next.

Then he stopped. A half smile played at his lips. The power and threat were enough—for now.

"A woman passed through a few weeks ago," Ruth blurted out, seizing on his hesitation. She instantly regretted it. Helena would have remained strong, and would not have helped the enemy. "Not from these parts. Jewish, I think."

Though the woman was not his present quarry, Wojski's eyes widened. "Did you see which way she went?"

"Over the fields." Ruth pointed in the opposite direction from which she had seen the woman go, praying that the policeman would not sense the lie.

She held her breath. Surely he would leave now. But he continued staring at her—did he think she had helped the woman? "I would have informed you, but I lost your card." She did not mention that the woman predated his earlier visit, having come just before he had.

Just then a loud wail came from the bedroom, Karolina awakening. The policeman raised an eyebrow. "You said you were alone."

Her breathing stopped. "One hardly counts a baby."

The policeman did not reply, but moved swiftly in the direction of the bedroom. Ruth leaped ahead of him, picking up Karolina before his outstretched hands could touch her.

"What a beautiful child," the police officer said, but there was no tenderness in his voice. "I do not have any myself, but I was a teacher once." As his crude finger rubbed the baby's soft apple cheek, Ruth wanted to slap his hand away. Her eyes traveled to Tata's hunting box, which sat high on the shelf. She did not know how to use the rifle as Helena did, had resisted Tata's attempts to show her. But she would try rather than let him hurt the children. "Is she yours?"

Ruth shook her head. "My sister."

He clucked his tongue. "That's a terrible burden to shoulder in these times. Families in Germany are paying dearly to adopt such Aryan-looking children. 'Lebensborn,' they call it. I could arrange for an application."

"No!" she blurted out with more force than she knew was left in her. Her anger boiled. To him, Karolina was a commodity, to be bartered for favor, or perhaps even money.

The policeman looked embarrassed. "Of course, I had not meant anything by it." He stepped backward, retreating. "Still, if you'd like to cooperate…" He licked his lips and his salacious tone left no room for misinterpretation. The man reached in his pocket and produced a pair of nylons like the very ones she had dreamed about. He held them out to her, the fine fabric soft as silk beneath her calloused fingertips. They weren't new and she could not help but wonder who had worn them, how he had come to have them in his possession.

She stared at the nylons, considering. Cooperating with this man would bring security for the family, perhaps even the gifts she'd heard about from the soldiers. It wasn't as if she had anyone else.

He reached in his pocket again and pushed a tin of sardines across the table. Ruth's mouth watered. "I could help you."

With difficulty, she handed both items back. There were some lines she could not cross. "That is very kind of you, but I really cannot accept these."

His lips curled in a sneer. "You think you are too good for me. This is my jurisdiction now. When the Germans come you'll be begging me, *pani*. You are a fool if you think you are safe here." He paused, as though expecting her to change her mind. Several seconds passed. "If you see the woman again, or hear anything unusual…" Then he turned and walked from the cottage.

Ruth stood motionless for several seconds, then raced to the window. The policeman strode in the direction of the barn and opened the gate. He led Bolek the goat from the pen. She gripped the window ledge, paralyzed. The Germans and their puppets were free to "procure" anything they wanted, and protesting would just give him more reasons to cause trouble. There was nothing she could do.

Watching the policeman retreat down the road with the goat, Ruth clutched Karolina, shaking so hard she thought she might drop her. Ruth dropped to a chair and looked around the room. There was no hint that the policeman had been there, other than a faint coating of mud on the floor that just as easily could have come from the children. Still, it looked wrong. Everything was tainted now by what had happened.

Setting Karolina back in her cradle, Ruth ran to the closet and pulled out one of Mama's sweaters, ignoring in her need to change and clear herself from the man's touch her earlier admonition to Helena to leave the clothes undisturbed. She hated to defile the soft, clean fabric with the man's filth, and she would have taken a bath then and there if it would not have aroused too much suspicion from the children. Her skin crawled. She caught a glimpse of herself in the mirror, her face now blotchy. Shame and loathing rose in her.

Her thoughts returned to the policeman. Once he had been a schoolteacher. What made someone like him turn against his own people—was it money or fear, or the need to find a better life or protect one's own? He had offered to arrange for the baby's placement. Ruth shivered. They must stay together at all costs. The war suddenly seemed closer, on their doorstep, large and menacing. As Ruth wrapped her arms tighter around Karolina, she understood then that she had not nearly begun to lose everything.

10

Helena made her way through the woods toward the city. The sky was pooling to the west with thick dark clouds that signaled snow. As she reached the place where the path broke off, she looked longingly in the direction of the chapel. She wanted to go and make sure Sam had made it back safely the previous day, and that he had not strained himself too much from the journey to the plane. But she needed to get to the city to see Mama as well as try to make contact with the resistance, and she had no idea how long that would take. And time passed so quickly when she was with Sam; if she went to him now, she would surely stay much longer than she intended. Plus, she had promised Sam she would help and he would be eager for information that would help him escape. She did not want to face him again until she had something to share.

As she continued up the hill, her doubts rose. She wanted to help Sam, and it had seemed like the right thing to do. But going into the city and asking questions meant even greater danger, and she owed her loyalty to the children and to keeping them safe. She imagined her sister's reaction if she had known what Helena was doing. Ruth would be furious. Helping the soldier survive was one thing—taking on his mission quite another. *This isn't our fight*, Ruth would say. But she would be dead wrong. Because aside from any feelings Helena might have for Sam, the truth was that Sam had come halfway around the world and risked his life to try to help them. How could they expect anyone else to fight for them if they did not stand up for others—and themselves?

Behind her, the wind grew stronger now, unabated by the pine trees. It pushed at her back, seeming to urge her forward. A sudden surge of energy raced through Helena, strengthening her legs, and she found herself walking with renewed vigor. Helping Sam was purposeful and real, more so than anything she'd ever done. It seemed in that moment as if she'd been waiting her whole life for this. She passed the point where the path divided. For the first time, she did not look in the direction that would take her away from this place, but instead focused straight ahead.

But as she climbed the hill above the city, her doubts bubbled anew. This time she questioned not whether she should help, but could she? She had offered to help Sam connect with the resistance without really thinking about how—or if she could even do it at all.

Pushing her questions aside, she descended the hill and crossed the wide steel railway bridge that spanned the Wisła River. Daylight, too bright for December, broke through the thick clouds, bathing Wawel Castle in dazzling, golden light. The soot-covered facades of the stone buildings below the fortress seemed to glow, as if saying defiantly, We have withstood war and suffering across the ages, and we will transcend this, too.

At the base of the bridge, she paused, looking toward Kazimierz. Should she go to see Mama first? No, better to try to make contact for Sam. Mama would still be there in a few hours, and perhaps Helena would be able to coax a bit of food into her.

Turning away from the Jewish quarter, Helena made her way along the high stone wall at the base of the castle. She turned onto Grodzka Street, taking care not to slip on the slick cobblestones. She had only seen the Old City from a distance before and she marveled at the sloping buildings that lined the winding medieval thoroughfare, their carved stone fronts and high windows elegant even in disrepair. Save for the automobiles, it was as if she had stepped into a storybook a hundred years earlier, making her feel awkward and out of place.

The street soon opened onto the *rynek*. Helena stopped, taken by the size of the massive square, divided by the long yellow Cloth Hall that housed merchants' stalls. A sharp breeze cut across the square, which was littered with bits of dirty snow at the corners. Drawing her coat closer, Helena was struck by how normal it all seemed, save for the swastika flags that billowed from the buildings. The shops were open and pedestrians walked easily along the pavement at midday. There was no Christmas market on the square, as there might have been in happier times, but festive wreaths hung in a number of the shop windows.

Helena hovered on the edge of the square uncertainly. Where should she begin in her search for the resistance? Ahead of her a little girl walked with her mother, eating roasted chestnuts. She looked slightly younger than Dorie, with silky blond hair peeking out from beneath a fur-lined bonnet. But Dorie would have eaten carefully without dropping precious bits to the pavement, as this girl did. Watching the child, oblivious to her own good fortune, resentment welled up in Helena. Why had fate chosen to treat this child so much more kindly than her own siblings?

Just then a horn called out above. Helena's gaze traveled to the towering spires of the Mariacki Cathedral, dark against the gray sky, where a trumpeter heralded each hour. The nurse Wanda had spoken of the church as a center of black-market activity when describing her attempts to procure more medicine. Helena knew little about the black market, since Biekowice was too small to have one of its own. But it sounded secretive and underground, so perhaps someone there might have a connection to the resistance.

Helena stepped from the curb, still looking up at the church spires. Something slammed hard into her, sending her sprawling to the pavement. Potatoes clattered to the ground around her. "Stupid!" a gray-haired man swore, diving after his fallen crate.

She sat up, ignoring the throbbing pain where she'd landed on her hip on the pavement. "Pardon me..."

"You clumsy girl, watch where you are going!" The man waved her off as she tried to help, then plucked a potato unceremoniously from beneath her. Helena could feel her cheeks grow red as he continued to berate her, drawing the attention of passersby.

"Halt!" A German soldier, noticing the commotion, walked over. At the sight of the glinting silver swastika on his collar, Helena's heart stopped. "What is this about?"

The man pointed at Helena. "This girl caused my potatoes to fall."

"That's all? Be gone with you, before I arrest you for causing a disturbance." As the man scampered off with his crate of potatoes, the German turned to Helena. He was Gestapo; she could tell by the insignia on his lapel, part of the police force that fiercely patrolled the city. But beneath the wide brim of his hat, he was not much older than she. "You must be careful, my dear."

Careful. She suppressed an improbable laugh at the irony. Then, catching the glint of metal from his waistband, her humor faded. Attracting the attention of the Gestapo was the very opposite of what she wanted to do.

The man held out his hand expectantly. Her breath caught. Would he ask for her *kennkarte*? She carried it with her, of course, the identity card that had been issued by the Germans at the start of the war. But it noted that she was from Biekowice and it did not have a stamp authorizing her to travel.

But the man took her hand in his. "Allow me," he said, helping her to her feet.

"Oh, thank you, sir," she said sweetly, doing her best impression of Ruth. "I don't know what I would have done if you hadn't come to stop that awful man." She lowered her eyes, then looked up again, marveling at the way the German's gaze followed her own, disarmed. The power she had as a woman was not one Helena had acknowledged before. Even as she availed herself of it to ward off the man's suspicions, she hated it.

The German lifted his shoulders. "It isn't a good idea for a woman to be out on the streets alone these days. May I escort you to your destination?"

"That's very kind of you but not at all necessary. I'm just going to the church." She pointed over his shoulder, watching for a reaction. The Germans hated not just Jews but all religion, and had stopped just shy of forbidding a devoutly Catholic nation of Poles from worshipping. "I need to say a prayer for my ailing mother. Sickness of the female parts," she added conspiratorially, knowing that the intimate reference would stave off further questions.

"I'm sorry." A look of what appeared to be genuine concern crossed the German's face as he stepped aside to let her pass. "I hope she is well soon."

"Thank you." Helena freed herself from his grasp and hurried onward, still shaking under the burn of his gaze.

Inside, she paused to calm her breathing, blinking in the dim light. The cathedral was grander than anything she had ever seen. An enormous crucifix rose from the nave to the cupola, set against an altarpiece embossed in gold. Solemn organ music played. She trembled, shaken in equal parts from the encounter with the German and the daunting task that stood before her. What was she doing? Looking up at the ornate stained-glass windows, it seemed hard to believe the kind of people she was looking for might be found here. But as her eyes adjusted, Helena could see the back rows more filled than they should have been on this weekday morning, mostly by young men. She slid into a pew across the aisle from them, trying not to stare as a flash of bills changed hands. Wanda had been right about the black market. Could one buy information there, as well? It had not occurred to Helena that she might have to pay for what she needed, and she had no means to do so.

Inhaling the scent of something that burned sweetly, she leaned over into the aisle. "I'm trying to make contact with the resistance," she whispered.

The man closest to her ignored her and turned away. "Seven o'clock at Pod Gwiazdami…" she heard him say to his companion before getting to his feet and swiftly leaving.

She reached in her pocket for a coin and held it out to the man who remained. He took it hurriedly. "The resistance," she whispered. He did not answer but pushed his hand down low as if to say wait. Then he, too, disappeared.

Helena sat alone now in the pew, watching people come and go from the church, including one stooped old woman clutching a rosary who actually seemed to be there to pray. *"Ojcze Nasz…"* the woman intoned in a low voice. *Our Father.* Thirty minutes passed, then forty. She scuffed her feet restlessly, uncertain what to do. A priest walked down the aisle and Helena held her breath, waiting for him to ask why she was lingering there, but he simply nodded as he passed. Outside, the trumpeter played again, signaling three o'clock. Helena's shoulders slumped. She had been duped.

Defeated, she got up and walked to the entrance of the cathedral, an ignorant village girl, unable to make her way in the city. Though still afternoon, it was getting dark and the lights had gone on above the shops, casting eerie halos in the mist. She had not yet gone to see Mama, but if she did not start home right now, she would never make it before it was completely dark. She did not want to risk, either, being caught out in the city after curfew. Would Mama notice that no one had come to see her that week, or had she gone to a place where time ceased to matter? She left the church, skirting the side of the building and cutting down Stolarska Street to avoid seeing the German soldier on the square once more. When she reached the railway bridge, she turned back, her eyes traveling remorsefully in the direction of Kazimierz. She had failed Sam, and had not seen Mama at all. She held her hand up in silent apology, feeling Mama in the cold, still air before her.

Three hours later, she reached the last hill. In the village below, the houses were shuttered, thin slats of light escaping drawn shutters. Quickening her step, Helena made her way down the deserted road, hopeful that no one would see her. They put the children to bed early in winter to stay warm and not burn the lights needlessly. Ruth would not be happy trying to corral all three by herself.

The house was dark as Helena entered, and for a moment she was hopeful that Ruth was asleep, too. But as she entered the bedroom, she saw in the moonlight her twin sitting up against the headboard, holding her knitting needles beneath the faint light of the lamp. She did not meet Ruth's eyes as she climbed into bed, but held her breath, waiting for the rebuke. But Ruth sat silently, clutching the motionless needles and staring into the darkness. Her lower lip was set in that way that it did when she was angry. Could she possibly know about Sam and the risks that Helena had just taken to help him? Helena noticed then that she was trembling. Not anger. *Terror.*

"What is it? Ruti, what's wrong?"

"Someone came to the house," Ruth said, her whisper so faint Helena struggled to hear.

An icy hand seemed to clutch at Helena's chest. "Who came?"

"A policeman." Not the Nazis, Helena thought, managing

to breathe. But the thought was only momentary comfort. The Polish police, headquartered in My´slenice, were little more than puppets for the Gestapo, and they seldom ventured into the sleepy village unless summoned. Had he come looking for Sam and his papers?

"What did he want?"

"Hoarding." Ruth pronounced the word with difficulty. "Someone told him that I'd been buying extra food at market. I haven't, of course," she hastened to add.

No, Helena thought guiltily. *I have.* It had begun innocently enough. Once last month as she'd started from town on her way to see Mama and visit Sam, she'd spied the green awning of the market that popped up in the town's tiny square twice weekly. On impulse, she'd walked toward it, fingering her mother's ration coupons. She'd purchased a few mottled carrots, ignoring the farmer's curious stare. Mama wasn't eating the food she brought these days, anyway. And Sam had seemed so appreciative. After that, she'd stopped at the market each week to find an extra bit of food to bring him. She hadn't imagined that someone would notice or take the time to report her. Only they had, and now it had caused the police to focus on their family. All of the reasons she should not have helped Sam were exposed and magnified a thousandfold before her.

Ruth inhaled a raspy breath beside her. Helena turned to her twin, who suddenly seemed smaller and more fragile. "Did he hurt you? Or the children?" Her voice rose with panic. Ruth shook her head. Helena exhaled, then put her arm awkwardly around her sister. The role of comforter was still not a familiar one to her. "Are you all right?"

"I'm fine," Ruth replied quickly, her voice oddly unemotional. She blinked, a slight hesitation, and Helena wondered if her sister was telling the truth. "The children don't even know," she added. "Michal and Dorie were out playing in the field. And Karolina was asleep almost the whole time."

Helena's body went slack with relief. Everyone was fine. But it could have been so much worse. *I should have been here*, she berated herself silently. *If it wasn't for Sam I would have been. Of course, if it wasn't for him, none of this would have happened in the first place.*

"He left just as suddenly," Ruth finished. Helena leaped up and raced to the window. "He took the goat," Ruth added, her voice cracking.

Helena bit her lip, fighting the urge to rebuke Ruth. The goat had been their last hope, providing a sour but drinkable milk. He, along with the mule, might have one day been a source of meat as a last resort. But it was just an animal, and her sister was in no condition for scolding. "It's not your fault," she offered as Ruth began to cry. "There was nothing you could have done to stop him."

"Oh, Helena," Ruth sobbed quietly now. "How could anyone think that we were hoarding?" Then she looked up questioningly. "Unless you…" Ruth trailed off, reluctant to finish the thought.

Helena did not answer. Her mind reeled back to a time when they were six and playing in Mama's armoire. Ruth had tried to hand her a bottle of perfume but it slipped between their fingers and shattered on the floor. Helena rushed to find a cloth to clean it up before Mama noticed, but when she returned, their mother was standing in the doorway. "Ruth!" Mama had cried out, taking in Ruth as the lone culprit. In the moment, Helena was pleased. She was always the one in trouble for breaking things or messing up. Immediately afterward, though, she began to regret her silence. Ruth always came to her aid when she was in trouble, with a kind word or shared treat to comfort her. How could she let her sister take the blame? But by then, it was too late—confessing her role in the accident days later would mean admitting she had lied. And so the secret had remained buried and nearly forgotten.

Ruth reached for her hand. Helena did not want to answer.

But she couldn't lie to her sister about this. "It was me." Ruth's mouth formed a small circle of surprise. "I'm sorry."

"But why? Surely not for yourself."

"No, of course not." They both tried so hard to eat as little as possible, passing on whatever they could to the little ones. Helena searched for a plausible alternative explanation. She considered telling Ruth that she'd taken the food to the hospital to bribe the hospital staff. But that would be another lie. Helena swallowed. She wanted to say nothing. Until now, Sam had been hers, only hers. She bit her lip, keeping the secret her own for just a few seconds more. Finally, she could hide it no longer. "A…man."

"I don't understand."

"Remember the night I thought there were bombs?"

Ruth nodded. "You were wrong."

"I was wrong." Helena brushed aside her annoyance. Why between them was it always about fault? "But the next day on the way back from seeing Mama, I discovered a man in the woods. An American soldier." Ruth gasped audibly and Helena realized how much had changed in the weeks that Sam had come. His presence, which had become so much a part of Helena's life, was nearly unfathomable to Ruth. "Sa— The soldier, was badly wounded." She did not share his name, keeping that one thing for herself.

"So you helped him." There was a disapproving note to Ruth's voice.

"Yes. Just some wood and a bit of food. You would have done the same," she added, daring Ruth to disagree.

Ruth's eyes were wide. "You never said a word." The sisters had never had secrets before. "So that's what the policeman was talking about."

"Better than that you didn't know and have to lie." Because Ruth could not keep a secret, hung the silent implication between them.

"He's still at the chapel?" Ruth asked, her voice breathy with disbelief. Helena nodded. "He has to leave."

"He can't. His leg is injured but healing. He'll be leaving soon. It's exciting in a way," she added. Beside her, Ruth stiffened. "I just mean, things before were so boring."

"Helena, do you *like* this man?" An amused note crept into Ruth's voice. "Surely you can't think—"

"No, of course not." Her sister's incredulousness was a kick to the stomach. Why was the notion of a man having feelings for her so impossible for Ruth to fathom?

"In any event, you can't see him again."

"But he has no food. Without me, he'll die."

"That isn't our concern. Don't you see?" Ruth's voice grew shrill. Then, glancing down at the children, she dropped to a whisper. "Every time you go there you're endangering us, them. If someone finds out, we'll be arrested or worse."

"That won't happen." But her voice wavered with uncertainty.

"It already *has*." Ruth's voice crackled with anger. She was right, of course. Helena had thought she was being so careful. Yet even a few extra vegetables and some cheese had not gone unnoticed.

Still, she could not stand the idea of leaving Sam on his own. "But he's here to help us."

"No one will help us but ourselves. Who is going to put food on the table or care for the children if something happens to you?" Helena did not respond. Ruth put her hand on Helena's. "I'm sorry," she said softening. "I'm sure you like him, but we have to think of the children."

"It's not that," Helena protested. But feeling the blush creep into her cheeks, she knew her sister would not be fooled.

"With Piotr…" Ruth began, then her voice trailed off.

"What?"

"Nothing." She was thinking, Helena knew, of what might have been. Piotr would have married Ruth if she had been willing to move away and leave her family behind. Ruth had refused, of course, and he had gone. Ruth had never said as much, not wanting her sister to feel a burden. But she was telling Helena now that she understood the sacrifice, demanding that Helena do the same: *I chose you.*

It was not the same, Helena told herself. Ruth could not have possibly felt for Piotr what she did for Sam. Despite that, Helena knew that she had no choice. "Fine," she relented.

As Ruth turned back to her knitting, Helena picked up a book of poetry that Michal had gotten at market some time ago. As she tried to read, her thoughts were interrupted by visions of the chapel just a few hours earlier, to Sam's admission that he cared for her, the proposal of a life together. Sitting in the warmth of his embrace had been the happiest moment she had ever known. But in the next minute it had been extinguished, a flame too tiny and new to withstand the stormy gusts of wind that surrounded it.

I could go with him, she thought. *Maybe we could send for Ruth and the others and it really would be all right.*

A while later, Helena gave up reading and set down the book. Ruth extinguished the lamp. Her fingernails dug into the back of Helena's hand suddenly. "So you promise, you won't see him again?" Her voice cut through the darkness, reading Helena's thoughts.

Helena hesitated, resting her hand on Michal's back. "I promise." But she remembered Sam as he sat against the wall of the chapel. Though she had told him that she wanted him to leave without warning, he had not said the same. No, she could not disappear without an explanation and have him think that she had deserted him. She had to return one more time to make him understand.

"Now perhaps things can go back to the way they were," Ruth mumbled drowsily. Helena did not answer. She did not want to go back, even if it were possible.

Ruth's fingers laced with her sister's, as if forming a protective arc over the sleeping children between them. They began to breathe in unison and soon it was hard to tell where Ruth's hand ended and her own began. *I promise.* The words echoed in Helena's mind in time with Michal's gentle snores, his back rising and falling beneath her touch. She saw Sam, alone by the fire in the chapel and with each breath the image seemed to grow dimmer and farther away, until it faded and was gone.

11

The next morning Helena made her way slowly through the predawn darkness of the forest, holding aloft the flashlight that Sam had given her. The silence, suffocating and deep, seemed to press down around her.

Something brushed against her face. A cobweb, she realized, swatting it away. As she did, a rustling sound came from the brush beside the path. Helena stopped. She was just steps from where she had heard a similar noise and found Sam. She walked to the bushes where he had lain. They were undisturbed and as she pushed them back she thought she might find him there again, helpless as a sleeping child. But a small brown mole glared at her disdainfully before scurrying away. Studying the bare earth, her heart swelled. What if she had never taken this route? Was having found Sam worth the knife that seemed to dig at her insides now, knowing that she would not see him again?

Helena forced herself to keep moving, her legs heavy and unwilling. Soon she reached the clearing before the chapel. The windows were dark. She had come at this hour deliberately, hoping that Sam would still be asleep.

She approached the church, clutching the package of food inside her bag. It was bigger than normal, and more than she should have taken. But she had not had time—nor would she have dared—to go to market again. This was to be the last visit, so she wanted to bring him as much as possible. Earlier, Ruth had heard her moving about and had come from the bedroom, eyeing the satchel she was packing, appraising its size. Helena had met her eyes defiantly, daring her sister to protest that she could not be taking all of that food to their mother. But Ruth had not said anything, and a minute later Helena left the house without explanation. Perhaps Ruth understood from her own loss of Piotr that Helena needed to come here once more to say goodbye.

Of course, she wasn't actually going to do that. Helena couldn't disappear without telling Sam—but she couldn't bear to see him again and to walk away, knowing it was the last time. She had scribbled a note: "I'm sorry that I cannot come to see you anymore, but my siblings need me at home. Be safe. Fondly, Helena." She had agonized over that last bit for some time, vacillating between ending the note "with love" or just her name, and finally settling somewhere in the middle. She hated to lie about the reason she could no longer come, but she did not want to tell Sam about the police, to worry him or admit that he had been right about helping him being too dangerous. She'd included a small photograph of herself as he'd asked.

Helena crept closer to the chapel door, the twigs beneath her feet seeming to betray her every step. She peered through the window. Sam lay by the nearly cold stove, curled up in a ball, much as he had been when she'd found him under the bush. But his face was peaceful now, his breathing even. Desire rose up in her and she desperately wanted to run through the door and lie down beside him, to revel in the embrace she had dreamed a thousand times but not fully experienced. She considered the idea: If it was to be the last time, why not have everything? Silent hands of reason seemed to restrain her. It was not that she thought it would be wrong—she felt whole with Sam in a way that transcended any social conventions. Rather, she knew that if she got that close to him she would never be able to pull away. That was the whole reason for coming now, before dawn, on her way to Mama instead of on the way home: if he was still asleep, she would not have to look in his eyes and tell him goodbye.

She swallowed over the lump in her throat. No, this was as close as she dared to get. She set down the package she'd put together, the extra food designed to last him as long as possible, the blanket and finally the note. She gazed once more at the only man she had ever loved, watching the visions of the life they might have had together rise and fade into the leaves like smoke. Then she turned and walked with leaden feet back into the darkness of the woods.

Two hours later, Helena made her way to the top of the hill above the city. As she surveyed the streets below, Sam's face appeared in her mind. It was midmorning now, and he would be awake. If he had ventured outside already, he would have found her note and realized that she was gone for good. She stopped, her sadness and disappointment exploding within her heart. She had failed him—not only was she abandoning him, but she had not been able to reach the resistance.

She crossed the Planty, the thin strip of parkland that ringed the Old City, now gray with dry, withered brush. Beyond the buildings to the north, the towers of the Mariacki Cathedral stood high against the slate-gray sky, beckoning her, and she wondered whether she should attempt once more to make contact. Helena knew that she should visit Mama quickly and return home, in case the policeman decided to pay another visit. But if she was to abandon Sam, the least she could do was to try one last time to fulfill her promise to help him. A quick detour would harm no one. Determined now, she started toward the Old City.

At the edge of the *rynek*, she stopped, contemplating the entranceway to the cathedral. She could try to make contact there again, of course, but there was no greater chance that anyone would be willing to help. She recalled overhearing the men whispering to one another. *"Pod Gwiazdami,"* one had said to the other, seemingly speaking about a planned meeting. *Under the stars.* It referred, she assumed, to a bar or *kawiarnia* of some sort—she'd observed that several establishments around the old city were called "pod" something-or-other, presumably because they were located beneath the streets of the market square, a subterranean maze of medieval cellars now serving food and drink.

She walked the perimeter of the square uncertainly, peering down the streets that fanned out in all directions. The sidewalks bustled with pedestrians navigating around parked trucks making morning deliveries. At the corner, a man selling stale *obwarzanki* pretzel rings that no one had the desire or coins to buy anymore eyed her curiously. Her skin prickled. Loitering much longer would arouse suspicion. She did not have time to search endlessly for the café and dared not ask someone on the street for fear of provoking questions. Finally, she walked down Florianska Street, which ended a hundred meters farther at the remnants of the medieval stone wall that had once surrounded the city. A decorative wrought-iron cluster of stars jutted out above one of the doorways, signaling the café below.

Looking down the stairway, she hesitated. Were such places even open this early in the day? She walked down the stone steps, holding the wall so as not to slip. The windowless brick cellar had been made into a café, with a half-dozen tables set at haphazard angles and a crudely hewn oak bar at the back of the room. Candlelight flickered long shadows against the walls, giving it the appearance of evening. A scrawny Christmas tree lilted in the corner. She lingered by the stairs uncertainly. There were no restaurants in Biekowice—people bought food at market or grew it or killed it and took it to their own homes to cook and eat. She marveled now at the way the handful of patrons sat among one another, each cluster or pair having its own conversation as though the tables on either side did not exist.

Behind the bar a man looked up at her and she realized she was supposed to ask for something to drink. *"Kawa, prosz̨e,"* she requested. It was the cheapest thing she could think of to order.

He waved toward the tables with disinterest. "Seat yourself anywhere." She slid onto a wood bench along one of the walls and scanned the room, then took a sip from the cup of black coffee a waiter placed in front of her. What now?

A man she had not seen arrive slid onto the bench beside her. As he pressed swiftly against her side, she stifled a gasp. He kissed her on the cheek, his breath a mix of tobacco and liquor reminiscent of Tata's. Before she could react, he did the same on the other side. "Oh!" she exclaimed in surprise.

The waiter returned and set a menu in front of her. *"Dzįeki,* but I don't want anything to eat."

"I think you do," the voice beside her said, sure and firm. Without looking up, she knew she had found someone who could help her find the resistance.

"Some bread, please," she said, too nervous to read the menu.

"I'll have the fish," the stranger added. "Put your arm around me," he instructed when the waiter had gone. The wool of his coat was scratchy beneath her palm as she complied. There was something calming and sure about his voice that made her obey, without questioning the odd command.

"I'm looking for the resistance."

"Shh!" She noticed for the first time a man sitting across the room watching them with interest, and understood then the fiction of being a couple. "You know you could be killed just for saying that?"

"Yes."

"Then don't say it again." She studied him. He was five, maybe six years older than her, with pale hair and a trim goatee. "I'm the one you're looking for."

"How did you know?"

"Someone told me you were asking for me at the cathedral." So the man who had taken the coin had kept his word. "I didn't think he'd told you where to find me, though."

"He didn't."

"Then how… Never mind." He pulled back, then stared at her expectantly. "What do you need?"

She hesitated. Now that she had found him, she was suddenly at a loss for words. "My name is Helena Nowak. I'm from Biekowice and I need to pass on a message to the partisans through the resistance. Do you have a name?"

"I do. Does it matter?" His words came out in short bursts, as if unable to spare more.

"I suppose not. But how do I know you can help?"

"You don't. You'll just have to trust." *Trust.* Could there have been a stranger word in these times? "I'm Alek. Alek Landesberg." Her jaw dropped slightly. So she had found him, after all. "Anyway, you wanted to make contact and I don't have a lot of time. What do you want?"

She inhaled, then took the leap. "There's an American soldier and he needs help."

"There *was* an American soldier," he interjected, cutting her off again. "He was captured, unfortunately."

Panic seized Helena. Had something happened to Sam? But the stranger could not possibly be talking about Sam, she realized. She had just left him. One of Sam's crewmates must have been found, after all. "Not that soldier. Another one." Alek blinked, trying without success to disguise his shock. "He's trying to make contact with the partisans in Czechoslovakia."

Alek raised his hand slightly off the table, signaling silence as the waiter reappeared. He twirled a match between his fingers as the waiter set down a plate of bread and smoked fish in front of them. Despite the faintly sour smell the mottled fish gave off, Helena's mouth salivated. She averted her eyes.

He pushed the plate toward her with a nod. "You can eat."

She thought of the few coins she carried with her when she traveled; surely they would not be enough. "But I don't have money."

"Don't worry, I can pay." She took a bite, the rich savory taste that filled her mouth a forgotten dream. "Where is he?"

Now it was Helena's turn to pause. Once she gave him Sam's location, there was no turning back. She passed him the note Sam had scribbled.

He took the note and scanned it. Then with one swift gesture, he struck the match under the table and raised the flame to the paper. "What is it that you want me to do?"

"Get him out of there and over the border." Helena forced the quiver from her voice.

"That's it?" He eyed her levelly. "Do you have any idea what kind of risk that would entail to our operations? I don't have time to help you. We've got hundreds of men fighting for our cause in the woods, Polish men in need of food and care and medicine."

"But he cannot stay where he is. It is essential that he get out!" Remembering the man at the other table, Helena dropped her voice. "His work is critical to the war effort."

"No single man is that important."

She wondered how much to reveal. "He is the only possibility of connecting the partisans to the west. He could mean reinforcements and provisions, which could make a difference for the whole war effort." She was stretching the truth now, saying more than she knew in her attempt to persuade him.

He stroked his goatee. "Let's say we were willing to help your soldier. How do I know that you can be trusted?"

He had a point. Though it seemed implausible, Helena herself could be a spy. "Because I want to help you." She had not planned to say this, but once she did, she realized it was the truth. "Beyond this, I mean."

He eyed her skeptically. "What is it that you think you can do?"

"Deliver messages. I'm good at getting around."

"Couriers I have." The man looked her up and down and a wrinkle of something, not disdain exactly but skepticism, crossed his face. Suddenly she saw herself as he must—young and inexperienced, a country girl. His doubts magnified thousandfold in her, exploding. Who was she, anyway, to think she could do this, or anything, to help?

An image flashed through her mind then of the German soldier atop the tank who had nearly caught her in the forest that day. He had just been ordinary, too, before he had chosen his wretched path. "I'm small," she blurted out. "And not at all what you expect. Isn't that sort of how your group operates? It's an advantage. After all, I found you, didn't I?" She did not wait, knowing he would not answer the question.

He stood abruptly and left some coins on the table. "I have to go."

"That's it?" Her heart fell.

"I wait tables at Wierzynek and the lunch preparations start in half an hour." She cocked her head. Unlike the modest café in which they now sat, Wierzynek was one of the finest restaurants in the city, forbidden now even to Poles who could afford it. It seemed like an odd place of employment for someone from the resistance. "You can learn a lot from such a place." Of course. Working in a restaurant was not only an effective way to transmit information without being noticed, but to gather a great deal from overhearing the patrons—especially in a café frequented by senior German officials.

"But…" Helena started to stand, unwilling to let him get away. She grabbed his sleeve, suddenly desperate and heedless who might hear. Alek looked down at her and there was something enigmatic about him that made her want to follow into his strange unknown world. "Please."

He pressed his hand on hers, willing her to remain seated. There was a gentle forcefulness to his touch she had never before encountered. "One week. Come again in one week and that will give me enough time to investigate your story and figure out what to do."

"And if I need you sooner?"

"You won't. Coming here was either very brave or very stupid. You must love this soldier a lot. Go now," he added before she could respond. "And you'd do well to avoid the checkpoint at Starowi´slna." He bounded up the steps and out the door.

12

Helena watched Alek leave, fighting the urge to run after him and ask more questions. She looked uncertainly at the plate of fish that remained before her. If only she had a way to take it back to Sam or the children. She took another few bites and then stood, eyeing the table across the room where the man watching them had sat. He was gone, and she wondered if he had followed Alek, or perhaps he had not been interested in them at all.

She took care not to move too quickly and attract attention as she made her way down the street. A wave of energy surged through her. She had done it—made contact with the resistance and found out...what, exactly? She had no idea, though, if Alek would or could help. And she could not even see Sam again to tell him. But there was no time to worry. She needed to get to Mama and then back home.

She took Alek's advice, rounding the block to avoid the cluster of military jeeps at the corner where Starowi´slna Street intersected with the *aleje*. Something was different, Helena noticed as she made her way through the backstreets on the way to the

Jewish quarter. From the hill above the city a few hours earlier, Kazimierz had looked unchanged. But, closer now, she could see that the neighborhood was even emptier than usual. Great piles of broken furniture and other discarded household items sat at the curb in front of several of the buildings, as though it were garbage day. A curious burning smell filled her throat. Uneasiness seeped through her as she mentally scanned the calendar for a forgotten holiday, a reason for the change, and found nothing.

Two blocks farther, she could see the back of the hospital. Looking ahead down the eerily deserted street, Helena desperately wanted to turn and run in the other direction. Steeling herself, she pressed forward, clinging closely to the buildings.

As she crossed Miodowa Street, there was a deafening explosion. The force of the blast flung her through the air and slammed her against the pavement. For a moment, she lay motionless, too stunned to move. Then she crawled into a doorway for cover, the still-shaking ground rough beneath her palms. Nothing, not even the sound she had heard the night Sam's plane crashed, had been anywhere near as loud. She wished desperately for the safety of the cellar back home, Ruth and the others warm beside her.

A clattering noise, rapid and repeated, reverberated off the buildings. Machine gunfire, she knew instinctively, though she had, of course, never heard it before. Helena ducked. The shots had come from the direction of the hospital. She broke into a run, heedless now of the need to blend in, not caring who might see her.

She started to turn onto Estery Street to reach the front of the hospital. Then she froze. Here in the heart of the Jewish quarter, all pretense of normalcy had been abandoned. The street thronged with men in uniform. Trucks and jeeps stopped haphazardly in the middle of the street and parked across the sidewalks. From the far end of Szeroka Street a cloud of smoke rose ominously toward the sky.

Aktion. The word formed slowly on her lips, though she did not know where she had learned it.

Helena crouched low behind a car, studying the front entrance to the hospital. Should she wait until it was safe, or flee and come back another day? But the less dangerous days were gone. She had to get to Mama now, or there might not be another chance. Not daring to step out onto the street, she retraced her steps, looking for another, less conspicuous way into the hospital.

She peered around the corner of the narrow alleyway that ran behind the hospital, then up at the windows of the tall apartment houses that rose on either side. The door to one of the buildings flew open. Helena leaped back. A family—mother and father, boy and girl—walked down the steps. Their unbuttoned coats were thrown on hastily and their feet were stockingless beneath their shoes. The girl clutched her brother's arm. The father splayed his right hand across the back of his son's head, as if to form a protective shield. The girl dropped something, a doll or toy perhaps, but her mother held her closely in place, forbidding her to reach for it.

Helena took a step toward them. Perhaps they knew what was happening here. But then she noticed that the father's other hand was raised above his head in a way that made his stomach stick out oddly. A German officer appeared from the doorway behind them, gun fixed at the man's back.

Helena tried to shrink back against the building as the officer marched the family down the sidewalk toward her. As they neared, the boy's eyes met hers, silently pleading for help. He was Michal's age but much thinner, eyes wide against his bony skull. And his skin was a shade of gray, like Sam's had been the day she found him, as if he had not seen the sun for a long time. She braced herself, terrified that he would say or do something to give away her presence. But he looked away, staring straight ahead, and a moment later they passed down the street and were gone.

Do something, a voice seemed to say. But what? She could shout, but there was no one to help anymore. *Breathe*, she willed herself. *Get to Mama.* I'm sorry, she mouthed silently, though the boy was no longer there. She raced around the corner. A wide exposed gulf of pavement stood between her and the back door to the hospital. She studied the windows of the buildings above, but the gaping holes were shrouded in darkness, giving no indication if anyone might be watching. She started quickly across the street, certain that at any moment she would be caught.

Seconds later, she reached the back entrance to the hospital. Struggling to catch her breath, Helena pried open the knobless door. Inside, she stood in shock: the hospital had been ransacked. Mattresses and chairs were piled high on either side of the hallway. Gone were the rhythmic, whirring sounds of the machines and the incessant moans of patients.

She peered into the nearest ward. The once-occupied beds were now empty, their sheets torn off and thrown to the center of the room, revealing bloodstained mattresses. Helena raced to her mother's ward, broken glass crunching under her boots. The beds nearest the door were also empty and stripped. Helena's body went slack with relief seeing Mama still lying in her bed on the far side of the room as she had during each of Helena's previous visits. Helena raced to her. A few patients still lay motionless in the other beds, wide swaths of blood marring their hospital gowns. Helena stifled a scream. A rasp of breath escaped from one of the beds. Someone was still alive.

But there was no time to help. "Mama!" she whispered loudly as she neared. Her mother showed no sign of harm. Her eyes were open, though, gazing toward the ceiling. Helena reached out, knowing before she touched her cheek that it would be cold. What had happened here? As she lowered her face, Helena smelled something chemical and foreign. A drop of clear liquid lingered at the corner of her mother's lips, slightly parted in an almost-sigh. Mama had swallowed something before the Nazis could get to her. She was gone.

Helena buried her head in her mother's lap. Mama's arm hung limply from the edge of the bed. Helena replaced it at her side, then rubbed her mother's shoulder, as if to bring her comfort. In reality it was for herself, and she sought to memorize every detail of the skin under her fingertips, holding on to the touch that she knew would be the last.

Helena looked up again. She had contemplated the end. Indeed there were times that she had thought it might be better for Mama for all of the suffering to end. But nothing had prepared her for the finality of it—all of the love and memories just gone, like an enormous gust of wind that had taken her very breath with it.

A hand clamped down on Helena's shoulder from behind. She opened her mouth to scream. "Shh," a female voice whispered. Helena turned to face the nurse Wanda. Her face was pale and the apron of her uniform smeared with blood. "You have to go."

Helena stood. "What happened?"

"The Germans came to liquidate Kazimierz and move the rest of the Jews to the ghetto." Helena remembered the nurse's erroneous prediction weeks earlier that some Jews would remain. "Then they came here." Wanda's eyes were bloodshot, her face aged years in an instant. "They started shooting the patients— No more than a bullet for each, I heard one of them say. We… the nurses, had always planned to give them something, to spare them the suffering if this happened. But we had no notice— there wasn't enough time to get to everyone."

"Why? Why now?"

"Reprisals." Wanda was sobbing openly now, cracking under the stress of what she had seen. Helena shifted uncomfortably. She had never been good with the tears of loved ones, much less a near-stranger. Regaining her composure, Wanda continued. "There are rumors that the Germans captured a foreign soldier, American maybe, or British. Whoever they caught killed a German in the struggle. So now we all pay. I took care of your mother first," Wanda added. *Took care.* It was a funny way to describe killing someone, even out of mercy. So that was what the coin she'd given Wanda had bought. "If they had gotten to her, her suffering would have been much worse."

Helena slumped to the edge of the bed. "But she wasn't even Jewish."

Wanda shook her head. "They don't care. Half-Jewish or whole, it's all the same to them."

"Half-Jewish... I don't understand." Helena noticed a strange expression on the nurse's face. "What is it?"

"Your mother... Surely you knew."

The ground seemed to wobble as it had from the explosion outside. "Knew what?"

"Your mother's mother was Jewish. I saw it once in the file."

Helena stared at her in disbelief. "That isn't possible. My grandparents..." She paused, remembering the photograph of Mama's mother and father taken years earlier. She searched for a reason that one of them could not have been Jewish, but found nothing. "Surely I would have known."

Wanda shrugged slightly. "I didn't ask her about it. It never occurred to me that you didn't know. But it's in her records."

Helena looked down at her mother's lifeless face, which seemed to have grown waxy. Why hadn't Mama ever said anything? To spare them the difficulty, the baggage that went with Jewish heritage in a time and place such as this. Suddenly she understood why Tata had been so closed off and suspicious of outsiders, Mama's dogged insistence that they go to church. It was a means of self-defense, protecting their family from prying eyes that might discover the truth.

"She isn't here anymore," Wanda added gently. She squeezed Helena's hand. "You need to go now."

Helena hesitated. She couldn't bear to leave Mama like this, but there was no other choice. "What about you?"

The nurse shook her head slightly. "There are others to help." Helena remembered the gasp of life she had heard from the bodies in the other ward. Wanda would not abandon her post until she had finished with the grim task of making sure no one was left behind to suffer.

Suddenly there came a noise, footsteps on the floor above. Wanda gripped her fingers hard. "Hide!" she whispered, pushing Helena beneath one of the empty beds. Helena lay flat against the ground, cheek pressed against the cold tile.

Seconds later, a pair of black boots came into view and neared the bed. Helena held her breath, bracing for certain discovery. Above her, Wanda let out a sharp yelp as the man flung her to the bed. Helena heard more muffled cries, and the sounds of cruel male laughter, of fabric ripping. Wanda's feet hung off the bed at a strange angle, her sturdy white shoes flailing. The mattress pressed lower, pinning Helena painfully to the floor with every horrid thrust, making her part of the assault.

Soon the bed went still and the black boots disappeared from sight. Helena waited for Wanda to recover and signal the all-clear. Her neck throbbed. She wanted to check on the nurse and make sure she was all right, but she did not dare move. Thirty minutes passed, then an hour. Finally, Helena untangled herself and slid out from beneath the bed. Wanda was gone. What had become of her? But there was no time to find out. The ward was now empty, but there were still men in the hallway, speaking in dispassionate tones as they moved the bodies about, finishing their vicious task.

Helena scanned the room, desperate for a means of escape. She crept to the nearest window and pulled hard on the latch, but it had been painted over and sealed shut. The voices grew louder now and she opened the door to the tiny supply closet and slipped inside.

Helena hid behind the door that she did not dare close fully, certain she would be discovered at any moment. Gestapo soldiers spoke crudely to one another as they walked through the ward, checking to make sure the few patients that remained were dead. She peered through the crack where the door met the frame. One of the Germans neared Mama's bed. She reached for the knife she carried, ready to leap out and protect her mother's body from any shame. Helena willed herself to remain hidden as the man inspected Mama with coarse hands, ransacked the drawer beside her bed for the valuables she did not possess. There was nothing she could do for Mama now, and it was more important than ever that Helena make it back home.

With nothing more to pilfer, the Germans finally left the ward. Breathing a slight sigh of relief, Helena leaned against the wall of the supply closet. Overhead bottles of laudanum sat high on the shelf. Her anger grew once more. The medicines her mother needed were not in short supply at all—that had simply been kept from the people who needed them most. Had Wanda known? Impulsively, she took two fistfuls of the vials that could not help Mama now and tucked them into her dress.

She peered out of the closet. Though the men had left the ward once more, there were voices in the hallway still, blocking her one route of departure and showing no signs of leaving. She looked around the tiny storeroom, fighting the urge to scream in frustration, grief and fear. The air was suddenly too thick to breathe.

She was trapped.

13

When at last the hallway was silent, Helena unfolded herself and stood. Her legs buckled, numb from remaining still for so long. She peered out into the now-silent ward. She did not know how much time had passed since she first hid in the closet, how many hours she'd been trapped as the Germans and their Polish laborers cleared bodies and furniture from the adjacent wards. They were gone now, just as quickly and inexplicably as they'd come.

Steadying herself, Helena walked to her mother's bed. At least she was still there, one of the overlooked—at least so far—in the harried cleanup. Stroking Mama's cool, waxy cheek, Helena tried to clear her mind. All the times she had sat by this bedside, she had tried to tell her mother something. But what, exactly? Even now, she struggled to find the words. She had wanted Mama just to notice her. It was more than that, though. She had yearned—even just for a second—for her mother to like her best. Now that would never be.

Helena took one last look at the beautiful face before covering it with a blanket. Mama deserved a funeral with prayers (though what kind, Helena was no longer sure), or at least a proper burial. But there was no way to carry her home. "I'm sorry," Helena whispered. With one last look, she walked to the door and, making sure that the hallway was clear, slipped out the back door of the hospital and onto the deserted street.

Helena started toward the corner, retracing her earlier route. A fine rain had begun to fall, filling the late-afternoon air with icy mist. She passed the steps of the apartment building where she'd seen the family earlier. The stuffed doll lay sodden and unclaimed where it had been left, abandoned and sad. Helena picked it up from the puddle and sat it up on the stairs in case the girl should return. Shame filled her. She should have done something, called out. She had always considered herself the strong one in their family, but when tested, she had failed.

As she neared the intersection, footsteps rang out. Helena ducked back around the corner. Boots, heavy and thudding, echoed off the pavement. A flashlight illuminated the way ahead, light licking the walls. The trucks had gone, but there were foot patrols, searching for any remaining Jews who might have escaped the net. Helena pressed against the wall, holding her breath. She looked around desperately for a better hiding place, but found none. She reached for her knife. Weeks earlier, when she'd almost encountered the Nazi jeep on the road, she'd been caught off guard, frozen in terror. But she knew now that she would sooner fight and bring on her own death than be taken.

Helena braced herself as the footsteps grew louder, preparing for her inevitable discovery. Suddenly they stopped, the air silent and still. *"Hier!"* a voice called in the distance. The footsteps came again but they were fading now as the patrol ran in the other direction. Helena exhaled, her shoulders slumping. Her relief was short-lived—rapid gunshots broke out, rattling the windows. They had caught someone else. Suppressing a scream, Helena ran down the alleyway, her own footsteps muted by the gunfire that rang ceaselessly against the stone buildings.

Forty minutes later, she reached the edge of the forest and raced for the cover of the trees. She paused for the first time since she'd fled Kazimierz, struggling to catch her breath. It was dark now, the familiar path ahead a veiled maze. Remembering the flashlight that Sam had given her, she pulled it out, holding it aloft to maximize the faint yellow beam. The rain had stopped and the air was cold and fresh. She breathed it in greedily, trying to clear the smells of burning and death that hung over the city.

Something moved behind her. Helena spun around sharply. But the path was deserted, the low brush still. *Easy,* she told herself. *Just an animal.* Still her skin prickled. She forced herself to keep moving. As she walked, the realization sunk in: *Mama was dead.* Her guilt rose. Helena had always accused Ruth of being the one with her head in the sand. Why hadn't she seen the disaster at the hospital coming and done something to save her? If she had not gone to find Alek, she would have been there, helped her mother. Instead, she had left her alone in her final desperate moments. And for what?

Helena saw her mother's face, finally at peace, and thought of the secrets she had kept hidden all of these years. A Jewish parent. *Half-Jewish.* The Jews she knew of were dark and strange. How could she possibly be one of them? Images from Helena's childhood clicked into place. She could remember her father's parents, who had lived with them when she was very young. Other than that, the family had been alone, no relations or even friends coming to the house. Mama's past had always been shrouded in darkness and she had airily laughed off questions about how she had come to be in their village, the family she had left behind in Masuria, Poland's northern Lake District. Now Helena saw her vagueness as deliberate, her break from the past as an attempt to hide the truth about her heritage. There was so much Helena wanted to ask her mother: Had she always known? Why hadn't she told them the truth? And then after escaping her past, to wind up in a Jewish hospital once more. She wondered whether Tata had put her there unwittingly, or had thought it the best way to protect her. Had Mama been aware enough to know that she had been returned to the very world she'd spent her life trying to escape? The answers lay buried forever now.

Grief ripped through Helena and she rocked backward on her heels, her head swimming. She had not expected Mama to live, had not labored under any of her sister's false hope. But reality set in now and a thousand images of her mother cascaded down upon her. It was not just Mama that had gone but all of her memories—and it was as if a part of Helena had died, too.

Mama was gone. Helena could not help Sam nor could she ever really be his. Tears did not come easily to Helena, not even in the darkest moments of night. But she cried now, the hot wet splashes rolling down her cheeks, foreign and unstoppable. She wiped them furiously, but they flowed unabated.

Helena began running through the woods, not feeling the twigs that snapped against her face and tangled her hair. Soon she reached the clearing and the shadow of the chapel loomed large in the darkness. She stopped short of the door. She had not planned to come here. Remembering her promise to Ruth, she started to turn. But the door opened then and at the sight of Sam, silhouetted against the chapel entrance, she could stand it no longer.

He raced to her as quickly as his half-mended leg would allow. "Lena!" In his surprise, he spoke too loudly, heedless of their usual caution. Then he embraced her with newfound abandon.

She fell into his arms sobbing. "What is it?" he demanded, holding her tighter. One of his crutches fell to the ground and his leg wobbled from the strain but he did not let go. "Are you hurt?"

"Mama's dead…and the Germans…" she began, and she could tell that without saying any more he understood. He lowered himself to the ground in the doorway, still holding her. She beat her hands against his chest. He grasped her wrists and drew her closer. Their lips met and she was kissing him then, not in the tentative way she had last time, but fiercely, letting her grief pour out through him.

"Helena…" He stiffened and she braced herself to hear once more that they should not do this because he was leaving.

"No." She kissed him again, drowning his protests. She felt his teeth behind his lips, tasted the saltiness of her tears. They needed to take this moment because it was all they might have. He pressed against her, matching her intensity, seeming to know that this was what she needed. And when they had finally broken apart, he drew her close to his chest and held her silently.

She drew her knees close and wrapped her arms around them. "She was alone at the end. I should have been there."

"Lena, no! There was nothing you could have done for her. You would have surely been killed, too. You said that she hasn't been lucid much when you've visited. Mercifully, she probably had no idea what was happening." Helena squeezed her eyes shut. She would never know the truth about whether her mother had been scared or in pain or whether she had simply drifted off into her memories forever.

He reached for a rag and pressed it against her hair, which she had not noticed was soaking wet from the rain. She inhaled the damp earthy smell that seemed to have permeated the fabric of his shirt, then shuddered as a series of images ran through her mind. "I saw a family arrested, old people murdered. A woman attacked. They were clearing the Jewish quarter—or what was left of it, anyway." Sam stiffened beneath her. She looked at him, surprised. "Did you know?"

"Not entirely," he replied, and she understood then the conflicted expression she had sometimes seen on his face when they spoke during her past visits. He had been trying to protect her from the truth, or as much as he knew of it. "I had some idea. But a hospital, I can't even imagine." He shook his head in disbelief. "Would it have done any good to worry you?"

He had a point, she conceded inwardly. Even if Sam had told
her that the sanatorium might be in danger, she would not have
been able to take her mother out of there.

"There's something else…" She looked up, her eyes meeting
his. "I found out that my mother is—was—half-Jewish."

He pulled back slightly. "What? How is that possible?"

"A nurse told me it was in Mama's file."

"And she kept it from you all of these years?" Helena nodded.
Sam's eyes widened. "That's quite a shock." For a second, she
was fearful—though Sam himself was Jewish, would he like her
any less because she was not the same person anymore?

"Being Jewish makes everything so much more dangerous
for you, Helena." His voice wavered and his expression was one
of grave concern.

She looked at him, puzzled. "I'm not a Jew. Part-Jewish,
maybe." That sounded odd. How could one be part anything?
Which part?

"Darling, the Jewish religion passes through the mother. So
if your maternal grandmother was Jewish, then your mother
was Jewish and so are you. And the Germans say that anyone
with even a bit of Jewish blood is a Jew." He took her hand.
"Do you mind?"

"No," Helena replied quickly, not wanting to offend him. She
meant it; it didn't bother her, really. For she loved him and he
was Jewish, and that could not mean anything bad or wrong.
But it was a strange idea, too—Jewish had always been something so foreign—how could it have been part of her all along
without her knowing it? She did not feel Jewish, whatever that
meant—she felt exactly as she had a few hours earlier.

"You can't possibly think about staying now that you know,"
he said, tightening his embrace. "The things that they are doing
to the Jews, well, you saw it yourself at the hospital."

She had not considered until then the ramifications of her
mother's religion. An image popped into her mind of the family

she had seen earlier being taken from their home. Innocents—
men, women and children—arrested on the streets of beautiful,
civilized Kraków because they were Jews. Arrested or worse,
she thought, remembering the bodies piled high in the hospital
hallway. *Because they were Jews.* Though Helena and her siblings
had lived as Christians their entire lives, they were now in the
same jeopardy. Was there no one to stop this from happening?
The family she had seen were her people, and she was now one
of them by virtue of her Jewish heritage. But shouldn't they have
been her people, anyway, regardless of faith?

Sam stroked her hair, then rested his chin against her head.
"Do you think some part of you knew?"

Helena considered the question. She had known, perhaps, that
she was different, not like the other girls in the village. But the
actual reality of being Jewish was so foreign...she could have
sooner imagined that she was from outer space. "I don't know."

She remembered then a visit to see Mama, months earlier,
before Sam. It was a Friday evening, and she was making her
way back from the hospital later than usual. She had passed one
of the synagogues, the large one on Miodowa Street with the
ornate glass windows. Alit from within, the temple seemed to
glow yellow gold, otherworldly. She had walked closer, drawn
to the low, methodical chanting from within that seemed to per-
meate the walls. Was it merely the beauty that had appealed to
her? Or was it some deeper part of her, something in her soul,
that had known the truth before she'd had any idea.

Sam chuckled. "What's so funny?" she demanded, caught
off guard.

"I don't mean to make light of things, not now. But a nice
Jewish girl, as they say back home, makes things so much easier. Being Jewish didn't seem to matter so much before the war.
But having been here and seen things, well, my faith is deeper
than ever. So I'm happy you're Jewish. It's almost like it's fated—
beshert, as my grandmother would say."

Helena wanted to tell him that she didn't believe in meant-to-be, not before and certainly not now after what she had seen in the city. "I want my children to be Jewish," he added. A lump formed in her throat. Was he really talking about a future together, the family that they might one day have? "I'm sorry if that was too forward."

"Not at all," she said, taking his hand. Here, in the quiet, removed world of the chapel, they could dream together and plan a future. For what else did they have but those dreams? Talking about it with him now, it almost seemed possible.

"There's something else," she said. "I went to the city and tried to make contact for you—twice actually."

"You did?" In comforting her, he had put his own need to escape aside. But now the urgency returned to his voice.

"I found Landesberg."

"Really? How?"

"I went to the church where the black market operates and asked."

"Helena, that's so dangerous! If you spoke with the wrong person, you could have been arrested."

Helena thought about this for the first time. It had been foolish, risking everything for Sam. But even now, she knew that she would do it again in an instant. "Well, it's done now and I wasn't. And I heard two men talking about a café where I could find him. So I went and I found Alek. Or rather, he found me."

He cut her off. "Helena, that's remarkable!" Then his face sobered. "Now we'll see if he comes through."

"He will." There was something about the man she sensed she could trust. Still, uncertainty lingered. "He liked me, I think."

"I'm not surprised, a beautiful woman like you," he said.

Helena blushed. "I didn't mean it that way." She would never get used to thinking of herself in such a way, especially not in such a disheveled state. But being with Sam made her feel somehow more feminine. "But I said I would help him. I have medi-cine for him and his men."

"You took medicine from the hospital?" he asked with dis-belief. "You never should have done that."

"I had to. It was the only way he would trust me and help you." Hiding in that closet had seemed so bad she had not con-templated any additional danger that stealing the drugs might bring. "I have to go back to the city in a week's time to deliver the medicine. I'll see what he can do to help you."

He straightened. "You mean you want to risk going back now, after learning the truth about your family?"

She considered this. "No one else knows the truth." To the rest of the world, she was still just a Pole—not a Jew. But some-thing about Sam's words nagged at her, as if the very fact she was half-Jewish, even unbeknownst to others, made things more dangerous. "What other choice do I have?"

He wrapped his arms around her. She looked down then. Her skirt was soiled from the floor of the hospital and the pave-ment and the mud kicked up from the forest path as she fled. But Sam did not seem to notice any of it. She leaned back, sa-voring his embrace and this moment that she thought just hours ago would never come again. "You are so brave," he said, his voice admiring.

Helena turned her head away. She considered Sam brave and hardly felt worthy of being included in such company. "It's no different than you coming here to help." But it wasn't about being brave. Now that she knew the truth, standing by was no longer an option.

His expression turned serious. He pulled away and rose with effort. "I want you to go now." She stood and stepped back, stung by the abruptness of his words. Had she done something to anger him? "It isn't safe for you to come anymore." No, his tone was one of pure concern.

She took another step back, pained as she had been the night he had rejected a second kiss. "I don't need to be protected." The words came out more harshly than she intended.

"Lena, this isn't about being brave or right. It's just about survival now. You helped me because you're a good person." *Good.* Helena had never thought of herself that way. Ruth had always been the good one. She was the good girl when they were little, and the one who was good with the children now. "But there's no room for good people in this war. Go home," he insisted.

"Don't you see, it doesn't work that way?" She threw her hands up in exasperation. "Even if I walk out that door now and never come back, it won't undo the danger." *Or my feelings for you*, she added silently. "There's no going back, only forward." He stared at her, not conceding.

Helena stormed from the chapel, shaking. When she neared the trees, she looked back. She did not want to leave Sam in anger, but she could not bring herself to apologize when she did not feel remorse.

The door to the chapel flung open. As Sam appeared, she raced back toward him. "Helena, I'm sorry." Her lips found his, silencing further apology. She pressed her whole self against him and he cupped the back of her head in his hands.

A moment later, he pulled back. "I'm sorry." She stared at him, unable to respond. He reached over and uncurled her fists, which she had not realized she was clenching so tightly that her nails had dug into her palms, breaking the skin and drawing blood. "You do that, you know, when you get angry." He paused. "Don't leave mad. I couldn't bear to have you thinking poorly of me."

She allowed him to draw her back inside the chapel. "I'm sorry I snapped," he said.

"It's understandable. This is stressful."

"It's more than that. Yesterday someone was nearby."

Her throat constricted, making it difficult to speak. "What?"

"I'm sorry to tell you now, on top of everything else. It was just before dawn and I heard footsteps at the door. At first I thought it was you but when I realized it wasn't, I went out the back and hid in a pile of leaves." Someone had been at the chapel. Helena was seized with terror at the notion. Sam did his best to keep the outside of the chapel looking the same so that a passerby would not know that it was occupied. But inside, on a moment's notice... "They didn't pass by like the time you were here—they stopped and lingered. I don't know if they actually came in. I heard whoever it was walking away." His eyes darted back and forth as he relived the terror.

"Did you see who it was?"

He shook his head. "I was more worried about staying out of sight."

She processed the information. It could have been nothing. The chapel was not far from the main road, so a passerby might have come this way. But who had reason to be out these days? The Germans had restricted travel among the provinces more so than ever and there was no work or real trade to be had in the city anymore. Once the hunters might have been up this way, but the hills had been picked so clean that most of the animals had died or gone elsewhere.

"So you see, I'm worried. Someone might know I'm here now and they might come back. That's why you can't come here anymore."

"I understand, and I'm worried, too. We can take extra precautions. My not coming isn't an option, though."

He looked as though he might protest more, then swallowed, deciding against it. "Helena, there's one other thing—if we are able to make contact with the partisans, will you come with me?" She opened her mouth but no sound came out. "I'd still have to be in the army, of course, but I could get you to America." He seemed to hold his breath, eyes searching her face expectantly.

"How?" she asked. "There are no visas now, not with the war."

"No, of course not, but it might not matter so much if we were married." He gazed at her squarely, not noticing or not caring about the redness that had crept into his cheeks. "I mean, that way we could go together and it would make things a bit easier." He was speaking quickly now, stumbling.

"Married," Helena repeated, the word thick and foreign on her tongue. Marriage was what her parents had, what Ruth almost had with Piotr. It was not something she had ever contemplated for herself. She had never viewed herself as someone's wife, or thought anyone might see her in that way—until now.

"Of course, I would understand if you didn't want to," he added quickly, misreading her hesitation as reluctance. "I don't come from much."

"It's not that at all," she hastened to reply. Material things had never mattered to her like they did Ruth. "I just never expected...married," she said again, as if trying it on.

"Yes." He faltered. "So you could emigrate with me. Not that it would just be a formality. I like you, that is, I think... I love you." *Love.* The word seemed to bounce around the cavity of her chest, tender and hollowed out from the pain and tears she'd shed. Was it possible to love someone you had only known for a handful of weeks? She loved her siblings, of course, and had loved her parents, but this real kind of grown-up love she had never expected to be hers, much less under these strangest of circumstances.

"I love you, too." The words tumbled out, as if not her own. *A woman should not give away her feelings so readily*, she could hear Ruth admonish. But Helena had no experience in these things and she'd never been skilled at hiding the truth. "I love you," she repeated the words, this time owning them. She leaned in to kiss him once, then again. Her heart felt as if it might burst. She could see it now: a life in America, married to Sam. Suddenly the role she'd never considered seemed like the only one in the world.

A moment later he pulled back. "I know that when we talked about leaving Poland, you said you couldn't go because of your mother." His tone was practical now. "But now that she is gone, surely she would want this for you."

She nodded, trying to catch her breath. Now that Mama was gone, there was even less reason for her to stay. But that didn't solve the problem of the children and the fact that she would never leave her siblings behind. "I'm not suggesting you go without your family," he added quickly, reading her thoughts. "But there's a possibility we could take them, as well."

Her heart skipped a beat. "A possibility," she repeated.

"There have been transports of children out of Poland to England. The Nazis have clamped down considerably on letting them leave. But there are ways." He hesitated. "If I can get them to the border, I'm pretty sure I can get passes for the children to England or America. You'd be too old, of course, but if we got married that would take care of things."

A knot formed in Helena's stomach. "That's a very good idea and I'm so grateful. But it won't work. You see, my sister Ruth is over eighteen."

His face clouded over. "She's too old for *kinder* transport, I'm afraid. But once we get to America we can send for her." His voice trailed off. He was unwilling to make promises he could not keep. No, once they were gone they would not likely be able to protect Ruth at all.

"Helena, we have to get you out. You saw what happened in Kraków. It isn't just in the big cities. In a village to the east, they burned a barn with Jews sealed inside," he said, his voice cracking, seemingly not able to hold back the things he had been keeping from her.

"The Germans have not come to Biekowice," she said, clinging to this one bit of hope. But it wasn't just the Nazis. There were centuries of distrust among the Poles of the Jews who lived among them yet remained strangers. She shivered. If some of their neighbors in Biekowice knew the truth, they would turn on Helena and her siblings as surely as they had on the Jews in the next village. It would not matter that they had gone to school or played together. The differences between them would transcend and wipe away all of that.

"They are coming," Sam replied, his voice full with certainty. He took her hand. "Come with me." His eyes were pleading. "Why won't you let me help you?" he asked softly. Because for so long it had been just herself, self-reliance the only certain way to survive. The others she had trusted had all gone. "You saved my life."

"You don't owe me anything."

"Is that what you think this is about, some sort of obligation or debt to repay?" He placed his hands on either side of her face, his fingers gentle but firm. "I love you, Lena. I'm not going to let you go because you're too stubborn to see it."

Helena noticed then the parcel she'd left for him outside the door earlier that day, still in the same spot unopened. He had not found it yet. For a minute she considered taking it and tucking it back in her bag.

But it was too late, she realized as his eyes followed hers. "What's this?" he asked, reaching for the package.

"Wait!" She tried to grab the note, but he unfolded the paper. She watched his face as he read it, the surprise and sadness and finally resignation blowing through like clouds on a stormy day. "You were just going to leave this?" There was no anger in his voice, just sadness.

"I wanted to tell you, but I couldn't bear it." She trailed off, ashamed. He had called her brave for everything she had done, but saying goodbye to him was the one thing she could not do. "The police have been to our house to ask about hoarding when my sister was there alone."

His jaw clenched. "They didn't hurt her, did they?"

She shook her head. "Just threats. She's fine. But Ruth, well, she's always been the nervous one and she's more scared than ever now. She doesn't want me to come here."

"And you?"

"No, I mean, yes. I want to come." She looked away, embarrassed by the effusiveness of her own response. "But I can't endanger my family."

Of course, the point was a moot one: that morning, Helena had thought she was walking away from Sam for good. Now that she was back here, though, Helena knew she could not stay away. Like her mother, this could all be gone in an instant and she would take the moments while they were here. She could no sooner leave Sam than leave herself.

"Dammit!" he exploded. Helena pulled back. "I hate that I'm stuck here. I can't protect you, can't help." He reached for his waistband. "I want you to take this," he said. He pulled out his gun, which dangled in the air between them.

"Oh, I couldn't," she said. "I mean, I don't even know how." It was not entirely true—she had used Tata's rifle, first as a child with him holding it steady and later on her own trying to find food for the children. But it was a far cry from the sleek pistol Sam held—which she might actually be expected to aim at a person.

"I'll show you." He stood with effort and she followed. "Here." She took the gun reluctantly. The steel felt cold and solid in her hand, but not as odd as she might have imagined. He moved behind her and put his arms around her on each side, adjusting her grip and then raising her arms to shoulder level. Her stomach fluttered as she felt his chest pressing warm behind her. "You brace like this," he said. "And squeeze slowly and evenly." Of course, they would not fire a real shot, not wanting to waste a bullet and for fear of attracting attention.

Wordlessly they sat down once more. "I'm not taking it,"

she said. "I still don't think I could use it." She did not tell him
the real reason—Alek's news of the other soldier's capture had
raised her fears that it was only a matter of time before the troops
searching the countryside came upon the chapel and she did
not want to leave Sam defenseless. "Anyway, it would be much
worse for me if I was stopped and found carrying an American weapon," she added. He pursed his lips, unable to disagree.

"Sometimes I wish you'd never found me," he burst out suddenly. She stared at him, hurt for a second. But it was understandable.

"Don't say that!" she cried. She could not bear to think what
would have happened to him. She paused, taken aback. Sam
was usually so optimistic. It was his desperation talking, giving
voice to the same thoughts she'd had in the dark of the night.

"We're in it together, you see, too far in it."

"If you hadn't found me, then none of this would have happened to you." He regretted the difficulty he had brought her.
He would have preferred to lay wounded in the brush, awaiting
animals or Germans or both, rather than put her at risk.

Sam had complicated her life to be sure, and she would not
glamorize that. But her world had changed indescribably and
she could not imagine putting it back the way it had once been,
or having it not changed at all. If she had never found Sam, she
would not have become involved in the spying—might never
have known she was Jewish. But she did not regret it.

"Anyway, we can't change it so let's not waste time thinking
about it, okay?" She looked out the window into the darkness.
"I have to go."

"You can't go now. At least wait until first light." She hesitated. Ruth would be worried sick but he was right, of course—
it was pitch-dark and navigating the rest of the way home, even
with the dying flashlight, would be impossible. She followed him
into the chapel. She lay down on the pile of leaves he called his
bed. He put his arms around her, resting them over her shoul-

ders in a way that suggested warmth and comfort but no more. His fingers grazed the back of her hand like the feeling of the grass about her ankles on the summer days they'd gone barefoot as children.

Helena thought Sam might try to kiss her again and was disappointed when he did not. She fretted silently for a moment that learning the secrets they had kept from each other—his about the mission, hers about Ruth—had created mistrust. But his arms held her more solidly than ever. She pressed against him, savoring his embrace even now.

Without warning her thoughts returned to the fact that she and her siblings were half-Jewish and the grave danger Sam said that could bring. "What is happening to them?" Helena asked. Though part of her did not want to know the answer, she could not turn away. "The Jews who are taken by the Germans, I mean."

Sam's body sagged as he exhaled, and she knew he was unable to lie to her. "Some are going to the ghettos, designated neighborhoods with walls." Helena understood then the construction she had glimpsed as she had crossed the bridge by Podgórze, the high stone fences that had seemed so impractical for the sprawling, industrial neighborhood. "And for others, the Germans have set up camps. For the Jews mostly." Once this last bit would have brought her comfort, but now it hung dark and ominous in the air between them. "But also for political prisoners and others who they don't like or they think don't fit in."

"What's the point—of the camps, I mean?"

Sam hesitated. "They're labor camps. The Germans only have use for those who can work."

"And for those who can't work? The elderly and the children and the sick?"

"I don't know." He turned away. Dorie's face appeared in her mind suddenly, causing Helena's stomach to twist. With her awkward limp, Dorie would be considered of no use to the

Reich. Baby Karolina would similarly be dubbed surplus. Michal might be technically old enough to be useful, but he wasn't strong enough to withstand hard labor. "Let's not talk about it. You will never go there, not you or your brother or sisters. I'd kill someone first. I did it once," he said in a hushed voice. "Killed a man."

"Oh." She found herself stroking his soft hands. A moment ago it would not have been possible to imagine.

"I just thought you should know. You didn't mention a sister so close to your age," he added, his voice now fuzzy with sleep. "I assumed that they were all younger."

"I guess it just never came up." She could hear the defensiveness in her own voice. It wasn't as if she had deliberately kept Ruth from him. But for once in her life she'd enjoyed being known as herself, not one of a set. "You'd like her." *More than me*, she added silently. Because everyone liked sweet, pretty Ruth more.

Helena pressed against him, eager to hide in the warmth of his embrace. Soon her breathing matched his and her eyes grew heavy as she drifted off into the deepest sleep she had ever known.

14

Chirping birds awakened Helena, signaling a dawn that had not yet broken through the thickness of the pine trees. Sam snored lightly beside her and she slipped reluctantly from beneath the warmth of his arm without waking him. A cold hollowness settled over her immediately. She lingered, wanting to see his eyes once more. But he needed his rest. Her mind whirled back to the previous night's kiss outside the chapel. There had been an intensity to his embrace that said he was barely able to contain himself, that he also wanted more. Should she have taken the moment further? Something had stopped her, saying that this was too big and important, and that if they crossed the line it would change everything in a way that neither of them wanted. Yet she wondered now if they had been wrong to hold back on the moment, the only one they might have.

She looked back at him once more, then stole quietly from the chapel and started for home, still thinking about their kiss. Her connection with Sam had not been imagined or one-sided. He wanted them to be together, to share a life beyond anything she had ever contemplated. But it was impossible—she could not go without Ruth.

Ruth. She shivered. Her sister did not know yet about Mama. The pain of yesterday's events rained down upon Helena like shards of glass. Mama was dead, and their attempts to keep her safe and well had failed. Each step home was heavy as lead as she dreaded the inevitability of telling Ruth what had happened. Perhaps she should not tell her at all. Helena stopped, considering the idea. She could keep going to the city each week and maintain the pretense to spare her sister the grief—and if Ruth did not know, Helena could keep going to see Sam. But sparing Ruth little realities was one thing—the truth about Mama quite another. She could never keep something like that from her sister.

Forty minutes later, Helena emerged from the forest. Smoke puffed faintly from the chimney of the cottage below. As she neared, the mule whinnied in greeting. The usual breakfast smells wafted from beneath the doorway. Helena grasped the doorknob, then paused, imagining for a second that things might be as they always had. Once she stepped through the door, that illusion would be shattered forever.

Ruth appeared from the bedroom, carrying Karolina. "Where have you been?" she demanded as she set the child down by the fire. Ruth was wearing one of Mama's sweaters, just weeks after forbidding Helena to take the same clothes.

From behind the house came the sound of the other children, laughing as they played. "I'm sorry, I couldn't get back. The Germans were everywhere in the city, and I had to hide in the hospital until they were gone." Helena cringed inwardly as her sister's eyes narrowed, scrutinizing the explanation that was just short of a lie.

"The Germans were in the hospital?" Ruth asked, imagining horrors so far short of the truth.

Helena knew then that she could not hide what had happened from her twin. "Ruti…" she began, but the words stuck in her throat. She shook her head. And with that single look, Ruth knew.

Ruth's face caved and for a moment she appeared as though she would break down. "Mama's gone." She spoke the words that Helena could not, her tone unquestioning.

Helena nodded, then waited for her sister to collapse into the tears that she always shed so readily. Ruth dropped into a chair and closed her eyes, then rocked back and forth. "How?"

"I don't know…in her sleep, I think." Not entirely a lie, for surely the poison Wanda had given their mother had first made her drowsy. "She died before the Germans got there." Helena wanted to spare Ruth from all that she had seen. "She's at peace."

Karolina toddled to Ruth, who picked her up and held her close. "You just left her there?"

"You don't understand, I had no choice." Helena stifled the urge to lash out. "The hospital is in ruins, and most of the nurses are gone. When the Germans left, I had to run. You have to believe I did everything I could to help her." She was begging now, pleading for Ruth to understand, not just about their mother's passing but that Helena had tried, really tried, to help her these past months.

Helena braced herself, waiting for Ruth to berate her further. But her sister sat numbly, staring through her fingers at the floor. "Ruti, there's something else…" Helena lowered her voice. "The soldier at the chapel thinks he can get us passes to leave." She held her breath, waiting for Ruth to rebuke her for breaking her promise and seeing him again, but she did not.

Ruth lifted her head. "Leave? I don't understand."

She nodded. "He believes that the Germans are coming to the villages, and if it's anything like the city, it won't be safe to stay here."

"Where would we go?" The perennial question was a refrain of their conversation just days earlier.

"Over the border." Karolina looked from Helena to Ruth and then back again, listening somberly.

"And then?"

"Away." Helena faltered, the incompleteness of the plan suddenly evident. "We can go to America with the soldier."

Ruth's eyes darted back and forth as she contemplated the magnitude of the journey. "He can get passes for all of us?"

"Yes, of course," Helena replied, too quickly. She had not intended to mention Sam's idea to her sister at all, but in her desperation to comfort Ruth, it had seemed like something. "There's a *kinder* transport for the children. And then you and I can get papers and go separately." She watched as Ruth processed the information, considering the idea.

"No," Ruth replied. "We can't put the children on a train without us."

"It won't be safe here. We would just send them ahead and meet them as soon as we are able. The children are strong."

"The children are children. We promised Mama we would stay together."

"But she couldn't possibly have known how things would change, how horrible circumstances would become."

Ruth shook her head, angrily swiping at a lock of hair that had fallen into her eyes. "It's too dangerous."

"But think about all of the things you could do in America. You could meet someone and get married." Ruth's face twisted at the mention of the painful dream, now abandoned. Helena continued quickly. "Or you could become a teacher."

"It isn't safe," Ruth persisted. "Those transports are intended for the Jews. If the Nazis find out they will become a target."

Helena hesitated, considering whether to tell Ruth the truth about Mama's Jewish heritage. Surely it would help her to understand the heightened danger for them here, the need to risk leaving. But Ruth was the most religious of them all, embracing Catholicism like a mantle, as though the church and its teach-ings might shield them from whatever transpired in the outside world. Helena could not possibly destroy the framework that had kept her sister going, not now when she had already lost so much else.

"You can't keep your head in the sand," she persisted instead.

"I'm not!"

"You saw it when the policeman came." Watching Ruth blanch, Helena felt a twinge of guilt for involving the painful memory. But she did not have a choice. "Don't you see, that one of these days there will be another knock on the door, only this time it won't be about hoarding?"

"I'm not in denial," Ruth replied again, this time with surprising force. "I'm not ignoring how bad things are, or what might happen. I just don't agree with you. Perhaps Father Dominik…"

"No!" Helena interjected loudly. The church had been a point of contention between them since Helena had discovered Ruth leaving mass one morning months earlier, head low beneath the hood of her cape. The church had always felt hostile to Helena, a place where she did not belong. Now she understood better why. And Father Dominik hated the Jews, spewing bile toward them in his sermons long before the Germans had come. He was the last person they could trust.

"I don't understand. If there's really trouble coming, then surely the church can help." Watching Ruth's face, Helena recognized even further then the depths of her sister's belief system, the elaborate world she had constructed to keep going. As the life she knew eroded around her, Ruth was clinging desperately to bare rock face, trying to find something to which she could hold.

Helena hesitated, not wanting to say too much, but unwilling to back off. "I just don't think we can count on anyone but ourselves anymore."

Several seconds of silence passed between them. "I have nightmares about it," Ruth confessed. "Running away." Helena was surprised—Ruth had always slept so soundly, it had not occurred to her to ask what she dreamed about.

"We could hide," Ruth added, her voice soft, almost sheepish. Helena opened her mouth to reject the idea, then thought better of it. Hiding was the other side of the coin, the one she'd tried not to think about. They could not hide in their own house, of course, but perhaps in the city. She remembered the now-deserted Kazimierz streets, the abandoned attic rooms beneath vaulted ceilings.

Before she could respond, Ruth took a deep breath and stood. She passed Karolina to Helena, then smoothed her apron with trembling hands. "Come," she said, putting her arms around Helena, signaling that the conversation was over. To Helena's surprise, Ruth led her to the armoire where their mother's clothing hung and began to riffle through the dresses. As she set Karolina down on the bed, Helena wanted to tell her that it was too soon, that there was no need to destroy the closet that she'd kept as a shrine for so long. But it was, Helena realized, Ruth's own form of grieving. She handed Helena a simple blue dress to replace her own filthy one.

When she had finished putting it on, Helena looked up. Ruth was holding Mama's pink church frock, staring at it. A hint of sage wafted from the collar. "I'll try this one." She tried to pull the dress over her head but, unlike the loose sweater she had already donned, it was too narrow for her round, full figure. Her face grew red with effort.

"Ruth…" One of the buttons burst and clattered to the floor. Ruth dove after it, but it fell between the floorboards and disappeared. She kept trying to reach for it, her fingers clawing at the coarse wood. "Shh." Helena dropped to the ground beside Ruth and folded her sister's scraped fingers into her own. She cradled Ruth's head as Ruth finally allowed herself to weep.

"I thought I could fit." Ruth was talking, it seemed, about something more than the dress.

"There, there," Helena soothed as her sister sobbed. "We're going to figure this out." But would they really? No one expected to find themselves in these circumstances, parentless with a household of children to care for. People in other times grew up and got married and had families, planning for life to carry on as it had for centuries. It was all different now, though—some of them would make it and some not, and it all came down to chance.

"It's not fair," Ruth sobbed, gesturing toward the window at the children. Helena nodded. But for Michal, the younger children scarcely had the chance to know Mama at all. "They should have so much more," Ruth added.

Helena thought of the spoiled blond girl eating chestnuts on the square. "They have us," she replied firmly, pushing the image aside. There was an unexpected moment of solidarity between them, a fleeting instant when their common goals outweighed their differences. Helena slipped her hand into Ruth's and suddenly they were six again, two girls in tattered dresses walking into school, them against the world.

Helena held up the dress that Ruth had thrown down. "We can cut this one down and make a dress for Dorie."

Ruth straightened and dabbed at her eyes. "The children, Michal and Dorie…should we tell them about Mama?"

"No, not yet, anyway." Ruth dipped her chin in silent agreement. They both knew it was best not to say anything. The children had accepted the status quo of Mama's absence and their parentless life. Why add to their grief with a loss they would otherwise never miss?

"I'm going to market," Ruth announced, walking to the mirror and blotting beneath her eyes. "I need a piece of carp, if there's one to be had."

"I can go for you."

"No," Ruth snapped, as if fearful to let Helena leave once more. They exchanged uneasy glances as the chill between them returned. They were not the same allies they had been when they were six. There was a kind of acrimony between them now, sharper than the rivalry of young girls vying for attention and space. They wanted different things, a conflict that brought with it an uneasy sense of distrust. "You've been gone all night and I can use the fresh air. Mind the children." Helena braced for the litany of instructions that Ruth always seemed to give, as if she were not an equal partner in their caretaking who could figure these things out for herself.

Ruth did not speak further, but simply donned her blue cape and slipped from the house. She needed time, Helena reflected, to process what had happened to Mama. "Come," Helena said to Karolina, who toddled after her. Helena walked to the window and looked up the hill longingly. Though she had returned from seeing Sam just hours earlier, she felt the desire to go to the chapel once more and be with him.

She turned to gaze out over the horizon—unseen beyond the tree line were the fog-clad peaks of the High Tatras. Once they had seemed to her a fortress, designed to keep trouble out. But now they were imposing, their high peaks an impenetrable barrier to escape. Helena's stomach twisted. It was only a matter of time before the Germans combed through the hospital records and learned the truth that Mama had kept so well for a lifetime. Then they would come looking for the family.

Helena peered around the corner of the house where Dorie and Michal played. She was seized with the urge to grab the children and run. But where? They would never survive winter in the forest. And the massive field behind the house was an open expanse, naked and exposed, with no refuge to be found. Hide, Ruth had suggested. Remembering the close stuffy closet at the hospital in which she had been trapped, Helena knew she could not do that.

She thought of Papa's rifle, high on the shelf. If the worst happened, and the Germans came, she would sooner shoot the

children herself, rather than let them suffer. The handful of remaining bullets would be just enough. Shame welled up in her.
She couldn't do that, not really. Who knew when all hope was
truly gone?

She looked up at the yellowed photograph of her parents on
their wedding day, their faces shining. Suddenly, the earth beneath Helena's feet, which she had walked for a lifetime, seemed
alien and full of secrets. She understood now why Mama always
preferred sweet, unquestioning Ruth, willing to take an explanation at face value.

What if people had known? Being a Jew would have been
awkward in the village before the war, but not altogether prob-
lematic. People would have whispered about it for a time and
then forgotten, or maybe remained a shade colder to the family
than they already were. But Mama's secrecy ran much deeper,
as if she sensed that things which had never been good for the
Jews would worsen, and the animosity bubbling beneath the
surface would suddenly boil over. Her anonymity, the fact that
people did not know she was a Jew, was a gift that she could
give to her family to protect them.

An image flashed through Helena's mind. She'd been seven
or eight and rummaging through her mother's cedar trunk idly.
The clothes did not interest her as they did Ruth, but she was
curious what else might be there, a bit of string perhaps, or
some felt. Her hand had closed around something metal and
cold and she pulled it out to discover a cup, more of a chalice,
really. Though it was tarnished she could tell that it was made
of real silver. Mama had come up behind her and snatched it
from her hands. "You should not go through a person's belongings without permission," she'd scolded. Helena had wanted to
point out that Ruth rummaged through the armoire for clothes
regularly without rebuke. But her mother was already gone and
the next time she snuck back to the trunk, the cup was nowhere
to be found.

Helena recalled now the ornate engravings on the cup, strange letters and symbols that she recognized now from the front of the hospital and other signs around Kazimierz to be Hebrew. The cup was the one tangible link between her Mama and the life she had tried so hard to keep a secret. Yet she had clung to it, despite the risks its discovery might have brought. And she had not sold it, even when the money had been sorely needed. It must have meant a great deal to her.

But what had become of the cup? "Wait here," she instructed Karolina, who now played contentedly by the warmth of the fire. Helena went to Mama's trunk, which sat at the foot of the bed, flinging open the lid. A mix of camphor and lavender wafted forth in an invisible cloud. She lifted a communion dress, rosary beads on top of it. Funny what people thought to save, the things that they thought would be meaningful a lifetime from now. Beneath it lay Mama's wedding veil. Helena thought of the wedding photo, the background dark and nondescript. She'd always assumed it had been taken at the parish church, but now the questions swirled—had it been somewhere else and, if so, where? Not that it mattered, but there were so many things she did not, could not, know—one little piece of certainty, no matter how remote, would help to ground her. She continued digging to the bottom of the trunk, tearing the clothes aside like pieces of earth until her hands scraped against the cedar wood. Nothing else.

Helena clumsily replaced the clothes as well as she could. Then she walked from the bedroom. Had Mama sold the cup, after all? It seemed unlikely that she would have discarded it after keeping it for so many years. Helena's eyes traveled to the mantelpiece. High above on the shelf there was a cabinet where Mama had once kept the medicines and other dangerous items she didn't want the children to find. Helena reached up into the space, but it was empty. She started to pull her hand out, deflated. As she did, she noticed that one of the bricks on the base of the cabinet sat at a strange angle, slightly higher than the others. She dug at the brick, lifting it with effort. Beneath was a small empty space. Her hand closed around hard metal.

She lifted out the tarnished, soot-covered cup and held it aloft, considering. It was a link to their mother and the past they would never know. She wished she had remembered the cup and thought to ask about it when Mama was still alive. Now it was too late and that, like so many other answers, lay buried forever. But the chalice was the most valuable thing in the house by far. Selling it would bring money for food and possibly their passage.

A clattering at the door jarred her from her thoughts. She replaced the brick and closed the cabinet, climbing down from the hearth as the children burst through the door. Quickly she walked to the hook where her coat hung, and slipped the cup into her bag. Michal and Dorie chattered, breathless from the snow and anticipation of the holiday that evening. "Boots off," she ordered, disliking the harshness in her own voice.

Then she stopped. She and Ruth were all they had now. Her hand rested on Dorie's head. The girl looked up, unaccustomed to her affectionate touch. "What is it?"

"Nothing," Helena said quickly. "How about a horse ride?" Dorie's face brightened, and she looked at Helena with such gratitude that Helena's insides crumbled. The children took it on blind faith that she and Ruth would do what was best for them—a promise she had betrayed when she'd risked their safety for Sam. She dropped to all fours heedless of the dirt against the hem of her skirt, giving Dorie a turn first, then Karolina. Ruth would scold her for riling up the children, but she did not care.

"Enough now. Wash your hands, and your sister's, too," Helena said a few minutes later, breathless from play. As they obeyed, she moved to set out the black bread and cheese Ruth had left for their lunch.

Watching the children eat, the earlier debate with Ruth played over in her head. Run or hide? Now knowing the truth, doing nothing was not an option. Perhaps Ruth was right.

"No," she said aloud to no one in particular. They would not hide only to be found like rats in a cage. They would keep going and if they were taken it would not be because they stopped trying.

15

The next morning Helena crept from the house before dawn. She searched the sky anxiously. Though the temperature seemed to have dropped ten degrees overnight, the weather was still relatively mild. In past years, there might have been as much as a half meter of snow. But now only a fine coating of white covered the ground. Her heart sank. A heavy storm was the one thing that might keep Sam from going. Then she stopped, taken aback by her selfishness. More snow would mean additional hardship for the family, burning coal and wood they could ill-afford and making it more difficult to find food. And it would keep Sam alone and freezing in the chapel, at constant risk of discovery.

Pushing the thought from her mind, Helena crossed to the forest quickly, feeling naked and exposed as though she might be apprehended—or worse—at any second.

She reached the trees, her breath calming as she began to climb. She had not woken Ruth to make excuses, for what reason could she plausibly give for going to the city now that Mama was gone? She had contemplated weaving a complex tale about trying to arrange for Mama's burial, the paperwork involved. Her lies would be unabashed—their mother's body was long since gone, making the possibility of a proper funeral nonexistent. Ruth would have known that she was going to see Sam. And in part that was true—but it was more than that. She fingered the packets of medicine that she'd stuffed into the lining of her coat. She'd gotten these for Alek in hopes that he might trust her enough to help Sam. Connecting Sam to the partisans was their only chance. Even now—especially now—she had to see this through.

Wait a week, Alek had said. Though it felt longer, it had, in fact, only been two days since she'd met him at the café. But things were worsening—she had to act now, or it would be too late.

At the fork in the path, Helena paused. She had left the house impulsively at her usual hour to start off into the forest. But she could not go to the café this early in the day. Alek would not be there; indeed, it would surely be closed, and she would not know where else to look for him. She hesitated, then started walking toward the chapel, joy and excitement rising in her as it always did when she was about to see Sam.

She knocked three times softly on the door, a habit she had formed in recent weeks, as though it was his proper house and she a visitor. Silence. Usually, Sam limped his way to greet her, or called to her from the other side. "Hello?" Helena pushed open the door. There was no answer. She inhaled sharply. Had Sam left, without saying goodbye, as she had asked him to do? No, she reasoned, his leg was not well enough for that. Perhaps someone had found him. She turned back toward the door, then stopped. Sam lay in the corner, leaves and a burlap sack piled over him. *Hiding.*

She approached Sam, her eyes adjusting to the dim light. Her stomach gave a little jump, as it always did when she first took him in. He was curled up on his side, back pressed against the wall, arms wrapped around one knee. His head was cocked at a slight angle as though he had seen something curious. His mouth was agape, eyes closed.

Nearing him, Helena's heart tugged. She ached to lie down beside him. She adjusted the burlap, and a wave of protectiveness arose in her. She knew in that moment that she would do just about anything to make sure he was safe.

She tried to move quietly as she knelt, but a twig cracked beneath her foot. Suddenly his head snapped up and he reached for his waist. "Wait!" She put her hand on his shoulder. "It's only me."

Sam's eyes cleared. "Lena. I must have dozed off." Deep half circles ringed the bottom of his eyes. He slept lightly, she surmised, fearful that someone might come and catch him off guard. He held out his arms to her. She folded wordlessly into them and lay down beside him. He kissed her, his full lips warm from sleep.

As they broke apart, she noticed her photo propped up against the wall of the chapel, placed close to where he slept. Warmth filled her as she imagined him looking at it at night, seeing her face before he closed his eyes, as she did his in her mind when she lay in the darkness with her siblings.

His face clouded. "What are you doing here so early? Is something wrong?"

"I'm headed back to see Alek and deliver the medicine."

She watched him wrestle once more with his concern for her versus his need to escape. "I thought he said to wait a week."

"He did. But I don't think I should wait." Their eyes met and locked in agreement.

He coughed then, a deep racking noise like heavy wagon tires on gravel. "You're getting sick," she fretted.

"No," he replied quickly. But with the constant dampness of the chapel and in his weakened state, it was inevitable. She pressed her hand to his forehead, noting with relief that it felt only slightly warm. Anxiety pressed at her stomach still. There was nothing she could do for him if he fell seriously ill, no medicine and certainly no doctor she could bring. He had to remain strong.

"Why don't you sleep while I'm here?" she suggested. "I'll make sure no one comes."

He looked at her dubiously. "You'll stand watch?"

"I suppose that's what it's called." She had intended only a brief visit, but he could not heal if he did not rest.

"That seems a terrible waste of our time together... I mean, your time."

"Not at all." He wrinkled his brow, tempted but not convinced. "You don't have to sleep. Just close your eyes for a bit while we're talking."

He did not lie down again, but leaned against her shoulder, burying his nose into her neck. She fought the desire to turn to him and find his lips. He closed his eyes and a moment later he was breathing against her skin, as evenly as before, only deeper. Moving slowly as not to disturb him, she reached with her free hand and covered him with the burlap, then sat back again.

Watching Sam's chest rise and fall, she was reminded of her father. An image flashed through her mind then of a January morning when she was twelve. Helena had risen early and discovered the fire had gone out, the cottage dangerously chilled, a frost growing on the windowpanes. Tata never let that happen. She had slipped from bed and found the space beside her mother empty. Alarmed, she put on her coat and went outside. Tata was passed out half inside the barn. She could not wake him and for a moment she thought he was dead, but his stale breath was warm. He might have died, frozen to death. She had used all of her strength to pull him into the barn, then gathered the wood and started the fire before anyone had noticed.

"It's chilly," Mama had remarked when she'd awoken, the cold still lingering, though the fire had burned brightly again.

A few minutes later, Tata came into the house, the faint stubble on his cheeks the only evidence of anything amiss. They exchanged looks, a silent vow, and she knew she would never say anything. And so it began, Helena covering for him, getting food and wood when he could not, making sure he passed out somewhere safely until that last night when she had so terribly failed. Mama and the others would not know, or chose not to guess, the truth about the extent of his drinking.

What if she had said something? she wondered now, as she had so many times over the years. If she had told Mama about the liquor, perhaps she could have done something, and Tata would be alive today.

Sam shifted beside her. He straightened and pulled away, leaving the spot where he'd nestled against her neck damp and chilled. Eyes open now, he propped his hands behind his head. "Hello." He smiled with a lightness that he could not possibly mean, given the grim circumstances. "I'm not tired anymore," he added before she could protest that he needed to sleep longer. "That was the best rest I've had in some time."

"You were smiling in your sleep. Was it a nice dream?"

"Oh, yes, we were at one of those dances I told you about, but you just kept eating bread and cheese as if we were here at the chapel." She chuckled but there was a note of truth to what he dreamed—even if they made it to America, she would somehow always be changed by the hunger and other struggles they had faced here.

Helena stood and went to the stove and made him some tea. Pouring it, she recalled Dorie looking for the cup a few days earlier by the fireplace. "My doll's cup," Dorie said, wrinkling her nose until the freckles formed a single red cluster. "I'm sure I left it here."

"You should be more careful with your belongings," Ruth scolded. Inwardly, Helena cringed, knowing that the fault was hers, not Dorie's. She wanted to own up to taking it, but could not afford the questions it would bring.

Helena shivered as she returned with the tea, noticing then how low the fire had gone. "Do you need more wood?"

He shook his head, gesturing to the pile in the corner. "I've just been keeping the fire low to be safe." He rose and limped to the stove and, before she could protest, added several more sticks. "It's a kind of cold that gets into your bones," he observed, holding his nearly healed leg.

She nodded. "I had to pour boiling water on the latch to open the barn door yesterday. Of course, it isn't nearly as cold there," she hastened to add, feeling guilty at the comforts of home, which she enjoyed and he did not.

He chuckled softly, seeming not to mind. "And to think I used to complain about Chicago winters. A hot bath," he said wistfully. "When I get home I'm going to climb into a hot bath up to my neck and not get out for a week." She blushed as the image of him naked in the tub penetrated into her mind.

They fell silent for several seconds. "Better today?" he asked gently, touching her cheek.

She shrugged, remembering the grief at losing Mama that had threatened to drown her just a day earlier. Sadness washed over her anew. It might have been any other visit to Sam, except that when she went to the city, Mama would no longer be there. The pain was a bit duller, like a cut just barely begun to heal.

"No, of course not," he said, answering his own question. "How stupid of me."

"More surreal, maybe. I don't know if it will ever get better." It would, of course. It had gotten easier with time after Tata's sudden death. But to acknowledge that now seemed like accepting Mama was gone, and she wasn't ready to do that. After Tata had died, she understood that people left—that she and her siblings would lose one another, one by one, separately, painfully. With Mama, she thought she had been ready. But all of the months of suffering had not prepared her for this. "I just never thought it would end this soon." She was talking about Mama, but the words seemed to mean so much more. "I feel so guilty," she added.

"You can't possibly blame yourself for what the Germans did at the hospital."

"I know that. My mother needed care and it was the only place. But Tata was so good at protecting her. I can't help but think that if he was alive, things might have turned out differently. And I think that's my fault, too."

"Your father dying? How can you possibly blame yourself for that?"

She recounted the story of finding him passed out in the barn years earlier. "I could have done more," she lamented. "If only I had said something about his drinking, maybe he would still be here—and Mama, too."

"You can't fix everything, you know." Sam was right. She had spent her whole life, it seemed, trying to make things right for others. "Your mother's cancer, for example, was out of your hands."

"Part of me knew how it would end with Tata's drinking, though. If I had told my mother that day, things might have turned out differently."

"That, I understand." His face dropped and she saw a darkness there she could not have imagined in his otherwise bright demeanor. "I didn't say much about my family before. It's not as cheery as I might have let on. My dad was a hitter, you see, mostly Mom, though my brother and I stepped in to take some of the pressure off her. See this?" He raised his hand to the scar on his temple. "I didn't fall. He pushed me into a table when I was nine."

"Oh!" Helena reached out to the spot where he had indicated, putting her hand over his. She felt the pain of his wound as she had the day she had found him with the broken leg in the woods. The hurt of the blow, and betrayal by his own father, reverberated through her, as though they were happening now and not a decade ago.

"My brother left for the army to get away from him, I think. I couldn't have abandoned Mom. But then things got worse." Sam pulled away from her touch, going somewhere deeper inside himself, a place that she could not reach. He licked his lips and she braced herself, intensely curious and yet filled with dread, as if she was about to walk down a dark scary hallway and open the door in spite of herself. "One night I caught him beating Mom worse than ever." His eyes darted back and forth as he relived the moment. "I tried to pull him off, but I couldn't. I got a baseball bat—just to break it up, you know? But then he tried to grab it and I was afraid he would use it on her." His voice cracked. "I hit him much harder than I intended and... and he died."

"Oh, Sam, no..." She searched for words but found none. How could sweet, gentle Sam, *her* Sam, have done such a thing? Because he had been protecting his mother—trying, as she had done by hiding Tata's drinking and on so many other occasions, to do the right thing—and getting it so horribly wrong.

"The judge said it was self-defense and he let me enlist instead of going to prison." Watching Sam's fists clench and unclench as he spoke, Helena understood then that his anger came from his determination to protect the innocent who had been caught up in this war, driven by his frustration that he could not protect his own family. Is that why he wanted to help her, as well?

His guilt washed over her then, dwarfing her own. She reached out and drew him close as Ruth might one of the children, trying to absorb some of the pain. "It's all right," she said, offering the pardon that was not hers to give. "It was an accident."

"I'm sorry I didn't tell you earlier. I thought you'd hate me."

"Not at all." His father had been a bully. And Sam, more so

than anything else, hated bullies. So did she. Though Tata had not been a violent man, Helena had instinctively taken on the role of gentle Michal's protector. "You were defending your mother, I understand." But how could she possibly? She'd been angry before at people, like the Germans at the hospital, and once a woman in the village had sneered at Dorie's limp and made her cry. Helena had wanted to throttle her. To actually have killed, though... Once she might have been horrified by Sam's story, judged his actions in terms of right and wrong. But everything was just so gray now—none of the old rules seemed to apply anymore.

He lifted his head, eyes damp. "I don't mean to burden you with my story now, on top of everything else. But I wanted to let you know I understand the what-ifs. And it might sound crazy, but even after everything, I miss my father."

"It doesn't sound crazy." So he had lost someone he cared about, after all. His grief and guilt were, like her own, inextricable.

His hand closed around hers tightly as though he were clutching to her for stability, trying to right himself. Was he worried that since he had shared the truth about his past, she would no longer want him? "You're the first person that I've trusted."

"Enough to tell, you mean?"

Sam shook his head. "Trusted at all. My brother was older, off living his life. And my mom was so busy trying to protect herself, I could never quite be sure she'd do the same for me." Helena shivered, picturing what he had been through. As difficult as their own lives had been with Tata's drinking and the lack of money and the secrets she had only just discovered, there had always been love. She tried to imagine the actual betrayal of those closest to her, but could not.

An ominous feeling overcame her then. "I found a chalice," she said, eager to change the subject. He cocked his head. She pulled it out and handed it to him.

"A Kiddush cup," he clarified gently. "Jews bless the wine and drink from it on special occasions."

"It was my mother's. That's Hebrew, isn't it?"

He nodded. "It's a beautiful piece."

"She kept it, in spite of everything."

"She must have felt a very special connection to it." Helena had thought only until now of the connection between the cup and her mother's secret Jewish identity. But what had it meant to Mama? Had it belonged to her parents, or grandparents? Helena saw then the generations of ancestors and lives that went with the cup, their stories hidden forever.

"It will make a wonderful addition to our home," Sam added. She stared at him in amazement. Things had never looked bleaker, yet he seemed more confident of their future together than ever before. His faith made her feel suddenly stronger, too. "Having it could be dangerous, though. Do you want me to keep it here for you?"

Helena hesitated. She knew he would keep it safe, but it would make things even worse if he was found. "No, I want it with me." She could not bear to tell him, either, that she planned to sell it.

"I wish we could just get married," he said abruptly. Her pulse quickened. Though they had discussed it before, the concept was still foreign to her. And it seemed remote, the questions of survival more pressing and immediate. "I mean, here we are, in a chapel…"

"It is ironic," she agreed. "But someday we will get married, in a real church—or synagogue," she hastened to add.

He shook his head. Someday was not good enough. "I mean now."

Sam took her hands solemnly and pulled her to her feet. What did he mean for them to do? He led her to the front of the chapel, where the pulpit would once have stood. "Do you take me as your lawfully wedded husband?"

She cut him off. "You want to say our vows here?"

But his face was gravely serious. He wanted to marry her *now*. She trembled, nearly shaking. "Take me as your lawfully wedded husband," he repeated, "to love, honor and obey?"

She cocked her head. "Obey?" It sounded like everything she had always disliked about the prospect of marriage.

"It's part of the American wedding vows, but we can leave it out. To love and honor?"

"I do."

"Well, I take you, too." He kissed her firmly on the lips. A moment later, he pulled back. "That will have to do for now." She nodded. It felt as real as if there had been a minister and church full of flowers. "Jews get married under a canopy, it's called a chuppa. It symbolizes the times they were in exile and couldn't get married in a temple."

"Oh." She looked up through the hole in the roof. "We don't even have that."

He shrugged. "We will someday. And the groom smashes a glass to break with the past." There was so much she didn't know about who he was and this unfamiliar people he now included her among. "The honeymoon will have to wait for another day," he quipped, his eyes twinkling.

She blushed and pulled away. "I didn't mean to offend you." He laughed.

"Not at all. But I need to go."

Sam followed her to the door. "I wish we could just stay like this."

"I know." But even if they stood in place, the world around them would not. Things were pulling them apart, and if they did not move with the powerful tides they would be swept away. She laced her fingers through his.

He brought his free hand to her cheek. "Be careful." His voice was almost a plea.

"I will," she promised, "and I'll see you soon."

Helena walked away uneasily. She turned back, wanting to see Sam one last time. But he had already disappeared back into the chapel. Longing welled up in her, stronger than it ever had, and she fought the urge to run back inside. *Enough*. She steeled herself. The sooner she made the connection to the resistance, the sooner they could be together.

16

Helena reached the top of the forested hill and gazed down at the city. Her eyes traveled in the direction of the Jewish quarter. From this vantage point, it seemed for a moment as though nothing had changed, and if she took her familiar route to the hospital she might find Mama still waiting there. Tears welled up unexpectedly, threatening to overflow. She blinked them back; this was not the time for mourning. Forcing herself to look away from Kazimierz, she plotted a route into the Stare Miasto, then started down.

German presence in the city was heavier now, she could sense as she crossed the bridge. The thin pretense of normalcy that had existed just days earlier was gone. The narrow, winding streets were clogged thick with military vehicles, and there were almost more Gestapo than locals on the sidewalks. Many of the shops were now closed at midday, some of their Christmas decorations taken down as though Christmas had already passed and was not still two days away. The faces of the passersby, ordinary Poles, were worn and haggard. Had liquidations come to the Old City, as well? Helena forced herself to walk calmly and keep her head level. To act as if she belonged. Once she had regarded the city as exciting, a place of intrigue and adventure. Now with every second she spent here, she risked discovery and capture.

As she drew closer to the *rynek*, she passed the stately Grand Hotel. Piano music tinkled from the ground floor *kawiarnia* as someone opened the door and stepped out, letting forth the smell of smoke and stale beer. *"Stille Nacht,"* a male voice sang in German, loudly and off-key. The merry sound seemed to hover above the grim street, a mocking caricature.

Hurrying on, Helena soon reached the entrance to Pod Gwiazdami. At the top of the stairwell, she hesitated. The voices were loud beneath, too boisterous for midmorning. Steeling herself, she started down. Halfway down, she stopped again, scanning the room below. The café, which had been almost empty on her last visit, was now lively with off-duty German soldiers. Some swilled beer, even at this early hour, while others drank coffee fortified, she suspected, with something stronger. There was no sign of Alek.

She scurried back up the stairs as leering eyes began to notice her, and she tripped in her haste. Righting herself, she reached the street, heart pounding. The café was her one link to Alek. She dared not loiter or ask for him there. What now?

Wierzynek, she remembered. Could she really go to the elegant restaurant where he said he worked as a waiter, with its *Nur für Deutsche* sign in the front window forbidding Poles to enter? She had no choice. She started toward the *rynek*.

As she reached the corner, she was suddenly thrown forward and slammed against the brick wall of a building. Her first thought was an explosion like the one that had rocked Kazimierz the other day? But no, this force was human, a strong male forearm wrapping around her throat to silence her scream before it reached her lips. She imagined one of the Germans had followed her from the café and struggled hopelessly to escape. She raised a foot to kick—

"Quiet," a familiar voice ordered. Alek turned her around and leaned in as though they were lovers, pressing her against the building, while two German officers staggered toward them. His jaw was dark with stubble and there was a stale, unwashed smell about him.

When the Germans had passed, he straightened, but did not release her. She stared up at him, blinking. "How did you find me?"

"It doesn't matter." He sounded annoyed, almost angry. "You don't listen, do you? I said a week."

"I couldn't wait. And I got you these." She reached in her pocket and started to pull out the packets of medicine. His eyes widened.

"Not here." He waved away her hand, then looked over his shoulder.

"You said you needed supplies. Surely this will help."

He sniffed. "Most certainly. But how did you get them?"

"I have my ways. And you can see my intentions are sincere. Now will you help me?"

"Go to ulica Bracka 7." He pointed toward a side street. "The brick beneath the third step moves. Leave the package behind it and then come back. Go now," he ordered. She started in the direction he indicated, turning onto Bracka Street, a winding residential lane tucked just off the bustling square. Number 7 was an elegant, four-story house, twinkling holiday candles behind each of its fir-adorned windows. A lone red poppy that appeared to have been stuck there rather than planted jutted defiantly from a snow-covered flower box. She glanced uncertainly in both directions. It seemed impossible that it was safe to leave anything here on this well-trafficked street. But the brick at the third step moved just like Alek said. Keeping her hands low to her sides so as not to attract attention, she slid the medicine in and replaced it.

She returned to the place near the *rynek* where Alek had intercepted her. He was smoking a cigarette, gazing upward at the cathedral spires.

"That house on Bracka Street, how did you know about it?"

"You should save your questions for things that matter." He wiped his hand across his brow. "It belonged to my aunt." Helena paused, considering this. She had once laughed at Sam's suggestion that Jews might be wealthy. To her, the ones she had seen in Kazimierz and in the village were hapless, even poorer than she. Looking at the house, Helena realized that she could not classify all Jews in a certain way. "And it still does, really, though the filthy Germans who live there might disagree," he added. She marveled at the audacity of keeping a drop box right under the nose of the Gestapo—perhaps the last place they might look for it.

Alek carefully extinguished his cigarette against the pavement and tucked what remained of it into his pocket. "So what was so urgent?"

She faltered. Did he really expect her to talk about it here on the open street? "To give you the medicine," she said in a low voice, "and to see if you found a way to get the soldier out." She still could not bring herself to say Sam's name in public.

"Again with the soldier. Why would you risk so much for an American you just met?" Alek's tone was chiding now. "Is he your lover?" Looking up, she saw him smiling for the first time.

"No!" she blurted out. "I want to help. That is, my mother's family is Jewish." Her words seemed to reverberate off the buildings, leaving her naked and exposed. "And I'm Jewish." It was the first time she had ever said this aloud to anyone but Sam. Somehow now it seemed an asset, a credential to make her motives plausible.

He raised an eyebrow. "Jews in Biekowice? That's unusual. Why didn't you say something last time?"

"I didn't know. My mother was in the Kazimierz hospital. We only just learned from the records."

His mouth twisted. "That's poor timing. Most Jews are doing what they can to hide their identities or themselves right now. You'd do well to do the same. I'm sorry about your mother," he added. Alek had heard of the hospital liquidation and knew without asking that the end had not been good.

"Thank you." Helena marveled that one who had surely seen much suffering and death could sound so sad about a woman he had never met. "She died that day, after I met you last time. I had to hide from the Germans at the hospital."

"Yet through all that, you had the presence of mind to steal the medicine." His voice carried an unmistakable note of admiration. "You have strength—and a good head."

"At least she did not suffer..." Helena added, only half hearing his compliment as she relived the horror of the hospital. She looked away, embarrassed by her thoughts, too personal to share.

"There's something else you want to ask me," Alek said, tilting his head, seeming to sense her question even before she had formed it.

"No, it's nothing," she said quickly. "Now about the soldier, you will help him, right?"

"You'd like to know more about your mother's past, wouldn't you?" Alek prodded, unwilling to let the matter go. "It's okay to want something for yourself. Come." Not waiting for a response, he grabbed her arm and tugged her into the alley and through a maze of smaller, unfamiliar streets. Helena struggled to keep up with his pace and not be dragged along. He led her quickly to the corner and joined a queue of people boarding a streetcar.

She pulled away. "We can't possibly ride." Streetcars were forbidden to Jews and though neither of them wore an armband, surely the police were more likely to check papers on one.

"Walking is more dangerous with all of the checkpoints."

They shuffled up the steps of the streetcar. No seats remained so they stood awkwardly in the aisle. Helena started to ask him where they were going, but a bell rang out and the streetcar lurched. She grasped the back of one of the seats to keep from falling, unaccustomed to moving at such a speed.

They did not speak as the streetcar glided through the mid-day traffic that thronged the *aleje*, wagons mixing with trucks and military vehicles. It stopped several more times to let off and take on passengers. A few minutes later Alek gestured that they should disembark. He led her through a strange neighbor-hood, turning right and left so many times she could not have found her way back if she'd wanted. A wind rushed down the narrow alleyways, kicking up the strewn newspapers and other debris at her feet. As they passed an *apteka*, the pharmacy win-dows now shuttered and drawn, something familiar stirred in her. They were in the Jewish quarter, she realized, taking in the high arch of one of the synagogues peeking over the top of a smaller building. They were simply approaching from a dif-ferent way than she had always come.

"Quickly," he said, urging her forward. She looked up at him puzzled, remembering the horrors she had witnessed in Kazimierz the night Mama had died. Surely they could not be safe here. But the danger was gone, because there were simply no Jews left to arrest.

They reached the corner of Miodowa Street where the mas-sive synagogue that had captivated her months earlier stood. Its windows were smashed, curtains blowing carelessly out through the jagged shards. They stared back at her like hollow eyes; shat-tered remnants of the stained-glass windows had formed on the ground beneath them like pools of tears. It looked so differ-ent from months earlier when it had been alight with song and prayer. *If only I had known*, Helena lamented. She might have gone inside and glimpsed the world Mama had kept secret. The

Jews were gone now, like some mystical fairy realm or ancient civilization that might never have existed at all.

Alek stopped in front of a hulking stone building that occupied an entire corner of the street. "Where are we going?" she asked finally.

"You helped me with the medicine. Now I can return the favor by getting some answers about your family." She opened her mouth to tell him that she wanted aid for Sam, not herself. Then she thought better of it. Alek continued, "This is the *gmina*, the Jewish center."

She looked at him with surprise. "After everything that has happened, it's still here?"

"For the moment, yes. You want information about your mother, and if anyone can help, the people who run this place can. They are quite pressed with other matters now, like helping those who have been moved to the ghetto find suitable quarters there, as well as caring for the sick and the orphaned." What, she wondered, could their own now-powerless leadership do for these hapless creatures, other than give them a bit of food or medicine? They could not offer shelter or safety.

He continued. "Their intentions are good, but I fear the *gmina* has become nothing but a puppet of the regime, processing the paperwork that ultimately will help the Nazis find us all," Alek added. "They'll close soon, now that all of the Jews have been sent across the river to the ghetto. But perhaps they have information to answer your questions." He eyed her levelly. "Or maybe you'd rather not go into the lion's den right now. You can still walk away from the truth."

"I'm already in—how much worse can it get?" He did not answer, his expression suggesting that she did not want to know.

Alek led her inside and up a spiraling marble staircase and knocked at a half-open door on the third floor. Behind the desk a wizened bald man in a skullcap faced away from them, loading books into boxes. "It's the Sabbath. We're closed." Then

he swiveled in his chair and, peering over the top of his reading glasses, smiled with more enthusiasm than she might have
thought his tired face could muster. "Alek!" He leaped to his
feet and pumped the younger man's hand heartily, the star on
his sleeve bobbing up and down.

While the men greeted each other, Helena took in the musty
office. There was an antique oak desk buried in stacks of yellowed paper, set against overflowing bookshelves that climbed to
the ceiling. Specks of dust danced in the pale light that filtered in
through the curtains. The walls were covered with photographs,
black-and-white-and-sepia images of weddings, family portraits
and pictures of holiday trips to the mountains and seaside. They
unfurled like a chronicle of the community now gone, giving
face to the hushed whispers that she had seemed to hear on the
street earlier and which hung from the rafters of the synagogue.
A polished silver menorah sat on the edge of the desk.

"As promised," Alek said, passing into the old man's palm
something she could not see.

"I wasn't expecting you, though with you one never knows
what to expect," the man said. "I wouldn't be here on a Saturday, but they've given us six days to pack and move." He gestured helplessly to the bookshelves.

"So you're going to the ghetto." Alek's voice was pained.

"I need to be where the people need help." It was not as if he
had a choice, Helena reflected.

"We won't take much of your time, Uncle. This young
woman is Helena Nowak, from Biekowice. Helena, this is Pan
Izakowicz, head of the Jewish community. Helena has some
questions. I'm hoping you can help her."

The man studied her. "You came all the way from the country?" His voice was curved with disbelief.

"She's stronger than she looks." Alek's tone was proud, almost proprietary. How did she look? Helena wondered. She had
always considered herself to be sturdy, but now she saw herself

compared to men like Alek and Sam as someone feminine and slight.

Before she could respond, Alek disappeared through the door, leaving her alone with the older man. "I'm sorry to bother you at a time like this…"

"Don't be. There isn't likely to be another sort of time." He gestured for her to sit. "What can I do for you?"

Helena glanced at the file cabinet behind him. Did she dare to ask? "The hospital that the Jewish community runs…"

"Used to run." A look of pain crossed his face.

"Yes. Well, I was wondering if the records were destroyed or if you might have them."

"Why, may I ask, is it of interest?"

"My mother, Ewa Nowak, was there."

"You are Jewish?" His voice was skeptical. It was more than just her appearance. He likely knew—or knew of—every Jewish family in the region. He did not know hers.

"Yes. I mean, no. I don't know," she confessed finally. "My mother is half-Jewish. Was." Would Helena ever get used to speaking about her in the past tense?

"There are no Jews in Biekowice. At least, none that we know of."

"She wasn't from Biekowice originally. She had kept her heritage a secret."

He rubbed his forehead. "I suppose it's not surprising. Jews and Poles have lived side by side for a thousand years in many places. They've become so intertwined that they scarcely have noticed. Take, for example, the crackers in the markets called *matzah*. That's a Hebrew word, derived from the unleavened bread we eat for Passover each spring. You didn't know, did you?" She shook her head. "For hundreds of years, our two peoples coexisted reasonably well." *Until now.*

He turned and riffled through the file cabinet behind him. A moment later he produced a sheet of paper. "There was a Nowak woman, from Biekowice no less, who came to be in the hospital last year. Younger than most."

"That's her." Helena's eyes filled with tears. It was all true.

Pan Izakowicz handed her the paper. She had hoped on some level that Wanda had been mistaken. But here it was in print, impossible to ignore: *Żyd*. It was not so much that Helena minded being Jewish—it brought her closer to Sam in a way that she liked. But she hated the idea that it had all been a lie.

She scanned the sheet. "It says here she was born in Krosno."

He nodded. "That is a few hours southwest from here."

"But…" Mama had always said she was from the far north—another lie. In fact, the whole truth had lain just a hundred miles from where they lived their entire lives.

"That region was prone to violence, even before the war. There were a number of pogroms during the tsarist years, and then more recently some Poles turned violently on the Jews there." Helena wondered if her father had saved Mama from danger, exactly as she had found Sam. Had Mama hidden the fact that she was Jewish from Tata, or had he known and loved her in spite of it?

"Do you think there might be relatives there, cousins perhaps?" she asked. Though the five of them often seemed quite enough, perhaps too many, Helena had often wished for an older sibling—a brother ideally—to help care for them and share the load. A glimmer of hope arose in her then, the prospect of the children having someone else.

But Pan Izakowicz shook his head. "The Jews from that village were among the first taken by the Germans—if any are still alive they might be in camps, but I don't know where."

So all of this time she might have known the truth and now it was too late. Helena handed the paper back to him silently. "And your mother never told you about being Jewish?" Helena shook her head. "I'm sure it is quite a shock. You know what this means, don't you, for your safety? I would forget about it, never speak of it again. I can even eliminate this record, though the Germans may have another in their central files. It is one thing for those of us who have been Jewish our whole lives to renounce our identity. But someone like you who never knew could hardly be blamed."

Helena considered this. She could just walk away. It would be understandable, even prudent under the circumstances, to obliterate any reference to their Jewish blood. But it would be a lie.

"You are alone?"

"No," she said, feeling somehow guilty that she had not yet mentioned her siblings. "I have three sisters and a brother." In that moment Ruth seemed like one of the younger children, her responsibility.

"Then take care of them, as your mother would have wanted. And do not speak of this again—for all of our sakes."

She jumped as the door to the office opened and Alek appeared. "I've come to collect you. This old man has got more to do than chat all day." But his voice was affable, tinged with a note of respect.

"Stop making trouble," Pan Izakowicz said. "And be careful. My brother would kill me if anything happened to you." The two men embraced and clapped each other on the back, lingering a bit longer, as if this might be the last time they met.

"Did he help you?" Alek asked when they had thanked Pan Izakowicz and walked from the building.

She considered the question. Pan Izakowicz had not been able to tell her anything new, but he had confirmed what Wanda had told her, the undeniable truth about her Jewish heritage. She wasn't sure, though, what she had been looking for in the first place—records would not tell the story of why Mama had come to hide. "I suppose." Pan Izakowicz had not been unkind, just practical—a man who could only save a few of his people, drops of water in an ocean of despair.

Alek led her away in a different direction than they had come.

She looked back over her shoulder at the remains of the synagogue. Even if the war ended and the allies managed somehow to drive the Germans out of Poland, it would never return to what it had been.

"The Jewish quarter is gone," she observed as they passed the shell of the synagogue.

He nodded grimly. "And the Jews in the ghetto will be, too, if the Americans don't come soon."

She wanted to remind him that this was why getting Sam out was so important. But he already knew. "You make it sound hopeless. And yet you fight." Admiration filled her then. People like Alek did more than simply survive—they rose up.

"Some say it is madness to struggle in the face of such hopelessness," he conceded with a nod. "My wife for one would probably rather I stay with her." *Wife.* She had not imagined Alek married. Hearing it, she felt more than a twinge of regret. In other circumstances, she would have introduced him to Ruth. "But when you love someone, their struggle is yours."

"Where are we going now?"

"*We* aren't going anywhere. I'm going to see you safely out of the city and get back to my work."

Helena bit her lip to keep from retorting that she could manage just fine on her own. "Wait, there's one other thing." She cleared her throat. "I'd like to sell this." She pulled the silver cup from her bag.

"You don't ask much, do you?" Alek's eyes widened. "You could be killed just for having that."

"I know."

His eyes narrowed. "How did you get it?"

Remembering the piles of belongings at the hospital, she understood his suspicion. "I didn't take it," she said hastily. "It was my mother's. Will you sell it for me?"

Alek shook his head. "No, but I will show you where you can."

Turning left, he led her down another street through a gap in two buildings. Behind the remnants of an abandoned factory sat a market not visible from the street. The tarp-covered stalls were not unlike those at home, but the market was many times bigger, sprawling across the rubbish-strewn lot. They had real food here, Helena noticed with surprise, fresh cuts of meat and other vegetables that she had not seen back home since before the war. The smell of roasting nuts tickled her nose, and for a moment she thought of buying a few for the children. But the price listed was ten times what she might have imagined.

The black market, she realized. She had heard of goods being traded, and had seen it peripherally when she had gone to the Mariacki Cathedral looking for Alek. The trading activity was everywhere. One woman unbuttoned her blouse without modesty to pull out the sausages she'd smuggled in an overstuffed brassiere. Another hitched her skirts to tuck her purchases in her stockings and hem. Helena shuddered. It didn't matter if one was caught smuggling one ounce or one hundred—the penalty would be the same: swift and severe.

A truck pulled up and began unloading boxes off the back and people ran to grab them. "What's that?"

"I've no idea. And they don't know, either. People will buy anything just to have it these days."

Helena hung back, watching uncertainly. "You haven't done this before, have you?" Alek asked. She shook her head, feeling her cheeks burn. "That's understandable. None of us were born to this life." He gestured across the market. "Go to the silver merchants there in the corner. Take it to Trojecki, not Lempe—he's a crook. Hand it to him still in the sack. And whatever he offers you, turn it down, take the cup back and walk away."

"But I want to sell it."

"Trust me. It's going to be too low. And he'll come after you. He isn't going to let an object like that get away."

Helena walked to the corner he indicated, feeling his eyes

on her. "Pan Trojecki?" She turned back, helplessly, looking to Alek for guidance, but he had disappeared.

The yellow-toothed man sitting on a low stool lifted his head. *"Tak?"*

She handed him the bag, then wiped the clamminess from her palms. He peered inside and though his expression remained impassive his eyes flickered. She realized that even the attempt to sell it brought its own danger. "I found this by the riverbank," she lied clumsily, hoping to ward off questions.

"What am I to do with that Jew metal?" the man asked. She was seized with the urge to reach out and slap him. But it was a bluff—she could see the glint in his eye as he appraised the quality of the workmanship, the thickness of the silver.

"Twenty," Trojecki said finally.

Her breath caught. Twenty was more than she had ever seen. It would buy food for weeks.

Then she remembered Alek's words. "No, thank you." She took the sack from his hands and started away, hoping she had not made a mistake.

"Wait! Twenty-five."

"Zlotys?"

"You were thinking dollars?" the man mocked.

Helena shook her head, ignoring his sarcasm. She cringed as he fingered the cup with crude, unappreciative hands. Though she had only seen it once before in her life, never even known its name, it seemed part of her, the link to Mama and the past and all of the secrets she could no longer explain. Her mother's Jewish background, though secret, had meant something to her, enough to keep the cup despite the dangers it might bring.

Helena snatched it back. "I've changed my mind."

"If you're trying to haggle..."

"I'm not." She put the Kiddush cup underneath her coat and turned to leave before the man could speak further. Around the corner, she stopped, shaking. She had wanted to get rid of the object to sever herself from this sudden unwanted history. But it seemed forged to her now, hot against her skin as if screaming out its presence to passersby, betraying her. She slipped it back into her bag.

Alek reappeared at the entrance to the market. "So you did it?"

She shook her head. "The price was too low." She was too embarrassed to tell him the truth—not being able to sell the cup felt sentimental and weak, and she did not want him to think less of her for it.

"That's too bad. I was hoping for a commission." She cocked her head. "Five zlotys. Standard practice. Anyone else and I would have taken ten. It's not for me. The money would buy food and supplies for the troops."

The troops. He sounded as if he was talking about a real army. "You won't win." She did not mean to be rude. "The Germans have rolled over half of Europe. How can a few boys—"

"Men," he interrupted correcting her, "and women."

"Make a difference?" she finished.

He started walking again. "So we should just lie down and die?" She did not answer. "We are showing the Germans, and our people, that as long as there is spirit in the heart, we are not defeated."

"You're a patriot."

"Don't make too much of me, or any one person," he cautioned, and she knew he was speaking of Sam. Helena blushed, feeling rebuked. "I'm just an ordinary man, dispensable as any other." There was a note of foreboding to his voice. "It's what we do when we find ourselves in such times that counts. Some will help the Germans, and that is unforgivable treason. Others will hide in their basements and that is okay, too." He did not sound as if he believed this last part. Would she have simply hidden, she wondered, if she had not found Sam and learned the truth about Mama?

They reached the corner where the *aleje* intersected with the road she took out of town and she knew they were to part ways. "You can manage from here?"

"Yes, but about Sam…" She blurted his name aloud without meaning to. "That is, the soldier. You didn't say how you were going to help him."

Alek's mouth pulled downward. "I wish I could. You did as you promised and proved I can trust you. But things have gotten much worse and this is a critical moment for our cause." His face grew stormy. "I can't do anything now that might compromise our entire southern operation."

She felt a painful thud, a kick to the chest. "But you said if I proved trustworthy you would help."

"Under normal circumstances, with fighting and weather, it would have been hard enough. But right now, it is impossible." He shook his head, unwilling to give her false hope.

She stood motionless. Alek had seemed so strong and confident that she just assumed he would be able to help Sam. "Are people getting out anymore? Ordinary people, I mean."

"There are no more transits. Better to wait it out here and hope for the best." He sounded oddly like Ruth then. "The war has to end sometime."

Does it? she wanted to ask. War had become such a default state she could not remember life before. And even if it did end, then what? Things could not go back to the way they had been.

"Here," he said, holding out a small parcel to her. The smell of sausage tickled her nose like a forgotten dream. "It's all I can spare." Helena hesitated. Had her hunger been so apparent? She did not want to take charity from him, but she could not let pride interfere with her getting additional nourishment for the children.

"I'm afraid," she confessed, more openly than she should have to this man she barely knew.

"You are wise to fear. Only the fool doesn't. But don't hide from your fear. Wear it like a cloak of armor."

"Thank you," she said. She wanted to ask him if there was anything else that might be done, so that she would have some morsel of information for Sam, some hope to give him.

Sirens whirred, growing louder in the distance. Helena turned toward the sound. "Run!" Alek hissed behind her. When she turned back, he was gone and she could not tell in which direction he had fled. It was as if he had disappeared before her eyes. The wailing grew louder, filling her ears, the danger almost upon her. Then obeying his words, she ran, too. The pounding of her soles echoed against the pavement and she kept going, heedless of who heard, desperate to get away. She ran until the city disappeared and the sirens faded into the wind behind her.

17

Ruth breathed in deeply as she walked past the barn, taking in the crispness of the air. Tonight was Christmas Eve and Helena was home, instead of traipsing off into the woods. Her muscles relaxed slightly, as they always did when they were all together and in one place. It was nearly noon, though, and market would be closing early for the holiday. She quickened her pace. She needed a bit of smoked trout, and some dill, if there was any to be had.

Then she stopped and cried aloud, her voice echoing into the emptiness of the field ahead. Mama was dead. Yet here she was planning *Wigilia* dinner, as though it still mattered. Suddenly her own breathing, carrying on when Mama could not, seemed disloyal. She looked upward at the sky, wondering where Mama really was now. Once she might have thought she knew the answer, but her faith, everything she once believed, felt shattered into pieces too small to reassemble. Perhaps they should not have the holiday at all. But she thought of Dorie's face, so excited as she explained to Karolina the tiny gifts that would be coming that evening. The children needed Christmas, and so she would keep going for them.

Fifteen minutes later, Ruth neared the village. At the corner by the school, she stopped, raising her hand to her mouth to stifle a cry. Hanging from the wooden frame where the children's swings had once been was a rope—a man dangled from the end, neck curved in a grotesque angle. Though his face was twisted, she recognized him vaguely as someone she had seen at market. She had always imagined death to be peaceful and slumberlike, but the man who hung from the makeshift gallows here had his mouth open and contorted in a silent scream. His pants were soiled front and back, perhaps the greatest indignity.

"What happened?" she asked aloud to no one in particular over the nausea that rose in her throat. People hurried by pretending not to see, as if nonplussed by the scene that had turned the peaceful square into a horror novel. Did they fear his cruel death was somehow contagious?

"Hoarding," a woman beside her whispered as she passed. Ruth's blood froze. The very crime of which the policeman had accused her—and which Helena had, in fact, committed. Reflexively, Ruth crossed herself. If the Germans would do this just for hoarding, what might the penalty be for stealing food for an American soldier?

Ruth forced herself to press onward, pushing the image of the man from her mind. Market was closing when she arrived, the sellers packing away their remaining foodstuffs and returning home early to enjoy the holiday with their own families, at least as much as they were able under the grim circumstances. The fishmonger was already gone. She would have to make do with what she had already purchased. Dejectedly, she turned away.

She turned toward the church at the top of the square, elevated slightly above the rest of the town. A good-size building and larger than the town might have needed, it had an unbroken sandstone facade, rising to a rounded cupola. Church bells no longer rang out as they had in past years but a slow line of parishioners streamed from the front door of the church, leaving an early mass. Ruth watched longingly. She had loved going to church as a family. Huddling together in the warm close pew, she had felt for a brief time like a part of something.

Even after they had stopped attending Sunday service, Ruth had made a secret weekly pilgrimage on her own until Helena had found out. It seemed ironic—confession itself being a secret. She had gone persistently, though in truth she had nothing new to say because nothing worth confessing ever happened, not here. She felt selfish, taking time away from her chores just to talk about herself. That was why she had hidden it. But it was the one time she could be sure that someone was listening.

Ruth moved closer to the church now, noting that the nativity that stood out front in past years was missing. Her eyes rose to the simple metal cross atop it and she thought of kindly Father Dominik, who had patted their heads and given them the occasional sweet as children. She passed the small graveyard that wrapped behind the church. The too-close stones lilted toward one another, as if being pushed from the ground below by unseen hands. Her stomach tightened. She had insisted on the proper stone for Tata over Helena's objections, using too much of the little money they had to pay for it, rather than allowing him to be buried in a pauper's grave. And she had chosen a spot by the edge of the cemetery deliberately, hoping that space might remain beside him when their mother's time came. Now that would never be.

Ruth walked against the tide of departing parishioners into the emptying church. Her eyes traveled to the front pew where Piotr's family sat on Sundays, toward the confessional. Once, the pouring out of her sins, even the little everyday ones, had brought her much solace. But it seemed pointless now. Instead, she went to the knave and lit a candle and she was praying then, for Mama's soul and for them all.

She looked up, wiping away a tear. The door leading to the rectory was open. Pushing Helena's admonition from her mind, she walked toward it. The gray-haired priest looked up, his expression instantly guarded. "I'm sorry," Father Dominik said as she neared, "but the charity baskets were given yesterday."

"I'm not here for charity," she said, struggling not to sound indignant. Her cheeks stung. She pulled her hood back. "It's me, Ruth Nowak." Had she really changed so much?

His watery eyes blinked once. "Yes, of course." She waited for him to rebuke her for not having come to church in so long. "How can I help you, my child?"

She swallowed. "My mother died."

His brow furrowed. "I had not heard. I'm so sorry."

"It only just happened."

"Death is very hard to make sense of..." he began, resorting to platitudes. "She was in the Jewish hospital, wasn't she?" His tone made it sound as though that had somehow contributed to her death. "Well, she is with God now."

"Do you remember her when she was younger?" Ruth was hungry for information, memories that might add to her own now that she could no longer do so.

"Your mother moved here not long after I came to the parish. She was from the north, I think. Your father had been on an errand there and had been taken by her beauty."

Ruth smiled at the familiar story. But how had Tata approached her mother, a strange woman he did not know? And how had he persuaded her to leave everything to go with him?

Remembering the man who hung from the swing set, anxiety flooded her once more. "Do you think we should leave?"

"I'm not sure I understand."

"Do you think it will be safe for people here in the village? Like that man who was hoarding..."

The priest raised his hand, willing her to be silent. A guarded look flickered across his face. "Each must follow his own conscience."

Isn't that what you are here for? Ruth wanted to ask. "But if one wanted to go, surely there are ways." She searched the priest's face, pleading.

His eyes widened. "I'm sure I don't know what you're talking about. I will call around to see your siblings," he said, in a way that suggested they were finished. Ruth opened her mouth to tell him that was not necessary. She was the only one who put stock in the church, and if the priest visited the house Helena would realize that she had come here against her wishes. Looking at his face, though, she knew she had nothing to worry about. There would be no visit. Her charitable side wanted to believe the priest was too busy with the work that the war had made for the church, so many needing help. But even without the war, the orphaned Nowak children were not a priority for the parish.

"Thank you." She walked down the aisle between the pews. The Virgin Mary seemed to stare down at her, demanding repentance. Ruth slipped from the church into the cold and dark and made her way to the edge of town, heading toward home.

As she started across the open field, her skin prickled with awareness. She turned sharply. A figure appeared from behind a tree, then disappeared from sight, dark and shadowy. The policeman. Surely he had better things to do than follow her. He was watching her, though, as if waiting for something to happen that she herself did not quite yet know. She quickened her step, praying that he would not come after her. When she reached the gate by the barn, she glanced over her shoulder. He was not there. But her relief was short-lived. Surely he would come again.

Calming her breath, she walked into the house. She was touched to see that Michal and Dorie had set the table and lit the candles, giving the room a merry feel. Michal's eyes dropped to Ruth's basket, which was as empty as if she had not gone to market at all, then darted quickly away.

"Where's Helena?" Ruth asked, looking around the quieter-than-usual cottage.

Michal shrugged. "She went out. Said that she would be back soon." Ruth's indignation rose. Helena must have gone to see the soldier again, on Christmas Eve no less. Struggling not to comment aloud, Ruth took off her coat and set about finishing the *babka* cake she'd made earlier with a dusting of sweetened flour.

A few minutes later the front door burst open. "Merry Christmas!" Helena strode into the cottage, her arms filled with a small evergreen.

"A tree!" Dorie exclaimed jubilantly as Helena set it in the corner and fetched the stand.

"Tee!" Karolina echoed, toddling toward it.

"But…" Ruth looked at her puzzled. "We agreed just to decorate the mantel."

"I know, but I thought…" She gestured toward the children, who jumped up and down merrily.

"You did what you wanted. Again." *And now you're the hero for it.* Resentment welled in her. Then watching the children, she softened and walked to the cedar chest. "Here." She handed Michal the box containing the few glass ornaments Mama had collected over the years. "Be careful," she admonished as the children set about hanging them quickly. In other years it would have taken hours to decorate the tree, but they could not spare the fruit and nuts they had once strung. The tree looked naked with just half a dozen or so ornaments. The children did not seem to mind, though, as they danced around it with excitement.

Helena went to the stove and lifted the lid on the pot that was simmering there. "*Golabki?* We always have carp," Helena said pointedly.

"There was none to be had. So tonight," Ruth snapped, "we are having cabbage rolls." The children watched, the tree forgotten, consternation on their faces. There was a level of acrimony between the twins they had not before seen, unheard of on the holiday when fences were to be mended. "Why don't you go look for the first star?" Ruth suggested, and they scampered to the window. By tradition, the *Wigilia* meal could not commence until they had seen the first star. She turned back to her sister, trying to find a way to ease the tension. Quarreling on the holiday was a poor omen for the year to come. But the gulf between them was too wide to bridge.

"I see it!" Dorie cried a few minutes later. "The first star!"

"'Tar!" Karolina echoed, pointing and jumping.

"Then let's sit down."

They all came to the table. Ruth produced a single *oplatek*, which she divided into pieces and gave to each of them. The breaking of the thin wafer between two people was a Christmas Eve ritual intended to symbolize forgiveness and letting go of the past. She reached across the table to Helena and extended the wafer. "Peace," her sister said as they broke the tiny piece between them. But the words were hollow, the kiss on her cheek stiff. How could one cracker heal so much division?

Ruth went to the kitchen and picked up the serving dish. Once *Wigilia* had consisted of more than a half dozen different seafood recipes. Now the only dish was *golabki*. She had boiled the last few cabbage leaves, which she had feared would be too tough for eating, then filled them with a savory mixture made from the apples she'd purchased at market and some ground nuts. She had been quite proud of the result, a plate of delicious cabbage rolls.

"No sauce?" Helena asked mildly when she had set out the feast.

Something burned white-hot in Ruth then and she stood, knocking several of the *golabki* from the plate beside her. "How dare you?" The children's eyes widened in surprise. Ruth hated for them to see this side of her, especially now. But she had slaved to make the best meal she could. She walked into the bedroom, trembling.

Helena followed, closing the bedroom door behind her. "Ruti, let's not fight on Christmas."

But Ruth was too far gone for that. Suddenly, it was about something much bigger than her cooking—or Helena's lack of gratitude. "You saw him again, didn't you?"

Helena's cheeks flushed. "I didn't mean to. I even left a note telling him I wouldn't come again. But then everything happened with Mama, and, well, I was so sad I just couldn't bear it."

"So you went to him." Helena had a man's arms in which to seek solace, Ruth realized with resentment. "Once or more than once?"

Before Helena could answer, Michal knocked tentatively on the door, then opened it. "Please don't... That is, it's Christmas and you're upsetting the girls."

"We'll be right out," Helena replied, waving him away. When Michal had closed the door again, she turned back to Ruth. "I have to help him," Helena said, her face animated in a way Ruth had never seen before. "His work is so important to the war." Then her expression grew serious. "But it's more than that... The soldier, he's Jewish."

"Is that so?" Ruth's lip curled involuntarily, her dislike of the soldier hardening. She waved her hand. "You said you would stop going. You lied." The words hung between them, heavy with accusation.

"I'm sorry, I tried not to go. But I won't abandon him, Ruth. I can't. I'm all he has."

Ruth's voice rose, and this time she did not try to control it. "You care about him more than us."

"That's not true! But yes, I do care about him." Helena was open and exposed in a way she never had been before. "Why must it always be one or the other?"

"Because life is about choices." She understood this in a way

that Helena did not. Ruth searched desperately for an argument
that would convince Helena to stop seeing the soldier. But Helena was loyal—it was one of the things Ruth loved best about
her, even as it infuriated her now.

They stared at each other, the issue looming unresolved between them. "I'm sorry about what I said about the cabbage
rolls." Helena shifted to an easier topic. "It was completely
thoughtless of me." Helena was genuinely contrite and she did
not try to justify what she had done. She held out her hand. Ruth
took it and returned to the table with her, somewhat mollified.
Dorie had picked up the cabbage rolls from the table, dusting
imaginary specks of dirt away. She stared hard at the table, not
meeting her sisters' eyes.

Michal squeezed her hand under the table as she sat down.
"They're delicious," he said a moment later. He would not, she
knew, ask about the quarrel for fear of restarting it.

Ruth sniffed. Cooking with little was hardly new. Mama
had taught her well how to stretch the broth for soup and other
meals. She had prided herself on being able to roll the dough for
pierogies thinner than any woman in the province. Of course, it
had been easier then; when the land was plentiful and not picked
over by starving people and animals, they had eaten with the
seasons—root vegetables in the long winter months, carp and
trout fresh from the stream when the waters flowed in spring.

They ate in silence. "Mischa," Helena said. "Remember the
year that Papa said the angels had brought you a lump of coal?"

Ruth smiled, joining in at the attempt to make light for the
children. "Of course, that was before he gave you the beautiful sled he'd made."

"That was funny," Michal said, his face brightening.

"I bet you didn't think so at the time," Dorie rejoined.

When they'd finished eating, Dorie and Michal cleared the
plates, more helpful than usual, mindful that Christmas gifts
were coming. "Come," she said when they'd finished, walking

to the chair by the fireplace and calling the children to her. The girls piled on her lap and Michal sat by her feet on the hearth. "*Mary*, a virgin, was living in Galilee of Nazareth and was engaged to be married to *Joseph*, a Jewish carpenter," she began. "An angel visited her and explained to her that she would conceive a son by the power of the *Holy Spirit*. She would carry and give birth to this child and she would name him Jesus." The children listened raptly as she told the Christmas story, trying to remember the words exactly as Mama had said them and get the inflection just right.

As she finished, there was a ringing sound; Helena held aloft the small bell that signaled an angel had left gifts at the door. The children rushed to claim them, discarding the brown paper wrappings feverishly. Ruth helped Karolina to unwrap the simple rag doll she had made. There were books for Dorie and a secondhand pair of boots for Michal that she'd managed to barter for some knitted mittens at market as Helena had suggested. Each child got a piece of candy, too. It should have been more, Ruth lamented. But they laughed and smiled excitedly, grateful for what was given.

As the children examined their gifts, Ruth gazed toward the door. For a moment it seemed that Tata might walk in. She turned toward the kitchen, straining to see Mama at the stove where she once had stood. Above the children's heads, her eyes met Helena's and held, their thoughts one, shared sadness transcending the differences between them. She batted back tears, unwilling to dampen the children's holiday.

Helena cleared her throat. "How about some *koledy*?" she suggested to Ruth, who had the better voice. Ruth nodded and began to sing, "Today in Bethlehem..." The children joined in, their voices gaining strength and rising to the rafters. When they finished the carol, she quickly began another, as though the music could keep out the sadness that surrounded them and maintain at least for a bit longer the pretext of Christmas.

"Off to bed with you," Ruth told the children when the last carol had been sung and the candles on the table burned low. They bounded to the bedroom still excited. Ruth smiled inwardly, pleased that they had made it a good *Wigilia*, after all. She kissed them each and tucked them in.

"Please tell us one more story," pled Dorie.

"But I've already told you the story of Christmas."

"Not that story. Our Christmas story." Dorie was asking about their Christmases past, the happy days that she could not quite remember and the spaces that Ruth and Helena could not quite fill.

"Once upon a time, there was a mother and a father, with five little children," she began. "Each Christmas, they had a great feast of carp and mushroom soup." As the children's eyes grew heavy, she tried to weave a tale of happier times that would not remind the children of too many things they now lacked.

When they were asleep, Ruth returned to the main room where Helena sat in the rocking chair before the fire. She considered raising the issue of the soldier again, then stopped, realizing it was futile. She hesitated, thinking of the man she had seen hanging from the rope, and Father Dominik's refusal to help. Maybe Helena was right about the dangers here. She wanted to tell Helena that she was ready to go, and that they needed to leave now.

"Helena, about leaving..." She stopped midsentence and looked over. Helena's eyes were closed and her mouth open, snoring slightly. Ruth took the extra blanket from the cedar trunk and covered her sister gently, straightening her head so it didn't press against the wood. Then she blew out the candles and went back into the bedroom.

18

The children were gone.

Ruth had put them to bed earlier, as she did every night. Then she had returned to the kitchen to wash the dishes and sweep. Not waiting for Helena to return from the city, Ruth changed into her nightgown and made her way to the bedroom. But when she pulled back the duvet, the bed was empty, the imprints of their tiny bodies still warm. She choked on the scream that seemed to rush forth from her bowels.

She sat bolt upright in the darkness, reaching wildly for the children that lay on either side of her. Feeling their warm skin, her body went slack with relief. It had been a dream, the same one she'd had each night since Helena had broken the news about their mother. Thankfully her scream had been imaginary, too, and had not woken them.

Ruth lay back down, trembling. The children were safe, but everything was far from all right. Mama was dead. There was always a moment each morning as she opened her eyes when she did not remember the truth. Then it quickly faded and the awful realization rushed over her anew like cold water.

Were they any worse off with Mama gone? Ruth drew the faintly musty blanket closer around her. Mama had been in the hospital for so long that the children had grown accustomed to functioning without her. As long as she had been in the hospital, though, there had been the thinnest sliver of hope she'd get well. There was some part of Ruth that had known, even as she'd kept her mother's dresses freshly hanging in the armoire, that she would never return. But she'd clung desperately to the vision of Mama walking through the door, putting her arms around Ruth and letting her be the child again. Now it was clear that it would always be this way, all of the responsibility their parents would have borne now eternally hers and Helena's.

Ruth lay awake in the darkness, still shaken from the dream. Helena slept on the other side of the children like a bookend, her breathing even and uninterrupted. She smiled and mumbled, then laughed faintly. Ruth bristled. There was so little to be happy about these days, even in one's sleep. She must be dreaming of her soldier. Ruth considered the man she had never seen with a twinge of envy, a shadowy image of a tall, handsome soldier forming in her mind. Why Helena? It might have been Ruth who had stumbled upon the chapel if she had been the adventurous one, instead of shut up in the house taking care of the children. But it was Helena who was always out and finding things, even when they were little. No, he hadn't chosen Helena at all. She had simply been at the right place at the right time.

Karolina stirred beside her, pushing her small feet against Ruth's stomach with surprising strength, as though she was trying to work her way inside. Pressed by the need for the toilet, Ruth sat up again reluctantly. She put one foot on the icy floor, feeling for her shoes. Then she froze. Someone was there, standing in the doorway to the bedroom. Ruth stood up with a start, wondering if Michal had gone to check the fire, but he snored undisturbed beside her.

It was someone else, Ruth realized. Her breath caught. Had the policeman come again? She hesitated, wanting to make a break for the gun on the mantelpiece but not daring to step away from the children. "Hello?" she called softly into the darkness, fighting the urge to scream, lest she wake the others. There was no response.

Ruth steeled herself, then took a step forward, still barefoot. A shape filled the doorway to the bedroom, familiar and unmistakable. Her heart soared. "Tata…" She waited for him to speak. He stood silently staring, as if exhorting her to do something. She stepped toward him. "Tata," she said again, closing her eyes and reaching out. Her arms closed around cold air. When she looked up again, the shadowy image had disappeared.

Ruth sunk to the chair by the door, weeping now. The image was gone, but it lingered in her mind with a certainty that chilled her. Was she going mad? She wanted to believe that Tata had come. Ruth had desperately wished that Mama would visit her in a dream, to tell her what to do or even just sit with her for a bit. But it was as if that part of her was blocked.

Ruth wiped her eyes and bent to put on her shoes. She walked from the bedroom, the smell of the pine boughs that still sat on the mantel two days after Christmas filling her nostrils. She put on her cape and walked outside to the toilet. As she returned to the house, Sergeant Wojski popped unbidden into her mind. The encounter with him, his awful hands drawing closer, replayed nightly in her dreams. Ruth had told Helena that he had been to the house, but she could not bring herself to share the rest of the story. Would Helena think that she allowed the attention, even invited it? She had done what was needed and distracted him so he would not notice the children—but that didn't make her feel any less shameful.

She returned to the house and splashed water on her face at

the basin. As she neared the bed, Ruth studied the sleeping figures in the predawn light. Her eyes rested on Helena. Something had shifted between them since Helena had told her about the soldier, a distrust, silent and persistent. Helena had kept a secret. Or maybe more than one: where had she really been the night she said she was trapped in the hospital? Though they had always been different, she and Helena had always been united by their common goal of keeping the family whole. Ruth would do anything to see them survive and stay together—but would her sister? Once she thought she knew the answer. Now she was not so sure.

Ruth climbed back into bed and drew her knees to her chest for warmth. Would Helena simply decide one day to keep going and not come back? Her sister was not demonstrative, spare with her hugs and affection. But there was a caring in the way she tirelessly made sure they had enough wood and food. And she was always thinking three steps ahead, anticipating the worst, looking around the corner for anything that might be a menace to their safety and well-being.

No, Helena loved them. But did she now love the soldier more? Helena had never been interested in boys—until now. There was something about this man that made her sister willing to risk everything else in order to help him. And she wanted them all to leave, an idea which was undoubtedly influenced by the soldier. Go to America, become a teacher, Helena had said. *Become.* Ruth had never considered in her life the notion of becoming anything, other than perhaps a wife and a mother, dreams which seemed out of the question now. It was always Helena who had been going and doing.

Here at least they had the house and one another. Why couldn't Helena see that? Because she'd always been restless, wanted bigger and more. Even before the soldier, she had liked going to the city each week, not just to see Mama, Ruth suspected, but for the excitement. And she would not give up, surely, on the notion of getting the children out. Helena was tenacious. When she got ahold of an idea, she clung to it stubbornly, a dog with a piece of meat in its clenched jaws. Ruth could continue to resist, but Helena would wear her down, or simply go around her. She might take the children herself and go with the soldier, leaving Ruth all alone.

Ruth climbed from bed again, all hope of sleeping gone. It was not yet dawn, but the sky behind the hills had begun to fade. Suddenly restless, she dressed and went outside. She paused uncertainly, surveying the trees silhouetted black against the sky. Fresh snow coated the ground. It was too early, in fact, for market, even if she had not used their ration coupons for the week. Impulsively, she started toward the hill. The fresh air was brisk and heady. Her hands grew light because there was no one clinging to them. Ahead the silence of the forest beckoned.

Ruth started into the trees. At the knoll the path split—the wider fork to the left, she recalled, joined the main road to the city. Overhead, a wind she could not feel tossed the tops of the pine trees, causing them to dance wildly with one another.

She walked down the narrower path, navigating between the fallen branches and stones. She had not understood until that moment how arduous the journey Helena took each week really was. Dawn had broken, but the trees clung to the darkness, holding on to the night for a bit longer. Ruth's ankle twisted and she caught herself to keep from falling down into the snow. Moisture seeped into the cracks in her boots. This was not her world, and for a moment she considered turning around and going back before anyone realized she was gone.

But then she stood and kept walking, the trees seeming to pull her in and hurl her forward. Suddenly she was not timid, but walked lightly among the roots and brush as she had when she was a girl, playing with her sister, before she had become ladylike and afraid. So this was what it was like for Helena—despite the harshness of the path and weather, she felt almost free.

It was not until she spied the chapel that she realized her plan: if Helena could not part from the soldier, then Ruth would do it for her. She would tell this man to leave them alone. If he truly loved Helena, he would not want to endanger her further.

Ruth reached the clearing, then stopped, imagining what it must have been like for her sister, coming to the chapel for the first time. The ground was covered by a fine, loose coating of snow and, looking at the unbroken white, Ruth knew that Helena had not been here in the past day. Ruth hesitated, ready to turn back for home, but a silent hand inside seemed to push her forward, stiffening her resolve.

Ruth knocked on the door of the chapel, and when there was no response she pushed it open. The soldier sleeping lay in the corner. He did not look intimidating as she expected, curled on one side, his forearm under his head for a pillow. He was handsome, beautiful, really, in a boyish way, with dark curly hair and a faint smile even as he slept. A dog nestled by his feet dark with a lone white paw, as if dipped in flour. As she took in the man's mouth and jawline, she was swept off her feet with a desire that she had not known since Piotr, or maybe ever. Her breath caught.

The man wore a familiar brown scarf around his neck, she noticed then. It was the one she had knitted for Piotr. Anger rose in her. How dare Helena give her scarf to this stranger? Her sister would not stop, it seemed, until she had taken everything.

The man stirred in his sleep. As he did, the dog leaped to its feet. It eyed her warily and she wondered if it might try to bite her. But it scurried past her and out the door.

As Ruth stepped backward to avoid the animal, her foot brushed against a familiar teacup that had been left on the ground. The sound reverberated throughout the chapel.

"Lena?" The soldier opened his eyes suddenly. Alarmed, he reached toward his waist. A gun, she realized.

"Shh. It's okay," she soothed, and at the sight of her he seemed to relax slightly. She felt as if she knew the soldier already; it had not occurred to her that coming here to confront this stranger unexpectedly might be dangerous. "I'm…"

He was staring at her, puzzled. The cape, she realized. The bright blue was such a sharp contrast from Helena's crude brown wool coat. Not wanting to alarm him, she slipped the cape from her shoulders and let it fall to the floor. His face relaxed.

"Lena, come here," he said, and her sister's ordinarily plain name was so full and sensuous on his sleepy tongue that it almost made Ruth blush. Ruth stepped forward and opened her mouth to tell the soldier who she really was, and demand that he stop seeing her sister.

Then she faltered. There was something about the broad contour of his shoulders that reminded her of Piotr. All of her anger dissolved and another wave of longing rose up inside her. She moved closer. This, or something like it, should have been hers. She desperately wanted to hold him just for a moment and feel what it was like to be inside a man's arms again, to feel a touch that was not about threat or shame.

She sat down on the cold ground beside him, not daring to breathe.

"Helena, are you all right?" he managed.

"Yes." The lie was out before she could stop it. But she did not want to lose the softness of his voice that came with his thinking that she was her sister. She reached out and, almost involuntarily, stroked his shoulder. Her hand jerked back, as if on its own. Then she reached out and touched him again.

At her touch, his eyes widened. It was her hands; they had always been so much improbably stronger than her sister's and the intensity of her touch was unexpected to him. She softened her caress to match Helena's, and his face softened. She had forgotten how it felt to have this power over a man. Suddenly she was light-headed.

The soldier smiled sleepily. He was handsome with a kind of

gentleness that she had not seen in Piotr. He looked at her with a light in his eyes that made her heart flutter. But Ruth knew that it was for her sister. She was seized with the impulse to lie down beside him. As she did, his hand ran over her back and it was as if his touch was wiping her clean, erasing the horrible stain of all that had happened with the policeman and Piotr, and making her anew.

Then she stopped. This was madness.

But the soldier reached for her hand. *"Kochana,"* he said in surprisingly good Polish. *Darling.* That one word told her every-thing she needed to know about what had transpired between this man and Helena. It belied the extent of the feelings he had for her sister, and it seemed to confirm everything that Ruth had suspected, her worst nightmare that her sister was indeed planning to leave without her.

Ruth considered again telling him who she really was and confronting him. But he reached out and pulled her closer. His scent and the warmth of his touch overwhelmed her. "I…" she began, but his lips were on hers now with an intensity that in-dicated it was not the first time. She waited for him to realize the difference, that the kiss was not Helena's. Instead, pushed forward by his desire, his hands traveled lower. He rolled on top of her now. The heat that rose in her as he lifted her skirt was reminiscent of the one time with Piotr in the barn. But Piotr's crude touch was nothing like this. The soldier's gentle fingers stroked her skin, inflaming her. She should stop the sol-dier, as she had Piotr, and tell him who she really was. She was too far gone now, though, wanting this to happen; his move-ments were frenetic, even as he tried to restrain himself and not hurt her. She found herself carried away by desire, a moment of wanting and being wanted, of feeling whole again in a way she hadn't thought possible. To know hands on her once again that meant tenderness and not threat. There was a sharp pain as he entered her, then a dull ache that seemed to radiate outward to her stomach and legs. Passion swept over her, washing away her jealously, her grief. She buried her head in his neck and let herself be carried by it.

When it was over, he lay motionless, his torso still pressed against hers. Then he rolled aside, still breathing heavily. "Darling," he repeated. "I'm so sorry, I never should have..." The remorse in his voice told Ruth that he and Helena had never let things go this far. "Are you okay?"

Ruth nodded, praying that he would mistake her silence for passion, or being overwhelmed by the moment. She needed to get out of there, quickly. But he threw one arm over her neck, preventing her escape. Then he wrapped his fingers around her own. "I love you," he said, and the intensity of his words broke her heart, for he meant them to her sister and not her.

He closed his eyes as if drained by their coupling, returning to the sleep she'd interrupted. She watched him, imagining. There had been an instant connection between them, a magic to his touch and the way their bodies fit together, as if they had known each other for ages. Perhaps she might be the right woman for him, after all. She closed her eyes, lulled by the warmth of his arms.

Ruth was awakened by a scream. She reached instinctively for the children, thinking that she was back home in Biekowice and that the Nazis had come. But her hand brushed the hard earth and she sat up, remembering lying with the soldier, their bodies pressed together. The clouds had shifted, freeing the early-morning sun, and the pale light now flooded the chapel.

The soldier was sitting upright, staring at her neck. He had seen her clearly now, seen the butterfly birthmark, and knew she wasn't Helena. His eyes widened. "You... Who are you?" he managed finally.

Ruth covered herself. Surely after everything that had happened, the passion that had transpired between them, he could not be angry. But his face was a mask of horror, mouth contorted with revulsion. She stood, buttoning her dress with shaking hands. She wanted to make him understand why she had done it, but that was impossible for she did not know herself. Should she apologize? She opened her mouth but no sound came out.

"I'm sorry," she managed at last, her voice barely a whisper.

"Get out!" he roared with an anger she had never heard.

Then she turned and ran.

19

Ruth raced from the chapel down the hill, stumbling over stones and fallen branches. After several minutes, she paused to catch her breath. She listened for footsteps, wondering if the soldier would come after her, imagining he might apologize for his outburst. But there was silence. How dare he? It was simply inconceivable that he would reject her, or like rough, tomboyish Helena better. For a moment, he had seemed different than other men. But once he had taken what he wanted he had pushed her away. He had been willing, even eager, yet he acted as if it had been her fault. No, he had used *her*, used both her and Helena, really. What other explanation could there possibly be?

Helena. Her sister could never know. Would the soldier tell her? Ruth's body ached in a way she had never before experienced, magnifying her shame.

She started forward once more. Her feet slid from under her and she landed on her bottom with a thump. Mud soiled her dress, icy dampness soaking through the fabric. This indignity was more than she could bear, and she burst out in tears, not caring who heard her racking sobs as they echoed through the trees. From a branch above a starling called back its own sad tale in refrain.

Finally, Ruth stood up, brushing the tears from her eyes, then the dirt from her bottom. She resumed walking, her sadness turning to anger once again, indignantly burning low and intense in her stomach. She had given the soldier everything and he had cast her out, wanting only Helena. Who did he think he was?

As she reached the edge of the forest, Ruth slowed, willing herself to breathe normally. She smoothed her hair. Coming from the forest would be remarkable enough, and she did not want to heighten any curiosity by appearing hysterical, as well. She started toward home. Soon the cottage nestled in the valley came into view, smoke billowing from its chimney. The barn doors, which had been closed when she'd left, were flung open now. Helena must have begun her chores. Usually, her sister's presence filled her with a quiet relief. But Ruth wasn't ready to face her yet, and she did not want Helena to see her visibly distraught.

Ruth gazed at the cluster of village rooftops, thinking of the green tarp awnings that filled the market square. Stopping at market would give her a bit of time to compose herself, and she could buy something to support her story, in case Helena asked where she had been.

She skirted the edge of the farm, fighting the urge to crouch down so as not to be seen. Past the edge of their property, she relaxed slightly. "Ruti!" A soft, lyrical voice pulled her from her thoughts. It was Michal, who had seen her coming from the hills and run out the door after her. He stopped at the fence. "What are you doing?"

"Going to market."

His brow crinkled and she waited for him to ask where she had been, if not to market already, or to notice she was not carrying her basket. "Helena and Dorie are working in the barn. Let me come with you."

Ruth hesitated, looking for an excuse. Usually she enjoyed Michal's calm, easy company, but right now she just wanted to be alone. "Who's watching Karolina?"

"She's asleep."

Ruth studied his face. Michal was her favorite, or would have been, if she permitted herself to admit that she had one. She'd known him instantly the second he'd been born. With the other children it was different—they were these strange squalling little creatures with open mouths and balled fists. But the first time she'd seen Michal he had looked up at her with calm eyes that bespoke a wisdom of ages. In that moment, even though Mama was there, well, it seemed that the baby was hers, a foreshadowing perhaps of what was to come, and the role that would someday be thrust upon her.

"Fine," she relented, too weary to argue. Michal fell in easy step beside her, not speaking. As they neared the village center, Ruth held her breath, remembering the man hanging from the makeshift gallows a few days earlier. She did not want to have to explain that to Michal. But someone had cut him down.

Ruth's relief was short-lived: something about the village was different this morning. A covered truck sat parked at the corner, large and looking out of place. A handful of men she did not recognize—crude laborers in striped overalls—swept the street under the supervision of a policeman (thankfully not the same one who had been to the house, Ruth noticed). A chill ran through her. It was as if the town was being prepared for something…or someone. The Germans were coming, just as Helena had said. Nowhere was too small to be overlooked anymore—not even Biekowice. She swallowed as the realization set in. Once there had seemed a tacit promise—keep your heads down and we will not bother you. But that agreement was now gone.

Ruth forced herself to keep moving. "I'm going to the book-seller," Michal announced when they reached the market.

She gripped his shoulder, as if letting go of him might mean imminent danger. Then she released him, not wanting to cause alarm by acting strangely. "Don't go far," she cautioned. "And come when I call for you."

She walked to the vegetable stall. In front of her making pur-chases stood a willowy young woman with lush raven hair pulled neatly into a knot at the nape of her neck. A French knot, Ruth had heard it called. She would have dearly liked to try such a style with her own hair if she ever had the time to spend on it.

"And some parsley, if you have it," the young woman said to Pani Kowalska. At the sound of the familiar voice, Ruth stifled a yelp. It was Maria, Piotr's fiancée. Although they had not met, Ruth had seen her once in town shopping with Piotr's mother. That time, Ruth had ducked behind a wagon to avoid the awk-wardness of the encounter. She looked around now, desperate for an escape.

The woman turned from the stand, clutching her parcel of vegetables. Ruth gasped, outwardly this time. Beneath the gap in her coat, Maria's stomach swelled with a slight yet unmis-takable roundness.

Shock sliced through her, making her dizzy and causing her to stumble. "Are you unwell?" Maria asked kindly.

"You're Maria," Ruth blurted. The woman cocked her head, puzzled but polite. She did not know who Ruth was. "Piotr's fiancée."

"Wife," the woman corrected quickly, giving off a faint hint of rosewater. "We were married a few months ago." Ruth did the math. The pregnancy would not have occurred while Piotr was still with her, she observed with relief. But it had come quickly after that, and certainly predated the marriage. Nor-mally, news of the rushed wedding would have burned through the town like wildfire. How had Ruth not heard?

That might have been me, Ruth thought, wistful for a moment as she took in the woman's glow and contented fullness once more. Of course, Maria was not so much better off than herself, pregnant with a husband off fighting at the front. But she was a wife and she would have his baby even if something happened to Piotr. Whereas Ruth... She stopped, unable to finish the thought. Her shame burned moist between her legs.

Maria followed Ruth's gaze. "It's the baby," she explained, thinking that Ruth was staring at her basket, which contained an enviable quantity of cheese and milk. "The state gives us a few extra coupons because of the pregnancy." Ruth considered concocting a story of a fiancé of her own, but feared Maria would see right through it. There were no men left—they had all gone off to the fighting and few had come back.

Then Maria pointed down at the hem of Ruth's dress where dirt and leaves clung to the fabric. "Did you fall?" she asked. Her tone bespoke genuine concern, but in that moment all Ruth could hear was Maria's superiority pointing out all that she was—and everything Ruth was not.

Ruth blanched; she did not want this woman's sympathy. She followed Maria's gaze to the mud and leaves that clung to the hem of her skirt, tangible proof of what had happened between her and Helena's soldier. The memory of their encounter burned so bright from within Ruth she was sure that Maria could see her betrayal. Ruth was more furious than ever at the soldier for coming here, for loving her sister and putting them all in this position.

"No, actually, I was in the forest searching for acorns," Ruth replied, the lie flowing so easily from her lips she might have believed it herself.

"Oh? I would have thought the ground picked clean by the squirrels."

Ruth cursed her own inexperience with the outdoors. "There's a patch in the woods just above our house that still has a few beneath the snow," she added, warming to the story. "But something startled me."

Pani Kowalska popped up from behind the vegetable stand, her gray head barely visible above the crates. "What was it?"

Ruth took a deep breath. "A man."

Maria's eyebrows raised high. "Someone from town?"

Ruth shook her head. "No one I've ever seen in these parts. A foreigner." The words were out of her mouth before she realized what she had done, the finality of not being able to take them back. "At first he'd startled me. But then…" She stopped again, realizing her error.

"He could be a Jew." The old woman leaned in, her eyes gleaming. "They say the Germans pay good money for those."

Ruth saw a shadow cross Maria's face. Maria might be her rival for Piotr's affections and the one who had won him, but she had a good heart, and was troubled by the notion of turning anyone over to the Nazis.

"They'll be here soon." The old woman jerked her head in the direction of the street sweepers. "The Germans are setting up quarters in the town hall. You should tell them, if you think he's a Jew."

"I don't know," Ruth said, suddenly loath to discuss the topic any longer. She picked up a handful of potatoes, passed her ration coupons hurriedly to Pani Kowalska. Then she turned abruptly away from Maria. "Let's go," she said to Michal, who had grown tired of looking at books and appeared behind her.

As she walked hurriedly from the village with Michal in tow, she caught Maria's startled expression, the hateful glint in the eyes of the old woman. A cool sweat broke out under her dress, making her skin clammy. What had she done?

"You saw a man?" Michal asked.

Ruth's vision cleared. "You m-must have misheard," she stammered, caught off guard.

But Michal was no longer a child, and too old to be fooled by a simple denial. "Who is he?"

"A soldier. But it's complicated, darling, and dangerous. We can't get involved." Which was exactly what she had just done by alerting the women at market to his presence. What would happen now? Surely the old woman, if not Maria, would tell someone. There would be questions, not just about the soldier but about the Nowak girls—how long they had known about the American, whether they had done anything to help him. By revealing his whereabouts, she had implicated herself and Helena and put the whole family at risk. She thought of the poor soul she'd seen hanging from the playground. If that was the penalty for hoarding, what might they do to those who helped the enemy? Helena was right; they would never be safe here. No, they needed to leave, now.

She turned to Michal. "You won't say anything to the others, will you? I wouldn't want to worry them."

He blinked. "I won't."

They soon reached the cottage. Inside, Helena was trying to help Karolina eat over her insistence that she do it herself. Helena appeared cross and out of her element, as she always did when left to care for the children alone.

"Where were you?" she asked tersely, not looking up.

Ruth tried to decipher whether there was a note of accusation to her sister's voice, then decided that there was not. "Market. I heard that there were extra apples to be had. There weren't." She waited for her sister to take in the lack of a basket and see through the lie, but Helena persisted in feeding the baby. The smell of Sam and their coupling seemed to ooze from Ruth's pores, filling the room. How could Helena not notice?

Helena looked up suddenly, cocking her head. "Are you all right?" Helena asked. Ruth realized then that despite her best efforts to compose herself, her cheeks were flushed, her hair disheveled and pulled from its knot at the edges. Hours later and she looked as though she had only just left the soldier's embrace.

"Y-yes, just a bit tired." She waited for her sister to suspect the truth—surely she would know that something was different. But Helena turned back to helping the baby.

"I was thinking about what you said," Ruth began. "You were right. We should go as soon as possible."

The spoon fell from Helena's hand, clattering to the floor. She did not pick it up, but stared at Ruth, puzzled by her sister's sudden change of heart. "Are you certain?"

Ruth walked to the kitchen and handed Helena a clean spoon. "Yes."

"Maybe we should wait a few weeks."

She was thinking, Ruth knew, of the soldier, wanting him to be strong enough to travel, rather than abandoning him. Ruth's anger flared. "Don't you see, we have to go now? You said yourself that if the heavy snows set in it will be impossible." A sharp wind whistled against the cottage walls, as if to underscore her point.

Helena bent to pick up the spoon. She was torn, Ruth knew, between asking about her change of heart and simply accepting her much-sought acquiescence. Quickly, Ruth recounted the preparations she'd witnessed in the village. "They say the Germans will be here anytime now," she added, stretching the story. A look that she could not decipher crossed her sister's face. "Of course, I'm sure we'll be fine," Ruth hastened to add. "All of our papers are in order and it's not as if Michal is old enough for the labor details."

Helena's hand, always steady, was trembling now. "What is it?" Ruth went to her sister and took the spoon from her, brought her hand gently to her lap. There was a furtiveness in Helena's eyes that suggested whatever secrets her sister was keeping were far worse than her own—though an hour ago she would not have thought such a thing was possible.

"How soon are they to be here?" Helena's voice wavered.

Ruth shrugged. "I don't know, but it could be any day."

"You're right, of course," Helena relented, reaching for her coat and bag. "I'll go to the soldier and figure out the best way for all of us to go together."

"No!" Ruth blurted out. Helena stared at her. Ruth struggled to recover as the full extent of her dilemma crashed down upon her. She did not want her sister going to the chapel—surely Ruth's deceit would be apparent then. But she believed Helena that Sam was their only hope for escape.

"Pack some bags," Helena instructed in a low voice. "In case he says we must go right away. Don't let the children see." Better not to provoke the questions they would have—they thought that the adults in their lives had all of the answers, which this time was simply not true.

"Wait!" Ruth faltered as her sister turned back. Helena could not go to the chapel. It was not really that she thought the soldier would tell—she knew that, despite his guilt, he would protect Helena from the awful truth rather than hurt her in the way. Now that Ruth had divulged news of a strange man in the woods, though, the Germans could find the chapel and apprehend Sam at any time and Helena could not be there when it happened. But Ruth could not explain this to her sister without telling her the truth. "It's dangerous," she said finally.

"It's always dangerous," Helena replied, sweeping a strand of hair impatiently from her forehead. "We have no other choice."

No, Ruth conceded silently. She had taken away that choice the moment she revealed Sam's existence at market. "Go now."

Helena was already at the door, buttoning her coat. Ruth watched out the window as her sister started up the hilltop. Despite his harsh rejection, she wished more than a little bit that it was her going to see Sam again. Did Helena suspect anything? No, it was still there—the same luminescent glow she had seen about her sister the first time she had returned from the chapel. Helena was happy in a way that she would never be again if she knew.

Her jealousy grew. Ruth could tell by the way that Sam had touched her, as if exploring a new country, that he and her sister had not been intimate. And surely he would not try to be with Helena now after all that had happened. Ruth willed her sister's feet to move faster, praying that she would reach Sam and leave again before the townspeople reported him, or found him themselves.

The time passed slowly. The children played inside, more quietly than usual. "Ruti," Michal said in a low voice, slipping away from the girls and coming to the chair where she knitted. "Helena's errand...does it have something to do with the soldier?"

"No," she replied, too quickly. She hated lying, but she did not want to alarm him. And how could she explain, when she did not have all of the answers herself? It was in a sense true— Helena's errand was not really about the soldier, but about their escape.

She looked around the cottage, desperate for a distraction. Once she might have suggested a craft, but one needed something to make it out of and there was simply nothing to spare. "Let's take a nap," she suggested, and they did not protest, but climbed into bed and huddled together for warmth. She cleared her throat and began to sing, her voice nowhere as good as Mama's. But the children did not seem to notice. Karolina snuggled in contentedly and let out a small sigh and fell quickly to sleep. Ruth stared at the ceiling, remembering how she had lain on the chapel floor with Sam just hours earlier.

She awakened sometime later and slipped out from among them to prepare dinner. Snow began to fall, heavy against the window, the wind whipping it into great circles. She fretted, thinking of her sister. Helena had made the trip in worse weather before, but surely the squall would slow her down.

She lifted the lid from the pot of soup she had prepared, then gave it a stir. Earlier, she had pulled a nearly empty sack from the cupboard and scoured the bottom for the last few remaining lentils, scraping the mold off them and depositing them in a dish as though each was a nugget of gold and adding the potatoes she'd bought. She remembered then as if from another lifetime a piece of meat that she had refused to eat as a child because it had been too charred. "It's a sin to waste food," Mama had said. "There are people who have to do without." Her mother's words now seemed a portent, their current suffering the price to be paid for her earlier waste.

In the bedroom, the children began to stir. Michal rubbed his eyes as he stumbled into the kitchen, a still-groggy Karolina nestled around his neck. Twenty minutes later, they had assembled at the table for dinner. No one needed to be reminded of mealtimes now. The children watched, hopeful but resigned, as she scraped the bottom of the pot, each trying not to beg for an extra morsel. They ate, quickly and silently. Even Karolina had stopped crying when her few drops of sweet milk were gone. Dorie was scraping at a bit of old porridge on the edge of the table and then when she thought nobody was looking popped it in her mouth.

Unable to watch them any longer, Ruth stood to clear the plates. Her eyes traveled to the calendar above the sink, marveling at how the days had blended together. How could she have forgotten Karolina's birthday, which always came in such a rush after Christmas? They did not have even a small gift for her. She pulled the jar of honey from the cupboard, the last remaining bits barely visible through the glass.

Ruth held it close to the stove, liquefying the thin coat of honey. She took a spoon and scraped the jar, holding it out to Dorie. Dorie paused for a split second uncertainly, as though it was a trick, then plunged the whole spoon into her mouth, eyes widening with glee. Ruth took another spoon, divided the rest of the contents between Michal and Karolina. The baby's face looked strange and for a moment Helena wondered if she'd made a mistake and the unfamiliar rich taste would make the child ill. But she squealed with delight.

Ruth looked down at the nearly empty jar, which called to her. One spoonful wasn't going to keep them from starvation. She could not keep them safe here and was powerless to help them escape. But she could give them this. She scraped the jar and then plunged the spoon into her mouth, the sweetness mixing with the salt from the tears she could no longer stem.

"*Sto lat*," she said aloud to Karolina. *May you live to be a hundred.* It was the child's second birthday.

20

Helena raced toward the chapel. It was bitterly cold now, the sky dark gray. Her breath rose in crystalline puffs, mixing with the falling snow. The few days since she had been to see Sam seemed a lifetime. She would have gone sooner, but sneaking out had proven impossible with the holiday. She recalled how the children had opened on Christmas Eve the small gifts she and Ruth had fashioned from whatever they could find around the house. Taking in the scene, she was flooded with guilt—it was a sham pretending to celebrate Christmas. But watching the children's faces, she knew that the happiness it brought was good, a respite from the suffering and worry that threatened to deny them their childhood.

She raised her feet higher to break through the ice that coated the ground, still puzzling over Ruth's change of heart. It simply wasn't like her sister to acquiesce. Had she finally lifted her head from the sand and seen just how bad things really were? It did not matter why Ruth had agreed to leave—the important fact was that she had done so. Helena imagined entering the chapel, telling Sam that they could go together now and have the life they planned. Would he be as happy about it as she was? She paused, considering. Making plans for a life together that was not possible was one thing, living out those fantasies quite another. Perhaps he would not want her for real.

Helena shook off the doubt that nagged at her. There simply wasn't time. She pressed forward and soon reached the chapel. She knocked and, not waiting for a response, pushed open the door. "Sam?" There was no response. Her heart fluttered slightly as she scanned the chapel to see if he was napping. He might have moved his sleeping place once more. But the floor was bare, the pile of brush he usually slept on scattered, as though someone had swept it away with a broom. Uneasiness licked at her stomach. The air was still and there was a strange musty smell she recognized from the day she had brought him here.

The fire, she noticed, was out, a little clump of ash visible through the open grate. Sam must have gone for wood, she reasoned. She stepped outside, a low buzzing in her ears. "Sam?" she called again, forgetting in her haste to keep her voice low. The trees seemed to muffle her words into silence. She held her breath for one second, then another, waiting for the familiar response that would make everything okay. *Nothing.* Terror seized her. Her eyes scanned the ground, searching for tracks. But the snow was unbroken. No one had come or gone from here since the fresh snow had begun to fall hours earlier. A pile of stones she did not remember lay in a semicircle just by the door.

Helena ran back inside. The cups and other small living items she'd given Sam were missing. The chapel looked as if no one had ever been there, and all that had happened these past weeks had been a figment of her imagination. Her photo, the one he had asked for, had been ripped from the spot on the wall near where Sam had once lain. A torn bit of paper, still stuck to the wall, was the only sign that anyone had been. Helena knew then that he was truly gone.

She stood motionless, her mind whirring with confusion. *Sam was gone.* She wondered if he had left on his own, made the break for the border he had talked about. He would not, she felt certain, have up and gone without at least letting her know, despite her once asking him to do just that. No, someone had come here, without warning. It could have been the police, or even the Germans. She looked around the room more closely now. There were no signs of a struggle. But her skin prickled. Whoever had come might be back. She must go.

Outside Helena paused, seeing him in the empty space before her. She turned back to the chapel, willing him to appear and run after her, as he had the day they had quarreled. But the door remained shut, and the windows dark. Her eyes stung with tears. She started quickly down the path toward home.

When Helena reached the fork in the road she stopped. Sam had disappeared, and with him their only hope of escape. Perhaps she had been wrong to trust him. Perhaps he had reconsidered his feelings for her. Seeing his solemn face as he had recited marriage vows just days earlier, it hardly seemed possible. No, he would not have abandoned her. But where was he? She saw his face in her mind, but the setting behind him was a blur. Was he hurt, or even dead? She doubled over in anguish.

A moment later, she straightened, swallowing back her pain. She had to try to find him, to know if he was all right. Alek, she decided, turning toward the route that led to Kraków. He had not been able to help Sam. But at least he might be able to tell her what to do.

It was nearly midday when she reached the city, breathless from running. The snow had stopped but clouds hung low, obscuring the top of the castle. Helena did not bother to climb to the top of the hill to plan her route—there simply wasn't time. Every passing minute meant that Sam might be farther away or in worse danger. Instead, she ran heedlessly across the wide railway bridge that spanned the river, footsteps clanging against metal and seeming to ricochet through the air.

At the top of Grodzka Street, she forced herself to slow down and walk normally for fear of attracting attention. She looked in the direction of the Old City, considering. Alek might be at the café now, but picturing the German patrons who had stared at her with interest, she knew she should not go there. Wierzynek, she thought, remembering the fine restaurant where Alek worked.

Wierzynek sat just above the market square, a two-story restaurant with a latticed iron balcony on the second floor and wide windows that swung inward to allow the fresh air on fine spring days. She hesitated outside the front door, smoothing her hair. Even if Poles were not now forbidden from dining there, she would not have dared enter the elegant establishment in such a state. She made her way around to the back of the restaurant where a truck sat idling. A moment later, a worker appeared, bobbling a stack of crates that rose higher than his head and gave off a sour smell. *"Prosz.e, pana,"* Helena said.

"Tak?" The crates wobbled precariously and Helena hoped that he would not be startled into dropping them.

"I'm looking for Alek Landesberg." It had not occurred to her until just that second that he might not work under his own name.

The man set down the crates. "Alek?" He shook his head. "He hasn't turned up for work in a few days. Something about a sick relative. The boss says he's going to let him go if he isn't back soon."

"Thank you." Walking hurriedly away, she considered the information. Though she had known him only briefly, it did not seem like Alek to miss the job he said was so valuable for obtaining information. Something was not right. Without thinking, she started toward Starowi´slna Street, the wide thoroughfare that would take her to the Jewish quarter.

A few minutes later, the bustle of the city center gave way to the quiet desolation of Kazimierz. Here the cobblestones had been hastily cleared of snow, leaving a slick coating, and she navigated them carefully, trying not to fall.

She reached Skawinska Street, pushed open the heavy door to the *gmina* and raced up the marble steps, her footsteps echoing eerily throughout the empty stairwell. The door to Pan Izako-wicz's office was open. She knocked. *"Dzie'n dobry?"* Silence greeted her. Her heart sank. She had hoped she might find him here, packing still. Some books remained on the shelves and the photographs still hung on the wall. But the piles of papers cleared from the desk and the menorah that had sat on the cor-ner were gone.

She sank to a chair, shaken. First Sam, then Alek and now Pan Izakowicz, too. It was as if the entire world had disappeared overnight.

A sudden noise came from the corridor. Footsteps. Helena jumped up. What would happen to her if she was caught here? The door pushed open and a toothless man in a wide black hat, not much older than Izakowicz, stood before her. They stared at each other uncertainly and she could tell from the fear in his eyes that he was supposed to be in the ghetto. Had he somehow escaped or not yet gone?

"I'm looking for Pan Izakowicz," she said.

"Why?" The man's voice was protective.

"I need to find someone and I think he can help."

"He isn't here anymore." Helena prayed he had not gotten into trouble for speaking with her about her mother. "They've closed the *gmina*." Sooner than the six days the Germans had promised him. "So he's in Podgórze now. Who are you trying to find?"

She hesitated, wondering whether the man could be trusted. "Alek, his nephew. I was hoping he could help me with some-thing."

She saw a glint of recognition in the man's eyes. But then he shook his head. "He's gone. To ground, I suspect, along with the rest of them." Alek had died? Her stomach twisted. "Hiding in the woods, that is," the man clarified. Helena exhaled. "Things have gotten very dangerous," he continued. More dangerous did not seem possible to Helena, but the man's grave voice left little room for doubt. "I doubt even Alek can help anyone now." The man walked past her and took one of the photographs from the wall. Was he connected to the people in it? "I wouldn't stay here long, if I were you," he added before walking from the office.

Helena raced down the stairs and back onto the street. Pan Izakowicz had been her last hope of finding Alek and for a moment she considered going to the ghetto. But if Alek was in hiding, no one—not even his uncle—would be able to find him. They were all gone, and with them her family's only hope of escape.

She stopped abruptly. The intersection ahead of her was blocked by two large jeeps. Her breathing stopped. Was it another *aktion*? No, there were no Jews left to arrest or kill anymore. Except her. Watching the police stop an ordinary pedestrian, Helena's heart pounded. It was a checkpoint, one that she might have seen if she had taken the time to survey the city before coming down. Her identity would not be apparent from her *kennkarte*, but if she was detained for unauthorized travel…

She ducked back against the building and headed in the other direction. At the corner she turned, and began walking blindly, taking a right and then a left turn, not caring which way she went, as long as it was away from the danger. A few minutes later, she stopped, leaning against one of the buildings to catch her breath. A drop of cold water fell from the roof overhead, running down her collar, icy against her neck. She was not quite certain which way she had gone, but there was something familiar about the street.

The black market, she remembered, taking in the abandoned industrial building at the corner. She reached into her bag and her hand closed around the cold metal of the Kiddush cup. She had nearly forgotten it was there. Holding tightly to it, Helena started forward. She slipped in between the two buildings. The market was much the same as it had been the day she had come with Alek, the traders seemingly unperturbed by the police presence just streets away. Amid the silver merchants, Trojecki sat in the same place as days earlier, as if he had not moved.

"You remember me?" she asked.

The man eyed her coldly. "Don't waste my time."

"I'm not. You said thirty, *tak*?" She bluffed the higher price, hoping he would not remember.

He shook his head. "Price has gone down. Twenty-five."

She stood. "Twenty-seven."

He waved her back. "Fine." He held out his hand.

Helena pulled out the Kiddush cup, then hesitated once more. She did not want to part with the item and reject her past as her mother had done. But the children needed food. She had believed in Sam and Alek, trusted them. That was her first mistake. She was back to that place now, where she could only depend on herself for their survival.

Helena waited until the merchant had passed her the money, then handed him the cup. Then she walked away quickly, the coins cold and heavy in her hand.

21

As she fed Karolina, Ruth watched her sister shovel coal into the stove, her movements leaden. When Helena finished, she did not shut the grate but stared blankly into the fire. Finally, Ruth crossed the room and closed the grate and put her hand on Helena's shoulder gently. Helena did not respond. Instead, she stood and swept the fine coating of coal dust from the floor.

It had been more than a month since Helena had returned shaken from her trip up the hill and confirmed in a whisper that she'd found the soldier gone. Sam, she'd called him. Ruth had not even known his name when she'd slept with him, though whether this made it better or worse she could not say. They had just sat down to dinner when Helena had come inside, snow covered and shaking. Ruth had watched her sister closely as she stood by the fire. Had Sam told her that she had been to the chapel? But as she drew near, she saw that Helena's face was ash pale and gutted. Her mouth tugged downward with sadness, not the rage she surely would have felt if she had learned the truth.

"What is it?" Ruth had asked, looking over her shoulder reflexively for any potential harm. She took stock of the children, making sure all were out of earshot.

Helena blinked several times, then swiped at her eyes. It was the closest Ruth had ever come to seeing her sister cry, and she knew as Helena shook her head wordlessly that the soldier was gone.

"Do you think he was taken?" she asked after the children had gone to bed.

"I don't know." Helena had lifted her arms, palms turned plaintively upward. "Sam wouldn't have just left. But there were no signs of a struggle. The chapel looked exactly like when he was there, as if he'd disappeared."

Ruth saw then the depth of despair in her sister's eyes as she grappled with Sam's leaving. Helena had believed, as Ruth had with Piotr, that Sam would never leave her, a notion that Ruth had wanted to dismiss as folly. Yet there had been something in Sam's expression that told Ruth he really did love Helena, and that, unlike Piotr, he would not have left by choice. A mix of resentment and guilt washed over her—she knew it was her fault Sam had gone.

Over the weeks that followed, Helena had become a shell of herself. It was as if her sorrow had manifested itself physically, causing her to lose weight and giving a gray pallor to her skin. Watching Helena now, Ruth's guilt rose until it seemed she might drown. She had not meant to hurt Helena like this. Her sister moved with a mechanical emptiness that Ruth recognized from her own days after Piotr had left. Helena had always been the practical one, though, with no time for what she called "sentimental nonsense." It was hard to imagine her getting close to a man, much less risking everything for him or letting the loss of him destroy her—even a man like Sam, with his gentle touch and soft chocolate eyes.

As she lifted Karolina from the high chair, Ruth saw Michal through the window, nearing the door with an armful of firewood that nearly reached his forehead, struggling to see over the massive stack. He stumbled under the weight and Ruth set down the baby and rushed to the door, flinging it open without stopping for her coat. "Here." The roughness of the branches scratched her hands as she helped him to lower it to the ground. "So much wood," she remarked.

"I brought extra in case…" His eyes traveled uneasily over Ruth's shoulder. The change in Helena's demeanor, her listlessness and faded strength, had not gone unnoticed by the children, and certainly not by perceptive Michal, who surely feared Helena was deteriorating mentally as Mama had. "In case it snows more," he finished finally. There was an undercurrent to his words that belied the deeper fears about Helena's ability not only to keep functioning, but to help contribute to their survival. But his stated reason was also true—winter had clamped down suddenly, a heavy curtain of snow dropped from above without warning. One day the ground had been dark and muddy, and the next morning it was a sea of unbroken white, drifts piled high and heavy against the door. It seemed to snow each night after that.

Once Ruth had loved the snowfalls, the way a heavy silence blanketed the house, muffling the outside world. Under other circumstances, the notion of being snowed in their cozy home would have been an attractive one. But now she hated it, for it seemed a constant reminder of just how trapped they really were. It was late January, the new year having slipped in weeks ago without notice on a night like any other. They should have left a month ago when the weather was better, Ruth reflected, and they were not as weak from lack of food. Now they would never survive the journey.

"That was good of you," she said to Michal, noticing how his lips were blue around the edges and his teeth chattered. The wood was not damp or green. How far into the forest had he gone to get the best pieces, and how had he managed to carry them all home? Michal had been trying in quiet ways to take over Tata's role, an effort that had become more pronounced now that Helena had become a ghost of herself. Ruth led him into the house and he let her pull off his coat and move him closer to the fire.

She poured him some warm beetroot tea and slid him a few of the nuts that they had been savoring since Christmas, then surveyed the room. Dorie and Karolina sat on the floor close to the stove, playing with the two threadbare dolls that had once been her and Helena's most prized possession. But their movements, too, were slow. Was it Helena's malaise rubbing off on them, or was all of the hunger and hardship wearing them down, squelching their youthful energy? Looking at their drawn faces, her heart broke.

Helena had returned from that last trip to the city with a small unexpected satchel of groceries, which she handed to Ruth without speaking.

"Where did you get those?" Ruth asked.

Helena had shaken her head. "The black market." Her answer explained only the food, and not how Helena had gotten the money. But her sister was in such a state over Sam, Ruth did not press. At the time, it had seemed like a feast. They had eaten bread first, before it grew moldy, and then the cheese. Only a handful of potatoes remained.

"They closed the border," Helena said grimly now. She was staring out the window at the endless blanket of white, speaking blankly into the air before her. Whether she had heard the news recently in the village or weeks ago was unclear. *So what?* Ruth wanted to reply. It was not as if they had any prospect of escape without passes.

Ruth saw the searching in her sister's face, knowing Helena was wondering what she had done wrong. It was a haunted feeling Ruth recognized all too well from the days following Piotr's departure, the nagging question of whether he might have stayed if she had somehow been different. Did Helena wish she had gone with Sam when she'd had the chance? She might have reached safety now, perhaps even sent for the others. Or she might have lost them forever.

It was her fault, Ruth knew. Helena would not say it, but Ruth could see the constant recrimination in her eyes. If she hadn't so stubbornly fought Helena's idea of leaving Biekowice, they might have reached safety by now. She looked over at pale, thin Dorie sitting by the fire and the full despair of the children washed over her. They would not see out the winter under such circumstances.

Ruth went to Helena's side and put her hand on her shoulder. "I can't feel him anymore," Helena said quietly, her voice hollow. "He really is gone, isn't he?"

"Yes," Ruth replied firmly. She searched Helena's face, desperate for some way to undo all of the pain she had caused. She put her arms around Helena. There was no good to come from keeping Helena's hopes alive falsely. Better she should accept the hard truth and move on to the next chapter of their lives.

Ruth considered again telling her sister everything, ripping to shreds what she had shared with Sam. Wouldn't it make things easier? "Helena…" Confession was in Ruth's nature. Even as a child, she was always tattling to Mama when they did something wrong, even before they'd gotten caught. Then she stopped. The truth would ease her pain but it would only hurt her sister. She was stuck with her secret guilt, alone.

Finally, she could stand it no longer. "Come," she said briskly, eager to break the heaviness that seemed to suffocate the entire room. "Let's walk to the pond."

The children looked up at her with surprise. It had always been Helena, at least in better days, who had urged them to go outside, Ruth preferring to remain home snug by the fire. And she hesitated to suggest it now, especially when Michal had barely gotten warm. She did not want them to overexert themselves and burn extra calories they could ill afford to re-place, aggravating their hunger. But she desperately wanted to do something to lift some of the sadness and return the color to their cheeks.

Outside Michal and Dorie ran ahead, dragging the sled Tata had fashioned years ago out of some spare wood. Dorie stum-bled. Michal held out his hand and helped her navigate down the steep path, his pace slow and patient. When she climbed onto the sled, he began to pull it.

Ruth walked more slowly alongside Helena, who carried Karolina on her shoulders. She looked out across the hills, be-yond the cloud of chimney smoke that hovered above the vil-lage to the smooth gray sky beyond. Gazing up at the tree line, she imagined the same stillness up by the chapel. Not that the soldier was there anymore. A flush of heat, equal parts desire and shame, ran through her, as it always did when she could not stop her thoughts of him.

But was it truly her fault that Sam was gone? Ruth consid-ered the question now for the hundredth time. He could have been planning to leave all along. But even as she thought this, she suspected that his departure was somehow related to her. Either he had felt so guilty at what had happened he had chosen not to face Helena again or... She could not finish the thought. His kind face appeared before her, his devastation at betraying Helena so apparent. Ruth had been angry and had spoken im-petuously that day at market, regretting the words as soon as they had come out. Had he been arrested as a result of her fool-ishness? She had heard no such rumors. Under normal circum-stances, news of the discovery of an American soldier by the Germans would have spread like wildfire through the town. But she seldom ventured out anymore and had scarcely been back to market since that day for fear of further questions. So it was possible she simply hadn't heard.

No, he had left on his own, Ruth insisted silently, as if con-

vincing herself would somehow make it true. Maybe he had recovered well enough and knew he had to flee before the weather
worsened. But deep down she knew the timing was too close
to be a coincidence.

The snows had come just days after Helena discovered him
gone. Just as well, she reflected. It would have been almost impossible for Helena to get back and forth to the chapel now.
Without her visits, he surely would have starved.

They walked wordlessly toward the pond, a small inlet of
water that formed off of the stream. The bare branches of the
willow trees, laden with snow, dipped low to the frozen surface. As Michal and Dorie slid on the ice, pretending that they
had skates, Ruth glanced out of the corner of her eye at her sister. Was it better or worse for Helena? At least with Piotr, Ruth
had known why he broke things off. Sam's sudden departure
would leave Helena always questioning why, wondering whether
he was safe. But unlike the finality of Piotr's farewell, Helena
still had hope. Ruth could see it in each furtive glance up the
mountainside, as though she thought Sam might appear, limping down the path toward her. She looked up each time there
was a scratch outside the cottage door. When he didn't appear
Helena's face would fall and she'd retreat inside herself, speaking
little and doing the bare minimum required for their survival.

Ruth's stomach turned and she wondered if the bit of milk
she'd mixed in with their porridge that morning had soured,
though none of the others seemed affected. But the discomfort
was more than digestive—she was tired these days in a way she
could not explain, that made her legs leaden and fearful to sit
down lest she fall asleep. Was it the grippe? She could not afford to be sick—there was no medicine to be had and no respite
from the things that had to be done for the children. It was the
exhaustion of trying to do too much without enough food, she
decided. All she wanted to do was sleep to stave off the cold
and the hunger.

Michal and Dorie had begun a snowball fight, their troubles momentarily forgotten. Ruth bent and formed a small snowball and handed it to Karolina, who licked it and squealed in delight. Then she formed a second snowball and gave it to Helena. "Go on," she urged. Her sister tossed it halfheartedly in Michal's direction.

Michal threw a snowball in retort, and it crashed into a tree above Ruth's head, raining a cool shower of white down upon her. As she ducked behind a tree to avoid being hit again, something at the base of the trunk caught her eye. It was a dead animal, stiff and motionless on a hard, unforgiving bed of snow. A raccoon or gopher, maybe. Animals that had succumbed to the harsh winter were hardly uncommon. The lifeless body might have startled her once, but after witnessing the man hanging from the swing set, a dead dog seemed unremarkable.

She started to turn away, then stopped at the sight of a white paw. It was the soldier's stray dog, the one who had slept by his feet that night. How had it come to be here? Sam did not seem the type to simply abandon the animal. Grimacing, she used her boot to bury it beneath the snow so Helena could not see.

The children's laughter subsided and a few minutes later they trudged back to their sisters, rosy-cheeked and tired of the snow and the icy water that seeped into their torn boots. The muted sky had shifted to the dark gray of late afternoon. As if by silent agreement, they all turned and started for home.

Helena stumbled, her foot catching an unseen tree root. Ruth reached out to steady her. "Careful." Ruth's eyes met her sister's and she pled with her silently to be strong, despite the pain that she understood so well. *I can't do this without you.* Guilt surged through her. She had brought this on, and she had no right to ask anything of Helena now.

When they reached the house, Helena tended to the fire while Ruth undressed the children from their wet snow clothes and put some soup on the stove to warm. Every meal was soup now—beet soup, cabbage soup, potato soup—thin and watery and indistinguishable from one another, designed to stretch the little that was left and to make the belly warm if not full. She glanced at the alarmingly low supply of potatoes in the cupboard. She should talk to Helena again about killing the mule for meat.

Ruth picked up a stack of plates she'd washed that morning. The location where Mama always kept them, halfway across the kitchen, had never made any sense to Ruth. She paused, then moved them to a spot closer to the sink.

"We could go, even without him," Helena said in a low voice after they sat down for dinner. Ruth stared at her in disbelief. Had she gone from depressed to delusional? But her eyes were clear and eager.

"We don't have passes. We don't even know the way."

"Yes, of course." The light in Helena's eyes extinguished and she withdrew into her melancholy once more.

Suddenly Ruth pictured Sam above her in the dim light of the chapel. Heat rose in her, mixing with bile, and she pushed back from the table. "Excuse me." She ran outside in time to be sick, heedless of the stench of her own vomit rising in the steam from the snow.

She straightened, gasping for air. It was not the food that had made her ill. She had been so tired the past few days, even before the climb. It was as if something was pulling the life from her, feeding on her as the way she sometimes felt the children did, only much more internal and intense. Children, she thought, Maria's swelling midsection appearing unbidden in her mind.

Ruth bent over to wretch again, then straightened, counting. Six weeks. Her stomach had ached weeks earlier with what she thought was her impending flow. But it had not materialized and she had been so caught up in everything that had happened she had ceased to notice. Panic rose in her. But it couldn't be, not from one time, not from her first time. But as soon as she thought it she had no doubt: she was pregnant with Sam's child.

Fear seized her then. Sam was gone. Her child would have no father. How could she possibly manage? And they couldn't hide it from the neighbors—they knew there was no man, they would ask questions and the dates wouldn't bear out her lying and saying it was Piotr. She would be disgraced. No, it could not possibly be true. She pushed the thought, too awful to contemplate further, from her mind.

Ruth returned to the house, wiping her mouth and trying to smile. "Are you all right?" Michal asked with concern.

She forced herself to stop trembling. "I'm fine. Just an upset stomach." Helena was staring at her strangely and she wondered if her sister did not believe the excuse.

They all went to bed early that night, tired from the walk to the pond. "The wood," Helena remarked in the darkness, and Ruth wondered how long it had taken her to notice that the pile had been replenished. Was Helena simply grief-struck or was her mind slipping as Mama's had done?

"Mischa brought it." Ruth considered pointing out to her sister the extra work her weakness meant for the rest. Then she stopped—Helena had enough to worry about. Helena did not speak further but soon began to snore. It seemed in recent months that they had switched places, Helena sleeping more soundly as if preferring her dreams to the life they had here, Ruth tossing restlessly with her guilt. She felt her own eyes grow heavy.

Sometime later, a noise in the darkness jolted her from sleep. Ruth looked up to see if Helena had gone to the water closet, but her sister lay beside her sleeping. She slipped from bed, checking all of the children beneath her fingertips.

Ruth walked to the kitchen. A loose shutter, perhaps. Closer to the doorway, she stopped again. This time, footsteps crunching against the snow were unmistakable. She opened her mouth to call for Helena but no sound came out. Fury rose in her as she remembered the policeman who had come, his near-violation. She considered going for Tata's gun, but even as she did, she knew she would never have the nerve to use it. Instead, her hand closed around the poker by the fireplace, cool and hard. She would not let him hurt her again and she certainly wasn't going to let him near the children.

There was a tentative knock at the door. For a moment she considered not answering it, but it would not stop whoever was on the other side. Taking a deep breath, she swung the door open, then stepped back and raised the poker. But before she could lower it and swing it at the intruder, something hit the ground by her feet with a heavy thud.

Ruth reached for the light and it flickered on. She gasped.

There, on the floor of the cottage, lay the American soldier, Sam.

22

Hearing a crash, Helena leaped from bed and raced to the front room. Ruth hovered over something on the ground, poker raised. As the lump unfolded, Helena gasped in disbelief. "Sam?"

She rushed forward to help him, concern and joy mixing with her shock. She touched his cheek to make sure that this was not a dream. He was here, really here. But his face was nearly as pale as the day she had found him in the forest and his eyes were half-closed. "Are you all right?"

Sam opened his mouth, but no sound came out. Helena assisted him into a chair. Then he wrapped his arms around her waist, and buried his snow-covered head against her, clinging to her tightly.

Feeling his chill against her midsection, Helena panicked. "Ruth, he's freezing." Her sister stood motionless, still clutching the poker and staring. "Warm some water, please. And bring blankets."

Karolina cried out then. "I'll get her," Ruth said, hurrying from the room.

Helena raised Sam's face to her, running her hands over his cheeks and chin, clearing the thick ice from them. She had expected never to see him again. She attempted to bat back her tears without success, then let them flow, heedless as they cascaded downward, pelting onto his cheeks and melting the snow that clung there. He looked different. Heavy stubble covered his jaw, reminding her of when they first met. His complexion was eerie pale. He was sweating profusely despite the cold and his breathing was labored, as though he had run a race. The trip, from wherever he had been, had taken everything he had, and perhaps more than his newly healed leg could handle. But he was here.

Ruth had not reappeared, so Helena rushed to pull a blanket from the cupboard and wrapped him in it. She pulled his wet boots and socks from his feet. His toes were a worrying shade of gray and she hoped he would not lose them to frostbite. She knelt and began to rub his feet to warm them.

As she worked, she studied him. It seemed so strange to see him here, in a house with real walls, a roof and furniture, instead of the bare chapel. Where had he been all this time? Tata's coat was gone and in its place he wore a thick brown leather jacket, worn at the elbows and seams. He looked more like the other Sam, the one she did not know. But even now, huddled and freezing in the chair, he seemed to fill the room with a kind of light.

"Thank you," he said in a hoarse voice, finally able to speak. "I'm sorry to come here unannounced—"

"Sorry?" She cut him off, her voice harsh with disbelief. "I've been frantic for some news of you. I had no idea what happened to you. I've been sick with worry." Tears welled up in her eyes again. "I thought you were dead." There was a moment of awkwardness between them, for even though he had returned, his sudden disappearance still felt somehow a betrayal.

"Excuse me," he apologized, looking over her shoulder. Helena was suddenly ashamed of the small room with its simple, worn furniture. But it wasn't the cottage he was noticing. Behind her, Dorie had appeared. She stared at the strange man who seemed to fill the room, eyes wide. Her lower lip quivered. "Hello," he said gently.

Helena stood up. "Sam, this is my sister Dorie." Ruth came back into the room, holding the baby. "And these are my other sisters Karolina…and Ruth." Helena could not disguise the note of reluctance in her voice.

"A pleasure," he said, starting to stand, but Helena put her hand on his shoulder, not wanting him to overexert himself. "You never mentioned that you had a twin," he said to Helena, his voice less surprised than it genuinely should have been. Helena glanced out of the corner of her eye at Ruth to see if she was angry at having been left out, but her face remained impassive.

Sam reached for her hand, but Helena stepped back, still stung by his betrayal, the scars deep from the weeks of worrying. She had been so certain he had left for good. She wanted to hit him, pound on his chest.

"I thought you'd been arrested or killed." Helena could not keep the pain and accusation from her voice as all of the uncertainty of the past few weeks finally broke free.

"I know. And I'm sorry for that. But they came for me, you see." Her eyes widened. "Your attempt to reach the partisans worked," he said. Her jaw dropped slightly. Alek had seemed so certain he could not help. "They came for me without warning and said we had to go right then."

"Alek found you?"

"Not him personally." No, of course not. To Helena, Alek was the face of the resistance. But in reality it was so much bigger than that. Sam's eyes darkened. "The partisans undertook some sort of action against the Germans. There were reprisals and, well, Alek is nowhere to be found." Helena's stomach twisted as she thought of strong, brave Alek, who had seemed to represent hope for them all. Sam continued. "The messenger who came for me was a young woman actually."

Helena looked at him levelly. "See, I told you that the women help, too." She was struck with more than a twinge of envy for this unseen female who had been able to do for Sam what she could not.

He ignored her remark. "She said that Alek had high praise for you and your bravery." Helena flushed, trying not to enjoy too much the note of jealousy now in Sam's voice. "He was able to radio the partisans and find their location. But I had no choice—had to go with her then, and I had no warning or way to get word to you. It was too dangerous to leave you a note. I tried to arrange the stones in a way you could recognize." So the pattern on the ground had been a message to her, after all.

"I understand." Helena's forgiveness was instant and complete.

"I buried the other items," he added apologetically. "The cups and such. They're all still there."

Helena waved her hand. Such things did not matter at all. "So what happened then?"

"We made it over the border."

"Then what are you doing here?" Surely his mission had not brought him back.

"I came for you," he said simply.

"You found the partisans and then just left again?" His courage loomed before her, larger than ever.

"They'll be none too pleased with me when I return," he conceded. So he had disobeyed orders, risked everything to come back for her.

"And the other men from your unit?"

He shook his head sadly. "Not yet. There are rumors of some Americans, though, in the partisan camps farther south toward Bratislava. They offered to take me there."

"But you didn't go."

"I told you that I wouldn't leave you. Here." He produced a tin of meat from his coat pocket.

Dorie and Karolina gathered hurriedly around the feast. "Slowly," Helena cautioned, breaking off pieces for them, which they devoured just as quickly. Only Ruth hung back. "You don't want to make yourself ill." She looked over her shoulder into the bedroom where Michal, always a sound sleeper, lay undisturbed by the commotion. Deciding against waking him, she found a cloth in the kitchen and wrapped a few pieces of meat in it so he would not miss out.

She turned back toward Sam. Joy and longing rose in her and she fought the urge to throw herself into his arms. Instead, she put a hand on his shoulder, holding on tight so he would not disappear again. "They're coming," he said to Helena in a low voice as the children ate. "The Germans—I sensed something different from the aircraft I saw going overhead, and the partisans I met confirmed it."

"They're already here," Ruth offered, stepping closer. Her eyes traveled to Helena's hand where it sat on Sam's shoulder and a small frown of disapproval crossed her face. "They've set up an administrative bureau in town."

"I mean the German *army*," Sam clarified. "Tanks and troops are headed this way."

So the countryside would no longer be spared. "Why now?" Helena asked.

"The Russians. Relations between Hitler and Stalin are deteriorating and there's bound to be war to the east." Helena processed this, remembering his comments months ago about Russian barbarity that made the Germans look almost civilized by comparison. "The Germans coming through, shoring up their position—and looking for any possible pockets of resistance." He turned to Helena. "We have to go now before they arrive. All of us."

"You're right." Helena stepped away from Sam and the chil-

dren toward Ruth. Her sister's mouth was open, ready to protest. "Ruth, surely you can see that he's right?"

Ruth looked out the window over her sister's shoulder at the
desolate expanse of night, the snow that stretched endlessly out
to the horizon. "But we promised Mama we would stay."

Helena stared at her, puzzled. Weeks earlier, Ruth had agreed
to go, had even urged her to get Sam's help. But now she was
rooted and fearful once more. "No, we promised her that we
would stay together and keep everyone safe—and we will. But
to do that, we must go. Everything is different now. Even if
the Germans are gone someday and we manage to survive, the
Russians will follow and God only knows what they'll want
with us. We're the parents now, Ruth, and we have to do what
we think is best. I know that it's scary out there. But we have
to take the chance."

Ruth did not respond, but shifted Karolina to her other hip.
"Don't you see?" Helena exploded, forgetting to keep her voice
low. "There is no safety in standing back and not taking a side."
Dorie stepped closer to Ruth, whose expression remained un-
convinced. Helena took a deep breath. "I'm afraid there's more
to it than that. You know that Mama was in a Jewish hospital,
right?"

"Of course. Tata said that they took her in for the money,
even though she wasn't Jewish. He had promised to do some
odd chores to pay for part of her keep."

"He lied." Helena swallowed. At the time it seemed a kindness
to withhold the truth about Mama from Ruth, forestalling yet
another chink in the fairy-tale armor her sister had constructed.
But now it was her best—and only—hope at persuading Ruth.
She had no choice. She prayed it would not be too much for her
sister to bear. "Mama was half-Jewish."

Ruth barked out a laugh. "That's not true!" she said in a pa-
tronizing tone. "Honestly, Helena, how can you say that? She

was the most religious of all of us—she went to church every week."

But Helena shook her head. "The nurse told me after Mama died. She had papers." Helena thought of the Kiddush cup she had sold. She wished she had the cup now so that she could show it to her sister. The Hebrew lettering would be physical proof, undeniable. "It's true. And sooner or later, there will be questions."

"No," Ruth insisted, but Helena could see the truth taking hold.

"I'm sorry I didn't tell you sooner," Helena whispered softly. "But with Mama gone I was afraid it would be too much. It's quite a shock, I know. But if the Germans check records and figure it out…" Helena did not finish the sentence.

"The Germans are very thorough," Sam chimed in. "In their eyes, a Jewish parent makes you Jewish, and if there's information in your mother's file they're going to know."

Helena tried again. "There's nothing left for us here. So you see now why…"

"We have to go." Ruth finished her sister's sentence decisively.

Helena started. "You understand now."

"Yes, we need to go as soon as possible," Ruth relented. Behind her, Helena felt Sam exhale. Ruth straightened. "I'll go gather our things."

But Sam shook his head. "There's no time for that. We have to go now or it will be too late. Just get everyone dressed, no more than the clothes on their backs, and perhaps a bit of food if it fits in their pockets."

"But, Sam, you need to rest. You'll never make it otherwise. Just a few hours," Helena soothed. "We'll leave before first light."

There was a creak from the bedroom door as Michal appeared. Before Helena could stop him, Sam rose with effort, then stepped forward. "You must be Michal." He held out his hand, offering a piece of meat that the girls had not yet devoured.

The boy gazed up at the tall man, his face a mixture of confusion and awe. He looked like such a child in his nightshirt beside the soldier.

"It's okay, Michal," Ruth reassured him. "This is Sam and he is a friend."

But Michal continued to stare at Sam skeptically, not convinced. Sam knelt down. "Do you like dogs?" he asked Michal, and the boy's eyes widened. "I have the most wonderful dog waiting to play with you." Dorie came to Sam's side then and slipped her hand in his. Helena knew then that all of the risks she had taken had been worth it and her instincts to place her faith in him correct.

"We're going on a trip with Sam," Helena added gently.

"But what about Mama?" Michal asked. Ruth and Helena exchanged uneasy looks over his head. They could not risk telling him the truth now, and have him break down right as they were about to leave.

"Mama wants us to go," Helena replied, regretting she did not possess the belief in the afterlife that might make such a statement more true. "She's fine where she is, and we'll send for her as soon as we've gotten settled." She hated lying to him, but there was simply no other choice.

"But we should go get her," Michal began again. "We can't just leave her all alone!"

"No more questions now," Ruth said firmly. "Back to bed, so we are all well rested for the journey." She started toward the bedroom, then turned back. "How are we going to get there?"

Helena faltered. She did not even know where "there" was, much less have a plan. "I don't know, but I'll figure it out with Sam, okay? Trust me."

When Ruth had ushered the children back into the bedroom, Helena set up a bed of blankets for Sam close to the fire. "Thank you," he said as he took the pillow, fingering it with a reverence that said after the weeks of laying on the ground this simple comfort was heaven. Helena berated herself silently that she had not done more to make the chapel more pleasant for him during the time he was there.

She sat down beside him. Despite her admonition that he needed to rest, she could not bear to leave him yet for fear that it was all a dream and he might disappear again. Seeming to read her mind, he pulled her to him and put his arms around her, pressing her close. "Lena," he whispered.

"I thought you'd gone forever." Her eyes filled with tears and she brushed them back. A single drop escaped and ran down her cheek.

"Not me. I knew I would find my way to you." He kissed the tear, catching it midflight with his lips. He kissed a trail up her cheek to her eyes, across her forehead, down toward her chin. He finally reached her mouth, but then hesitated, pulling back, his lips nearly grazing hers. A worried expression crossed his face, then disappeared.

"What is it?"

He shook his head, then pressed his lips to hers, and for a moment it was as if they were back in the chapel. But they weren't, she reminded herself. Ruth and the children were in the next room. She pulled back, forcing her desire down.

He straightened. "I saved a bit of food for you," he said, pulling some meat wrapped in paper from his pocket. "Because I knew you never would for yourself." She started to protest. "Eat it. You need your strength, too. Lena, you're starving."

She started to say that she was fine. But he was right. Day to day she did not notice it. Hunger was so much the default state, the gnawing in her stomach omnipresent. She was a little more tired perhaps. But she saw herself now as he did—after weeks apart, the change was more visible to him, how her cheeks were sallow and sunken. "It's the rations," she confessed, taking the food he offered gratefully.

Warmth surged through her blood at the unexpected nourishment. "What's the plan?"

"The partisans have a base camp not far over the border."

"But Alek had said that his entire southern route might be compromised."

"It's true. There's no clear path anymore, so we will just have to make our way. It will have to be by foot."

Helena looked out the window, imagining the peaks which stood jagged and menacing between them and the destination he had indicated. Then she shook her head, gesturing slightly toward the bedroom, thinking of Dorie. She could not remember if she had told Sam about her younger sister's limp, or if it had been apparent before the children had gone to bed. The mountains would have been difficult even just for the two of them, but impossible with the children. "No," she said slowly. "Some time ago, you said something about trucks."

He shook his head. "The roads are closed now, and even if the trucks could get to us, we'd never clear the checkpoints. They're all but taking them apart looking for stowaways. No, it's the only way."

She wondered if he had any idea the enormity of the risk or how difficult the journey might be. Of course he did—he had just come that way. But there was no other choice—what awaited them here was surely that much worse. "There's a train station about nine kilometers to the southeast," she began slowly, still thinking. "If we can make it there by 5:00 a.m., there's a freight train that stops. It will take us across the border." She had seen the train weeks earlier from the loft in the barn as she watched for him in the predawn hours.

"East," he echoed. Then he lowered his voice. "Lena, no. The German army is headed that way, and getting closer by the second."

"We can make it, Sam. We must try." It was as if they had switched places, her strength bolstering his.

"Fine," he relented, brushing her hair from her forehead. She tilted her face upward, drinking in the touch for which she had longed these many weeks.

"Tell me more about the partisans," she said. "That is, if you're not too tired."

"That morning, before dawn, someone came for me, a young woman with dark hair." She tried not to feel jealous this time. "And she took me over the border to the partisans. They wanted to move me farther south to reconnect with my unit, but I knew if we went that far there would be no turning back. Three days, I begged. Three days to come back and find you. I told them how you had helped me and how much I owed you. They refused, said the effort could not be held up for any one person. So I left." She tried to fathom what he had gone through making the dangerous crossing not once, but twice.

"I was afraid I wouldn't make it," he confessed, and she heard real fear in his voice. "The path was even worse than you described. But I could not bear to have you think I'd just left you." His words filled Helena with deeper consternation, for if he could barely survive the trip on his own, how would they manage with the children? "And I know where they are—or at least where they were—and I have the passes." He pulled out a folded card. "This is a temporary passport, identifying you as my wife and granting you an entry visa to America."

"How did you...?"

"I lied. I told them that I wouldn't go back myself if they sent back papers for all of you. They have forgers—artists, really—quite remarkable at making documents, especially under such primitive circumstances. But I couldn't be sure they would follow through, so I took the documents and left."

Recognizing the photo she'd given him, now affixed to the card, she laughed. "So that's why you wanted my picture?"

"Just in case. But I didn't want to get your hopes up—or argue with you about not going." He held up another document. "And these papers will put the children on a youth transport out of Czechoslovakia. We don't necessarily have to send them, of course. But the papers will give us the pretext to get them over the border."

"And what happens when we get to Czechoslovakia?" Her doubts redoubled. "That's occupied, as well."

He dipped his chin in acknowledgment. "True. But the border is much more porous, and closer to the west."

"And Ruth?"

Sam's expression fell. "Nothing yet. But we'll take her with us, of course, and I'll think of something." His face bore the same grim determination she had seen when he talked of escape and she knew he would not relent until he had gotten them all across the border to safety.

Helena looked over his shoulder out the window. In just a few hours it would be light. "You should rest." She fought the urge to lie beside him as she had in the chapel. But it would not be proper and the children might see. "Good night." She bent to kiss his cheek.

Sam closed his eyes with the ease of someone who had become used to spending nights in strange, uncomfortable places. Helena adjusted his blanket, her hand lingering on his back. She crept back to the bedroom, feeling Sam on the other side of the wall as though he were beside her. She crawled in among Ruth and the children. For this one night, they were all together under one roof, just as it should be. But it would be their last time together in the giant bed and she could not help but wonder where they would next lay their heads, or if they might all sleep together just like this again somewhere else. From the other room, Sam snored faintly and she breathed in unison with him, trying not to imagine the treacherous road that lay just ahead.

In spite of herself, her eyes grew heavy. Sometime later she awoke with a start, cursing herself for drifting off. But the room was still dark. She turned to reach for Ruth to tell her it was time to wake the children. She felt beside her to an empty spot, a coolness on the sheets where there should have been warmth.

Seeing the emptiness, she let out an involuntary cry. Michal was not there.

23

Hands shook Ruth from sleep. "Mischa's gone." Helena's voice, low and urgent, cut through the darkness.

Ruth sat up, banging her shoulder on the bedpost. "Don't be silly." It was usually Helena accusing her of being melodramatic, not the other way around. "He probably just went to the water closet."

"No, I already checked. He's gone."

Gone. The word reverberated in Ruth's head as she searched for a plausible alternative explanation. In daylight, Michal might have been tending to the animals, or fetching wood if he had not done that yesterday. But even then, he would not have left without telling one of them.

"I'll go find him," Helena whispered, and hurried out of the room. She was trying not to wake the other children, or Sam. If he awoke he would surely insist upon helping with the search, instead of conserving his strength for the journey ahead.

Ruth dressed quickly. In the main room, Sam slept peacefully by the fire on the bed of blankets Helena had carefully made.

His head was nestled in his arm exactly as it had been that morning she had gone to the chapel. Averting her eyes, Ruth went to the window and watched as Helena strode across the field and disappeared behind the barn, holding a lantern aloft before her. Another thick snow had fallen overnight. Ruth's mind raced. Like herself, Michal was not suited to the rugged terrain, and he seldom ventured farther than the edge of the property unless necessary. She had awakened in the middle of the night and felt Michal sleeping soundly beside her. He could not have been gone more than an hour.

Helena returned twenty minutes later, breathless and alone. "I looked everywhere—the barn, the fields." She did not bother to lower her voice now. "I even went as far as the pond." Fear sliced through Ruth. Other than Helena's trips to the city to see Mama or to the chapel, the five of them had always been together—until now.

Sam stirred then beside the fire. "What time is it?"

"Just about three."

He struggled to stand, grimacing. "We should go."

"There's a problem. Michal's gone."

Sam's frown deepened. "Any idea where he might have gone?"

"There were faint tracks headed toward the forest. I think—" Helena glanced nervously between her sister and Sam "—that he's gone to the city...to get Mama." Even as Helena spoke the words, Ruth knew she was right. Michal, not knowing about Mama's death, had been clearly distressed at the idea of leaving without her.

"We should have told him the truth," Ruth lamented. But who knew what he might have done then?

"The train is leaving in two hours," Sam interjected gently. "This is our only chance."

"We can't go without him," Helena insisted. Ruth shook her head in firm agreement.

"I understand. But if we don't leave now, none of you will

get out. This is our only chance," he repeated. "I'd send you both ahead and go find him myself, but you're going to need me to find the partisans."

"You take the little ones to the station with Sam," Ruth blurted out. "I'll find Michal."

Helena's brow furrowed. "Don't be ridiculous. You can't possibly do that."

Hearing Helena's dismissiveness, Ruth's resolve hardened. "I'm perfectly capable."

"But you're so much less familiar with the forest. You've never been to the hospital on your own."

Ruth looked away, avoiding Sam's direction. She couldn't tell her sister that she had been through the woods more recently than she knew, on her secret, ill-fated trip to the chapel. "I can do it," she replied firmly.

"Let me," Helena protested again. "I'm stronger." Once that might have been true. It should be Helena going through the forest, Ruth caring for the children. But Helena had grown so much weaker during Sam's absence. It was almost as if they had traded places in the past few weeks, Ruth drawing on her strength where Helena's had failed.

"No, I can do this. Anyway, you'll need to carry Dorie if she gets tired. I can't manage both of the little ones all the way to the train station. You can. I'll meet you there."

Helena opened her mouth once more. "There's really no time to argue," Sam interjected. "The Germans are getting closer." As if on cue, a rumbling came from the distance, low and ominous, shaking the ground beneath them.

"Fine," Helena relented. Their eyes met in silent agreement: this was the only way. She would let her sister help.

Ten minutes later they stood in front of the house. Together she and Helena had bundled every conceivable piece of clothing onto the younger girls, who stood like plump little balls of wool, scarcely able to move. Ruth had hurriedly extinguished the fire, but left a light burning, as though they might be back in an hour. She looked over sadly at the mule they had never bothered to name. Helena had pitched the last of the feed into his bin, but it would last a day or two at most. Then what? They could not ask anyone to care for him.

Helena closed the door to the house. "You can't wear that," she said, taking in her sister's blue cape. Her disdain for the impractical garb amplified all of the reasons why she considered Ruth ill-prepared to make the journey up the mountain, why she thought she should be going instead. "You'll trip, and it's too easy to see you in that."

"But I love it." To Ruth, Mama's cape was a kind of armor that would protect her against the dangers and hardships ahead.

"Wait," Helena instructed, then ran back into the house. She emerged a minute later with Tata's old brown hunting jacket and put it on over the cape, large and bulky. Helena tucked the hem of the cape into Ruth's boots then straightened. "That's better. At least the color will make you harder to spot in the woods."

Helena pulled Tata's hunting knife from her pocket. "You should take this, too."

But Ruth shook her head. "I could never use it." They both knew it was true. Helena tucked it back in her pocket. "Are you taking the rifle?"

"It's too bulky. Anyway, Sam has his gun." Ruth noted with a touch of envy the confidence in Helena's voice that she and Sam would be together and that he would protect her.

Ruth handed her sister the small bag in which she had gathered whatever food had been left in the house that might be eaten on the trip. "Remember that the baby needs…" she began, then stopped herself. Helena knew these things and she would take care of them.

"Here," Sam said, holding out his hand to Ruth. Clutched in it were a card and one of the pieces of paper. "The paper is for the youth transport. And the card…" He hesitated, turning slightly to Helena, who nodded. "The card is for you."

Ruth took it. It was a pass bearing her sister's photograph and granting transit to Helena Rosen, wife of an American soldier. Her jaw dropped slightly. "Helena, you're not married, are you?"

Helena flushed. "Not formally. Not yet, anyway. But this pass will get you across the border."

Ruth stared at the card uncertainly, not moving. "But it's yours."

"It's ours," Helena corrected. "We were always going to leave together."

So Helena had not planned to leave her, after all. Guilt washed over Ruth as she remembered all of her suspicions about Helena, and the awful things they had prompted her to do.

"Take it," Helena insisted. "No one will notice the difference between us." As the card passed from her hand to her sister's, a kind of healing forged between them, like the *oplatek* wafer on Christmas Eve, but much stronger.

"What about you?"

"Sam will get me over the border." There was a confidence in her sister's voice, a certainty that the man she loved could protect her, would not let her down. Ruth couldn't help the envy that formed in her stomach.

"I'll find Michal and meet you at the train station." Helena nodded. Ruth could travel more swiftly with just him and catch up with them. Ruth lifted her head, meeting Sam's eyes directly now, her concern overtaking any lingering awkwardness between them. "Take care of them," she ordered.

He nodded so gravely she thought he might salute. "I will."

"And, Helena, you get those children on the train no matter what." Ruth stared deep into her sister's eyes, understanding for the first time how inseparable they were, two halves of the same being.

"I will. We both will." Her confidence sounded forced now, like a line from a book she had been told to read aloud.

Sam stepped up and put his hand on Helena's shoulder. "We should go."

They all walked past the barn and through the gate wordlessly. At the base of the hill, they stopped.

Helena pointed up into the forest. "You know that the path splits farther along. The fork goes to the chapel and you can keep on that way through the woods, or you can follow the main road toward the city." She faltered, her eyes darting back and forth, as if trying to figure out what other guidance she could give. But who knew which way Michal had gone, or how far he had gotten? He could not possibly make it all the way to the city, and if he did there would be nothing there but certain danger. "If you stay close to the brush by the side of the road you should be safe," Helena finished lamely.

They looked at each other, any last remaining bits of acrimony fading and disappearing in the wind. It simply did not matter anymore. The sisters were one breath, inhale and exhale, and how could one exist without the other?

"Quickly!" Sam growled in a low voice, looking anxiously over his shoulder across the open field toward the Slomir farm. They could not afford to be seen leaving.

But Ruth hesitated, kneeling by Dorie. There was a quiet fear in the child's eyes that said she understood what was happening. Ruth straightened Dorie's collar and closed the top button of her coat, biting her lip. Tears had always come too easily to her. "You listen to Helena," she managed, fighting to keep the urgency from her embrace.

"No!" Dorie clung to the hem of her coat. "I want to go with you."

"I'll meet you at the station in a little while." Her eyes flickered and she wondered if Dorie believed her. Then she picked up Karolina and handed the baby to her sister. "She likes to be patted to sleep this way," she said, moving her arms in a slow circular motion, unable to resist one last bit of advice.

She started to turn, but Helena grabbed her arm. "Please…" she said. "Find him, Ruti. Because I don't think…" Ruth nodded, understanding. She, too, would not be able to go on without their brother.

"I promise." Ruth pulled away.

Then she turned and disappeared into the woods.

24

As Ruth vanished into the cover of the trees, Helena turned and looked out over the horizon. Above the birch forest to the south, the bare branches slashed together like barbed wire. She swallowed over the lump that had formed in her throat, then reached down and pulled Dorie's hat lower against the wind, which was bitingly cold. The predawn sky was pale gray with the threat of more snow.

Sam touched her arm, his hand strong and reassuring through the fabric of her coat. "We need to get to the station. Which way?"

Helena gestured southwest. "Through the woods." His eyes traveled in the direction she was pointing. The open field adjacent to the Slomir farm lay between the spot where they stood and the cover of the trees. Their eyes met uncertainly. She shook her head slightly, in response to his unanswered question as to whether there was a less exposed path. "Let's go," she said, forcing a note of brightness into her voice for Dorie's benefit.

Sam squared his shoulders and took her hand, his glove-clad fingers intertwining thickly with her own. "Quickly, then."

They started across the field in silence. Above, the clouds shifted and the nearly full moon peeked through, illuminating the snow-covered field. Helena snuck a peek over her shoulder at the cottage. She had wanted to leave this place a thousand times. Now she was actually going for good as she had dreamed, with Sam. But it felt ominous, their future uncertain.

"Where's Michal?" Dorie asked, too loudly, her voice billowing across the field.

"Hush, Dorie." Where indeed? Helena wondered how swiftly Ruth was going, and how she would know which path to choose when the road forked. "You know how he's always dawdling," Helena whispered, trying to make her voice light. "Ruth's gone to hurry him along and then they'll meet us." She held her breath, not expecting the answer to satisfy ever-curious Dorie.

Helena shifted Karolina higher up on her hip. Sam held out his free arm. "Do you want me to take her?" Helena shook her head, not wanting to wake the now-sleeping child.

Beside her, Dorie's awkward gait crunched loudly against the frozen snow, every second step seeming to reverberate through the air. Helena cringed, not wanting to rebuke the child for something she could not help. With each second, she felt the cold more intensely. Though she had been walking through the forest for months, it was somehow different trudging through the unbroken expanse of white fields. A dull ache seeped through her boots, clutching at her feet like iron bands. It was a sensation she remembered from playing in the snow as a child. But then, there was a fire to come inside to, Mama's hands to rub her feet and warm milk for her insides. Now there were only miles of cold stretching endlessly before them. Soon her feet went numb and it was as if she were walking on nothing at all.

When they finally reached the trees on the far side of the field, Helena looked back, half expecting to see someone coming after them. But the frigid expanse was empty. Taking in the edge of the still-sleeping village, she remembered what Alek had said about the war ending someday. What would this place look like a hundred years from now? Time and life would go on here, but they would not be here to see it.

They pressed forward through the birch forest. At least the route to the railway was mercifully flat, Helena reflected. But as they took cover in the trees, she almost wished for the hills. Here there was no worn path and lifting her feet from the soft, sodden earth required great effort. The tangle of roots and brush, obscured by the snow, threatened to trip them with every step. The trees were thinner, too, narrow rods of birch, their bare branches offering scant cover compared to the lush pines in the hills above.

Helena pulled away from Sam and took Dorie's hand to make sure the child did not fall. She looked over her shoulder hopefully, as though Ruth and Michal might magically appear. But the trees had closed in, eclipsing the life that they had left behind. "This way," she said, trying to make her voice sound confident once more as she led them through the low brush. Though she struggled to see in the near-darkness, the terrain was familiar to her, letting her guide them in a way that Sam, even with all his military training, could not.

They trudged along through the woods without speaking. Helena's arms ached from carrying Karolina, who in her bundle of warm clothing seemed twice as bulky and heavy to hold. She regretted not taking Sam up on his earlier offer to help with the child. Beside her, Dorie clung hard to her hand, seeming to pull her downward. The child stumbled over a large tree root, going slower even as Helena silently willed her to make haste. "I'm tired," Dorie announced suddenly, her sharp voice breaking the silence once more. Helena cringed as though someone might hear, but the sound disappeared into the trees.

Before Helena could respond, Sam knelt. "May I carry you?"

he asked gently, holding out his hand grandly and patiently, as though offering a dance. Helena started to protest: How could he possibly carry a full-size child with his own leg scarcely mended? Though Dorie was emaciated as the rest of them, she was still nearly fifty pounds. Dorie looked up at Helena uncertainly. "You can ride on my back, like a horse," Sam added gamely, turning away from the child. Dorie climbed on his back and, in that moment, Sam irreversibly became one of them—a part of their family they had never expected, and until then had not known was exactly what they needed. A part they simply could not do without.

Helena smiled gratefully as Sam straightened, trying not to grimace from the effort. He reached out and squeezed her fingers quickly, then dropped them again, too soon. He had a way, even now, of making things seem all right. She started walking again with newfound strength.

A crackling sound broke the silence ahead. "Hide!" Sam whispered, pushing them low into the bushes and onto the icy ground. Awakened by the sudden movement, Karolina squawked and tensed up in a way Helena knew meant she was about to bawl. Desperately, Helena pressed her forearm against Karolina's mouth, stifling her cries, and trying to leave just a bit of space for air. The child squirmed for several seconds, then seemed to relax. Helena squinted through the trees, trying without success to identify the source of the noise, which was too loud to be an animal.

Footsteps, she realized. They grew louder now, branches breaking under them. A girl, older than Karolina but younger than Dorie, appeared between the birch trees, running in the direction in which they were headed, heedless of who might hear her. She was nearly naked, but for a thin cotton shirt and torn rags where her shoes should have been. Watching the child, vulnerable and alone, Helena's heart tore. She could not possibly survive long in these conditions. In her hand, she held something balled. A red plaid scarf, Helena could see, with some sort of gold emblem on it.

Helena started to stand. She wanted to call out to the girl, for the child could not keep going alone in such a state. "We must help her."

Sam held her down firmly. There was pain in his eyes, too, as he took in the helpless girl and her nearly certain fate. But he shook his head, signaling that they could not afford to make their presence known to anyone. "It's no good. We've got no way to help her and we can't carry another child. We have to keep going."

He was right, of course. Once they might have shared shelter and clothing. Now they had no assistance to offer, and they could not risk their own safety for strangers. But Helena remembered the family she had seen arrested in Kraków, the promise to herself that next time she would do something to help. "She's a child," Helena persisted, starting to unbutton her own coat. How could they leave the girl to die in the cold?

Sam gestured downward. "So are they." Helena started to argue, but the point was moot: the girl had disappeared into the trees. What had happened, Helena wondered, to separate the child from her parents? She needed someone to tell her to wear the scarf, the only warm thing that she had. Helena reached up to touch Dorie's head and drew Karolina closer to her. The baby was limp, she noticed. She held Karolina's motionless body aloft, panic rising. Had she gone too far in silencing her? "Karolina!" she whispered fiercely. She pinched her cheek, and a moment later, the baby began to move. Helena went slack with relief.

Sam was tugging her to her feet with uncharacteristic roughness. "How much farther?"

"A few kilometers. But, Sam…" She pulled away. "If the girl was running from danger, then maybe we shouldn't continue this way."

He hoisted Dorie once more. "We don't have a choice, do we?"

Helena stepped ahead of him, starting through the woods once more. "This way, and then we have to go across a small bridge..." A sudden clattering burst out ahead, illuminating the forest in ghostly white. She jumped back, covering Karolina's mouth, muffling her inevitable squeal. Then she turned, following her instinct to run in the other direction. She choked back a scream as another round of gunfire lit up the trees like skeletons.

Sam grabbed her and began pulling her sideways into the brush once more. Helena stumbled to the ground. Pain shot through her leg. Her cry rang out in the stillness, inviting someone to discover them but it was muffled by a third round of gunfire. She lay on the ground, half atop Karolina, paralyzed by terror and pain, wondering if she had been shot. Had they walked right into some sort of fighting?

When the gunfire did not come again, Sam crouched low beside her and rolled her over. "Hold this," he said, producing a lighter from his pocket and flicking it so a small orange flame appeared, casting a faint glow. He handed the lighter to her, then pulled up her skirt, heedless in his haste of any propriety. A large branch with a sharp pointed end had pierced Helena's thigh when she fell. Sam's forehead wrinkled with worry. "I have to get this out," he said decisively. Before she could respond, he pulled the stick from her leg. She bit her lip, stifling the urge to scream. The children looked on, wide-eyed.

"I'm sorry," Sam said. "It had to be done." He swiftly cleaned the wound with snow, then took the scarf from around his neck and wrapped her leg in it. But his brow was still furrowed. "We need to get you somewhere to have that examined before it becomes infected. When you get to Czechoslovakia..."

"We..." she corrected.

"Yes, of course," he said quickly. "We need to get some alco-

hol on that cut, even if it is just liquor. It will burn like hell, excuse my language, but you don't have a choice. Can you stand?"

Helena rose with effort, struggling not to cry out against the
burning pain that shot through her leg. "What was that? Some
sort of battle?"

He shook his head. "I don't think so. It could have been a
skirmish but the shooting was only coming from one direction."

"Michal... Ruth." Helena started back toward the river.

But Sam grabbed her and drew her close, pressing her to his
chest. "You can't," he whispered. "Think of the children. Anyway, Michal likely went in the other direction toward the city.
There's no reason to think they'll encounter any fighting."

He was right. Ruth would have gone in the other direction,
following Michal toward the city. But Ruth was not as strong
as she, did not have Sam to guide her. How would they ever
get to the station?

"We can't keep going that way, though."

"No." She considered the terrain ahead, trying to think of an
alternate route. The path that had just been cut off was the only
way she knew to get to the station. "Let's just keep on through
the trees," she suggested. He eyed her dubiously. "We'll have
to find a way around."

Sam reached down for Karolina, who still sat on the icy
ground. Helena took Dorie's hand and steered them slightly
south. She forged a path through the trees, trying to ignore the
burning pain that seared upward from her thigh with every
step. As she breathed deeply, Tata's face appeared suddenly in
her mind. It was as if he were leading her now, showing her
the route as she turned instinctively through the winding trees.
She held her hand out in front of her to clear the branches so
they did not scrape against Karolina, a padded ball beneath the
blanket in Sam's arms.

The birch forest ended abruptly at an open field like the one
they had crossed earlier, leading to the mill and river. But they

were well south of the bridge they needed to cross, still unable
to reach it without nearing the gunfire they had heard. The
sky was lightening, making it easier to see and at the same time
urging haste. Sam turned to her with a desperation in his once-
confident eyes that scared her more than anything had so far.
He was looking to her, she realized, for the answer. She turned
away, ashamed that she had failed him.

"We need to get downstream," she said suddenly, gazing at
the water. "There's another bridge a few miles south, but if we
walk we'll never make the train."

"Look." He pointed. Several meters away stood a small shed
by the riverbank. Piled alongside it were the dinghies used by
the millers to ferry goods downstream. But the open field still
stood between them and the river. "I'll go first," he whispered.
Not waiting for an answer, he dashed across the field, his body
doubled over Karolina protectively.

As he reached the other side, a shot rang out. They had been
spotted. Watching Sam and Karolina dive for the cover of the
bank, Helena's heart stopped. How had they come to be here,
running from gunfire through the forest like hunted animals?
Mere hours ago they had been safe and warm in bed. Perhaps
Ruth had been right. She'd dragged them all from the safety of
home, only to die in the cold.

A second later, Sam's arm rose from the brush, gesturing to
her and she knew she had no choice. She lifted Dorie up and
buried her as deeply in her arms as she could. "I've got you," she
soothed as she felt the child stiffen with fear. Helena hunched
over and ran despite the searing pain in her wounded leg. A
bullet whizzed past her head and she waited to feel the pain.
But there was nothing and she kept going. Sam had risen from
the bank and stepped out to divert any fire toward him. She
reached him and he yanked her and Dorie toward the water's
edge. The ground was softer beneath their feet here, giving off a
damp peat smell. The river was beginning to freeze, fine sheets

of ice forming on the surface. Sam went to the dinghies and dragged one toward the bank. It was no more than a raft, really, some logs roped together, cracks filled with hardened pine sap. It was not intended for so many passengers, but it was the best they could do.

He set the raft into the water, holding it steady as Helena climbed on.

Sam handed the children to her, his movements jerky with haste. "It's all right," she soothed, feeling Dorie's body tighten once more.

Sam pushed them from the bank, soaking one leg in the icy water. "Stay low," he whispered.

Helena clutched the children close as Sam leaped aboard, causing the raft to wobble slightly. "Careful," she cautioned. None of them would survive even a few minutes in the freezing water. She pressed them flat to the raft and placed herself atop them, bracing for another shot to ring out. But as the current carried them, the air grew still. Whoever had fired at them seemed not to have followed.

They began to drift sideways downstream. Tree branches bowed above them beneath the weight of snow and icicles that hung from them in an arch like jagged, menacing teeth. A piece of discarded burlap lay on the raft. Helena covered the children with it, then draped one hand protectively across them. She began to paddle with the other hand, the water biting into her skin until it went numb and she could no longer feel the cold. Sam paddled on the far side, the two of them moving in tandem, willing the raft through the icy water.

Farther along now, the hills on either side of the river grew steeper and the trees gave way to sheer rock face, worn by the water that had coursed through the gorge for centuries. She had been here once as a child on a summer rafting trip so distant she might have imagined it. The current moved them more quickly now, pushed by the heavy fall rains and snow.

"There!" Helena pointed, spying the break in the gorge that would bring them to the bridge, but the current threatened to hurtle them beyond their target. She paddled harder, steering them toward the bank. Sam reached for a branch that jutted out, trying to pull them into the shore. The raft banged into a rock and lurched suddenly, sending him flailing into the water.

"Sam!" Helena cried too loudly, forgetting the risk of being detected once more. She could not reach him without letting go of the children. Desperately, she steered the raft in his direction. It was no use—they were losing him.

Sam reached his arms high above the surface of the water, clutching the edge of the raft, and hoisted himself up. It wobbled precariously under his weight and she clung to the children desperately, willing the wood craft to level. Sam lay across the raft, gasping for air. Helena moved to dry his face with the fabric of her skirt, but he waved her away. "You'll freeze, too."

Helena looked at the shore. They had come so much farther than they should have and they had to find a place to pull in on the far bank before they were carried past the navigable part of the river to the shoals that would tear the raft to pieces.

Sam sat up, seeming to sense her urgency. "There." He indicated a narrow break in the rocks on the far shore. They paddled furiously for several minutes, seeming to stand still against the current. "This isn't working," she began. Sam rose to his knees, causing the raft to tilt dangerously. As they neared the bank, Sam leaped off, grimacing at his re-immersion into the frigid water that reached his calves as he pulled them in.

Abandoning the raft, Helena and Sam carried the children up the steep bank. They pushed forward for the cover of the trees, the final swath of forest that separated them from the train station. Sam's labored breathing matched her own as they navigated the unfamiliar slope.

They reached the top of the hill. The land here was not even, as Helena had expected. Instead, it dropped off into a steep gorge. As they caught their breath, Helena looked down into the bottom of the chasm. She could see something stacked there, snow-covered and piled higher than her head if she'd been standing beside it. At first she thought it was additional rafts, broken ones perhaps, piled high for scrap or repair. She took a step closer to the edge, stumbling and nearly slipping down the hill. Sam grabbed her. "Helena, no." His voice was terse with caution.

They were not boats, she realized looking closer, but bodies. A pile of corpses filled the gaping hole in the ground. Sam turned swiftly away so that Dorie could not see, but Helena stood transfixed. It was not just the elderly and infirm as it had been in the hospital, but people of all ages, women and children, lifeless and frozen into the earth. They were naked, stripped of their glasses and their clothes and the possessions that linked them to the outside life they had once known, meshed together arms and breasts and hair. Even without their clothing, Helena knew that they were Jews.

"Darling, don't..." Sam drew her close, trying to shield her view, but it was too late. She pulled away from him, unable to look away or deny the truth any longer. It was not just about labor camps and ghettos, she realized then. This was about the shooting they had heard, why the little girl was running away, what Sam had been trying to save them from. Had he known the full truth? She had faulted the Americans for failing to see. But she was no better living just miles from the destruction and burying her head in the sand. This was no longer just pity, though—the fate of those poor souls might well have been their own, and still could be. Helena sunk to her knees. She simply could not go a step farther.

She looked back across the horizon, thinking of her brother and sister, now miles away. Though she had never before believed in God she found herself looking up at the sky with more faith than she had ever felt, asking Him and their parents and whoever else might be up there to help them make it through.

Then she stood. For Dorie and Karolina's sake, she had to keep going. "Sam?" She turned to find the space behind her empty. Sam, too, had crumpled to his knees, shaking.

"We're not going to make it," he said hollowly.

Helena was flooded with panic. Sam was her strength and to see him like this was unfathomable.

Then steeling herself, she took his hand and knelt before him. It was no less terrible for her, but she forced herself to focus on the path ahead. "Don't say that. We can do this. You owe me a dance, remember? I'd like a trip to the seaside, too. Come." She helped him to his feet, careful not to show her fear at how Sam's wet clothes had already begun to freeze. It was her turn to be the strong one now. She peered through the trees in the direction of the station. Though it surely stood just a kilometer or so to the other side of the forest, it seemed a lifetime away.

Sam and the girls watched her, helpless and expectant, unable to make it on their own. Helena took off her scarf and fashioned a sling for the baby. "Get on my back," she instructed Dorie, who eyed her skeptically as she knelt. When Dorie complied, Helena straightened. "Don't let go." Dorie nodded in silent assent. Helena staggered under the weight of the two children and the searing pain in her leg. She stumbled and started to say that she could not do it. Then she sensed Alek's presence, showing her how to be strong. Energy surged through her.

But Sam still knelt motionless. With her free hand, Helena reached down and touched his shoulder. He looked up, eyes wild and desperate. Her fingers cupped his chin. "We can do this." Seeming to draw strength from her, he stood uncertainly. "Come." Lacing her fingers in Sam's, Helena half led, half dragged him through the forest. The station was just ahead now, a lone light in the woods.

25

Ruth started up the hill, stepping with great effort through the snow, which soaked through her stockings at midcalf. But after only a few minutes, she stopped, panting and weary in that way she had been in recent days. She looked up hopefully, but saw that she had only gone a few meters. The cottage was still near, and the path ahead through the forest long and steep. Suddenly the magnitude of the task she had taken on unfurled before her. She had volunteered from a place so deep that she scarcely recognized it, a need to redeem herself for all that she had done to hurt Helena, for assuming the worst about her sister and all of the consequences that flowed from that. But now she faltered, remembering how difficult the journey through the woods would be. She had only gone as far as the chapel last time and that was almost too much. She could not fathom how to find Michal. If she did find him, she would have to tell him the awful truth about Mama in order to convince him to leave. And even if she managed that, how would they possibly reach the others?

Snow began to fall gently around her. Ruth turned back over her shoulder, seized with the urge to call Helena for help as she had done so many times over the years. If she ran after Helena and the others now, she could still catch them and go with them. Helena would understand. She would concede that her sister had been right, that she was not strong enough to make the journey. Surely Helena would agree that they should switch places. But Helena and Sam had already crossed the field and disappeared into the woods with the younger children. Ruth was too late.

Sam. As she forced herself to press onward, she relived the moment when he'd collapsed onto the cottage floor the previous night. Ruth had stared at him in disbelief. Sam could have saved himself and fled for good. Instead, he had returned to the danger. He had risked it all...for Helena. After, when they'd stood awkwardly on opposite sides of the room, Ruth feared the tension between them would be so palpable that Helena would guess what had happened. But Sam's face had remained blank as he addressed her, as though meeting Ruth for the first time. It was as if, in his joy at reuniting with Helena, he had simply forgotten.

Sam had spoken to the children of a dog. But it wasn't the dog who kept him company here, she thought, remembering the frozen mongrel down by the river. No, Sam was talking about one back home, and the life they would all have in America. Ruth could picture it then, Sam and Helena happily married, a home for the children—a picture complete without her. He would make, she realized with sadness and longing for all that could not be, a wonderful father.

From below there came the sound of a vehicle. Ruth spun around once more. Was someone coming for her? A military jeep emerged into view through the trees and drove directly to the cottage below. She wondered if it was the policeman who had come again. But three men emerged from the jeep, and even from this distance she could tell their uniforms were German military. Fear gripped her. It was no coincidence that they had come to the house now, so soon after the family had gone. No, the neighbors must have seen them slip away and reported them—or perhaps someone had betrayed Sam.

Waves of recrimination rose in her mind: if Helena had not found Sam and he had not come back for her none of this would have happened.

No, her sister had been right, Ruth realized. Even if they had done nothing and the truth about their family had not come to light, it still would have come to this eventually. The Germans would not have spared them if they stood quietly by. And it did not matter who was to blame. In just minutes, the men at the house would realize the family was gone and fan out, searching. She could not wait. She turned and ran up the hill, in her mind willing Helena and Sam to move faster with the children.

Soon, though, her gait slowed. Her legs—her right leg more precisely—inexplicably began to burn. The air was bitingly cold now and snow began to fall more heavily in icy daggers against her face, cutting into her cheeks. She could feel her cracked lips begin to bleed. In the distance, a noise like thunder crackled, though of course, that was impossible. This sound was sharp, but she wouldn't let herself think about guns and bullets. The wind whipped harder, as though it had a will of its own, trying to prevent her progress.

An image of Mama flashed into her mind, the secrets she had kept buried for so many years. Ruth was suddenly angry—she had thought herself closer to their mother than anyone, yet her mother had kept this enormous lie from her. All of the emotions she'd managed to sequester for so long welled up, threatening to burst forth. Ruth fought back her tears. She considered, for a moment, simply giving up.

Something pulled at her stomach then, like the love she'd felt for Karolina and the others, only deeper and more intense. "No," she said aloud. It was about more now than just herself,

about even more than Michal. Joy surged through her, eclipsing her anxiety like a great wind snuffing out a tiny flame. She
had this one thing, and it was wholly her own. A feeling rose
in her, strong and maternal. There was new life inside her—she
knew that for certain now—and she could protect this child.
But to do so, she had to survive. Her child had no future here.
Their best—and only—hope for safety lay not in the one place
that had always been shelter, but in going to the unknown. She
owed it to her baby, to all of them, to try.

Should she have told Sam that she was pregnant? No, Sam
had blocked out what had happened and moved on. Soldier
that he was, he knew he had to focus on their survival—which
was exactly what she needed to do now. Ruth turned back,
shoulders squared, steeling herself. Michal was out there in the
woods somewhere, alone and undoubtedly scared. She was the
only one who could find him. Now she was needed. She had
a purpose, a place.

Something slammed into her from behind without warning.
She flew into the snow, breastbone thudding against an unseen
tree stump. A wolf, she thought fleetingly, remembering the
warnings Helena had given. But then a voice snarled in her ear
low and deep. *"Gdzie idzie?" Where are you going?* It was the policeman, Wojski, all pretense of courtesy now gone and his grip
vicelike on her shoulder.

Ruth glanced desperately out of the corner of her eye. Had
the men in the jeep reached her so quickly? But the policeman
was alone, his mission personal. His hands traveled lower. She
opened her mouth to scream but no sound came out. She remembered the knife Helena had pressed her to take. If only she
had it now. Her hands flailed, and she desperately grasped hand-
fuls of snow and ice as he reached for her skirt. She managed to
rise to her hands and knees and kicked backward, her foot tan-
gling in her cape. Her boot grazed the policeman, who let out a

wild cry, inflamed by her attempt. He reached beneath her skirt, pressed his weight upon her. She pushed back, swinging wildly.

Ruth fell forward again, slicing her cheek against something sharp. She reached for it; her fingers closed around a rock, swinging backward but missing. The policeman slammed her face into the snowdrift with an angry grunt. Closer now, he pressed his forearm against the back of her neck. She gasped for breath as ice filled her mouth and nose. She prayed that she would lose consciousness before the assault. *"Kurwa,"* he snarled. *Whore.*

Something snapped in her then. Ruth swung blindly with the rock a second time, letting forth her rage, and connected with a sickening crunch. The policeman fell away from her and was still. She pulled herself up, shaking. Wojski lay on the ground, a halo of blood fanning out around his head and seeping into the snow. Whether he was breathing, she could not tell. Her vision blurred. Standing, she wiped at her cheek and ran farther into the forest.

When she had gone another twenty meters, she looked back. The policeman had not followed her. Her stomach spasmed. Something warm trickled down her leg and she found herself praying it was not blood, for she now desperately wanted to hold on to this life inside her. She had to keep going. Gulping for air, she started again with new vigor, more determined with every step. She could do this. Her limbs were strong from lifting children, eyes keen from protecting them from the worst.

Ruth forged ahead, pressing into the wind. The ground shook and in the distance behind the house the sky glowed red, filling her with terror. How close were Helena and the girls to the fighting? She pressed on, more desperate than ever to get to Michal.

At the fork, she paused, wishing Michal might have left a clue as she did in the game she played with Dorie. Helena had explained that the path divided, but she had not told Ruth which way to go, leaving that judgment to her in the moment. The chapel was much closer, so she could check there first. But if she was wrong, the detour would put her even farther behind Michal.

She peered into the woods ahead. Something flickered, so faintly she might have imagined it. It was a light, coming from the direction of the chapel. Of course—Michal had known about the chapel from Helena and must have gone there to take shelter. She imagined him sitting by a small fire, waiting for her. She had found him, and the first part of the journey was over.

Above the chapel in the trees, Ruth envisioned Sam and Helena with the children, starting a new life. But she did not feel angry or sad now, just contented that she had put things right. She had her own child to think about now. And Michal was waiting for her, waiting for her to bring him home.

26

Helena paused to catch her breath. She released Sam and he slumped to the ground beside her, resting on one knee. Though a light snow still fell, the wind had eased. In the distance the sky began to brighten, pink against the dark silhouette of the low station, signaling equal parts hope and despair. They had nearly made it, but as the sun rose, their cover would be lessened, worsening their chances and making discovery more likely.

"Come." She pulled Sam, willing him to go faster, though she herself could not. "When we get over the border..." she began. There was a slight tug at her hand as he faltered. A strange look crossed his face.

"What is it?"

He shook his head. "Let's just get to the train."

Minutes later they neared the station, approaching slowly from behind it. It was nothing more than a freight depot where logs could be loaded, a simple building, now mercifully deserted.

Helena scanned the platform hopefully for Ruth and Michal. "They aren't here."

"They will be." His voice wavered.

Helena was not comforted. She and Sam, already slowed by the children they had to carry, had been delayed by the detour and the unexpected necessity of taking to the water. She had hoped, almost expected, that her sister would have found Michal quickly and gotten here first.

"Would she have been caught behind the field where we heard the shooting?" he asked.

Helena shook her head. "They should have been able to go around." A pit formed in her stomach. "I should have been the one to go. I'm so much stronger."

"You've gotten these two here. Come."

She took his hand once more. Then she released it as something wet and warm seeped through her mitten. *Blood.* She remembered how he had risen to shield her as she ran across the field. "You were shot?" Not waiting for an answer, she pulled back his coat and sweater to reveal a small hole at his waist that oozed red with each breath he took. How could he have not said anything... How could she not have noticed?

"It's nothing," he protested, but there was a paleness to his face that said otherwise.

"You're hurt," she said, feeling the pain as though it were her own. Her panic rose. Sam's earlier breakdown had been more than just shock at seeing the bodies—his wound must be deep and the growing pain almost too much to bear. "We have to get you help."

Before he could reply, a train whistle sounded long and low in the distance. Now Sam, seeming to find new strength, was pulling her as she half carried and half dragged the girls to the platform. She scanned the tree line behind her, willing her sister and brother to appear. "I never should have let her go," she repeated desperately. Ruth, despite her protestations, was not strong enough to do this alone. Something, Helena knew, had gone terribly wrong.

She willed the train to slow down to give them more time. But its lights appeared in the darkness, a threat as well as a promise. "We have to go back," she said desperately as the train neared the station, lights like two giant eyes, searching.

Sam grasped her firmly by the shoulders. "Lena, don't you understand?" he panted, with more breath than voice. "There is no going back." His words were an echo of her own weeks earlier when she refused to let him push her away. He looked down at the children. "People will have noticed you gone by now," he added more softly. "They'll be at the house." *They.* "You can't undo things, darling, as if they never were."

"We could hide here until the others arrive." Even as she said this, she knew it would not work.

Sam shook his head. "The Germans have already closed most of the borders. The trains won't run for much longer. And the army will be here soon, and then the passes will be worthless."

The train screeched to a stop, drowning out his last words. Sam pulled them hurriedly into the shadow of the station as the engineer stuck his head out. When it was clear, Sam opened a door to one of the freight cars to reveal a gaping black hole. Helena hesitated. She had not expected a parlor car, exactly, but the massive cargo space, dark and cold, terrified her.

Sam helped Dorie up into the car. "Take care of your sisters," he ordered, and the girl nodded, wide-eyed.

Realization dawned on her then. Helena stared at Sam in disbelief. "You're not coming with me, are you?" He had known he was going back and had kept it from her, knowing she would not go without him. "You lied."

"Lena, I'm going back for your sister and brother. I'll find them for you." Helena waited for him to say he would find her, as well. But he would not make that promise. They had found each other once, no twice—and such a miracle would likely not happen again.

"You can't possibly keep going. You're shot."

"It's just a flesh wound. I'll be fine."

"But my leg," Helena protested. If his wound would not dissuade him, then perhaps her own. "I can't possibly go on without you." She stopped, hearing how weak and desperate her own voice sounded. She hated herself for it. But she would do anything to make him stay. "Without you, how am I to get to the partisans?"

"Once you are over the border, head toward the town of Polomka. In the woods to the east you'll find a small encampment. Tell them you're my wife and that I sent you." Sam paused, his eyes betraying doubt that his plan would work. In that moment of hesitation, she knew that she could persuade him to come with her. But Ruth and Michal were still out there, and Sam was the one person who might be able to find them. The others needed him if they were to have a chance to survive.

Yet still she persisted. "I don't have my pass." The ground rumbled then from an unseen explosion and Helena clutched Karolina tighter as she struggled to maintain her footing.

"I know, but you'll think of something. You're smart, resourceful. Look at everything you did in Kraków. You'll manage. You have to. Don't you see—I'm going back for you. You saw it," he said, his voice hushed. He was talking, of course, about the mass grave. Seeing it then, she had understood everything he had tried to shield her from. Now she could not deny the truth that awaited them if they stayed. She had Dorie and Karolina and she had to get them out; she owed it to them to take this chance and not turn back, no matter how painful.

"Here," he said, pressing the gun into her hand, its cold steel now familiar. This time she did not argue, but took it and slipped it into her pocket. "Take these, too." He pulled the chain from his neck and handed it to her. "My dog tags. If you make it to the Americans, these should mean something."

"But then you won't have them with you if..." She couldn't bear to finish the thought.

"That's not gonna happen," Sam said, his voice full of bravado. He reached out to touch her cheek. "I'm coming back to you, Lena Rosen." She blushed as he gave her his surname. Then taking in the red sky behind her, his voice grew serious once more. "You can do this."

"Fine," she managed. He took a step away.

"No!" It was Dorie who cried out this time, her voice high and plaintive and dangerously loud. "You aren't leaving us, are you?" Her lip quivered. She had known Sam for only a few hours, but she trusted him as immediately as Helena had herself. Dorie had lost her father and mother and the war seemed to be chipping away at the rest of her family. This additional break was too much.

"He's just going to get Ruti and Mischa," Helena said. "Then we'll all be together." She forced certainty into her voice. Sam turned to go. "Wait." Helena clung to his arm desperately, knowing that if she let go, it would be the last time. She would never see him again. She wanted to beg him to stay with her, to hold on to this moment they had only just found. But Ruth and Michal appeared in her mind. Sam was their only hope. And she could tell by the fierce look of determination in his eyes, his grimly set jaw, that there would be no changing his mind now, even if she wanted to.

He pressed his lips against the top of her head. "Just get them to safety," he murmured. Looking at Dorie, something broke open within Helena then. She had been keeping the children at a distance for so long. She had convinced herself that she had been tough for their own good, but it had been as much for her, the distance a means of self-preservation. They were no longer just her siblings, or even her own children, but a part of her, and a part that must survive.

Still, she could not let Sam walk away. "No," she cried as the full realization of what was happening unfurled before her. She pressed herself against him as though she might make them one being, inseparable.

He wrapped his arms around her and breathed in her ear. "Save me a dance, okay?" She nodded, unable to answer. "Until then, I'll see you in my dreams." He kissed her long and hard, then broke away. Then he took Karolina from Helena and placed her into the boxcar where Dorie took her hand.

Helena started to reach for him, then stopped. She looked desperately across the horizon. She could not bear leaving Michal and Ruth, but going back now with Dorie and Karolina meant certain death for them all. The three of them at least still had one another. Helena owed it to the children to try. Reluctantly she boarded the freight car.

Sam ducked from sight in the shadows of the station and Helena pulled the children farther into the car as the driver stuck his head out to inspect the train again. A whistle sounded. Helena traced the air in front of her, as though Sam still stood before her. She stared out at the dark silhouette of the trees against the barely lightening sky, a scene she had known her entire life but would surely never see again. Smoke amassed in a cloud to the east. Ruth and Michal were out there, somewhere, though whether together or alone, safe or in peril, she could not say. They were torn and scattered, their one promise to Mama broken.

As the train began to move, Helena sank down, clutching tightly to the children as if they, too, might disappear into dust. The children sat down on the floor of the boxcar, too unfamiliar with trains to expect seats. There was no heat and a fine glaze of ice covered the door frame. The smell of rotting grain and manure hung heavy in the air.

She looked down the platform, hoping in vain to see one or both of her missing siblings. A faint ray of sunlight peeked through the clouds, illuminating the fading smoke above the hills. Helena thought of Alek and the other resistance fighters. But for the children, she might have stayed and helped them, maybe even fought herself. But Alek would not have been able to save her family. Sam, a different type of hero, had put them first. Now, she would do the same.

Helena wrapped her sisters tightly beneath her coat. They clung to her, Karolina to her neck and Dorie to her hand as if she were Ruth, and Helena understood in that second that something had changed forever. She was both mother and father to them now. She rocked Karolina the way Ruth said, singing to her in a low voice as she never had before, surprised as they relaxed into her at the comfort she had not known was hers to give.

As the station disappeared from view, Helena gazed one last time at the tree line. In the distant direction of the chapel, the sky glowed bright orange. Her stomach skipped a funny little beat and then the light slipped from view as they pulled away.

Epilogue

New York
2013

When several seconds have passed without my responding, the woman with the ponytail turns to the police officer. "I think we're all set here," she says brightly. The policeman turns, eager to be dismissed.

"There," the woman says when he has gone. "That's better, isn't it? I only brought him to help me find you and make sure I could visit," she adds apologetically. I nod. It has been decades and I still cannot see a policeman or hear a siren without wondering if they are coming for me. I am shaped irrevocably by all that happened. But I've been changed for the better, too, like the way that seeing a young American soldier in uniform on the street still fills me with a sense of nostalgia.

"Excuse me…" The young woman's voice, tugging and insistent, pulls me from my thoughts. I blink my eyes and look up. "May I come in?"

"Please." I step back. "*Herbata?* I mean, would you like some tea?" A mention of Biekowice and the old ways begin to creep back into my blood.

"No, thank you." She sits, perching on the edge of the chair I've indicated. Her hands dance around each other, reminding me of the restlessness I have long since abandoned. "Mrs...."

"You can call me Helen."

Her eyes widen. "Did you say Helen? I'm sorry, I don't mean to be rude, but I thought..."

"You thought that I was Ruth." *And that Helena was dead.* "I'm not." I hear the brusqueness in my own tone. "You still haven't told me who you are."

"I'm sorry. My name is Rabbi Farber." She says this as though she hopes the title will convey a sense of trustworthiness, but it comes out sounding stiff and silly. I process the information: a female rabbi. Once I would not have believed it, but I have seen enough in my years that few things surprise me anymore. "Elizabeth Farber. I'd like to talk to you about your hometown of Biekowice."

I should be surprised at this unexpected visitor, asking about a place I've not seen in more than half a century. But in some sense this is a visit for which I have waited my entire life. "That was our village, yes."

"Not far from your house there was a small church, more of a chapel, really. Are you familiar with it?"

"That's where Sam..." I hesitate, not sure whether to speak of such things, even after all of these years. "It was in the forest. It wasn't really part of our property."

"No, but you were the landowners of record closest to it."

"Why are you asking about all of this?"

"There's some development going on in the area," the woman explains vaguely. Does she think I will not understand the details? "Near the chapel site."

Now it is my turn to be surprised and I do not bother to mask it. "It's still there?" The woman shakes her head. "Oh." I don't know what I expected. A simple wood structure—there had not been much left but the walls seventy years ago. In my mind it was ageless; I can see every cracked windowpane and rotting floorboard like it was yesterday. But there was no reason to think it had actually withstood the test of time.

"I'm afraid the chapel burned down some time ago."

I push down the pain, reminding myself that I should not care, that it was never the chapel that mattered. But I cannot help but grieve for the sweetest place I ever laid my head, a bed of leaves with a canopy of stars above. "So you know it?" she prompts gently.

"That's where Sam hid after his plane crashed. I found him in the woods and helped him to the chapel. He stayed there while his leg healed and we fell in love."

"But…" Her forehead wrinkles in confusion. "Maybe you could start at the beginning."

"Maybe you could tell me why you're asking in the first place."

"Some bones were found at a development site close to where the chapel had been. Bones are a big concern in Poland because so many Jewish cemeteries were destroyed and are unmarked. The Orthodox rabbis worry that there may have been a cemetery there, or that the bones may have been Jewish. I'm here to ask you."

"There was no cemetery there." She exhales visibly. "Whether the bones were Jewish is more complicated." I take a deep breath. "I was born Helena Nowak. I had a twin, Ruth, who I think you expected to find here, as well as three younger siblings. We were raising them at our cottage in Biekowice after our parents died." I swallow. "The bones…they're male, aren't they?" I know the answer without looking up to see her nod.

"Yes, they were on the thin side so at first we thought female. But forensic tests confirmed it."

"Michal…"

"Michal," she repeats, the name unfamiliar on her tongue.

Even if she had researched the history of what had happened in
Biekowice, there was no reason she would have heard of him.

"My little brother. He was twelve. Sam had arranged for
our escape. He was an American paratrooper, you see. But as
we were about to leave for the border, Michal disappeared. We
thought he went to the city to save our mother in the hospital. We had not told him she had already died. Ruth went to
find him. It began to snow and he must have taken shelter in
the chapel."

The woman's eyes dart back and forth as she tries to grasp the
enormity of my tale. Finally, she says, "That would be consis-
tent with what we found. Some bones of an adolescent male that
showed signs of being at the chapel at the time it burned down."

It is as if someone had punched me in the stomach. Michal
is dead. Remorse, unbridled by the years, washes over me. We
had tried to spare the younger children the worst by not telling
them about our mother's death. But in the end the belief that
she was still alive sent Michal into the woods after her, making our escape together impossible. "I had told him about the
chapel once and he must have taken shelter there." An image
forms in my mind. I see Michal opening the grate of the woodstove to stoke the fire, transfixed by the orange flames. Lulled
by the heat, his eyes grew heavy. Just a small rest, he must have
told himself, to give him strength for the rest of the journey.
Or perhaps he knew that we would come looking for him and
thought one of us would be there soon.

In my heart I had known—if he were alive, he would have
come to me, found me and the others somehow. But I had been
able to construct a fantasy world where he had grown to a man,
had a family and children, a life. Now he was gone. I see his
body lying on the cold ground of that Małopolska hill, a bed
of pine needles beneath him, vacant eyes staring up at the sky.

"One can learn so much from bones. The age of a person at
time of death, and often the gender, though that proved to be

wrong here. We can learn about the position which the person was in, and that can often tell us much about how he or she died." But not the things I really want to know, like why he had gone to the chapel and for how long he had waited, why Ruth did not reach him in time. Those are secrets for the bones to keep.

"There were a few other items found, like fragments of a cup." Buried things that could survive so much longer than humans.

"We couldn't find Michal," I continue, forcing my voice to remain even. "Ruth insisted on going after him. It should have been me. I was the stronger one. But I went with Sam to take the other children to the train station. We made plans to meet there. But Ruth and Michal never arrived. I wanted to go back for them, but Sam wouldn't hear of it. He put me and the children on the train and he went back to look for them, even though he had been shot as we escaped."

"He never found either of them?"

"No. I later learned that Ruth was arrested and sent to Auschwitz." I imagine now the Germans drawn to the woods by the fire at the chapel, happening upon Ruth, who was going in the same direction. I wipe my eyes as I think of my twin sister, the sacrifices she had made. "The Germans thought it was me because she was carrying my transit pass when she was arrested."

She nods. "That's why I expected to find Ruth here, not you."

"Yes." I had not corrected the records. The comingling of our names, my living as Ruth, seemed fitting. Part of me had died there with her, and part of her lived on in me still.

"What happened then?"

"We made it to the border."

"It must have been hard living all of these years without him," she says. "Sam, I mean."

"All of these years? My Sam died last spring..."

Her jaw drops slightly. A Jewish soldier wounded and alone in the occupied Polish countryside. The odds of survival were nonexistent. I had thought so, too, when he pushed me on the train that morning and ran off to find my brother and sister, still bleeding from his wound. I was sure I would never see him again. But he had survived—and he had found me.

One June day some four years later there was a knock on the door of the Lower East Side boardinghouse where Dorie, Karolina and I shared a room. "Hello," Sam said, and there was a moment's shyness, meeting as strangers in the unfamiliar setting. He extended a hand. "May I have this dance?" I stared at him in wonder—his survival was nothing short of a miracle.

Then Dorie appeared behind me. "Sam!" she cried, wrapping herself around his legs, and just like that, we were a family.

"Lena, wait, I need to give you this." He held a box in his cracked hands.

"Oh!" I gasped as I opened it, tears springing to my eyes at the familiar blue. It was Ruth's cape, or rather a portion of it—the hood and a bit of the shoulders. I closed my eyes and tried to block out the visions of what might have caused Ruth to be separated from her beloved cape, or the garment to be torn into pieces so violently. "I went back to get them, just like I promised. Oh, Lena," he said, breaking down as all of the tears he had hidden for so long rushed forth. "I'm so sorry. I told you I would…"

"And you did," I replied, offering the absolution that would never be quite enough. He reached out to touch my face, and I fell into his arms, as if we were back in the chapel once more. I kissed him, not caring that Dorie was watching or that we were on the steps of the boardinghouse or what people might think. "Thank you," I added, clutching the cape. "For bringing this back to me." I took a deep breath, then grasped his hand to lead him to shelter once more.

"Sam came to me after the war," I told Rabbi Farber. "Only later was he able to tell me the whole story of how he tracked Ruth to the camps and learned of her death there." Nothing

I had experienced before—not losing my mother or father—had prepared me for the fact that Ruth was gone. Now hearing what I have always known about Michal, the scar is ripped open again. Had Sam known about the chapel burning and tried to spare me further pain?

"I was in Poland researching and I found this." Rabbi Farber pulls out a copy of a black-and-white photograph. "They wouldn't let me take the original." A bald woman in a striped uniform stares back at me. "Is that her?"

I sink to the ground. The woman in the photo is skeletal, but eyes a mirror image of my own stare back. It is the notion of my sister's locks, her pride and joy, shorn to the scalp that brings me to my knees. I take the picture, clutch it to my chest.

Rabbi Farber helps me to a chair. "I'm sorry if I upset you."

"Why are we here, if not to cry for those who have gone?" I look at the photograph once more, my own name penciled beneath. "You've heard of how amputees sometimes have phantom pains where their missing limbs once were?" She nods. "That's me. It is as if Ruth has been here with me this entire time, talking, living. I still turn to her to tell her things, almost every day." Ruth had been with me since my first breath and, somehow, I assumed she would be there until my last. "We never knew about Michal, though, until now."

"Of course, we don't know for sure. If you'd like to be more certain, there are DNA tests."

"It's him. I'm sure of it." Tears stream down my face now. "Oh, my sweet Michal."

I will have to tell the others, Karolina and Dorie. Of course, to them our brother is just a shadowy image. When we first left Biekowice they asked for Ruth and Michal incessantly. But a child's mind is mercifully short of memory and as we had escaped, finally landing in New York, the excitement and new unfamiliar sights that assaulted the senses pushed their pain away until the questions came only once every few days, then weeks

and months between. When they were old enough I'd sat them
down and told them the truth about a brother and a sister and
parents they had never really known, and they'd listened gravely
but their concern had been more for my tears than any real sense
of sadness. Our family had become the stuff of once upon a
time, bedtime lore or a fantasy world that had not truly existed.

"I'm so sorry," Rabbi Farber says again.

"It's all right. I knew when we couldn't find Ruth that something had happened. My other two sisters survived. Dorie is a
doctor now. She lives about fifteen minutes from here with her
family and I see them almost every week. And my baby sister,
Karolina—Kari, she's called now—is a grandmother of five."
We are generations because of Sam's heroism.

"And Sam?"

"A heart attack, two years ago. But we had a wonderful life
for many years." I worried that Sam would never find us. "I
don't think he ever forgave himself, though, for not being able
to save the others—or find out what happened to Michal. Years
later we checked the records in Poland, Tel Aviv, even Moscow
after the wall came down. It became something of a fixation
for Sam. He said it was about genealogy, constructing his family tree. But I knew that a boy from Chicago had no real cause
to be poking around in all those archives. You see, Rabbi—"

"Elizabeth, please call me Elizabeth."

I continue. "Elizabeth, he was doing it for me, trying to find
the truth. We knew it was virtually impossible that Michal had
survived. He was only twelve. Still, he was a strong boy and
so smart and resourceful, so part of me always hoped… Well,
never mind. He's at peace now." But the questions still haunt
me. Had Michal been cold? Had he suffered?

"Did you have children of your own?" she asks, her voice
round with kindness as she tries to change the subject.

"Not biologically." The doctors had never been able to find
anything wrong. My body, they suggested, was just too rav-

aged from the starvation and other hardships, to prove hospitable. But I knew that the reason ran deeper: after all I had seen, how could I bring a child into the world and live with the cold terror of knowing I might not live long enough to protect it?

"Of course, there was Max." I gesture proudly to the photograph on the windowsill of the tall, slight man, now graying himself. Elizabeth cocks her head, not understanding. In my mind's eye, I see Sam as he appeared on my doorstep that day so long ago. After Sam gave me the box with the scrap of Ruth's cape, I started to lead him inside.

But Sam pulled back. "Lena, wait." I noticed then a child of nearly four, undersized from malnourishment, clutching to his leg. I looked up at Sam questioningly. Had he rescued a child, brought him here for us? Then the child looked up at me with eyes as familiar as my own. "I don't understand..." Sam's face broke then with more pain than I had seen or known possible. "Ruth," he whispered, and I knew then that, although my sister was dead, Sam had returned and against all odds found this child with her perfect blue eyes that would carry her legacy.

"Sam brought Max home from the war." Holding tight to this piece of my sister, I saw birth and death like bookends then. The child did not have Ruth's auburn hair, though. His was black, and something about the too-close eyes was also familiar. Staring at the child, I understood then that Sam's commitment came from a deeper place. "Max was Sam's child with my sister and he rescued the baby from the camps." Rabbi Farber's eyes widen. "Sam slept with my sister." It is the first time I have shared this with anyone.

"I was angry at Ruth for a very long time for trying to take that one thing from me. I wanted to see her again to ask her why but I never got that chance. But in the end she was gone and I forgave her. It was my fault, you see. My secret of sheltering Sam poisoned things between us and caused all the rest to happen." I should have known what Ruth was facing, how Sam's presence would have threatened her. And then later, there were signs of what had happened, but I didn't want to acknowledge it. "I was angry at Ruth and I let her go up the hill when I was the stronger one." We all paid the price for my lies.

"No amount of strength could have saved her or Michal," Elizabeth interjects gently.

"No, of course not. But I should have been the one who died at the chapel. Or maybe, if we had stayed…" Perhaps there was a chance. In my mind, there has always been part of me still living in the cottage with my brother and sisters, all of us together. I clear my throat, eager to change the subject. "You mentioned some development by the chapel."

"Yes, a resort with a golf course." She watches me expectantly, wondering if I will object to such a trivial use of the grounds.

For a moment, I am saddened, thinking of the rugged landscape being hewn down and smoothed to look like everywhere else. Then I shrug. It is not mine to worry about anymore. "Something nice for the people in the region. There's been so much suffering. And maybe it will bring some people to visit. It really is a lovely area."

"Have you ever been back?"

I shake my head. "There's nothing left there for me."

"But your family was—"

"No." I can hear the stubbornness in my own voice, still there after so many years.

"Anyway," Elizabeth says smoothly, "we were trying to figure out the identity of the bones to see if they are Jewish and whether they can be moved so the development can proceed."

"They're Jewish," I reply firmly.

"But I don't understand. If the bones were your brother's, then how could they possibly be? The provincial records…"

Would have given no indication that we were Jewish, I finish silently. "You see, shortly before we fled Poland, we learned that my mother's mother had been Jewish. So that meant…"

"That you were Jewish, too," Elizabeth finishes for me.

"I didn't find out until partway through the war," I say. "So once we knew, things were even more dangerous." I smile slightly. "You don't seem surprised."

"I'm not. In a country where Jews and Poles lived side by side families mingled, secrets were kept. Many Poles have some Jewish blood."

"To their chagrin."

"Perhaps. But things are changing there, slowly." I do not answer. I want to believe that people get better. But some memories are ingrained too deep. "And lots of Jewish identities are being discovered every day, even in places like Kraków. There are young Jews in the synagogue now." One synagogue, where there once would have been a dozen. "There's a Jewish community center and a cultural festival." Places I once thought gone forever breathing with new life. I wonder, though, whether those who once walked the streets would have been happy about the revival or thought it a mockery?

"You raised your sisters Jewish?" I nod. In the new world, there had been no need to be afraid. People treated us as Holocaust survivors and I felt guilty at that because we had escaped so much of what the known Jews had suffered. But Mama was Jewish, and Sam, too, and suddenly it was who we were and as natural as slipping into an old sweater.

"Ruth died in the camps. But not because she was a Jew." That was the irony. The records for Biekowice and the hospital had not been reconciled when they found Ruth. They arrested her as a political prisoner, accused of helping the resistance.

"And they shot her when she wouldn't talk, presumably."

"Because she couldn't talk—she didn't know anything. I did."

Suddenly it is as if the past sixty-plus years have been erased and I am a young woman once more. "Tell me," I say, now hungry for news. "What of my family's home? Was it destroyed, too?"

The woman shook her head. "It's still there. A Polish family named Slomir owns it now."

I stifle a laugh. Pan Slomir had gotten the property, just like he had always wanted. "You know, if you want to get it back, there are ways. A property restitution law has been passed."

I shake my head slightly. I have no interest in such things. I now have the only belongings I want: the memories in my mind—and the truth about what happened to my brother.

"So are you okay with the development proceeding? We can have Michal's bones brought here and reburied in a Jewish cemetery."

"Yes." It will be good to have him close again.

"You know you should be recognized for what you did for Sam. Your name should be in Yad V'Shem and the Holocaust Museum, not mistakenly listed among the victims at Auschwitz."

But I shake my head. "I had more than sixty years with Sam and a family to love, and that's more reward than any plaque or ceremony. I'm proud to have my name among the victims. They're my people, my sister. A part of me did die there."

"And you've never told anyone?" I shake my head. "Mrs. Rosen, I mean, Helena, if you'll forgive my saying, you have to do it. People should know."

I smile faintly. "Everyone who needs to know already does." Of course, they are almost all gone. I raise my hands. "I just don't have the words."

She reaches in her bag and produces a small recorder. "You don't have to write, you can just push this button and talk. Or we could have coffee and you could tell me. Even if you never do anything with it. Someone should know." She stands and brushes the lint from her pants, then passes me her card. "I don't want to bother you further. I'll be in touch about the bones. And thank you for your time." I stand motionless as she closes the door behind her.

Someone should know. Her words linger in the now-empty

apartment. Once again I am that girl in the chapel, swaying with a solider in the semidarkness to a tune hummed low.

I think of Sam, of my siblings. Dorie and Karolina are too young to remember. But someone should know. I press the button. "My name is Helena Rosen…" And then I begin to speak.

★ ★ ★ ★ ★

Acknowledgments

Many years ago when I was working at the Pentagon, I had the good fortune to accompany a delegation of senior U.S. officials to Europe and Asia for fiftieth anniversary commemorations of the Second World War. Our first trip was to a tiny cabin in the mountainous woods near Banská Bystrica, Slovakia, where several American intelligence officers had been captured and later executed during an attempt to assist the Slovak uprising. The Americans had been aided in their mission by a young Slovak woman. I was immediately taken by the tale and have long sought to create a story inspired by theirs in one of my books.

A few years later, when I was posted to Poland for the State Department and working on Holocaust issues, I became acquainted with the issue of the bones. Because the Nazis destroyed so many Jewish cemeteries and killed and buried so many people in unmarked graves, human remains are sometimes found in unexpected locations. This can present problems regarding identification of the bones, making sure that they are buried properly and ensuring that sites which were cemeteries are not disturbed.

After two decades, I am still processing my time in Central and Eastern Europe. My experiences with the commemoration in Slovakia and the bones in Poland came together to create a tale of a downed American airman, rescued by a young Polish woman, and their possible connection to remains found more than a half century later. I placed the setting to a fictitious village in Poland for reasons of story and (as a mom of twin girls myself) gave the heroine a twin to explore the dynamic between sisters. Thus, *The Winter Guest* was born.

As always, I'm so grateful to Susan Swinwood and her entire team at MIRA, who make the publishing experience sheer joy. Deepest thanks also to Scott Hoffman for his wonderful time and talent. Finally, my greatest love and appreciation are reserved for my "village": my husband, Phillip, and our three little muses, my mom, Marsha, brother, Jay, in-laws Ann and Wayne, and friends and colleagues too many to name. Without you, none of this would be possible—or worthwhile.

PAM JENOFF
THE WINTER GUEST

Reader's Guide

Questions for Discussion

1. Which sister did you identify with more closely, Helena or Ruth? If you have a sibling, were you able to relate to their rivalry, camaraderie and the distinct role each of them played in the family?

2. Under what circumstances would you make a decision like Helena's—one that put yourself and potentially the ones you love at risk? Would you have helped Sam, or looked the other way to protect your family?

3. Despite the horrors of war, a romantic view of WWI and WWII abounds in historical novels. What is it about wartime that drew men and women together so powerfully, like Helena and Sam? Do you believe it is possible for people to fall in love so quickly and for such a love to last?

4. How did each of the sisters' strengths and weaknesses come to light in the story—and what role did Sam play in how they were revealed?

5. Discuss the sisters' relationship as it evolved throughout the book. In what ways had it improved or deteriorated by the end?

6. The Nowak sisters were living in an environment and coping with situations that were completely overwhelming, especially for such young women. What do you think each really wanted out of life, and in your view were those dreams achievable?

7. Did you identify with any symbolic items or places throughout the book? What did they represent to you?

8. Helena's feelings toward the Jews—and the Poles' views of the Jews—were multifaceted. What was your reaction to these varying perspectives?

9. Were you surprised to learn what had happened to the Nowak siblings in the epilogue? Did you feel it was the appropriate ending for each of the characters?

Read on for a special sneak peek at
The Woman with the Blue Star,
the next breathtaking tale of historical fiction
from Pam Jenoff.

Prologue

Kraków, Poland
June 2016

The woman I see before me is not the one I expected at all.

Ten minutes earlier, I stood before the mirror in my hotel room, brushing some lint from the cuff of my pale blue blouse, adjusting a pearl earring. Distaste rose inside me. I had become the poster child for a woman in her early seventies—graying hair cut short and practical, pantsuit hugging my sturdy frame more snugly than it would have a year ago.

I patted the bouquet of fresh flowers on the nightstand, bright red blooms wrapped in crisp brown paper. Then I walked to the window. Hotel Wentzl, a converted sixteenth-century mansion, sat on the southwest corner of the Rynek, Kraków's immense town square. I chose the location deliberately, made sure my room had just the right view. The square, with its concave southern corner giving it rather the appearance of a sieve, bustled with activity. Tourists thronged between the churches and the souvenir stalls of the Sukiennice, the massive, oblong cloth hall that bisected the square. Friends gathered at the outdoor cafés for an after-work drink on a warm June evening, while commuters hurried home with their parcels, eyes cast toward the clouds darkening over Wawel Castle to the south.

I had been to Kraków twice before, once right after communism fell and then again ten years later when I started my search in earnest. I was immediately won over by the hidden gem of a city. Though eclipsed by the tourist magnets of Prague and Berlin, Kraków's Old Town, with its unscarred cathedrals and stone-carved houses restored to the original, was one of the most elegant in all of Europe.

The city changed so much each time I came, everything brighter and newer—"better" in the eyes of the locals, who had gone through many years of hardship and stalled progress. The once-gray houses had been painted vibrant yellows and blues, turning the ancient streets into a movie-set version of themselves. The locals were a study in contradictions, too: fashionably dressed young people talked on their cell phones as they walked, heedless of the mountain villagers selling wool sweaters and sheep's cheese from tarps laid on the ground, and a scarf-clad *babcia* who sat on the pavement, begging for coins. Under a store window touting wi-fi and internet plans, pigeons pecked at the hard cobblestones of the market square as they had for centuries. Beneath all of the modernity and polish, the baroque architecture of the Old Town shone defiantly through, a history that would not be denied.

But it was not history that brought me here—or at least not *that* history.

As the trumpeter in the Mariacki Church tower began to play the Hejnał, signaling the top of the hour, I studied the northwest corner of the square, waiting for the woman to appear at five as she had every day. I did not see her and I wondered if she might not come today, in which case my trip halfway around the world would have been in vain. The first day, I wanted to make sure she was the right person. The second, I meant to speak with her but lost my nerve. Tomorrow I would fly home to America. This was my last chance.

Finally, she appeared from around the corner of a pharmacy, umbrella tucked smartly under one arm. She made her way across the square with surprising speed for a woman who was about ninety. She was not stooped; her back was straight and tall. Her white hair was pulled into a loose knot atop her head, but pieces had broken free and fanned out wildly, framing her face. In contrast to my own staid clothing, she wore a brightly colored skirt, its pattern vibrant. The shiny fabric seemed to dance around her ankles by its own accord as she walked and I could almost hear its rustling sound.

Her routine was familiar, the same as the previous two days when I watched her walk to the Café Noworolski and request the table farthest from the square, sheltered from the activity and noise by the deep arched entranceway of the building. Last time I had come to Kraków, I was still searching. Now I knew who she was and where to find her. The only thing to do was to summon my courage and go down.

The woman took a seat at her usual table in the corner, opened a newspaper. She had no idea that we were about to meet—or even that I was alive.

From the distance came a rumble of thunder. Drops began to fall then, splattering the cobblestones like dark tears. I had to hurry. If the outdoor café closed and the woman left, everything I came for would be gone.

I heard the voices of my children, telling me that it was too dangerous to travel so far alone at my age, that there was no reason, nothing more to be learned here. I should just leave and go home. It would matter to no one.

Except to me—and to *her*. I heard her voice in my mind as I imagined it to be, reminding me what it was that I had come for.

Steeling myself, I picked up the flowers and walked from the room.

Outside, I started across the square. Then I stopped again. Doubts reverberated through my brain. Why had I come all of this way? What was I looking for? Doggedly, I pressed onward, not feeling the large drops that splattered my clothes and hair. I reached the café, wound through the tables of patrons who were paying their checks and preparing to leave as the rain fell heavier. As I neared the table, the woman with the white hair lifted her gaze from the newspaper. Her eyes widened.

Up close now, I can see her face. I can see everything. I stand motionless, struck frozen.

The woman I see before me is not the one I expected at all.